WARRIORS
SUPER EDITION

SQUIRRELFLIGHT'S HOPE

WARRIORS

SUPER EDITIONS

WARRIORS
SUPER EDITION

SQUIRRELFLIGHT'S HOPE

ERIN HUNTER

HARPER

An Imprint of HarperCollins*Publishers*

Squirrelflight's Hope
Copyright © 2019 by Working Partners Limited
Series created by Working Partners Limited
Map art © 2019 by Dave Stevenson
Interior art © 2019 by Owen Richardson

Library of Congress Control Number: 2019939329
ISBN 978-0-06-269880-3 (trade bdg.)
ISBN 978-0-06-269881-0 (lib. bdg.)

19 20 21 22 23   PC/LSCH   10 9 8 7 6 5 4 3 2 1
❖
First Edition

Special thanks to Kate Cary

ALLEGIANCES

THUNDERCLAN

LEADER   **BRAMBLESTAR**—dark brown tabby tom with amber eyes

DEPUTY   **SQUIRRELFLIGHT**—dark ginger she-cat with green eyes and one white paw

MEDICINE CATS   **LEAFPOOL**—light brown tabby she-cat with amber eyes, white paws and chest

JAYFEATHER—gray tabby tom with blind blue eyes

ALDERHEART—dark ginger tom with amber eyes

WARRIORS   (toms and she-cats without kits)

THORNCLAW—golden-brown tabby tom

WHITEWING—white she-cat with green eyes

BIRCHFALL—light brown tabby tom

BERRYNOSE—cream-colored tom with a stump for a tail

MOUSEWHISKER—gray-and-white tom

POPPYFROST—pale tortoiseshell-and-white she-cat

LIONBLAZE—golden tabby tom with amber eyes

ROSEPETAL—dark cream she-cat
APPRENTICE, BRISTLEPAW (pale gray she-cat)

LILYHEART—small, dark tabby she-cat with white patches and blue eyes

BUMBLESTRIPE—very pale gray tom with black stripes

CHERRYFALL—ginger she-cat

MOLEWHISKER—brown-and-cream tom

CINDERHEART—gray tabby she-cat

BLOSSOMFALL—tortoiseshell-and-white she-cat with petal-shaped white patches

IVYPOOL—silver-and-white tabby she-cat with dark blue eyes

STEMLEAF—white-and-orange tom

EAGLEWING—ginger she-cat

DEWNOSE—gray-and-white tom
APPRENTICE, THRIFTPAW (dark gray she-cat)

STORMCLOUD—gray tabby tom

HOLLYTUFT—black she-cat
APPRENTICE, FLIPPAW (tabby tom)

FERNSONG—yellow tabby tom

LEAFSHADE—tortoiseshell she-cat

SPOTFUR—spotted tabby she-cat

LARKSONG—black tom

HONEYFUR—white she-cat with yellow splotches

SPARKPELT—orange tabby she-cat

TWIGBRANCH—gray she-cat with green eyes

FINLEAP—brown tom

SNAPPTOOTH—golden tabby tom

FLYWHISKER—striped gray tabby she-cat

SHELLFUR—tortoiseshell tom

PLUMSTONE—black-and-ginger she-cat

QUEENS (she-cats expecting or nursing kits)

DAISY—cream long-furred cat from the horseplace

SORRELSTRIPE—dark brown she-cat (mother to Baykit, a golden tabby kit with white splotches and Myrtlekit, a pale brown she-kit)

ELDERS (former warriors and queens, now retired)

GRAYSTRIPE—long-haired gray tom

MILLIE—striped silver tabby she-cat with blue eyes

BRACKENFUR—golden-brown tabby tom

CLOUDTAIL—long-haired white tom with blue eyes

BRIGHTHEART—white she-cat with ginger patches

SHADOWCLAN

LEADER **TIGERSTAR**—dark brown tabby tom

DEPUTY **CLOVERFOOT**—gray tabby she-cat

MEDICINE CAT **PUDDLESHINE**—brown tom with white splotches

APPRENTICE, SHADOWPAW (gray tabby tom)

WARRIORS   **TAWNYPELT**—tortoiseshell she-cat with green eyes

DOVEWING—pale gray she-cat with green eyes

STRIKESTONE—brown tabby tom

STONEWING—white tom
APPRENTICE, LIGHTPAW (brown tabby she-cat)

SCORCHFUR—dark gray tom with slashed ears
APPRENTICE, FLAXPAW (brown tabby tom)

SPARROWTAIL—large brown tabby tom

SNOWBIRD—pure white she-cat with green eyes
APPRENTICE, POUNCEPAW (gray she-cat)

YARROWLEAF—ginger she-cat with yellow eyes
APPRENTICE, SPIREPAW (black-and-white tom)

BERRYHEART—black-and-white she-cat

GRASSHEART—pale brown tabby she-cat
APPRENTICE, HOLLOWPAW (black tom)

WHORLPELT—gray-and-white tom
APPRENTICE, HOPPAW (calico she-cat)

ANTFUR—tom with a brown-and-black splotched pelt

BLAZEFIRE—white-and-ginger tom

CINNAMONTAIL—brown tabby she-cat with white paws

FLOWERSTEM—silver she-cat

SNAKETOOTH—honey-colored tabby she-cat

APPRENTICE, SUNPAW (brown-and-white tabby she-cat)

SLATEFUR—sleek gray tom

CONEFOOT—white-and-gray tom

FRONDWHISKER—gray tabby she-cat

GULLSWOOP—white she-cat

ELDERS

OAKFUR—small brown tom

RATSCAR—scarred, skinny dark brown tom

SKYCLAN

LEADER

LEAFSTAR—brown-and-cream tabby she-cat with amber eyes

DEPUTY

HAWKWING—dark gray tom with yellow eyes

MEDICINE CATS

FRECKLEWISH—mottled light brown tabby she-cat with spotted legs

FIDGETFLAKE—black-and-white tom

MEDIATOR

TREE—yellow tom with amber eyes

WARRIORS

SPARROWPELT—dark brown tabby tom

MACGYVER—black-and-white tom

DEWSPRING—sturdy gray tom

PLUMWILLOW—dark gray she-cat

SAGENOSE—pale gray tom

HARRYBROOK—gray tom

BLOSSOMHEART—ginger-and-white she-cat

SANDYNOSE—stocky light brown tom with ginger legs

RABBITLEAP—brown tom

MINTFUR—gray tabby she-cat with blue eyes

NETTLESPLASH—pale brown tom

TINYCLOUD—small white she-cat

BELLALEAF—pale orange she-cat with green eyes

PALESKY—black-and-white she-cat

NECTARSONG—brown she-cat

QUAILFEATHER—white tom with crow-black ears

PIGEONFOOT—gray-and-white she-cat

FRINGEWHISKER—white she-cat with brown splotches

GRAVELNOSE—tan tom

SUNNYPELT—ginger she-cat

QUEENS   **REEDCLAW**—small pale tabby she-cat (mother to Kitekit, a reddish-brown tom, and Turtlekit, a tortoiseshell she-kit)

VIOLETSHINE—black-and-white she-cat with yellow eyes (mother to Rootkit, a yellow tom, and Needlekit, a black-and-white she-kit)

ELDERS   **FALLOWFERN**—pale brown she-cat who has lost her hearing

WINDCLAN

LEADER   **HARESTAR**—brown-and-white tom

DEPUTY   **CROWFEATHER**—dark gray tom

MEDICINE CAT   KESTRELFLIGHT—mottled gray tom with white splotches like kestrel feathers

WARRIORS   NIGHTCLOUD—black she-cat

BRINDLEWING—mottled brown she-cat

GORSETAIL—very pale gray-and-white she-cat with blue eyes

LEAFTAIL—dark tabby tom with amber eyes

EMBERFOOT—gray tom with two dark paws

SMOKEHAZE—gray she-cat

BREEZEPELT—black tom with amber eyes

CROUCHFOOT—ginger tom

LARKWING—pale brown tabby she-cat

SEDGEWHISKER—light brown tabby she-cat

SLIGHTFOOT—black tom with white flash on his chest

OATCLAW—pale brown tabby tom

HOOTWHISKER—dark gray tom

HEATHERTAIL—light brown tabby she-cat with blue eyes

FERNSTRIPE—gray tabby she-cat

QUEENS   FEATHERPELT—gray tabby she-cat

ELDERS   WHISKERNOSE—light brown tom

RIVERCLAN

LEADER   MISTYSTAR—gray she-cat with blue eyes

DEPUTY   REEDWHISKER—black tom

MEDICINE CATS   **MOTHWING**—dappled golden she-cat

WILLOWSHINE—gray tabby she-cat

WARRIORS   **DUSKFUR**—brown tabby she-cat

MINNOWTAIL—dark gray-and-white she-cat

MALLOWNOSE—light brown tabby tom

CURLFEATHER—pale brown she-cat

PODLIGHT—gray-and-white tom

SHIMMERPELT—silver she-cat

LIZARDTAIL—light brown tom

HAVENPELT—black-and-white she-cat

SNEEZECLOUD—gray-and-white tom

BRACKENPELT—tortoiseshell she-cat

JAYCLAW—gray tom

OWLNOSE—brown tabby tom

ICEWING—white she-cat with blue eyes

NIGHTSKY—dark gray she-cat with blue eyes

SOFTPELT—gray she-cat

DAPPLETUFT—gray-and-white tom

BREEZEHEART—brown-and-white she-cat

HARELIGHT—white tom

GORSECLAW—white tom with gray ears

ELDERS   **MOSSPELT**—tortoiseshell-and-white she-cat

SQUIRRELFLIGHT'S
HOPE

GREENLEAF
TWOLEGPLACE

TWOLEG NEST

TWOLEG PATH

TWOLEG PATH

CLEARING

SHADOWCLAN
CAMP

SKYCLAN
CAMP

SMALL
THUNDERPATH

HALFBRIDGE

GREENLEAF
TWOLEGPLACE

HALFBRIDGE

CAT VIEW

ISLAND

STREAM

RIVERCLAN
CAMP

HORSEPLACE

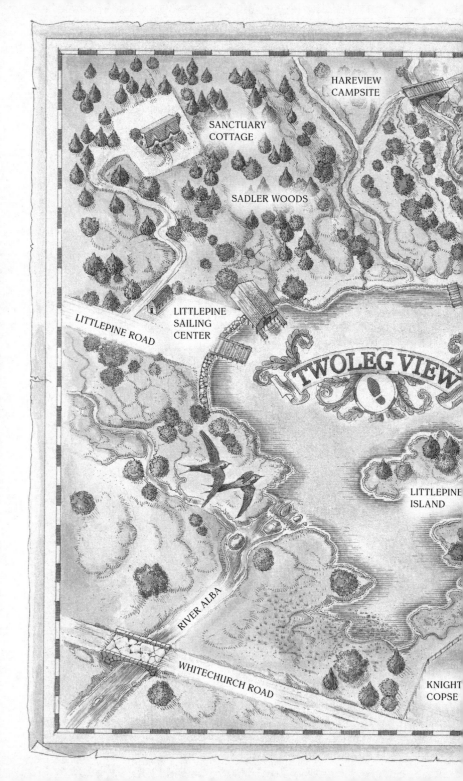

PROLOGUE

Squirrelpaw tasted the air. A soft breeze was spiraling into the sandy ravine, thick with the scent of moss and prey. Her paws pricked with excitement. She was about to explore her Clan's territory, something she'd only smelled until now, for the first time. *Hurry up, Dustpelt.* On the other side of the clearing, her new mentor lingered beside Firestar while Cinderpelt and Sandstorm chatted next to them. She blinked at Leafpaw. "Couldn't they have done their talking before the ceremony?" she mewed. "I want to explore the forest."

"Me too!" Leafpaw's fur was fluffed with excitement. "Cinderpelt promised to show me where coltsfoot and burdock grow. I'm going to make my first poultice this afternoon." Her amber eyes sparkled. "Wasn't the ceremony great? Everyone was looking at us like we were real warriors already and not kits anymore."

"We're *not* kits anymore!" Squirrelpaw remembered with a shiver of pleasure how Firestar had said her apprentice name for the first time. He'd looked so proud. She began to pace in front of Leafpaw, unable to keep still. "And we'll be a real warrior and a real medicine cat soon. I hope I don't have to train for too long. I want to be a warrior by leaf-bare. Then I can lead patrols." Her thoughts were racing. "I wonder what my warrior name will be!"

"Slow down! You only just got your *apprentice* name." Leafpool nudged her with her muzzle.

"But *everyone* gets to be a 'paw. I want a name that's all my own."

"I can call you Squirrelface if you like," Leafpaw purred.

"Very funny." Squirrelpaw glanced at her sister. "Do you think Firestar will name me Squirreltail? I hope not. I'd rather be called Squirrelflame or Squirreldash." Her thoughts sped ahead. "But I won't care what my warrior name is as long as I can be Squirrelstar someday." She stopped and looked earnestly at Leafpaw. "Do you think I'll be leader one day?"

Leafpaw whisked her tail. "Of course!"

Squirrelpaw felt a rush of pleasure. "I'll be leader and I'll have kits and they'll rule the whole forest."

Leafpaw nodded eagerly. "And I'll be the best medicine cat and I'll share prophecies with StarClan every day, and together we will be the most powerful cats who ever lived."

Squirrelpaw paused. "Did StarClan tell you that?" she mewed hopefully.

"No." Leafpaw glanced at her paws shyly. "But it's obviously true."

Across the clearing, Firestar turned away from Dustpelt. Squirrelpaw's heart leaped. "They're done talking!" She looked eagerly toward Dustpelt and Cinderpelt. Disappointment dropped like a stone in her belly as *they* began talking. "What else is left to say?"

But Firestar and Sandstorm were headed across the clearing.

"How does it feel to be an apprentice?" Firestar meowed happily as he neared.

"Great!" Leafpaw hurried to meet them.

Sandstorm swished her tail. "Do you feel different now that you're 'paws?"

"Of course!" Leafpaw wove around her mother. "Squirrelpaw's already planning her warrior name."

Squirrelpaw fluffed out her pelt. "I've been planning my warrior name for moons!" She looked earnestly at Firestar. "You won't name me Squirreltail, will you?"

"One step at a time," Firestar purred, his eyes shining with pride. "First you must finish your apprentice training."

"That'll be easy!" Squirrelpaw's tail shivered with excitement.

Leafpaw frowned. "It'll be easy for *you*. *You* don't have to remember the name of every herb in the forest."

"But I have to remember every prey-scent and paw print," Squirrelpaw pointed out.

Sandstorm blinked at them fondly. "I know you'll both make us proud."

"What if Leafpaw gets her medicine-cat name before I get my warrior name?" Squirrelpaw fretted. "That would be embarrassing."

"It won't matter," Firestar assured her. "You each have your own path to tread."

Sandstorm stretched her muzzle forward and touched her nose to Squirrelpaw's and then to Leafpaw's. "As long as you have each other, you'll both stand tall."

Squirrelpaw's fur prickled with happiness. She looked at her sister. "Leafpaw and I will always stick together." She meant it with every hair on her pelt.

Leafpaw twined her tail around Squirrelpaw's. "And we'll always help each other," she vowed. "Nothing will ever drive us apart."

CHAPTER 1

✿

Greenleaf was giving way to leaf-fall, and shriveled leaves were already drifting along the forest trails. Ahead, a stream babbled, tumbling its way toward the lake, and beyond it the moor rose against a blue afternoon sky. Squirrelflight padded from beneath the trees and tasted the air. She could smell heather, dusty and browning.

Eaglewing, Plumstone, and Bumblestripe fanned out beside her.

"It's quiet," Eaglewing murmured.

Plumstone gazed at the heather stretching ahead. "It's perfect hunting weather."

Eaglewing stared at the trees as though he might see through them. "We'd best be on our guard."

Squirrelflight nodded, knowing that the young warrior was probably thinking of Ambermoon, his former mentor, who had been attacked by an owl a moon before on a day very much like this. She had died. *It's good to remember,* Squirrelflight thought, *that even the clearest days hold their dangers.*

Squirrelflight narrowed her eyes, straining to make out a dark shape near the top of the moor. She was leading the border patrol and had promised to report back on their neighbors. It had been nearly three moons since the Clans had redrawn their borders to make room for SkyClan, and the new scent lines had remained unchallenged. Bramblestar was happy—the new peace suited him—but he'd confided in her that he was worried that it was too good to be true.

The dark shape dipped beneath the heather. Another darted after it. "Is that a WindClan patrol?" Squirrelflight wondered.

Bumblestripe followed her gaze. "I think so."

"They're heading away." Plumstone narrowed her eyes.

Squirrelflight shifted her paws. "We'd better check the border to make sure it hasn't been crossed."

Eaglewing padded forward and sniffed the edge of the stream. Plumstone headed along the bank.

Squirrelflight flicked her tail toward the stretch of prickly gorse beyond. "The border's been moved," she reminded them.

"Yeah, but the stream is where the forest ends." Eaglewing blinked at her.

"We have to get used to our new borders, too." Squirrelflight glanced at the ginger she-cat, surprised that a young warrior should already be so rooted in Clan traditions. Did her sister, Plumstone, feel the same way? "Have you ever marked the new border?"

"Thornclaw said there was no point," Plumstone told her. "He says ThunderClan cats don't hunt on moorland. We hunt in the forest."

Squirrelflight widened her eyes, surprised. A strong Clan

should adapt to change, not ignore it. Bramblestar would have to speak to his senior warriors. *Has the peace only held because the Clans haven't been trying to enforce our new borders?* She padded downstream to where stones jutted out of the water, and hopped onto the first one. "ThunderClan cats hunt on ThunderClan land," she called back to her Clanmates. "From now on we mark all our borders." She scrambled onto the next stone, uncurling her claws as her pads slipped on the wet rock. Then she leaped onto the far shore. The air tasted peaty here and stringent with gorse scents. She was surprised that it could be so different only a few paces from the tree line. But the moor wind was brisk, always carrying fresh smells. In the calm of the forest, scents hung longer in the air.

Behind her, Eaglewing and Bumblestripe looked distrustfully at the crossing stones.

"Are you coming?" Squirrelflight whisked her tail impatiently.

Plumstone brushed past her sister and leaped onto the first stone. "Come on!" She pricked her ears. "We've never been on WindClan land before."

"It's *ThunderClan* territory now," Squirrelflight corrected her. The stretch of moorland had clearly been left unhunted. The grass was untrampled, and no prey-scent sweetened the air. And yet ThunderClan hadn't gone hungry since the border changes. It had been a good greenleaf. Prey had been plentiful. But when leaf-bare drove prey underground, they'd need this precious hunting territory. They had, after all, given a good swath of their forest to SkyClan.

Plumstone hopped onto the bank and stopped beside Squirrelflight. "It smells like WindClan here."

Squirrelflight sniffed again as Bumblestripe and Eaglewing crossed the stream. There was a hint of WindClan, but the scent wasn't fresh. "It's probably the wind carrying the smell down from the high moor," she told Plumstone.

Plumstone sniffed the grass. "*Everything* smells like Wind-Clan here."

Bumblestripe reached them. "It was their land for a long time," he commented, looking warily toward the moor. "I guess it'll take a while for ThunderClan scent to take hold."

Squirrelflight headed toward the line of gorse that marked the border. "It'll take hold quicker if we leave scent marks." She grazed her cheek along a branch, wincing as the prickles snagged her fur. Bumblestripe padded stiffly along the border, leaving marks as he went, while Eaglewing and Plumstone plucked at the grass, rubbing their scent into the earth.

"I can't smell any WindClan scent markers." Eaglewing looked puzzled. "They haven't marked the new border."

"Perhaps they've been busy. Remember, Whitetail died recently, and they would have had her vigil. Wait till the weather starts to turn," Squirrelflight warned her. "They'll be more careful about borders when prey is scarce."

Bumblestripe jerked his muzzle toward the forest. His ears pricked with excitement. Eaglewing stiffened as she followed his gaze.

"Rabbit!" Plumstone darted toward the stream as a fat buck bounded from the forest.

Bumblestripe and Eaglewing pelted after her. They scrambled over the crossing stones that spanned the stream and raced into the trees toward their quarry. The rabbit squealed in panic as it saw them and fled for cover. But Bumblestripe was fast. With one leap, he crossed the stretch between hunters and prey and pinned the rabbit to the ground. He killed it with a bite before Eaglewing and Plumstone reached him.

Squirrelflight watched them as they took turns sniffing the juicy fresh-kill, their pelts fluffed with excitement. Her Clanmates were clearly happier hunting in the forest. She rubbed her cheek on another branch and padded back to the stream. Bramblestar would have to remind his warriors to keep the markers on this border fresh. If they didn't make this land their own, there might come a day when the WindClan scent markers on this stretch of land wouldn't be stale anymore.

"It won't feel like a real Gathering." Squirrelflight glanced at the night sky as she padded beside Bramblestar. "There's no full moon."

"It's *not* a real Gathering," Bramblestar reminded her. "Just a meeting of the leaders and deputies."

Beside them, the lake lapped sluggishly over the shore. Beneath Squirrelflight's paws, the pebbles were still warm from the day's heat. She looked anxiously toward the island. Silhouettes moved across the tree-bridge. She couldn't make out who they were. She tasted the air but smelled only moorland scents and remembered her patrol with Bumblestripe,

Plumstone, and Eaglewing. Did Harestar want to challenge the markers they'd left? Surely he couldn't complain. It was ThunderClan land now. "Why did Harestar call the meeting?"

"Emberfoot didn't say." The WindClan warrior had visited the ThunderClan camp while she'd been resting after her patrol. "He just brought the message. Harestar wants to talk." Bramblestar moved closer, letting his flank brush hers. "The moon may not be full, but it's very bright tonight." He glanced at her affectionately. "It's nice to be alone."

She leaned against him. "I can't remember the last time it was just us."

"Do you remember when this territory still felt new?"

She did. "You'd just been made deputy."

"We used to sneak out and explore after the camp had gone to sleep."

Squirrelflight purred. "You were terrible at sneaking. I don't know why we were never caught."

"Probably because I was deputy," Bramblestar whispered.

"More likely because our denmates were kind and pretended not to hear us. Even *Dustpelt*, and he was always a stickler about young warriors getting enough sleep." Happiness warmed her pelt as she remembered her old mentor. It seemed countless moons since she'd been his apprentice. How young she'd been without realizing it. Recalling suddenly how she and Leafpool had planned great futures for themselves, she glanced self-consciously at her paws. *I guess we haven't done so badly.* She didn't feel old yet, but it had been a long time since she'd felt the rush of excitement she used to feel in her first moons as a warrior, whenever she was picked to go on patrol or attend a Gathering. She pressed closer to Bramblestar. "Do you miss being young?"

He shrugged. "I miss being irresponsible. Back then, the only thing we had to worry about was our next hunt. That was before we became leader and deputy, and before we had kits to look after."

Squirrelflight felt a pang of longing. Sparkpelt and Alderheart were grown, and she'd never had a chance to know their littermates, Juniperkit and Dandelionkit, who had died. She'd been hoping to have a new litter by now—tiny kits to nurture and love. But they'd had no luck. "Having kits didn't make me feel old. I liked the responsibility. It'll be good to feel that way again." She glanced hopefully at Bramblestar. When he didn't comment, she prompted him. "Don't you think?"

"Of course." He didn't look at her.

Anxiety prickled beneath her pelt. She'd wanted him to sound more enthusiastic about kits. "Let's pretend we're young again now. It's almost like we're sneaking out of camp." Squirrelflight kept her mew light. "Half the Clan are already in their nests, and the rest will be asleep by the time we get home."

"I wish we could." Was that a sigh in Bramblestar's mew? "But we can't be late for the meeting. And we have to go straight back to camp afterward; Birchfall and Lionblaze will be waiting to find out what happened."

He was worrying about the Clan again. He was a good

leader; he always put his Clan before his own needs. But she couldn't help wishing he could put her first this time. Disappointment jabbed at her heart as their moment of closeness passed, but she ignored it and focused on the meeting. "Surely Harestar can't have anything serious to talk about. It's been peaceful since the storm. It finally feels normal to have Sky-Clan with us beside the lake, and the other Clans seem happy with the new borders."

"Then why call a meeting?" Bramblestar meowed.

"There could be sickness, or Twoleg trouble."

"It's pointless to guess. Let's go find out." Bramblestar quickened his pace. When the island was near, he broke into a run. Squirrelflight hurried after him, and as she followed him across the tree-bridge, she glanced down at the moon-dappled water. Pebbles crunched on the shore behind her. She looked back and saw Mistystar and Reedwhisker. She nodded a greeting, but the two cats had already plunged into the water and were swimming the short stretch of lake to the island.

On the far shore, Bramblestar pushed his way into the long grass. Fresh scents lingered here. SkyClan's, WindClan's, and ShadowClan's leaders had already arrived. Squirrelflight pushed her way among the stems, following the passage Bramblestar had opened to the clearing.

As she emerged on the other side, she saw Tigerstar, Harestar, and Leafstar in a pool of moonlight at the center. Cloverfoot, Crowfeather, and Hawkwing hung back, exchanging watchful glances. Bramblestar was already hurrying to join them. As Squirrelflight caught up to him, branches swished overhead. The breeze tumbled fallen leaves across the ground. Squirrelflight shivered. She was used to the clearing teeming with warriors and apprentices, their scents and voices crowding the air.

Harestar nodded a greeting as they reached him. "Thank you for coming."

Squirrelflight searched the WindClan leader's eyes, but his gaze was unreadable. She could see stiffness and tension in the others that made her wary. Were she and Bramblestar the only ones who didn't know what this meeting was about? She glanced over her shoulder as the long grass swished and Mistystar and Reedwhisker padded, dripping, into the clearing.

"Harestar." Mistystar bowed her head respectfully as she reached them.

Harestar acknowledged her with a blink, then swept his gaze around the gathered cats. "I called you here because there's a problem with SkyClan's territory."

Surprise lit Leafstar's gaze. "A problem?"

Mistystar, Harestar, and Tigerstar were staring coolly at the SkyClan leader. Alarm pricked through Squirrelflight's pelt. Had Harestar already discussed this with the other leaders?

Bramblestar narrowed his eyes. "If there's a problem with SkyClan's territory," he meowed stiffly, "why isn't Leafstar bringing it to us?"

"She clearly hasn't noticed it," Mistystar meowed pointedly.

"Have your Clans been talking behind SkyClan's back again?" Leafstar's fur ruffled.

Hawkwing moved closer to his leader. "We hoped those days were over."

"It's not a question of talking behind your back." Crowfeather whisked his tail. The WindClan deputy seemed impatient. "If you'd lived here longer, you'd have seen the problem already."

Squirrelflight stared at him. Was he trying to insult Sky-Clan?

"We settled the issue of SkyClan's territory three moons ago," Bramblestar growled. "We all agreed."

"It was the best plan we could think of at the time." Tigerstar shifted his paws. The division of land had been the ShadowClan leader's idea. Was he regretting it now?

Harestar was still staring at Leafstar. "Three moons has given us time to see the flaws in that plan."

"What flaws?" Leafstar demanded.

"We shifted our borders to make room for SkyClan." Harestar glanced around at the other leaders. "We were happy to do it. We know SkyClan belongs beside the lake. StarClan has made that clear. But moving borders means that now some of us have land we can't use."

"The water channels on the land RiverClan gave us make it hard for us to patrol," Tigerstar agreed.

Mistystar fluffed out her fur. "Yet they're full of fish that only RiverClan can catch and eat," she meowed.

"And you were given moorland." Harestar nodded at Bramblestar.

Bramblestar's pelt ruffled along his spine. "We use the land beyond the stream."

"Really?" Harestar looked unconvinced.

"Larksong caught a rabbit there yesterday," Bramblestar told him.

"Only one?" Harestar narrowed his eyes.

"One was all we needed."

Harestar pressed on. "Today your patrol barely crossed the stream."

Squirrelflight felt heat beneath her pelt. Had the Wind-Clan leader been spying on them? "It was a border patrol, not a hunting patrol," she pointed out.

"And yet you hunted." Harestar stared at her. "But in the forest, not on the moorland."

Bramblestar shifted his paws. "We hunt wherever the prey runs."

"And catch one rabbit where we would have caught three," Harestar meowed.

"Are you insulting my warriors?" Bramblestar's hackles lifted.

"Of course not." Harestar swished his tail. "We're more experienced at hunting on moorland, that's all."

"*We'll* be experienced at hunting there eventually," Squirrelflight put in. "We all just need time to adjust to our new territories."

Leafstar turned to Harestar and puffed out her chest. "What are you trying to say?" she asked. "Do you want Sky-Clan to leave again? If you—"

"No cat thinks you should leave," Harestar said quickly.

Leafstar went on. "If you want us gone, you'll have to take it up with our ancestors!"

Squirrelflight felt a rush of sympathy for the SkyClan leader. "Haven't they moved enough?"

Harestar met her gaze. "All I'm saying is that territory is being wasted. WindClan is growing—Featherpelt is expecting kits—and we need every bit of land we can get."

"You act like you need land more than we do. But Sky-Clan is growing too!" Leafstar blinked at him. "Violetshine has kits."

"All the Clans are growing," Harestar meowed evenly. Squirrelflight shifted her paws self-consciously. It seemed everyone was having kits except her. The WindClan leader went on. "Which is why no Clan should hold on to land it can't use." He looked pointedly at Bramblestar.

Bramblestar met his gaze. "ThunderClan uses *all* its land."

Squirrelflight stared at the ground. Perhaps she'd been wrong to insist that ThunderClan adapt to its new territory. The Clans might work better hunting land that they were used to. "We don't use the moorland as much as we should," she admitted. "The border had barely been marked before today."

Bramblestar swung his gaze toward her. "We're not giving up territory. It would leave us with less than the other Clans."

"I'd happily give RiverClan's marshland back," Tigerstar meowed. "But SkyClan would have to return our forest."

Bramblestar lashed his tail. "No cat takes territory from SkyClan. We all fought too hard for this settlement. If we destroy it now, we'll be back where we started."

"But is it fair to give SkyClan prey-rich land in exchange for marsh we can't use?" Tigerstar blinked at him.

"You should have thought of that before you suggested it!" Bramblestar snapped.

Tigerstar glared at the ThunderClan leader. "How could I know that WindClan would have to watch your warriors waste their prey?"

Bramblestar bared his teeth. "My warriors don't waste prey!"

Squirrelflight's tail bushed. She couldn't let them fight. "Perhaps there's another solution," she mewed quickly. "One that means no land will be wasted, but SkyClan will still have equal territory." Her thoughts whirled as she reached for a plan offered many moons ago before the Clans had come to their final arrangement. At the time, the leaders had been wary of a plan that would place SkyClan far from the others. But now it seemed like the most sensible solution. "What about the land beyond the abandoned Twolegplace?"

"Where's that, again?" Leafstar narrowed her eyes.

"At the far edge of ThunderClan and ShadowClan's forest." Squirrelflight looked at her eagerly, hoping the SkyClan leader would like the idea.

But Leafstar looked unconvinced. "If that's such good hunting territory, why hasn't ThunderClan or ShadowClan claimed it already?"

Squirrelflight blinked. "When there were just four Clans, no cat needed it."

"We'd have no access to the lake," Hawkwing meowed.

Tigerstar pricked his ears. "Why do you need the lake? You don't catch fish."

"You'd be nearer the Moonpool," Harestar meowed encouragingly.

"What about herbs?" Leafstar countered. "There are some plants that only grow on the lakeshore."

"They could keep a narrow strip of forest," Squirrelflight meowed quickly. SkyClan shouldn't be cut off completely. "Enough to let them get to the lakeshore. And there might be herbs on the new land. We don't know what lies up there, except forest. It might be richer territory than this, for all we know. It must be worth exploring."

Leafstar narrowed her eyes. "We've only just built our new camp and marked our borders. Why should we have to build another new home?"

"You're right," Tigerstar agreed. "That wouldn't be fair. But if it's better for all the Clans, then it's the right thing to do. And this time we will help you." The ShadowClan leader looked at the others. "I'm sure *all* the Clans will help."

Hawkwing stared at the ShadowClan leader, clearly unconvinced. "When was the last time any cat visited this land?"

Squirrelflight tensed as the cats glanced doubtfully at each other.

"I'm not sure any cat's ever fully explored it," Mistystar admitted.

"Then why should *we*?" Hawkwing snapped. "It might be infested with foxes or Twolegs."

Squirrelflight leaned forward. "But it's worth looking at, isn't it? What if it's perfect Clan territory? We'd all have enough land to hunt on, and nothing would be wasted."

Leafstar flicked her tail irritably. "You want to exile us again."

"It wouldn't be exile," Squirrelflight objected. "You'd be living right beside us."

Leafstar looked unimpressed. "Beside you, not among you. You'd always see us as outsiders."

Tigerstar narrowed his eyes. "That would be up to you."

Squirrelflight ignored the ShadowClan leader. "We'd see you at Gatherings. And you'd still share borders with ThunderClan and ShadowClan."

Harestar nodded. "SkyClan wouldn't be left out. We are one beneath StarClan now. We share ancestors."

Leafstar looked thoughtful for a moment, as though she were seriously considering the idea. Then she seemed to blink the thought away and squared her shoulders defensively. "Moving into unknown territory would be dangerous and difficult. Who knows what's hiding in that forest?"

"SkyClan is no stranger to dangerous situations," Mistystar meowed. "I'm sure whatever challenges await you, you will face them with courage and skill."

Leafstar snorted. "Try telling that to my elders and queens."

Squirrelflight felt Bramblestar shift beside her. He was watching the others, his eyes dark with rage. She blinked at him hopefully. "We'd help SkyClan with the move, wouldn't we?"

Before he could answer, Harestar spoke. "New land for a new Clan! This could be the best solution." He sounded delighted.

Hawkwing flexed his claws. "Nothing's changed here. You carve up territory as it suits you, without listening to what we want."

"We didn't carve up territory." Tigerstar's pelt ruffled. "We came up with the best plan we could." He met Hawkwing's gaze. "You're one of us now. Surely you care about our problems as well as your own? We only want to please StarClan. Don't you?"

Leafstar's ears twitched. "Would moving us yet again please them?"

"If it brings lasting peace, perhaps it would," Squirrelflight meowed quickly. "Let's consult with our medicine cats. To make sure that StarClan approves."

"And what if StarClan doesn't send a message?" Leafstar's gaze darkened. "They've been silent since the storm."

Mistystar whisked her tail. "That's probably because there's nothing to worry about. They'd warn us if we were doing something wrong."

Bramblestar growled softly. "So we can move a Clan off their land as long as our ancestors don't complain." His pelt twitched. "Is that how the warrior code works now?"

"Our complaints matter too," Tigerstar told him. "The warrior code tells us to respect the living as well as the dead."

Harestar tipped his head thoughtfully. "Let's at least think about Squirrelflight's suggestion," he meowed.

Mistystar nodded. "We don't need to make a decision until everyone is happy. Perhaps if SkyClan has a chance to get used to the idea." She glanced hopefully at Leafstar.

The SkyClan leader frowned. "Come on, Hawkwing. We're wasting our breath here."

"No, you're not—" Squirrelflight began. But Leafstar and Hawkwing were already heading away.

"I hope they'll come around." Tigerstar looked uncertainly at the other leaders.

"It would solve all our problems," Harestar agreed.

"Leafstar is a sensible cat." Mistystar glanced after the Sky-Clan leader.

Bramblestar grunted. "Let's go." He beckoned to Squirrel-flight with a sharp flick of his tail.

Mistystar dipped her head as he marched away. "It was a good plan, Squirrelflight."

"Thanks." Squirrelflight turned to follow him.

At the edge of the clearing, she darted in front of Bramble-star. As he stopped, she blinked at him eagerly. She had kept the leaders from fighting. But her heart lurched as she met his gaze. He was glaring at her.

"What's wrong?" she mewed.

"I don't think SkyClan should move," he growled.

"I know," Squirrelflight mewed sympathetically. "But something needs to change. Tigerstar's solution might have been the best one at the time. But the Clans are growing. We all need territory. This plan means that no one has to give up land."

"No one except SkyClan," he muttered darkly.

Squirrelflight blinked at him. "They'll have new land. They're used to moving, and this might be the last move they ever have to make. This land beyond the abandoned Twoleg-place might be perfect for them."

"*Might* be." Bramblestar's tail twitched angrily. "Or it might be overrun with snakes, or dogs, or foxes. Warriors might *die* thanks to your idea."

Squirrelflight's heart pounded. Why was Bramblestar so angry? "SkyClan is strong and resourceful. They have survived so much. They can survive this."

"Why do they have to *survive* anything?"

"Land is being wasted!" Frustration burned beneath Squirrelflight's pelt, but she kept her voice low, aware that the other leaders were watching them from across the clearing. "Bumblestripe and Plumstone didn't even want to mark the WindClan border today. I don't think Eaglewing had ever crossed the stream. And the same thing's clearly happening in ShadowClan. Who ever heard of a ShadowClan cat getting their paws wet? They're never going to hunt on that marsh-land."

Bramblestar turned away and began to pad into the long grass. "They'll get used to it, just like we'll get used to the moorland beyond the stream."

"But we'd all have bigger territories if SkyClan moved." Squirrelflight hurried after him. "And you heard Harestar and Leafstar. The Clans are growing. There'll be more kits by newleaf, more mouths to feed, more apprentices to train—"

"More kits!" Bramblestar lashed his tail. "Is that all you think about now?"

His words stung like claw marks. She watched him disappear into the grass, her chest tightening. "Don't *you* think about it?" She pushed after him, but he was already hurrying ahead. He was on the tree-bridge by the time she caught up to him. She followed him over it and jumped onto the far shore.

She fell in beside Bramblestar, breathless as she tried to keep up. "Don't *you* think about kits, Bramblestar?"

"I have kits," he snapped.

"Alderheart and Sparkpelt? They're grown up now!"

"I know!" Bramblestar didn't look at her. "They're old enough to look after themselves. Why are you so desperate to be responsible for new lives? Isn't being deputy enough?"

"It should be, but it's not." Squirrelflight felt panic welling. "I'm getting older with each season. One day I won't be able to have more kits. I just want another litter before it's too late."

"I know." Bramblestar sounded weary. "And of course I want kits. Just not as much as you do."

Squirrelflight stopped and stared after him. "Don't you love me anymore?"

Bramblestar turned, his eyes sparking with exasperation. "Yes! But I am responsible for our Clan. And if the other Clans are planning to start up more trouble with SkyClan, I need to focus on that. I don't have as much energy as I used to. I'm getting older too."

"No, you're not!" Anger flared in Squirrelflight's chest.

"You have more lives than me—" She broke off as a realization washed over her like ice water. Was that why he didn't care about kits? He had plenty of time to have kits in the future, maybe even with another mate, when she was dead. The thought made her feel sick. Bramblestar's next litter might have a mother who wasn't her. She stared at him, unable to speak.

His gaze shimmered suddenly as though he saw her pain. "I'm sorry." He hurried to her side and pressed his muzzle against her cheek. "I shouldn't have said anything. I was angry. I felt you weren't on my side at the meeting. I was trying to protect SkyClan."

"So was I!" She pulled away indignantly. "I was trying to find a solution that would keep the peace."

"Maybe you're right. But that isn't the point. You're my deputy." His tail twitched. "You're supposed to back me up in front of the other Clans. We need to look united. You know how quickly Tigerstar smells weakness, and how he exploits it."

"It's not weak to have different opinions." Squirrelflight's pelt pricked.

"It looks a lot like weakness when a deputy disagrees with her leader in public." Bramblestar shifted his paws. "You should know better! You should have discussed your idea with me in private and we could have taken it to the other Clans together."

"It might have been too late by then." Squirrelflight paused. She didn't want to argue. And besides, the issue with Sky-Clan wasn't what was worrying her now. "I'm sorry I spoke up without talking to you first. But is that really why you said you don't want to have kits?"

Bramblestar gazed at her, his eyes round. "I'm sorry if I made it sound that way. I do want to have kits with you."

"Really?" Her heart lifted.

"Yes. If that's what you want."

Squirrelflight stared at him. There was resignation in his eyes. Grief twisted her belly as he stared back at her blankly. She turned away. *I want you to want it too.*

They followed the trail back to camp in silence. When they arrived, Larksong was guarding the entrance. His eyes flashed in the darkness as he saw them. "How was the meeting?" The black tom hurried forward. "What did Harestar want?"

"It was the usual argument," Bramblestar meowed heavily as he ducked through the thorn tunnel. Squirrelflight let Larksong slip in front of her and followed them into camp. Birchfall and Lionblaze were waiting in the moonlit clearing as Bramblestar had predicted. As the three warriors clustered around Bramblestar, Squirrelflight hesitated.

They hardly seemed to notice she was there. She felt barely there herself. The argument with Bramblestar buzzed in her head. *He might have kits with another cat when I'm dead.* She'd never really considered before that he would likely outlive her—by several lifetimes. Her heart sank as she understood suddenly, for the first time, that she would never become Thunder-Clan's leader. The kithood dreams she'd shared with Leafpool would come to nothing. Bramblestar would outlive her, and she'd only ever be the leader's mate. Sadness swamped her.

What would she leave behind when she died? Would another cat replace her as soon as she was gone?

Quietly, she padded toward the warriors' den. She'd sleep in her old nest tonight. Her heart ached too much to lie beside Bramblestar now.

❧

"It's going to need repairing before leaf-bare." Brackenfur looked up.

Squirrelflight followed the old warrior's gaze and saw holes in the roof of the elders' den. Sunshine streamed through them, dazzling her. She looked away. "I'll organize a patrol to fix it," she promised.

Graystripe stuck his head through the entrance. "Are you going to patch up that roof?"

"Of course," Squirrelflight told him.

"She's going to patch it up!" Graystripe called over his shoulder to Millie, who was lying outside in the sunshine.

"She's going to *what*?" croaked Millie. The old she-cat was growing increasingly deaf.

"Patch it up!" Graystripe yowled.

"Who with?" Millie sounded confused. "Has she been quarreling again?"

Alarm flashed in Squirrelflight's chest. Did the Clan know about her spat with Bramblestar? They must have noticed she hadn't slept in his den last night.

"The roof!" Rolling his eyes, Graystripe headed outside.

Squirrelflight shifted her paws self-consciously. She was

deputy as well as Bramblestar's mate. She couldn't appear at odds with the leader. Bramblestar had been right when he'd said that they must show a united front, and not just to the other Clans. Their own Clan should feel their relationship was strong. A quarrel between a leader and deputy could send ripples through the whole Clan.

Brackenfur twitched his tail. It jerked her from her thoughts. "When will the work start?" He was still staring at the roof.

"I'll ask Dewnose and Thriftpaw to start work on it as soon as they get back from training."

"Thanks." Brackenfur padded to his nest and settled into it. "It's been good to let sunshine into the den, but we can smell leaf-fall coming, and Cloudtail worries about Brightheart getting cold."

"We'll pad all the walls," Squirrelflight promised. "It'll be as warm as a mouse nest in here."

She ducked outside, nodding to Millie and Graystripe as she passed them, and glanced around the camp. Bramblestar was sunning himself on the Highledge with Thornclaw. She didn't look at him, afraid to catch his eye. She'd avoided him since she'd woken at dawn. Her grief had eased with sleep, and common sense had returned on waking. Of course Bramblestar loved her, and if he wanted kits less than she did, at least he'd been honest with her. She knew she'd overreacted. Why should he want exactly the same things that she did? And yet she still wasn't ready to speak to him. She'd assigned herself to the dawn patrol and then gone hunting.

But she couldn't stay out of camp all day, and it was sunhigh now. There were no more chores until dusk patrol. Hesitating at the edge of the clearing, she looked for something to keep her busy. Hollytuft and Flippaw were back from training, nosing eagerly through the fresh-kill pile. Jayfeather and Alderheart were heading out of camp, Jayfeather leading the way as usual despite his blindness. Outside the nursery, Daisy was chatting to Lilyheart and Rosepetal, while Rosepetal's apprentice, Bristlepaw, nosed about in the ferns at the edge of the camp, clearly looking for mice. Squirrelflight wondered if it was time Daisy moved to the elders' den. It must be lonely in the nursery. But she was such a help to expectant queens. What if a warrior announced she was having kits? No one should have to sleep in the nursery alone. A pang of grief jabbed Squirrelflight's heart. *I should be there by now.* Her thoughts quickened. How could she have kits now that she knew that Bramblestar didn't want them? *He does want kits!* she corrected herself. *Just not as much as I do.*

But it hadn't been just the kits he'd been upset about. She'd contradicted him in front of the others. *But they were close to fighting!* Squirrelflight flicked her tail indignantly. *And I have a right to my own opinion.* Her plan for SkyClan could be the perfect solution. She couldn't have held her tongue even if she'd wanted to. Bramblestar had implied that a good deputy would have kept quiet. She shook out her pelt. Was that what Bramblestar thought—that she wasn't a good deputy? Hurt sharpened its claws on her heart once again. She closed her eyes. Chasing thoughts like this wasn't going to help her feel better.

"Bristlepaw! Flippaw! Look what I caught!" Thriftpaw's mew surprised Squirrelflight, and at his littermate's call, Flippaw looked up from the mouse he was eating. Bristlepaw stuck her head out of the ferns, her eyes wide.

The dark gray she-cat was standing at the camp entrance, Dewnose beside her and a small rabbit at her paws.

Bristlepaw dashed from the ferns and skidded to a halt beside her sister. "It's almost as big as you!" She sniffed excitedly at the rabbit as Flippaw hurried over.

"Did you catch it by yourself?" Flippaw looked impressed.

Thriftpaw glanced at her paws. "Not exactly by myself."

Dewnose purred beside her. "Thriftpaw tracked it and caught it. I just helped with the killing bite."

"Can we eat it now?" Thriftpaw asked.

"Put it on the fresh-kill pile and take something smaller," Dewnose told her. "We can share the rabbit later with the elders."

Thriftpaw glanced toward the heap of prey at the edge of the clearing. The long body of a weasel lay on top. Her eyes widened. "Is that a weasel?"

Flippaw nodded. "Mousewhisker caught it this morning."

"But weasels are vicious," Thriftpaw mewed, her eyes widening.

"That one was," Flippaw told her. "Mousewhisker's in the medicine-cat den right now covered in bites."

Squirrelflight pricked her ears. Mousewhisker must have returned while she was in the elders' den. "Is he badly hurt?"

"I don't know," Flippaw told her.

Squirrelflight headed toward the medicine-cat den.

"Imagine being wounded by prey," Bristlepaw murmured.

"Imagine being *killed* by prey!" Thriftpaw mewed.

"Put your rabbit on the fresh-kill pile," Dewnose told her again. "When you've had something to eat, we're going to practice battle moves."

Squirrelflight glanced back at the gray-and-white tom. "Can you take a look at the elders' den when you're finished? The roof needs mending."

"Sure." Dewnose swished his tail as Squirrelflight ducked through the brambles that trailed over the entrance to the medicine-cat den. Inside, cool shadows swathed the wide stretch of earth. Herb scents filled the air. Her littermate, Leafpool, glanced up warmly as Squirrelflight entered. "Well, hello."

Mousewhisker sat stiffly in the middle of the den. Leafpool returned to lapping ointment into his wounds.

"Are you badly hurt?" Squirrelflight crossed the den and stopped beside them. "I see Leafpool is taking good care of you."

"She is. And it's just a few bites," Mousewhisker told her.

"There are a couple of deep ones," Leafpool reported. "But I've cleaned them and put plenty of herbs on them. They should heal quickly." She looked earnestly at the gray-and-white tom. "But if you get any fever or the pain keeps you awake tonight, come straight to me."

Mousewhisker nodded.

"Where did you catch the weasel?" Squirrelflight was curious. Weasels were rare in this part of the forest.

"Near the beeches," Mousewhisker told her.

Squirrelflight realized she'd been wondering if he'd caught it on ThunderClan's strip of moorland. "Not the moor?"

Mousewhisker looked at her, puzzled. "Why would I be hunting on the moor? That's WindClan territory."

"The stretch beyond the stream is ThunderClan territory now," she reminded him, twitching her tail in irritation.

"Oh, yes." He sounded surprised. "I keep forgetting. It feels so unnatural to hunt in the open."

Squirrelflight stifled a sigh. Harestar had been right about the wasted land. "We all need to learn," Squirrelflight prompted.

"Of course." Mousewhisker peered distractedly at a bite mark on his shoulder. "I just hope hunting in the wind doesn't make us as stunted as WindClan warriors."

Leafpool used her paw to fold the leaf she'd mixed the ointment on. "WindClan warriors are only smaller than us because their ancestors were smaller, not because of the wind."

Mousewhisker sniffed. "So what made their ancestors small?"

Leafpool shrugged. "Only StarClan knows."

"It was probably the wind."

Squirrelflight caught her sister's eye and swallowed back a purr. Was Leafpool going to argue with that kind of logic?

"Go and rest in the sunshine," Leafpool told Mousewhisker, changing the subject. "It'll dry out your wounds."

"Thanks, Leafpool." Mousewhisker dipped his head and headed for the entrance.

"Wait," Squirrelflight called after him. Mousewhisker turned to her questioningly. "Have you patrolled the edge of ThunderClan territory lately, beyond the abandoned Twoleg-place?"

Mousewhisker frowned. "I was up that way a quarter moon ago with Larksong and Cherryfall."

"Do you know what the land's like beyond the border?" Her fur pricked along her spine. Bramblestar wouldn't be happy if he knew she was asking these questions. "Are there any strays living there, or foxes?"

"Occasionally there are unfamiliar scents on the border. But if there are strays or foxes up there, they're smart enough to know not to cross into our territory."

"Thanks, Mousewhisker." Squirrelflight nodded at him, and the gray-and-white tom pushed his way out of the den.

"What was that about?" Leafpool was staring at her.

Squirrelflight sat down and curled her tail over her paws, relieved to have a moment alone with her sister. "Last night's meeting with Harestar was tense."

"I heard that they want the borders to go back to the way they were before SkyClan." Leafpool's gaze was dark with worry.

"Not exactly," Squirrelflight explained. "No cat wants to deprive SkyClan of a home. But the new borders have left ShadowClan with land they can't hunt. And we have a strip of moorland that, clearly, we hardly use."

Leafstar's pelt ruffled. "But we can't go back to our old borders. What would happen to SkyClan?"

"That's why I was asking Mousewhisker about the area beyond the abandoned Twolegplace. It might make great territory for SkyClan."

Leafpool looked curious. "Would they move there?"

"They might if they knew it was good land." Squirrelflight looked at her sister hopefully.

Leafpool didn't look convinced. "It could work, but does Bramblestar know about this idea?"

Squirrelflight puffed out her chest. "I suggested it at the meeting last night."

"You did?" Leafpool's ears twitched nervously.

"I had to. It would solve all our problems," Squirrelflight insisted.

Leafpool frowned. "I really don't think SkyClan should have to move. They've been through enough. Can't the Clans get used to their new borders?"

"We all need more land," Squirrelflight pointed out, swallowing back frustration. She'd been hoping Leafpool would agree with her.

"What does Bramblestar think?"

"He thinks SkyClan should stay where they are."

"I'm glad someone's on their side." Leafpool picked up the folded leaf between her teeth and carried it to the back of the den. She dropped it beside the pool. "ShadowClan has been trying to push out SkyClan since they got here. Now RiverClan and WindClan are joining in. I know change is difficult, but the Clans aren't even trying to change. They seem to want everything the same as it used to be. I'm surprised StarClan hasn't said something."

Squirrelflight pricked her ears. "Will you ask them next time you're at the Moonpool?"

Leafpool shrugged. "I can, but I don't know if they'll answer. They've been silent since the storm. We figured it was because they had nothing to tell us." She glanced away, frowning. "Now I'm not so sure."

Squirrelflight tensed. "Do you think their silence means something?"

"I only know that it's unnerving touching my nose to the Moonpool and seeing nothing but the moon's reflection." She padded back to Squirrelflight. "You said Bramblestar thinks SkyClan shouldn't move." She tipped her head enquiringly. "Did you argue about it?"

Squirrelflight looked away. "What makes you think we argued?"

"I saw you come out of the warriors' den this morning." Leafpool gazed sympathetically at her sister.

"He says I should have backed him up."

"It might have been best to discuss it with him first. Sky-Clan needs time to find their paws and establish themselves beside the lake. I'm not sure moving them now would be a good idea."

"But if they stay where they are, these tensions over the borders will only grow." Why couldn't Leafpool and Bramblestar see what would happen if they didn't solve the land dispute quickly? "Tigerstar's like a fox with a bone once he's got an idea in his head."

"True," Leafpool conceded. "But do you think Tigerstar—
or any of them—will let go of *this* idea now? What if SkyClan
decides it doesn't want to move?" She frowned. "No wonder
Bramblestar's upset. You've stirred up quite a bee's nest."

Squirrelflight swished her tail irritably. "We didn't just
argue over moving SkyClan." She wanted to tell Leafpool
the whole story, but she hesitated. The subject of kits was a
tricky one with Leafpool. Many moons before, she'd had a litter of kits with Crowfeather, a WindClan warrior. Because
Leafpool was a medicine cat, forbidden from taking a mate,
and because the kit's father was in another Clan, Squirrelflight had agreed to raise the kits with Bramblestar as though
they were her own. Those kits were Jayfeather, Lionblaze, and
Hollyleaf, and Squirrelflight had loved them as much as any
mother could. But she knew it must be hard for Leafpool to
understand her desire for another litter. She had already had
the chance to be a mother twice, something Leafpool could
never experience.

Her littermate stared at her, her eyes glittering with curiosity. "What is it, then?"

Squirrelflight let out her breath. *Never mind the awkwardness—
Leafpool will understand.* And she needed reassurance. "He said
he doesn't want more kits as much as I do."

Leafpool's eyes rounded with sympathy. "Oh, Squirrelflight."

Squirrelflight nodded. "I know. It's—" *Selfish of me,* she was
about to say. *Because I've already mothered two litters.* But Leafpool
didn't let her finish.

"That must have hurt," Leafpool said softly, dipping her head. "I know how much you want another litter."

"Bramblestar says he's getting old and that the Clan is enough responsibility." She trailed into silence, the memory of the argument stinging her afresh.

"I'm sure he'd love kits if you had them," Leafpool mewed. "But I can see how he finds the thought overwhelming."

Squirrelflight blinked at her. "Do you think I'm being unreasonable, wanting more kits? I know I . . ."

"No, of course not. But you already have Alderheart and Sparkpelt. And, in a way, Jayfeather and Lionblaze."

Squirrelflight nodded, but her heart ached. "They don't need me anymore."

"They'll always need you," Leafpool mewed. "Just not in the same way as when they were kits. And the Clan needs you, doesn't it?"

"It's not the same."

Leafpool stretched her muzzle forward and touched her nose to Squirrelflight's cheek. "I'm sorry you're hurting. I'm sure Bramblestar wants kits. Just give him time."

"What if there isn't time?" Squirrelflight felt suddenly weary. "What if I'm too old?"

"You're not too old." Leafpool pulled away. "Don't rush so much, Squirrelflight." She gazed fondly at her sister. "Stop trying to sort out every problem at once. One day you'll have more kits, and Bramblestar will forget he ever had doubts. And the Clans will sort out their borders. Slow down and let things happen naturally."

Squirrelflight dipped her head, grateful that Leafpool was her sister. She was gentle and wise, and she always tried to understand. But Squirrelflight knew they were looking at the border dispute from different angles. Leafpool was a medicine cat—of course she thought the new borders should remain. She didn't understand that warriors valued hunting land too much to let it go to waste without a fight.

And as far as kits went . . . Leafpool didn't understand what it felt like not to be needed. Leafpool was needed every day. The Clan depended on her, sometimes for their lives. It was different for Squirrelflight. Even as deputy, she was just one warrior among many.

She got to her paws. "Thanks for listening, Leafpool." She felt her sister's gaze follow her as she padded out of the den. Hunger tugged in her belly, not for food but for something she couldn't quite put her paw on. She needed to do something. She couldn't just accept the way things were. She headed for the camp entrance. Last night's meeting still nagged at her. There must be some way to convince Bramblestar that her idea was the perfect solution to this new disagreement among the Clans. She remembered Leafstar's hesitation; the Sky-Clan leader had looked thoughtful for a moment before she'd squared her shoulders, as though she was weighing the possibility of moving. Perhaps there was a way to persuade her. If Squirrelflight could approach her quietly, without the eyes of the other Clans, she might be able to make her consider the idea seriously. Mousewhisker had said that there were few signs of danger beyond the border. If she took this information to Leafstar, it might be enough to change the SkyClan leader's mind.

Lifting her tail, Squirrelflight marched out of the Thunder-Clan camp and headed toward the SkyClan border. She knew what she must do. She had to speak to Leafstar.

CHAPTER 3

Squirrelflight fluffed out her pelt as she neared the SkyClan border and peered between the trees. She'd wait for an escort. There was no point rubbing Leafstar's fur the wrong way by crossing SkyClan territory without permission. The heat of the morning had given way to dampness as clouds rolled in from the mountains. Squirrelflight could smell rain, and the first drops began to fall as she waited, straining to glimpse movement beyond the SkyClan border.

She heard ferns rustle and snapped her gaze toward the sound. Black-and-white fur flashed between the fronds, and Palesky, a SkyClan warrior, slid into the open, warily tasting the air. "I smell ThunderClan."

Tree padded out beside her. "We're near the border, right?"

Squirrelflight lifted her tail. "Tree!"

Palesky turned first. "Squirrelflight? What are you doing here?" As Tree turned around, she stalked toward Squirrelflight. Around them, raindrops splashed onto the leaves.

Tree hurried after her. "How's Twigbranch?" he called.

"She's fine." Squirrelflight's mew rang through the trees. She glanced over her shoulder, wondering if ThunderClan warriors were near. She didn't want to be seen talking to the SkyClan cats. Lowering her voice, she called more softly. "I want to speak with Leafstar."

Palesky reached her, narrowing her eyes. Squirrelflight could see curiosity in her gaze, but the black-and-white she-cat dipped her head respectfully and didn't ask any questions. *Sometimes it's useful to be a Clan deputy,* Squirrelflight thought. "She's in the camp. I'll take you to her."

Tree looked surprised. "But Squirrelflight knows where the camp is. She can find it herself and we can finish our patrol."

Palesky flicked her tail impatiently. "We can't let cats from other Clans wander around our territory unguarded."

"But she's alone." Tree looked unconvinced. "What harm could she do?"

"She might be a spy, or have come to hunt our prey," Palesky told him. She looked quickly at Squirrelflight. "I know you aren't," she added respectfully. "But we must follow the rules."

"The rules make no sense," Tree objected. "But fine, we'll do it your way."

Squirrelflight glanced at him, amused. *Once a loner, always a loner.* Would Tree ever understand the warrior code?

Palesky nodded for Squirrelflight to cross the border. Squirrelflight scanned the forest once more for ThunderClan warriors, then padded into SkyClan territory and followed Palesky toward the SkyClan camp.

"How are your kits?" she asked Tree as he fell in beside her.

The yellow tom purred proudly. "They're growing fast."

Frecklewish had reported at the last Gathering that

Violetshine had given birth to Tree's kits. Her sister, Twig-branch, had been overjoyed and had asked to be allowed to visit her new kin, but Bramblestar had been reluctant to let one of his warriors foster such close ties. "Violetshine is Sky-Clan. Twigbranch is ThunderClan," he had said. "No good can come from such divided loyalties."

Squirrelflight glanced at Tree as she followed Palesky through a clearing thick with brambles. "Twigbranch is dying to see them, but I think she'll have to wait until their first Gathering."

"Violetshine can't wait to show them off." Tree's eyes shone.

The rain was falling more heavily now, drumming on the canopy and dripping into the forest. Squirrelflight shook drops from her pelt. Her heart quickened as they neared the camp. Would Leafstar be willing to listen to her?

The camp wall showed ahead and Palesky hurried forward. "Stay with her, Tree," she called over her shoulder. "I'll warn Leafstar she's coming."

Warn? Squirrelflight's ears twitched nervously. "I only want to speak with her," she called as Palesky disappeared through the entrance tunnel.

"What do you want to speak to her about?" Tree asked.

Squirrelflight lifted her chin. She wasn't used to being questioned by warriors. "You'll hear when Leafstar wants you to hear."

Tree glanced at her but said nothing and escorted her into camp.

Violetshine looked up as she entered. The young queen was

sharing a mouse with Reedclaw beside the nursery, ignoring the rain dripping from their ears. Bellaleaf sheltered in the nursery entrance, lapping her swollen belly. Four kits were splashing noisily through the puddles already forming at the edge of the clearing. None of them were more than three moons old. The two smaller kits—one black-and-white and one yellow—stopped when they saw Tree and hurtled across the clearing to meet him.

The black-and-white she-kit reached him first. "Tree!"

Squirrelflight hopped out of the way as the other kit caught up and began weaving eagerly around Tree's legs.

"Hi, Rootkit." He cuffed the yellow tom-kit fondly with his paw, then nosed the black-and-white she-kit. "How's it going, Needlekit?"

"Can you play with us now?" squeaked Needlekit.

"Violetshine says she's tired." Rootkit looked like a tiny version of Tree.

Tree purred. "I can play with you after our visitor has left."

Needlekit looked up at Squirrelflight, her eyes widening. "Who are you?"

"I'm Squirrelflight." Her heart ached with longing. How much longer would she have to wait to have her own kits? "I've come to speak with Leafstar." She glanced at the two larger kits, left behind in the puddles. She hadn't realized SkyClan had so many kits. They would need all the territory they could get soon. "Who are they?"

"Reedclaw's kits," Tree told her. "Kitekit and Turtlekit."

"They're going to be apprentices a whole moon before

us." Needlekit looked indignant. "But Frecklewish says we're growing really fast. We'll be as big as them soon."

Rootkit was sniffing Squirrelflight warily. "You don't smell like us," he mewed.

"I don't smell like SkyClan," Squirrelflight told him. "I'm from ThunderClan."

Rootkit pricked his ears. "Like Twigbranch?"

"Yes." Squirrelflight purred. Violetshine must have told them about their ThunderClan kin. She gazed around the clearing. Harrybrook and Plumwillow were watching her from the other side of the camp. Frecklewish glanced up from the herbs she was sorting outside the medicine-cat den. Dewspring and Nectarsong stared at her from beside the fresh-kill pile.

Macgyver padded sleepily from the warriors' den, his nose twitching. "I smell ThunderClan."

Needlekit bounded toward him, her black chest puffed out. "It's Squirrelflight. She's come to visit."

As Macgyver turned his watchful gaze on Squirrelflight, Palesky ducked out of a den, and Leafstar and Hawkwing slid out after her, their eyes dark with suspicion.

"Squirrelflight," Leafstar greeted her coldly, stopping a tail-length away. "What do you want? Where is Bramblestar?"

"I was hoping to talk to you." Squirrelflight shifted her paws as the SkyClan leader glared at her. "Alone."

Hawkwing narrowed his eyes. "I think you said enough at the meeting."

"But I didn't," Squirrelflight meowed quickly. "If I had,

things might be different. I just want to see if we can come to an agreement." The curious stares of the SkyClan warriors, watching from around the clearing, seemed to burn through her pelt. "Perhaps we could talk somewhere private."

Leafstar didn't move. Rain ran along her whiskers.

Squirrelflight lowered her voice. "I don't want to put ideas into the heads of your Clanmates."

Leafstar snorted. "You seemed happy to put them into the heads of the other Clans."

"I'm sorry." Squirrelflight dipped her head. "Perhaps I shouldn't have spoken out, but I was trying to keep the peace."

"At our expense, as usual," muttered Hawkwing.

"Just let me speak to you." Squirrelflight gazed imploringly at Leafstar. Had she imagined the SkyClan leader's moment of hesitation at the meeting? Perhaps Leafstar had never even considered moving SkyClan to new territory. Her breath caught in her throat. *But she has to!*

Leafstar flicked her tail. "Okay." She jerked her muzzle toward her den. "But I can't spare much time. I have a Clan to take care of."

Squirrelflight hurried through the rain and waited at the den entrance for Leafstar to go in first.

"Join us, Hawkwing," Leafstar ordered as she nosed her way inside.

Needlekit blinked at Squirrelflight. "Leafstar doesn't like you much, does she?"

"Not at the moment," Squirrelflight told her softly. "But I hope I can change her mind."

She followed Leafstar inside, Hawkwing at her heels.

It was dry inside the den and stuffy from the morning's heat. Squirrelflight wanted to shake the rain from her fur but didn't dare. She'd soak Leafstar and Hawkwing. Instead she blinked the raindrops from her eyes, ignoring the dampness seeping deeper into her pelt. "I know I am asking a lot of you," she began. "You have suffered more than most Clans, and you've been without a real home for too long. But Harestar was right about land being wasted. I think we undertook these new borders with the best of intentions, but even if we learn to hunt the moorland we were given, ShadowClan will never fish in their marshes, and RiverClan will have to watch prey that once belonged to them go uncaught. We simply can't adapt to this new territory, and that makes the new borders unworkable."

Hawkwing stood as still as rock. "How is that our problem?"

"It'll be everyone's problem eventually. The Clans are growing, and not every season is as kind as greenleaf. When Clans go hungry, battles start. The peace we have now won't survive a prey-scarce leaf-bare if WindClan and RiverClan are forced to watch territory that was once theirs go to waste." She saw a flicker of interest in Leafstar's stony gaze. "It was the best solution we could come up with at the time. And it is not fair to ask you to move again," Squirrelflight meowed earnestly. "I know that. Every cat knows that. But it might be the only way to keep a lasting peace."

"You want us to leave the lake," Leafstar growled.

"No!" Squirrelflight thrust her muzzle forward. "You must never leave the lake. You belong here. But the territory beyond the abandoned Twolegplace might be a great home for you. If it is, this quarrel over land will be ended before it starts."

Leafstar didn't move. "If it's so important," she meowed icily, "why are *you* here and not your leader?"

Squirrelflight felt the sting of her words but didn't react. Leafstar was right to be angry. "Bramblestar doesn't know I'm here," she admitted. If she was going to win the SkyClan leader's trust, she needed to be honest. "He thinks you shouldn't move. But if he could see what a great piece of territory you'd be moving to, he'd have to admit that it's the best plan we have."

"You're going behind his back?" Leafstar looked surprised.

"I'm trying to find a way to convince him." Squirrelflight blinked at the SkyClan leader earnestly.

Hawkwing narrowed his eyes. "And you want us to help you?"

"It'll help SkyClan too. It'll help *all* the Clans." Squirrelflight stared at the SkyClan deputy. Surely he could see that! "Why should five Clans try to live on four Clans' land when there's plenty to spare on our borders?"

"We don't know it's to spare," Leafstar grunted. "It might be home to rogues or foxes, or Twolegs."

"That's why we need to go there." She gazed at Leafstar. "You and me. We could take a look at it; then you can decide. If it's not safe for SkyClan, no one will make you move."

Hawkwing's pelt ruffled along his spine. "You can't explore

unknown territory," he told Leafstar. "It's too dangerous. Let me send a warrior patrol—"

"No." Leafstar cut him off. "The Clan mustn't know that we're even thinking about this until I know it's a real possibility."

Hope flashed in Squirrelflight's heart. "So you'll come with me to look at the territory?" She searched Leafstar's gaze, relieved when she saw curiosity there.

"I don't like that you're deceiving Bramblestar," Leafstar meowed. "But that's your issue, not mine." Squirrelflight ignored the worry sparking at the edge of her thoughts. She was too excited to hear Leafstar go on. "I'll come with you and see this land for myself and, if it's not suitable, SkyClan will not move and we'll never speak of it again."

"I understand." Squirrelflight whisked her tail. "And I agree. SkyClan should only live where you can thrive."

Leafstar nodded to Hawkwing. "Tell the Clan that I'm escorting Squirrelflight to the border. I'll return as soon as I can."

"You may not be back for a while," Squirrelflight warned her. "It's a long way, and we'll need to investigate the territory thoroughly before you come to a decision."

"If I'm not back tonight," Leafstar told Hawkwing, "cover for me."

"What do I tell them?" Hawkwing mewed, his pelt bristling anxiously.

Leafstar narrowed her eyes, clearly thinking. After a moment she spoke. "Tell them I'm visiting each of the Clan leaders to get to know them better."

Hawkwing flicked his tail. "I don't like this. You're putting yourself in danger. Let me come with you, at least."

Leafstar shook her head. "I need you here to take care of the Clan."

"Then let me send Sagenose with you, or Plumwillow."

"No." Leafstar was firm. "There's no point starting rumors in the Clan. And if there are any dangers to be faced, I have more lives to spare than my warriors."

Respect swelled in Squirrelflight's chest. Leafstar was ready to sacrifice her own lives to protect her Clan. She dipped her head as the SkyClan leader padded past her and slid out of the den. "I'll take care of her," she promised Hawkwing.

Hawkwing's eyes were dark. "I hope you'll take care of each other. I don't like the thought of telling Bramblestar that something bad has happened to you."

Squirrelflight hesitated. Would Bramblestar forgive her if she never came back? Would he care? She padded from the den. Rain was pounding the camp. The kits were gone, the clearing empty. The SkyClan cats had retreated to their dens. She could see eyes flashing from the shadowy entrances as they watched her. Leafstar was already heading toward the bramble tunnel, and she hurried to catch up.

Outside the camp, the scents of moss and prey pressed around her, sharpened by the rain. The smell would be washed away soon, but for now it hung tantalizingly in the air. For a moment, Squirrelflight was tugged back to the day she was made an apprentice. She remembered standing beside

Leafpaw as forest scents spiraled into the camp. Her heart seemed to shiver with excitement. She'd dreamed of being leader as a kit, and now she was thinking like one. She puffed out her chest. Once again, she was heading into unknown territory.

Squirrelflight's excitement ebbed as she and Leafstar crossed into ThunderClan land and made for the distant border. Rain dripped through the canopy and seeped deeper into her fur. But the rain wasn't making her shiver. She wanted to see the new territory, but she knew she was being deceitful. She was sneaking out, knowing that Bramblestar would not approve. What if a Clanmate saw her? How would she explain what she was doing leading Leafstar through their territory? Guilt pricked at her belly and quickened her paw steps as she led Leafstar along the rise, which curved toward the abandoned Twoleg nest.

"Mousewhisker says that rogues and foxes rarely cross the border from the new territory," Squirrelflight told Leafstar.

"That doesn't mean there aren't any beyond it." Leafstar narrowed her eyes against the rain.

Squirrelflight tried to gauge Leafstar's mood. Was the SkyClan leader keeping an open mind about the land? Or would she find any excuse to object to it? "You'll be closer to the mountains," she encouraged. "There'll be plenty of prey."

"And more hawks to compete with." Leafstar ducked under a trailing branch. "I hope it's not too exposed."

Squirrelflight hopped over the branch. "It might be good

to be away from the dampness of the lake."

The stone walls of the crumbling Twolegplace showed among the trees. She veered along a trail that would take them around it, instinctively wary of anything that had once attracted Twolegs. As she leaped across an old streambed, she heard voices. Stiffening, she tasted the air. Through the rain she smelled ThunderClan. *A patrol?* Her paws tingling guiltily, she looked at Leafstar. "Someone's coming," she hissed. "Hide!"

Leafstar's eyes rounded. She ducked quickly behind an oak, snatching her wet tail from view as Squirrelflight turned to meet her Clanmates. Her heart quickened as she smelled Sparkpelt's scent.

Orange fur flashed through the undergrowth, and Sparkpelt slid from between the dripping ferns, Larksong at her heels. The young warrior clearly hadn't smelled her mother's scent. "Lionblaze said that Harestar is causing trouble." Sparkpelt's voice echoed between the trees.

"That's a refreshing change," Larksong answered. "It's usually Tigerstar who starts arguments among the Clans. Did he say what it was about?"

"He said it was best not to start rumors," Sparkpelt told him. "In which case, why say anything at all?"

Squirrelflight wondered whether to hide beside Leafstar. It would be easier if they weren't seen. But what if Sparkpelt or Larksong spotted them? What if they picked up their scent? It would be uncomfortable to be caught hiding, especially from her own daughter. Best to face them head on. "Hi!" She lifted her tail and hurried through the rain to meet Sparkpelt, whose ears pricked with surprise.

"Squirrelflight! What are you doing here?"

Squirrelflight wondered what to tell them. "I'm checking on something." Larksong scanned the forest warily. Squirrelflight could see him tasting the air. "Why are you two this far from camp?"

"We're hunting," Larksong told her. "It's been a while since anyone hunted this part of the forest. We thought we might find some juicy prey."

Sparkpelt was eyeing her mother curiously. "What are you checking on?"

Squirrelflight shifted her paws, hoping that the rain had slicked down her ruffled fur. "I came to look at the border."

"Which border?" Sparkpelt glanced around. They were deep in ThunderClan territory.

"The far edge of our land," Squirrelflight explained.

"Why?" Sparkpelt frowned.

Squirrelflight hesitated. It felt wrong to go behind Bramblestar's back, and worse to lie to her own daughter. Her tail drooped. She couldn't do it. "I want Leafstar to see the land outside," she confessed. She jerked her nose toward the tree where Leafstar was hiding. "She's here with me."

Leafstar padded out, her gaze wary.

"I *knew* I smelled SkyClan!" Larksong's hackles lifted.

Sparkpelt looked puzzled. "What's going on? Why does Leafstar need to see the land beyond our border?"

Squirrelflight lifted her chin. "I had an idea at the leaders' meeting. I wanted to stop the Clans from fighting over land again, so I suggested SkyClan move to new territory." She looked toward the border. "The land there is unclaimed. It might make a good home for SkyClan, but we're going to check it out first. We need to make sure it's not overrun with rogues or Twolegs."

Larksong frowned. "Wouldn't it be safer to send a patrol?"

Squirrelflight hesitated. "Bramblestar isn't *sure* about the plan," she explained at last, deciding to stretch the truth a bit, "so I brought Leafstar to see it. If she likes it, she can confirm to Bramblestar that she wants to move SkyClan there."

"I haven't agreed to anything yet," Leafstar grunted.

"No," Squirrelflight mewed quickly. "Which is why I don't want any cat to know about this."

"Not even Bramblestar?" Sparkpelt asked.

"Not even him," Squirrelflight answered, glancing awkwardly at Leafstar to gauge her reaction. The SkyClan leader was just watching her, clear-eyed. "If the Clans find out what we're doing, it could create expectations that might never be met. I don't want Leafstar to feel forced into anything."

"But what if something happens to you?" Sparkpelt's eyes glittered with worry.

"We'll be careful," Squirrelflight promised, leaning forward to rub her cheek against Sparkpelt's. "Don't worry. I'll be home soon."

"When, exactly?" Larksong gazed doubtfully toward the border.

Squirrelflight shifted her paws. It seemed unlikely that

they'd be able to explore the new territory before dark, and the thought of spending the night in a strange forest, far from her Clan, made her nervous. But she had to see this through. "Tomorrow," she mewed decisively.

"*Tomorrow?*" Sparkpelt looked alarmed. "But Bramblestar will be worried if you don't come home tonight. I can't act like I don't know anything."

"You have to." Squirrelflight looked at her urgently. "One night of worry to keep peace among the Clans. Surely you see that it's worth it?"

Sparkpelt's ears twitched nervously. "I guess."

"I'll be home as soon as possible," Squirrelflight told her. "But we have to do this properly. We need to cover as much of the land as we can."

Leafstar was watching, her eyes dark. "I won't ask SkyClan to move unless I'm sure about where we're going."

Sparkpelt looked at them both, then nodded. "Okay," she meowed. "We'll keep your secret . . . for now."

Relief washed over Squirrelflight's pelt. "Thank you." She nuzzled Sparkpelt's ear gratefully. "I promise I'll be careful." She fluffed her fur against the rain and turned toward the border. Glancing at Leafstar, she lifted her tail. "Ready?"

"Yes." Leafstar looked determined, her pelt spiked with raindrops.

"See you soon." With a quick nod to Sparkpelt and Larksong, Squirrelflight struck out past the Twoleg nest.

The forest grew thicker as they crossed the border, the slope beyond steepening sharply until they found themselves scrambling between rocks. The earth had turned to mud here and was slippery underpaw, but the rain was easing. Squirrelflight sniffed the air. The musky odor of Clan markers faded and disappeared behind them. Fresh prey-scents mingled with the smell of bark and earth. Pines clustered around them, blocking out the sun. Out of breath, Squirrelflight paused and looked up the slope, disappointed when she saw that trees hid the top.

Leafstar pushed past her, her ears flat with determination. Squirrelflight hurried at her heels as the SkyClan leader zigzagged between the rocks. At last, the slope began to flatten once more. The trees thinned, and they broke from the forest and found themselves on an open hilltop. As they paused at the peak, sunshine beamed through the clouds and lit the landscape ahead.

Squirrelflight caught her breath. Mounds rose before them, giving way to rocky mountain slopes in the distance. Forest sprouted here and there, opening into swaths of land where grass covered the rolling hills like a pelt. Squirrelflight could see streams cutting through the valleys like claw marks. Cascades of boulders clustered in ravines. "That looks like a good hunting ground." Squirrelflight nodded toward a sunny hillside. "I think I can see rabbit holes."

Leafstar didn't comment. She was staring at the view, her nose twitching. Fresh mountain scent mingled with forest and water, and the smell of prey hung heavy in the air. Squirrelflight scanned the hillsides for signs of Twolegs, but there were no stone nests here. A Thunderpath cut its way along one edge, heading for the mountain, but no monsters patrolled it.

Hope welled in Squirrelflight's chest. It seemed like good territory. She glanced at Leafstar, trying to hide her excitement. This had to be Leafstar's decision.

Leafstar narrowed her eyes. "Let's take a closer look." The SkyClan leader crossed the hilltop and headed into the valley below. Brambles rose around them, cut by sandy tracks and growing thicker as they neared the bottom. Had Leafstar noticed the prey trails? What else could have carved those pathways? Squirrelflight fell in behind her as she veered onto a steep path down. At the bottom a stream chattered over a stony bed. Beyond it, woodland reached the bank. The stream was shallow enough to wade across, and Leafstar led the way.

Cold water swirled around Squirrelflight's paws. She was glad to hop out the other side and follow Leafstar into the woods. There were wider tracks through the undergrowth here, and Squirrelflight's fur bristled nervously as she smelled a familiar scent. Other cats had been here. *Loners or rogues?* She tasted the air. The scent was faint, almost washed away now, and there was no sign of movement between the trees. She glanced at Leafstar. The SkyClan leader's pelt was slick from the rain, ruffled along her spine. Had Leafstar smelled the cat-scent too?

Leafstar slowed as they headed deeper into the new territory, her whiskers twitching. Squirrelflight sensed her caution and moved closer to her, scanning the trees as they skirted a hillside and followed the woodland down into another valley. As they neared the bottom, the forest opened. Shrubs clustered on the far side, sheltering a wide stretch of grass that covered the valley floor. Squirrelflight felt sunshine break through the clouds to warm her pelt and shook out her fur, relieved that she'd be dry soon. "This would make a good place for a camp," she murmured.

"Look." Leafstar nodded toward moss piled at the foot of a bush. Beside it, earth was scraped from beneath the branches to form a hollow around the trunk.

Squirrelflight stiffened. "It looks like someone's made a camp already." She jerked her muzzle around, noticing gaps between branches and patches of flattened grass. Her pelt spiking, she sniffed the ground. *Cats!* She couldn't tell how many. The scent was no more than a trace; the rain had washed the place clean. "It smells like it's been abandoned."

Leafstar's tail twitched. She looked around warily. "Why would they abandon this place?" she mewed. "They've taken a lot of trouble to make it their home."

Squirrelflight uncurled her claws, hoping Leafstar was wrong. Her heart quickened as a breeze whisked into the valley. It carried fresh cat-scents.

Leafstar moved beside her, pelt bushing. "Some cat's coming."

"I know." Squirrelflight's breath caught in her throat. She suddenly felt a long way from home.

"Let's get out of here." Leafstar turned and froze.

Squirrelflight followed her gaze. A huge she-cat was staring at them from beside a dogwood. The cat's long, fine gray fur was bushed out, and her eyes glittered with hostility.

Squirrelflight's heart raced as the cat stalked toward them, growling.

"We're going to have to fight our way out," she whispered to Leafstar.

"I don't know if we can." Leafstar nodded to the brambles at the side of the valley as three more cats, each as large as the first, padded out. Four cats followed the gray cat from the dogwood, and three more slid from beneath a juniper bush on the other side of the valley. "We're surrounded."

CHAPTER 4

The gray cat narrowed its eyes. "Why are you here?"

The other cats moved closer, pelts bushed, eyes flashing menacingly.

"We're exploring. We didn't realize . . ." Squirrelflight's mew trailed away as she saw that the gray cat's belly was round. She was expecting kits!

Leafstar shifted beside her. "We thought the camp was abandoned."

"The rain had washed away your scent," Squirrelflight mewed quickly.

The gray queen exchanged glances with a young white she-cat near the brambles. As the white she-cat flicked her tail, her gaze flashed back to Squirrelflight. "You must have seen our tracks and our dens."

"Yes." Leafstar leaned forward. "And we were just going to leave."

"But you said you thought this would be a good place to make camp." The queen was still glaring at Squirrelflight. "Why?"

"We were looking for new territory," Squirrelflight told

her. "We didn't realize this land belonged to a Clan."

"A Clan?" The queen tipped her head.

Leafstar growled. "Why are you explaining yourself to these cats?" she snapped at Squirrelflight.

Squirrelflight looked at her. What else was she supposed to do? "They outnumber us, or hadn't you noticed?"

"I noticed." Anger glittered in Leafstar's gaze. "But they're rogues, not a Clan!" She turned back to the queen. "I'm Leafstar, leader of SkyClan."

"I'm Moonlight, and these are the Sisters." The queen nodded toward her campmates.

"We only came to find out if this land was empty," Leafstar snarled. "Now that we know it isn't, we'll leave." She began to pad forward, but Moonlight hissed. The Sisters fanned out until every stretch of grass was covered.

"Wait!" Squirrelflight swallowed back panic. They'd never be able to fight their way out of here. She looked imploringly at Moonlight. "We just want to go home."

Moonlight's gaze flicked over her. "Are you one of the cats from the lake?"

"Yes." Had Moonlight and the Sisters been watching the Clans?

"I didn't think you ever strayed past your scent markers," Moonlight meowed.

"We don't, usually," Squirrelflight told her. "But as I explained, we're looking for territory."

"And you think you're going to take this land?" Moonlight's eyes narrowed into hard slits.

"We were just *looking*," Leafstar growled. "But we don't *need* it. Keep your land."

Moonlight didn't move. "Who says it's our land?"

"You live here, don't you?" Leafstar shot back.

"For now." She shook out her fur suddenly and sat down. Squirrelflight sensed the other cats relaxing around them. She let her fur smooth and glanced at Leafstar, hoping the SkyClan leader would do the same. These cats clearly didn't *want* to fight. Why provoke them? Moonlight lifted a paw and licked it. "We're not like you lake cats." She drew her paw over her ear. "We don't make boundaries or leave markers."

"If you did," Leafstar muttered, "we might have stayed away."

"True." Moonlight nodded to the white cat, who padded to her side. Her snowy pelt was sleek and well-groomed, and she sat down noiselessly as Moonlight went on. "But other cats don't show much interest in our land. They come and go; they hunt, then continue on their way. They leave us mostly in peace." She licked a paw and washed her other ear.

Squirrelflight wasn't surprised that other cats left them alone. The Sisters were larger than Clan cats. Their broad shoulders and wide paws were intimidating, and she wondered if even a trained warrior could fight more than one of them. The three males she could make out seemed younger than the other cats and smaller, but they were sleek and well-muscled, as though they'd never suffered a harsh leaf-bare or gone to sleep with an empty belly.

Leafstar looked around the camp, her gaze sharp. "You said

you only live here for now. Are you going to stay long?"

Squirrelflight pricked her ears. Leafstar sounded curious. Was she considering this territory?

Moonlight followed the SkyClan leader's gaze. "We'll stay until my kits are ready to travel."

Leafstar glanced at her belly. "Will you ever return?"

"It's a good place for birthing," Moonlight told her. "But if it's occupied when we come back this way, we'll find someplace else." She sounded unconcerned.

Hope flashed beneath Squirrelflight's pelt. The Sisters didn't want this land, and Leafstar sounded interested in making it SkyClan's home. "Will you move SkyClan here?" she asked Leafstar.

"It's good land," Leafstar told her. "Once Moonlight and her friends have moved on, I will send patrols to explore more and discuss a future here with my warriors."

Squirrelflight's heart soared. Her plan had worked! She couldn't wait to tell Bramblestar. He'd see what a great idea it had been once he heard about the land and knew Leafstar was open to moving SkyClan there. She looked at Moonlight's belly again, trying to guess how long it would be until she had her kits. They would be ready to travel before leaf-bare. Surely the Clans could wait that long to redraw their borders? "Let's go back and share the news," she meowed eagerly.

"I don't want to tell the other leaders until I've made a definite decision." Leafstar's pelt rippled along her spine.

"But once they know you're willing to think about moving, they'll be happy to live with the current borders for a few moons longer," Squirrelflight argued.

Leafstar dug her claws into the damp grass. "We're not announcing anything until we've checked out the whole territory and found it safe."

Why was Leafstar being so stubborn? The peace of the Clans depended on SkyClan finding new territory. This was better land even than the forest. "But it's perfect!"

Leafstar glared at her. "Why doesn't ThunderClan move here, then? We can go back to the Clans and suggest it—"

"No cat is going anywhere." Moonlight was watching them, her tail twitching.

Squirrelflight stiffened. The queen's mew was determined. "What do you mean?"

Moonlight shifted her weight. "I can't let you go back to your friends. Not yet. We don't want swarms of strange cats trekking through here."

Leafstar's ears twitched. "We won't come back until you've left."

"We want to go home and tell our Clans that this land will be free soon," Squirrelflight added.

Moonlight narrowed her eyes. "You've only just arrived, and already you're arguing about which Clan should take our home. Do you expect me to believe that you won't want to get your paws on it as soon as you can?"

"We will respect your right to this territory until you're ready to move on," Squirrelflight promised.

"*You* might," Moonlight mewed. "But your campmates might not."

The white she-cat nodded. "We've heard enough about the Clans to know that when they see something they like, they believe they have a right to it. Now that you've discovered this land, your Clanmates will want to take it by force."

"ThunderClan would never do that!" Squirrelflight bristled.

"And the others?" Moonlight gazed at her evenly. "Would they respect our right to be here too?"

Squirrelflight hesitated. Would Tigerstar leave these cats alone? Was Harestar patient enough to wait? Would Mistystar deny her Clan if she thought there was something better for it? "We want this land for *SkyClan*," she meowed firmly. "And you already have the word of SkyClan's leader not to take it until you've left."

"We've learned not to invite trouble if we don't have to." Moonlight flicked her nose toward a den at the edge of the clearing. "You will sleep there until the time comes for us to move on."

"But our Clans will come looking for us," Squirrelflight insisted.

"Will they find you?" Moonlight glanced toward the end of the valley, where one hill rose into another. Squirrelflight realized how deep they'd ventured into this territory. And the forest was wet with rain heavy enough to have washed away their scent. She gazed toward the hilltops, feeling suddenly how small she was and far from home.

Leafstar was frowning at the gray queen. "You can't hold us here against our will."

Moonlight didn't reply, but the other cats shifted around them, as though reminding Leafstar of their presence.

Leafstar bared her teeth.

"Stay calm," Squirrelflight whispered. "They won't be able to watch us all the time. We'll be able to slip away."

The white she-cat padded around them, sniffing curiously. Leafstar gave a warning growl.

"Quiet!" Moonlight's mew was suddenly fierce. "Snow is our sister. Show her respect."

Leafstar's growl turned into a hiss.

"Hush!" Squirrelflight nudged the SkyClan leader sharply. Snow stopped and stared at Leafstar, a threat in her eyes. She was big, with muscles visible even beneath her pelt. Leafstar held her gaze, refusing to be cowed. Snow stalked back to Moonlight's side, her fur bristling.

"Forgive Leafstar." Squirrelflight ignored Leafstar's sharp hiss. "She's a warrior. We're not used to surrendering. But if you fear our Clanmates so much, we will stay as willing captives until you are ready to move on."

Moonlight dipped her head. "Thank you. You will be treated as our campmates." She nodded to a tabby she-cat. "Tempest, bring food from the prey-hole for our visitors."

As the tabby padded to a large juniper bush and began digging between the roots, Squirrelflight surveyed the camp. The sun was sinking toward the hilltop, and shadow reached into the valley. She saw now how well the surrounding bushes hid the camp, so that anyone climbing down the side of the valley would see only undergrowth until they reached the bottom and pushed through to the grassy clearing. The dense bushes that lined the sides of the valley would make it easier to hide if she and Leafstar managed to slip away. And she knew Bramblestar would find them eventually, no matter how hidden the camp seemed. Her heart quickened. What would he think when he discovered that she'd gone behind his back and brought Leafstar here without his approval? Things were already tense between them. This would make it worse. She wondered, her paws pricking nervously, how long Sparkpelt would keep her secret before she told her father where they'd been heading.

Moonlight's campmates glanced at one another, as though unsure of what to do. Two of them sat down; the young toms padded to the edge of the grassy clearing and watched their captives while the others moved closer and murmured to one another, their inquisitive gazes flicking over Leafstar and Squirrelflight.

Leafstar leaned toward Squirrelflight. "These cats are strange," she hissed under her breath.

"I don't think they want to hurt us."

Leafstar snorted. "They're holding us captive."

Squirrelflight tried to keep her tone bright. "At least it looks like they're going to feed us."

"I guess," Leafstar conceded, her gaze flitting over the Sisters. "They don't look like they know what hunger is."

Squirrelflight saw Moonlight watching her and lifted her muzzle. "What's the hunting like here?" she asked the queen loudly.

"You can see for yourself." Moonlight nodded toward the tabby.

Tempest dragged two fat mice from a hole beneath the juniper. She lifted them in her teeth and shook the earth from them with a sharp toss of her head. Then she padded across the grass and dropped the mice at Squirrelflight's paws.

The mice smelled good, and Squirrelflight realized that she was hungry. She nodded to the tabby. "Thanks."

Moonlight stood up and flicked her tail toward the young toms. One darted toward the prey-hole and began fishing for more food. Another ducked behind a bush at the edge of the camp and dragged out a dead rabbit. The other cats slipped away and came back with more prey. Squirrelflight guessed that the group had been returning from a hunting patrol and dropped their catch outside the camp when they'd smelled intruders. The prey-hole must be where they stored prey left over from one day for the next. She wondered how the cats decided who ate yesterday's prey and who ate fresh. A tortoiseshell carried two voles to Moonlight and laid them on the ground in front of her. She padded away as Moonlight nodded her thanks, and settled on the grass between two young ginger she-cats.

Squirrelflight lowered herself onto her belly and pulled one of the mice close. "Eat," she whispered to Leafstar.

Leafstar ignored her, sitting straighter and staring at her captors.

She hoped that the SkyClan leader wouldn't start a fight. Didn't she realize they only had to play along until they had the chance to slip away, or until their Clanmates came to free them? Why risk hurting another cat or getting hurt themselves?

As she bit into her mouse, she watched the Sisters relax. They shared prey and tongues like Clanmates. Moonlight swallowed a mouthful of vole. Beside her, Snow was eating a shrew. With a sigh, the queen shifted onto her side to ease the weight away from her swollen belly. She blinked calmly at Squirrelflight. "I hope you will find your stay with us comfortable. It seems better to enjoy the company of others rather than resist it. The Sisters don't like violence, and we avoid it when we can."

"The Clans avoid violence too, when possible," Squirrelflight told her. "Peace is better for every cat."

Tempest had settled beside the young toms. She looked up from the mouse she was eating. "How long will it be before your Clan wonders where you are?"

"A quarter moon at least," Squirrelflight told her. She guessed that Bramblestar would send a patrol sooner, but rescue would be easier if the Sisters weren't expecting it.

Leafstar huffed beside her. "My Clan will be missing me already," she meowed pointedly. "They'll send out a search party. It won't take long for them to find me."

As Squirrelflight swallowed back frustration, Tempest glanced at Moonlight, alarmed. "Perhaps we should let them go. We don't want trouble."

Moonlight hooked up another vole with her claw. "There won't be trouble. Keeping these cats will send an important message to their Clans."

The tabby-and-white tom beside Tempest frowned. "What message?"

"That we don't fight easily, but we don't scare easily either," Moonlight told him. "And they're less likely to start anything if it might endanger their Clanmates' safety."

The tom scowled at Squirrelflight. "If they hurt us, we hurt you!"

Moonlight blinked at him coolly. "Keep your claws sheathed, Stone." She glanced at Tempest. "Your kit reminds me of his father."

Tempest's tail twitched self-consciously. "He's young, that's all."

The tom looked like an apprentice, not yet fully grown, but old enough to be a skillful hunter and fighter. The tom beside him looked the same age. He was white with tabby splotches on his legs.

"Are you brothers?" Squirrelflight asked. Stone nodded.

"I'm Grass," his brother added.

Squirrelflight looked at the only other tom in the group. He was moons younger than the other two—barely more than a kit—and ginger, like the she-cat beside him. The she-cat nodded to her. "I'm Furze," she said, "and this is my kit, Creek."

Squirrelflight greeted her, then leaned toward Leafstar. "Have you noticed that there are no grown males here, only youngsters?"

"Now that you mention it . . ." Leafstar narrowed her eyes. "I wonder what happened to their fathers."

"Maybe they ate them." Squirrelflight glanced at Leafstar,

joking, yet she couldn't help feeling that the absence of adult toms was strange.

Moonlight pointed to a yellow she-cat crouching beside the juniper. "That's Sunrise." Sunrise nodded as Moonlight's gaze flicked past her, toward two young ginger-and-white she-cats sharing a thrush a tail-length away. "They're Flurry and Sparrow. Hawk's their mother."

Leafstar jabbed her mouse with her paw. She hooked it up and inspected it. "We don't need to know every cat's name," she mewed. "We won't be here long."

Moonlight glanced at her thoughtfully for a moment, then returned to her vole as though dismissing the SkyClan leader's claim.

They finished their meal in silence. Squirrelflight was aware of the Sisters snatching watchful glances at her as they ate. Some of them clearly weren't comfortable with Moonlight's decision to keep them. But Sparrow and Flurry stared with open curiosity, and Squirrelflight couldn't help warming to the pair. They reminded her of apprentices, eager to start training.

Dusk was creeping over the valley. As shadow swallowed the hillside, Squirrelflight glanced around at the bushes encircling the camp. There were gaps here and there where she and Leafstar could slip out. The Sisters would have to sleep eventually, and it might be possible to sneak past even the most careful guard. Once they were out of the camp and in the thick undergrowth of the valley, it would be hard to follow them. Her thoughts flitted back to ThunderClan.

Bramblestar would be worried that she hadn't returned. She felt guilty about asking Sparkpelt to keep her secret. It wouldn't be easy for her daughter to sleep while her father fretted. Perhaps she'd tell him, and Bramblestar would be angry. Would he send a search party straight away? *No.* Even if he was angry with her for coming, he'd respect her enough to let her finish the mission she'd started and only worry when she hadn't returned in a day or two.

Moonlight beckoned Tempest with a flick of her nose and, when the she-cat hurried to speak with her, murmured something first to Tempest and then to Snow. The white cat got to her paws and followed Tempest across the clearing. They stopped in front of Squirrelflight and Leafstar.

Tempest nodded toward the juniper bush. "Moonlight says you're to sleep there."

Snow hung back, watching through narrowed eyes as Squirrelflight and Leafstar stood and padded toward the juniper bush.

Leafstar glanced over her shoulder at the white she-cat. "I don't care how big she is," she hissed to Squirrelflight. "If she snarls at me again, I'll claw her fur off."

Tempest stopped beside the juniper bush. "She's protective of her campmates, that's all." She blinked apologetically at Leafstar. "And she doesn't trust strangers."

Squirrelflight sniffed the bush. The warm scent of bracken hung around it. Tempest nodded to a small gap between the branches. "You'll find nests inside. Snow will guard the entrance. If you need anything, ask her and she'll let me know."

Squirrelflight dipped her head. "Thank you."

Leafstar pushed past her and strode inside.

"Do you have to make this difficult?" Squirrelflight followed her in. The entrance opened into a small den. Bracken and moss were piled at the edges. It had clearly been slept on. "Cats have given up their nests so that we can sleep comfortably."

"They wouldn't have to if they let us go." Leafstar sat on one of the piles and curled down stiffly into the moss. "I don't know why you're treating them like friends."

"Why make this any more uncomfortable than it is?" Squirrelflight mewed irritably. "Besides, I saw a gap beside the dogwood that looks like it might lead to a track through the brush. I doubt we'll get past Snow tonight, but if we play along, the whole group might be less watchful and we'll be able to slip away tomorrow."

"'Play along,'" Leafstar grunted. "I thought we were warriors." She turned her back on Squirrelflight and tucked her nose into the bracken, grumbling. "Held hostage by a bunch of rogues."

Squirrelflight settled onto the bracken beside her. She sympathized with the SkyClan leader. It was humiliating to be kept prisoner here, but conflict could be dangerous, not just for them. What if Moonlight's unborn kits were hurt in the fight? She rested her muzzle on her paws and closed her eyes. Tired after the long trek into new territory, she pushed worries from her mind and let herself sink into sleep.

A screech woke her. It split the air and she jerked her head up. In the darkness, it took a moment to remember where she was. Another shriek sounded. With a sickening jolt, Squirrelflight realized that Leafstar wasn't beside her. She scrambled from her nest and darted outside.

Snow had pinned Leafstar to the grass. Her pelt bushed, the white she-cat snarled at the SkyClan leader and pressed her shoulders harder against the earth. Leafstar struggled beneath her, hind paws churning. But Snow had twisted out of reach. The white cat glanced up as Squirrelflight skidded to a halt behind them. "I don't like to start fights any more than Moonlight," she hissed. "But I'm more than willing to finish them." She let go of Leafstar and backed away, her ears flat.

Flurry and Sparrow had hurried from their den. Stone and Grass watched from across the clearing.

Moonlight padded toward them. "What's going on here?"

"She tried to escape," Snow hissed.

Leafstar pushed herself to her paws and shook out her pelt. Rage shone in her eyes.

Squirrelflight hurried forward. "She was probably just going to make dirt," she mewed quickly.

"No, I wasn't," Leafstar growled.

"Get inside," Squirrelflight hissed. Did she want more trouble? She smelled blood and saw that Leafstar was wounded. "You're hurt!"

Leafstar snorted and turned toward the den. Squirrelflight's chest tightened as she watched her limp inside. Snow was glaring at her, eyes glittering. Stone and Grass glanced nervously at each other.

Flurry stepped forward. "We can guard if you like," she told Snow.

Sparrow pressed beside her. "You can get some sleep."

Snow narrowed her eyes. "I'll finish what I started," she mewed ominously.

Moonlight flicked her tail. "Make sure your friend stays in her den," she told Squirrelflight. "I don't want any more disturbances tonight." She turned back to her own den.

Squirrelflight followed Leafstar inside to find her lapping her hind paw. "Let me look at your wound." Squirrelflight nosed her muzzle out of the way and inspected the ragged fur. Blood oozed from a deep scratch on her leg. Her heart sank. It would be harder to escape now that Leafstar was injured. "Make sure it's clean," Squirrelflight told her.

"What do you think I was doing?" Leafstar began licking it again.

Squirrelflight looked around the den, relieved to see cobwebs crowding between the branches above her head. She reached up and grabbed a pawful. "Dress it with these when you've finished cleaning it."

"Thanks." Leafstar took the cobwebs from her.

"Tomorrow we'll see if we can get herbs to treat it." Anxiety fluttered in Squirrelflight's belly. Why hadn't Leafstar waited, as they'd planned? "Were you planning to leave without me?"

"I was trying to see if there was an easy way out of the

camp," Leafstar told her. "If I'd found one, I would have come back for you."

"Okay." Squirrelflight believed her. Leafstar wouldn't abandon another warrior. She sat down. Slipping away was going to be harder than she'd thought. Were they going to have to fight their way out of here? She forced her fur to remain flat. Fighting these cats would be dangerous. The Sisters seemed peaceful, but they were clearly willing to be aggressive if they needed to. "Next time you come up with an escape plan, tell me first."

"I don't know if there will be a next time." Leafstar began wrapping cobweb around her paw. "I think we'll have to wait for our Clanmates to rescue us."

Squirrelflight met her gaze darkly. She didn't want ThunderClan cats to get hurt because she'd made the mistake of coming here. Guilt wormed in her belly. She should never have gone behind Bramblestar's back. "They might not watch us so closely tomorrow," she mewed hopefully. "We might get away."

Leafstar eyed her doubtfully. "These cats won't let us go easily."

Squirrelflight shifted her paws anxiously. Leafstar was right. Escaping was going to be hard. And even if they managed, she wondered what kind of reception would await her in the ThunderClan camp.

CHAPTER 5

Squirrelflight sat down and curled her tail over her paws. She yawned, sleepy after eating the fat vole Sparrow had brought her at sunhigh. Across the clearing Tempest, Stone, and Grass were digging earth from beneath a low gorse bush. Its thick branches spilled onto the grassy clearing, and the three cats had opened a gap in the front and were taking turns hauling dirt from around the central stem. Squirrelflight nodded to Leafstar. "It looks like they're building a new den."

"If Moonlight let us go, they wouldn't need another den." Leafstar lay outside the juniper bush where they'd slept for the past two nights. The wound on her leg was still raw. The Sisters had treated it with herbs and there was no sign of infection, but they had no hope of slipping away from the camp now. The Sisters watched them day and night, and even if they could escape unnoticed, there would be no way Leafstar could outrun a patrol if they were followed.

Besides, Squirrelflight had found she was content here. The Sisters had treated them well, sharing prey and accepting them as though they were new members of the group. Even Snow, who was still watchful, had begun to warm to them. Last night she'd brought poppy seeds to the den in case Leafstar's wound kept her awake. Leafstar too seemed to be growing used to living in the valley camp. She'd stopped complaining about the crisp scent of the hills and the fact that fresh-kill here tasted more of sweet herbs than the dank flavors of the forest.

Squirrelflight wondered if ThunderClan or SkyClan had sent search patrols yet. The thought made her belly tighten. She felt sure by now that Bramblestar would be angry and she'd have to defend her reasons for coming here. And she felt guilty that the Sisters might face a patrol of hostile warriors because of her.

Flurry pushed her way through the ferns that masked the camp entrance. She was carrying herbs in her mouth. Squirrelflight tasted the air and smelled marigold leaves. The ginger-and-white she-cat crossed the clearing and stopped beside Leafstar. She dropped the herbs beside the SkyClan leader and shook out her pelt. "How does your leg feel?" she asked Leafstar.

"It's sore, but it's feeling better." Leafstar moved her leg closer as Flurry leaned down to look at it.

Squirrelflight had been impressed by how many of the Sisters were skilled in using herbs. Sparrow, Flurry, Sunrise, and Hawk had all tended to Leafstar's wound in turn. "Do you all know how to treat wounds?" She watched Flurry strip the marigold leaves from the stem.

"Of course." Flurry kept her eyes on her work.

"The Clans have only a few medicine cats," Squirrelflight told her.

"What if they get sick?" Flurry blinked at her. "Who looks after them?"

Leafstar stretched her muzzle forward to sniff the marigold. "They look after one another. And they have apprentices," she mewed.

"I guess we're all apprentices here," Flurry explained. "The mothers teach their kits, and the sisters learn from one another." She began to chew the leaves into a poultice.

Squirrelflight was beginning to get used to the strange way the Sisters addressed one another. The younger cats often referred to the older cats as Mother, whether a she-cat was their mother or not, and cats of a similar age called one another Sister. Names were used sparingly, except for the toms, who were only ever referred to by their names.

As Flurry began to lap the poultice gently into Leafstar's wound, Moonlight padded into camp, trailing long honeysuckle vines from her mouth. Snow, Creek, and Sparrow followed, dragging more vines after them.

"Is that for the new den?" Leafstar had stopped hiding her curiosity and was as quick now to ask questions as Squirrelflight.

Flurry finished applying the poultice and looked at her campmates. "We're building Moonlight's birthing den."

"Are her kits due soon?" Squirrelflight hoped her estimation that the Sisters might be gone by leaf-bare was correct.

"The kits will come in about a moon," Flurry told her.

Moonlight dropped the vines beside the gorse bush and headed across the clearing. "Is the wound healing, Sister?"

she called to Flurry as she neared.

"Yes, Mother. The swelling has gone down," Flurry told her.

"Good." Moonlight stopped beside her and nodded politely to Squirrelflight and Leafstar. "Have you eaten?"

"Sparrow brought us prey," Squirrelflight told her. She dipped her head. "I wish you'd let me help with the hunting. I don't like being treated like an elder."

"An elder?" Moonlight looked puzzled.

Leafstar stretched her injured leg tentatively. "An elder is an old cat. In the Clans, when warriors become elders, they only hunt if they want to. Younger warriors and apprentices make sure they are well fed and cared for. Elders need never leave the camp."

"I could never stay in camp all day," Moonlight meowed.

"I don't like it much." Squirrelflight flicked her tail-tip irritably. "I need to stretch my legs."

Leafstar's ears twitched. "If you let us go, we could both stretch our legs."

Moonlight sniffed Leafstar's wound. "We'll let you go when we move on. For now you'll have to put up with living like your elders."

Squirrelflight looked on as Creek and Sparrow wove the vines between the branches to build the gorse den. "Can I help here, then?" Two long days of doing nothing had left her restless.

"That would be kind." Moonlight straightened. "Leafstar should rest this leg, though."

"I'm happy to watch," Leafstar told her.

Moonlight led Squirrelflight across the clearing. Flurry padded after them. Stone was still scraping earth from the den. He paused as Squirrelflight reached him. She peered inside and saw that he'd created a wide dip around the central stem. Branches had been broken off to open up the space inside, but the remaining walls were still thick enough to keep the den cool. It looked a lot like a warrior den.

Tempest padded around the pile of vines. "We'll need more."

Moonlight nodded to Snow. "Sister, take Creek and fetch more," she meowed.

Snow dipped her head. She made her way out of camp, Creek hurrying behind her.

Tempest beckoned Stone and Grass with her tail. "Use these to reinforce the back of the den," she told them.

"Sure." Stone glanced at his brother. "You weave from the inside and I'll weave from out here."

Grass picked up a vine in his teeth and dragged it into the den while Stone hauled another vine around the back.

As Tempest watched them disappear, Squirrelflight saw sadness in the tabby's gaze. Was she thinking about their father? Where was he?

"We'll work on this side." Moonlight pulled the remaining vines around the back of the den.

Squirrelflight followed, glancing at Tempest. "It must have been hard for her, raising her kits alone."

Moonlight's eyes widened. "She didn't raise them alone. She had us."

"But she must miss her mate."

Moonlight tucked a vine into the den wall and began to draw it through, tugging at it with her paws. "Why would she miss her mate?"

"Doesn't she love him?" Squirrelflight pressed a vine through a gap.

"I don't know," Moonlight told her. "We prefer to live without toms. Tempest could have stayed with him if she'd wanted to, but she chose to travel with us and raise her kits among her sisters."

Squirrelflight couldn't imagine raising kits without Bramblestar. And how could she think of living without him? Even though she hadn't been gone long, she missed him. Would he forgive her for coming here? Suddenly her heart quickened. She wanted to see him, to explain why she'd crossed the border. He'd understand when he realized how important it was to her.

"Here." Moonlight pushed a stray tendril toward her. "Pull this one through."

Squirrelflight tugged at it while Moonlight fastened the other end into the wall. "If you prefer not to have toms around, what will happen to Grass and Stone? They're your kin. Can they stay?"

"No." Moonlight sat back on her haunches and inspected her work. "They're old enough to leave us. We've been waiting until the stars are in place."

Squirrelflight wondered for a moment if the Sisters had their own StarClan. She glanced at Moonlight. "What do you mean?"

"Wait until tonight," Moonlight told her. "You'll see."

"Do they want to leave?" Squirrelflight wondered how the Sisters could send their young away.

"Of course they want to leave. They're toms. They have a deep connection with the land. They must travel it as they wish, not be tied to our path."

Squirrelflight couldn't imagine being separated from her kits no matter how old they were. "Won't Tempest miss them?"

"At first," Moonlight told her. "But there will be new litters to take care of." She glanced at her belly. "And we are each mother to all the young."

"Where will Stone and Grass go?"

"Wherever they choose." Moonlight reached for the end of Squirrelflight's vine and began to tuck it between the branches. "They might travel together, or become loners or join rogues, or live with Twopaws. Their ancestors will guide them."

"Twopaws?" Squirrelflight asked.

Moonlight tipped her head. "The furless animals that build big stone dens to live in."

Twolegs. Squirrelflight shuddered. "But why would any cat choose to be a kittypet?"

"Our ancestors were *kittypets,* as you call them," Moonlight told her. "All the Sisters are descended from den-bound cats. Our first Mothers were one family."

Squirrelflight let go of the vine and Moonlight pulled it. She suddenly understood why the Sisters looked so similar.

Their large frames and thick, long fur marked them as different from most of the warriors and rogues Squirrelflight had met. It made sense that they were descended from a single family. She was eager to know more. "Flurry said that you all have medicine-cat skills."

Moonlight glanced at her. "What's a medicine cat?"

"In the Clans, we have cats who have special knowledge about healing herbs," she explained.

"Surely it is safer to share such knowledge?"

"There's more to being a medicine cat than knowing about herbs. They have a special gift. They can communicate with our dead ancestors."

"They speak with the dead?" Moonlight looked suddenly interested. She rested her forepaws on the ground. "Is their gift passed from mother to kit?"

"Medicine cats don't have kits."

Moonlight blinked. "Why not?"

"It's forbidden. They devote their lives to caring for their Clan."

Moonlight frowned. "That must be hard. I couldn't imagine life without kits."

"Nor could I." Squirrelflight thought of Leafpool. How hard it must have been for her sister to watch Squirrelflight raise Jayfeather, Lionblaze, and Hollyleaf, to pretend all the time that she wasn't their mother. How much simpler it was here. Kits were born and the Sisters raised them together. They could take mates where they liked. There were no rules about falling in love with cats from other Clans. Or about who could have kits and who couldn't. And yet they had to send their sons away. She glanced at Moonlight's belly. "Aren't you frightened you might have sons who'll have to leave you?"

"We can't hold on to those we love forever," Moonlight told her.

"What about their father?" Squirrelflight hesitated. "I hope you don't mind me asking, but did you love him?"

Moonlight purred, as though she thought the question was funny. "I liked him. But Jack's an everkit—a den-bound cat. He was fun to be around, and handsome. And I was ready to have another litter. But my life is with my Sisters."

Squirrelflight's heart suddenly ached for the litter she dreamed of. "Will you see him again?"

"I'll visit the barn where he lives and show him his kits when they're old enough to travel," Moonlight told her. "They may want to know him, and they might even choose to live near him when they're old enough to leave our group. We let our young decide how they want to live. Not every cat wants a life like ours.."

As she spoke, Creek and Snow pushed through the ferns at the entrance, dragging long vines behind them. They dropped them beside the birthing den, and Stone took one inside while Moonlight fetched more for the wall. Squirrelflight noticed how peacefully the cats worked, quietly helping one another until Sunrise and Furze padded into camp carrying prey.

As the sun set, the Sisters finished their work and then settled around the clearing to eat. Moonlight pushed a young rabbit toward Squirrelflight and glanced at the purple sky, where stars were beginning to show. "Look."

Squirrelflight followed her gaze toward a patch of stars that seemed to stretch in a line toward the horizon.

"The Claw Stars are pointing toward the sunset." Moonlight glanced across the clearing to where Grass and Stone sat close to their mother, sharing a squirrel. "It is a good night for our sons to begin their wandering."

"Tonight?" Squirrelflight's heart ached as she saw Tempest nudge Grass fondly and tear off a strip of flesh for Stone. "Does Tempest know?"

"She'll have seen the stars by now," Moonlight told her matter-of-factly. The gray she-cat padded to join Tempest and the toms.

Squirrelflight carried the rabbit to Leafstar and laid it down before her. The SkyClan leader was dozing, her muzzle resting on the grass. She lifted her head sleepily as Squirrelflight sat beside her, and blinked at the rabbit. "Is the den ready?"

"Not yet, but we made good progress." Squirrelflight looked at the half-finished den. "We can weave in the rest of the vines tomorrow. I might suggest that they lay a branch across the entrance to stop the kits from getting out."

Leafstar pushed herself into a sitting position and sniffed the rabbit. "You sound so at home here. Are you planning to stay?" She eyed Squirrelflight accusingly.

"No, of course not." Squirrelflight lifted her chin. "But I might as well make myself useful while I'm here."

"Don't make yourself too useful," Leafstar grunted. "They might decide to keep you forever."

Squirrelflight tore a hunk of rabbit from the carcass and settled down to eat it. The Sisters had a good life here, but she missed her Clanmates. She wondered what it was like to live without the warrior code. The Sisters had a code of their own, but it seemed very loose. Cats were allowed to come and go as they pleased, and she wondered what stopped the group falling apart, especially when they faced the hardships of sickness or hunger.

The shadows deepened as she ate, and the moon rose into a star-speckled sky. Moonlight got to her paws. Wordlessly, she headed toward the camp entrance. The rest of the group followed her, Grass and Stone padding close to their mother.

Furze stopped beside Squirrelflight. "Moonlight says you're to go with them." She glanced at Leafstar's injured leg. "She can stay here with me."

Squirrelflight looked at Leafstar. "Grass and Stone are leaving. They're going to say good-bye," she told her. "Will you be all right here by yourself?"

Leafstar sniffed. "I won't be by myself. I'll have Furze to keep me company." She sounded unimpressed, but Furze didn't seem to take offence. Instead she sat down beside the SkyClan leader and sniffed at the rabbit's remains.

"Do you mind if I take a bite?" she asked Leafstar.

"Sure." Leafstar shrugged.

Squirrelflight left them and hurried after the others. Sunrise was waiting for her as she pushed through the ferns at the entrance to the camp. "Which way did they go?" Squirrelflight gazed up the slope rising ahead. Bushes hid whatever path the Sisters had taken.

"Follow me." Sunrise ducked beneath a gorse bush and led Squirrelflight up a winding trail through the undergrowth. Squirrelflight could smell the Sisters' paw prints on the grass, fresher with each step, until she glimpsed Snow's tail flicking away through a swath of bracken ahead. Sunrise quickened her pace and Squirrelflight followed, pushing past the ferns, surprised when she broke into the open to find that they'd reached the top of the hill.

The Sisters were lined along the crest, gazing at the land beyond. The starlit sky stretched over hill after hill, rolling away to the mountains. Grass and Stone stared into the distance, their pelts ruffled by the wind. As they looked back at the Sisters, Squirrelflight could see excitement glittering in their eyes. Were they glad to be leaving? Slowly, the Sisters gathered in a circle around them. Moonlight padded toward them and touched her nose to Grass's ear and then Stone's. "I wish you well," she murmured.

Snow took her place as Moonlight returned to the circle, nuzzling each tom fondly before stepping away. One by one, the Sisters said good-bye to the toms. Squirrelflight's throat tightened as Tempest approached them. Grief glittered in the tabby's eyes as she pressed her muzzle to Grass's cheek. "Take care of yourself," she whispered. Then she turned to Stone. "Be happy."

Stone's eyes shone with sadness, and he ran his nose along his mother's cheek. "We will always remember you." He pulled away and glanced at Grass. They seemed to share a moment of understanding, then blinked and looked away.

Tempest padded back to join her Sisters. Hawk and Snow pressed either side of her as Moonlight dipped her head to the young toms. "This is the beginning of your great adventure," the gray she-cat told them. "You must walk through the night, never looking back, and at dawn you will have left your kithood behind and become true toms. May the ancestors who walk the land find you and give you guidance."

Stone dipped his head. "Thank you, Mother."

Grass shifted his paws, seeming suddenly uncertain.

"Wander in peace," Moonlight meowed.

The Sisters raised their voices to the sky. "Wander in peace."

They moved, opening the circle they'd made, and Stone and Grass padded away, following the slope of the hill down into the next valley.

Squirrelflight glanced back over her shoulder. She wondered if she could ever give up the toms in her life. *No.* From here she could see the edge of the forest beside the lake. *ThunderClan territory.* She gazed wistfully toward it. What was Bramblestar doing right now? Was the Clan settling down for the night? Or was a patrol already searching for her? Guilt tugged beneath her pelt. Was Sparkpelt still keeping her secret? It would be a heavy burden to bear. She couldn't let her daughter or her Clan worry any longer. She had to find a way home.

Grass and Stone had disappeared into shadow, but the Sisters stood watching silently as though breathing every last scent of them. Tempest leaned softly against Snow, her gaze misty.

Squirrelflight's heart twisted with sadness. Tomorrow, once the Sisters' loss was less raw, she'd ask Moonlight again if she and Leafstar could leave. If she explained how much she missed her Clan and her kin, perhaps the Sisters would understand her longing to go home. Would they believe her promise not to let her Clanmates come here until the Sisters had left? Her belly tightened. Was it a promise she'd be able to keep?

CHAPTER 6

Squirrelflight jerked awake, her nose twitching. The air was thick with the scent of nighttime dew. She could smell another scent in the darkness, one that made her heart quicken, filled with the warmth of memory and home. She scrambled to her paws. *Bramblestar!* He was near. She could smell Thornclaw too, and Larksong and Sparkpelt. "Wake up, Leafstar!"

The SkyClan leader lifted her head blearily. "What's going on?"

"Quick!" Squirrelflight darted to the entrance. "They're here. A rescue party's here!"

As she spoke, wails shrilled outside the den. Alarm bristled through her pelt. She couldn't let them fight. No cat must be hurt. "Stop!" She exploded from the den, skidding to a halt as she saw Clan warriors facing the Sisters.

Pale in the moonlight, Snow and Tempest had puffed out their fur. Ears flat, lips drawn back, they hissed at the warrior patrol. Bramblestar, Thornclaw, and Larksong snarled back at them. Furze, Sunrise, and Hawk slid like hissing snakes around their sisters as SkyClan cats—Hawkwing, Plumwillow, and Tree—fanned out around the ThunderClan patrol.

The cats glared at one another through slitted eyes.

"Wait!" Squirrelflight flung herself between the Sisters and the warriors. ThunderClan and SkyClan outnumbered the Sisters. Blossomheart, Macgyver, and Sagenose appeared, pushing between their Clanmates, as Berrynose and Amber-moon stepped out from behind the ThunderClan warriors and bared their teeth. "You mustn't fight!"

Confusion clouded Bramblestar's gaze.

Leafstar limped from the den and stopped at the edge of the clearing, her eyes round with alarm. "Listen to her."

Hawkwing stared at her, as though trying to understand.

"They haven't harmed us," Squirrelflight told him. She knew that it was a lie. Snow had wounded Leafstar, but only because the SkyClan leader had tried to escape. There would be time for honesty later; right now it was more important to defuse the rage sparking around her.

Creek, Flurry, and Sparrow darted from the shadows and stood beside their mothers. Moonlight hurried from the back of the clearing and wove between her campmates. She stopped at the front of the group and stared at Bramblestar.

Squirrelflight was shocked to see how small the Clan cats looked in front of the Sisters. She'd grown used to these cats, forgetting their size. She realized once more how different they were—their fur was longer, their bodies larger than any warrior or rogue Squirrelflight knew. Even Bramblestar seemed overshadowed by their size. She wondered suddenly if, for all their training, the Clans could win a fight with these cats. She brushed the thought away. *Of course they can.* Skill would always beat strength. And yet, how could she be sure the Sisters didn't have as much skill as strength?

Moonlight lashed her tail. "What are you doing in our camp?" She curled her lip as she glared at the warrior patrol.

Bramblestar answered, his ears twitching with rage. "We've come to fetch our Clanmates." He didn't look at Squirrel-flight.

Worry wormed in her belly, as she guessed that some of his anger was directed at her. He'd be wondering why in StarClan she was defending her captors and why she'd come here without telling him, putting herself and Leafstar in danger. She'd gone against his wishes. What would he have felt if any other of his warriors had ignored his orders so blatantly? Her mouth felt dry. *What would I feel if one of our warriors ignored my orders?*

"They shouldn't be here," he growled.

"Your Clanmates are our guests," Moonlight told him.

Hawkwing jerked his gaze toward Leafstar. "Is that true?"

Moonlight answered for her. "We have treated them like sisters."

Bramblestar flicked his tail angrily. "They haven't stayed here voluntarily. No warrior would! You've held them against their will."

"It was necessary," Moonlight growled.

Hawkwing glared at her. "Why?"

Squirrelflight looked from Moonlight to Bramblestar as she stood between them. "They were scared we'd bring our Clanmates here if they let us go."

Bramblestar looked puzzled. "But they must have known

we'd come looking for you."

"They're not Clan cats," Squirrelflight explained. "They didn't realize you'd try so hard to get us back."

"They've only been here two days." Moonlight scanned the warrior patrol curiously. "That's not long to be away from home. Don't any of you ever wander?"

Hawkwing growled. "We're warriors, not loners. We stay with our Clan."

The Sisters exchanged glances, but no cat spoke.

Bramblestar let his pelt smooth. Around him the Clan cats shifted self-consciously, as though suddenly wondering what they were doing here, if Squirrelflight and Leafstar didn't seem to be in danger.

Squirrelflight padded to Bramblestar's side, her heart quickening out of habit as his scent filled her nose. She reached her muzzle toward him. Did he feel the same way? Or was he too angry with her to feel relieved that she was safe? "I'm glad you came to get us."

He pulled away, blinking at her. "Are you okay?"

"I'm fine."

Leafstar limped toward her warriors.

"Not so fast." Snow darted from the group and blocked her way. "We haven't said you can leave."

"Why keep us now?" Leafstar blinked at her. "Our Clan-mates know where your camp is. There's nothing left to hide."

"No," Snow agreed, her pelt rippling along her spine. "But as long as you're our guests, your friends will have to respect our boundaries."

Squirrelflight looked at her in surprise. "I thought the Sisters didn't have boundaries."

"Not permanently," Snow conceded. "But when one of us is ready to kit, we must mark out some sort of territory to protect her and her newborn."

Bramblestar's gaze flitted around the Sisters, stopping as it reached Moonlight. He dipped his head. "I should have seen that you are expecting kits."

Squirrelflight blinked at him. "Do you see why I couldn't let you fight?"

He ignored her. "But you can't keep Leafstar and Squirrelflight here. They're coming home with us now."

As he spoke, Tree pushed his way to the front. The Sky-Clan tom's eyes were on Moonlight. Squirrelflight watched him, alarm sparking in her belly. Why was Tree glaring at the gray she-cat so resentfully?

"Hello, *Mother*."

Squirrelflight blinked. *Mother?* Had he once been part of this group? She stiffened as another thought flashed in her mind. Were they *actually* mother and son? Tree—small, muscular, thickly pelted—looked nothing like the broad, long-furred, bushy-tailed she-cat. And yet there was a dark determination in his amber gaze that reminded her of Moonlight.

Moonlight stared back at Tree, blankness giving way to excitement as she recognized him. "Earth!" Sunrise, whose coat was the same shade of yellow as Tree's, stepped forward, her tail rising in excitement, but paused at Tree's next words.

"I'm not Earth anymore." Anger hardened Tree's mew. "I named myself Tree after you sent me away."

"Tree." Moonlight repeated his name, as though testing it. She tipped her head. "I like it. It suits you. You were always a strong-minded kit."

"Is that why you abandoned me?"

"Abandoned you?" Moonlight looked surprised. "You were old enough to hunt."

"Barely."

"But the Claw Stars were pointing to the sunset. It was time for you to wander."

"You let the stars dictate my fate." Tree held his mother's gaze scornfully for a moment longer, then looked away.

Squirrelflight glanced around at the Sisters. They shifted uncomfortably. Sunrise was staring guiltily at her paws. Perhaps their way of life wasn't as uncomplicated as she'd thought. She saw Creek shoot a nervous glance at his mother. Was he anxious about leaving when his time came to wander?

Bramblestar moved beside him. "Tree is one of us now. If he wishes to know you better, that's up to him, but he came here for the same reason we did. You are holding our Clanmates against their will. Let them go!" He flexed his claws. "You may be carrying kits, but that doesn't mean we won't fight to get our Clanmates back."

As Moonlight hesitated, Squirrelflight saw Plumwillow and Berrynose drop into battle stances. Hawkwing and Thornclaw bared their teeth. Her breath caught in her throat. "They only want us to stay here until Moonlight's kits are ready to travel," she mewed quickly.

Bramblestar swung his gaze toward her. "Do you want to stay with them until then?" he growled.

"Of course not!" Squirrelflight blinked at him. "But they meant us no harm. If we wait, this territory will be free for SkyClan to take in a moon or two."

Bramblestar stared at her coolly. "That is a decision for Leafstar and SkyClan to make."

Leafstar whisked her tail. "This is good land. I think Sky-Clan would be happy here." Relief washed Squirrelflight's pelt. Leafstar was backing her up. She looked gratefully at her as the SkyClan leader went on. "I'm willing to give the Sisters a moon to move on. Two if they need it." She switched her gaze to Moonlight. "But they must let us return to our Clans. I'm not staying here another day."

Moonlight dipped her head. "You can go." She lifted her gaze to Bramblestar. "We're bigger than you, and stronger," she told him. "Any battle between us would be bloody. But there is no need to fight if you leave us in peace."

Bramblestar narrowed his gaze. "Strength doesn't always win battles," he snarled.

Plumwillow showed her teeth. "You held our leader captive!"

"She looks wounded," Sagenose growled.

Did the Clan cats want revenge? Squirrelflight gazed pleadingly at Bramblestar. "Let's go."

Larksong padded forward. "If they're letting Squirrelflight leave, there's no need to fight. Leafstar's wound will heal faster if she returns home right away."

Squirrelflight looked at the young tom, grateful for his sense. He was thinking with his head, not his claws. Sparkpelt had chosen a good mate.

"Very well." Bramblestar signaled with his tail, and the Clan cats began to turn toward the fern entrance.

Squirrelflight lingered, catching Moonlight's eye. "Thanks for sharing your fresh-kill."

"I am sorry that we met under such circumstances," the gray she-cat meowed. "If we meet again, I hope that it will be as friends."

Leafstar eyed Moonlight but didn't speak. She was clearly less than grateful for the Sisters' hospitality. She nodded curtly and limped after her Clanmates as Squirrelflight dipped her head to Moonlight.

"I hope your kitting goes well."

"Thank you." Moonlight swished her tail.

"Are you coming?" Bramblestar stopped at the entrance and glared at Squirrelflight, his pelt prickling along his spine.

"I have to go." Squirrelflight headed toward him, irritated at being called away like a kit.

Bramblestar waited for her to push through the ferns, then followed her out of camp. Her Clanmates wound their way out of the valley. She padded after them, relieved to be heading home.

"What in StarClan were you thinking?" Bramblestar fell in beside her.

She dipped her head, bracing herself for the argument she knew must be coming. "I'm sorry."

"Going off like that on a hare-brained mission without telling me!"

She could feel his gaze burning through her pelt. "You'd have stopped me if you'd known," she mewed.

"Of course I would have!" he snapped. "Now look what's happened. You've found a whole new group of cats to fight with over territory. As if ShadowClan and WindClan weren't enough!"

"But we don't have to fight with them," Squirrelflight objected. "They're happy for SkyClan to have the land when they're finished with it." She stopped and looked at him. She'd made a mistake coming here as she had, but it was obvious she'd found the answer to the Clans' problems. "Don't you see? I've found SkyClan the land they need! Now the Clans won't have to fight over territory ever again."

"Don't be naive." Bramblestar stared at her. "New territory will probably mean new battles. Since when was any Clan satisfied with what they have?"

"When each Clan has enough, then the fighting will stop." Why was he being so negative? "We haven't gotten the borders right until now. But once SkyClan moves, every Clan will have plenty."

Bramblestar brushed past her and padded after his Clanmates.

Squirrelflight caught up to him, irritation spiking her fur. "I had a good idea and I followed it through," she snapped. "Leafstar likes the new territory, and now SkyClan will have somewhere they can finally make a real home. You just don't want to admit I was right!"

"Nonsense!" Bramblestar lashed his tail. "I'm Clan leader. I welcome ideas from any of my Clanmates, and if it's a good idea, I'm happy to be proved wrong."

"My idea *is* a good idea!" Squirrelflight swallowed back frustration.

"You're only seeing it from your point of view," Bramblestar growled. "Have you really thought about what it would be like for SkyClan to move again so soon? To build yet another camp? To learn about new territory? How do you know there aren't Twolegs here? Or a family of foxes? Have you checked every tail-length of this land? What if one of their kits is killed by a snake here? Will you take responsibility?"

"Life is risky!" Squirrelflight ignored the doubt shimmering at the edge of her thoughts. "There will be risks wherever SkyClan lives!"

Bramblestar ignored her. "And how does it make SkyClan look—agreeing to live where the other Clans choose *again*? Do you think the other Clans will treat them as equals once they've finished pushing them around?"

"That's not my problem!" Squirrelflight shot back. "It's up to SkyClan! Leafstar *wants* to move. She knows what she's doing."

"I hope so." Bramblestar paused and looked along the track as it steepened and disappeared among boulders. "Are you sure that, after a few seasons living among these hills, SkyClan won't feel like they've been pushed outside the Clans again?"

"Why should they? This land is right next to ours, and ShadowClan's. And they'll have a strip of territory right down to the lakeshore. They'll be as much a part of the Clans as we are." Squirrelflight hurried after him, following the path as it snaked into a narrow gorge. Ahead, their Clanmates padded beneath overhanging rock. The star-specked sky showed in a narrow band above them. As the trail opened into another valley, Bramblestar spoke again.

"I was worried about you, you know?" His mew was husky.

"I know." Guilt rippled beneath her pelt. "I didn't know I'd be away so long, and I told Sparkpelt where I'd gone, just in case."

"Sparkpelt was worried too," he told her. "More so because you asked her to keep your secret. She didn't know whether telling me was betraying you, or remaining silent was betraying me. You should never have put her in that position."

Squirrelflight shrank beneath her pelt. "I know," she mewed softly. "I just wanted to make the Clans okay again. How was I to know we'd be taken prisoner?" As she spoke, resentment bubbled in her chest. Bramblestar wasn't even trying to understand. Was he enjoying making her feel bad? "But we weren't hurt, and it was good to see how other cats live. The Sisters have an interesting way of life."

"And we don't?"

"That's not what I meant and you know it!" He was acting like a kit! "They treated us well."

"What about Leafstar's wound?"

"She tried to escape."

"And you didn't?" He shot her a reproachful look. "Did you like the Sisters so much that you didn't want to come home?"

"Don't be mouse-brained!"

"'Mouse-brained'!" He glared at her. "You force me to lead my Clanmates into hostile territory on a rescue mission and you call *me* mouse-brained. You're Clan deputy, for StarClan's sake! You're supposed to be protecting your Clan, not putting them in danger. And you're my mate. If there's anyone I should be able to rely on in ThunderClan, it should be *you!*"

"You *can* rely on me!" The ground seemed to shift beneath Squirrelflight's paws. Didn't he trust her anymore?

"Not when you behave like a reckless apprentice." Bramblestar glared at her. "From now on, I want you to run every decision by me. No more going off on your own ridiculous missions. No more arguing with me at Gatherings. If a deputy can't support her own leader, perhaps she's not fit to be deputy." With that, Bramblestar pulled ahead, his shoulders stiff, and followed his Clanmates as the path wound into a wooded ravine.

Some of the ThunderClan warriors shot Squirrelflight sympathetic glances. It only made her feel more wretched. *Did my own mate just threaten to replace me as deputy?* She trailed behind. What was the point of talking to him? He seemed determined to twist her words, and he clearly didn't want to admit that her mission might have helped the Clans. Suddenly she missed the amiable calm of the Sisters' camp. In her days there, no cat had argued or worried about territory or fussed about whether their campmates were following the warrior code. They seemed to take life as it came, without judgment or complaint. As they neared the Clan border, Squirrelflight's chest tightened as she felt the forest begin to close in on her.

She could sense that Bramblestar wasn't going to forgive her anytime soon.

CHAPTER 7

❧

Flippaw stopped as he crossed the clearing, a bundle of fresh moss for the elders' den between his jaws. He dropped it as he reached Squirrelflight. "I'm glad you're back. Hollytuft said the Sisters wanted to keep you captive forever." He blinked at her eagerly. "She said they were twice the size of normal cats. Were they scary?"

Squirrelflight twitched her tail. She'd lost count of the number of times she'd answered questions about the Sisters since she'd returned yesterday. "They were nice," she told him patiently.

Flippaw looked puzzled. "But they held you hostage."

"Yes, but they shared their prey with us and took care of Leafstar's wounded paw." Why were her Clanmates so surprised that cats could be kind and yet still stand up for themselves?

Flippaw tipped his head to one side. "Is that why you didn't try to escape?"

Squirrelflight swallowed back irritation. "Leafstar's injury made it hard to escape, and I wasn't going to leave her."

"But you said they were nice. She would have been okay."

"It wouldn't have been right to escape by myself." Didn't young cats understand loyalty?

But Flippaw had moved on. "Were they rogues?" He stared at her intently. "Bristlepaw said they used to be part of Darktail's Kin."

"Of course they weren't." Squirrelflight flicked her tail sharply. She was relieved to see Hollytuft padding from the fresh-kill pile.

The black warrior looked sternly at Flippaw. "Shouldn't you be cleaning out the elders' den?"

His tail drooped. "I wanted to find out about the new Clan."

"I told you," Hollytuft mewed. "It isn't a Clan. It's just some cats who live near the mountains. Squirrelflight was unlucky to run into them."

"Why were you near the mountains?" Flippaw blinked at Squirrelflight. "Are we moving there? Thriftpaw says one of the Clans has to move before leaf-bare or we'll all starve."

"No one is going to starve." Hollytuft looked at Squirrelflight apologetically. "Trying to stop apprentices gossiping is like trying to stop birds singing."

Squirrelflight's gaze drifted around the clearing. The whole Clan had been talking about her time with the Sisters since she'd gotten back. Now her Clanmates were settling down for a midday meal. Whitewing and Honeyfur carried mice from the fresh-kill pile. Larksong dropped a vole at Dewnose's paws. Finleap and Twigbranch settled beside the warriors' den, snatching glances at Squirrelflight before tucking into a rabbit. Rosepetal blinked at her sympathetically, as though she'd just recovered from an illness.

Graystripe sat beside Millie outside the elders' den. Millie looked gaunt, and Graystripe sat close to her. "You must be glad to be back, Squirrelflight," he called across the clearing. "Another cat's food never tastes as good as your own."

"Imagine!" Cloudtail stretched beside him. "A group of cats with no toms. Who's heard of such a thing? I hope they didn't give you any ideas." He blinked teasingly at Squirrel-flight. "I don't know what Graystripe and I would do if Millie and Brightheart threw us out."

Millie purred roughly. "The den would be a lot neater."

Graystripe nudged her cheek with his nose. "But you'd miss me, right?"

Millie nosed him away, her eyes shimmering with affection. "Of course I would, you old fool." For a moment the fragility that had appeared in the old she-cat's face since the start of greenleaf vanished.

Small stones showered from the rock tumble, and Squirrel-flight looked up to see Bramblestar scrambling down from the Highledge. She looked away to avoid catching his eye. Since she'd returned from the Sisters' camp, he'd been polite but formal. Her heart ached at being kept at tail's length, but she understood why he was still angry. She'd caused a lot of worry and disruption in the Clan. But she wished he hadn't told her he was thinking about replacing her as deputy. She'd been taken captive by the Sisters only because she had been trying to find a way to keep the peace among the Clans. He wanted peace too. Why couldn't he support her plan instead of criticizing her for it?

"Squirrelflight." He padded toward her, his gaze cool.

She dipped her head. "Bramblestar."

"Who do you plan to send on dawn patrol tomorrow?" He glanced around the Clan.

"I haven't decided yet."

Bramblestar frowned and padded softly into the shadow of the Highledge. He beckoned Squirrelflight closer with a twitch of his tail. "I thought I asked you to let me know in advance of any decisions you make as deputy," he mewed, lowering his voice.

Anger flared in her belly. "I never decide who's going on patrol until the morning," she told him icily. "I like to see who's awake. It's no use waking one warrior when another warrior is already itching to get out into the forest."

"That's sloppy. A warrior should know if he's going on patrol and be ready." Bramblestar's ears twitched. "From now on, I want to know who's going out on dawn patrol the night before."

Squirrelflight flexed her claws. "Is that how it's going to be now? Are you going to make up mouse-brained rules just to prove you're in charge?"

"You're my deputy," he told her. "I need to know that you can follow orders."

"Or you'll replace me. I know. I get the message." Squirrelflight glared at him.

Bramblestar met her gaze evenly. "I need to know I can trust you."

"Of course you can trust me! I love you and I love my Clan. I would never do anything to hurt you or them." The Sisters' life seemed suddenly appealing. The idea that Moonlight would invent pointless rules for Snow and the others to follow seemed ridiculous. Bramblestar was supposed to be her mate. Why couldn't he *talk* to her instead of trying to make her feel small?

Bramblestar sniffed. "I'm just worried that your judgment is not as sound as it should be."

"Not sound?" Squirrelflight stared at him in disbelief. "Because I came up with a plan and tried to follow it through?"

"Because your plan put SkyClan and ThunderClan in danger." He stared at her accusingly.

"The Sisters aren't a danger to any—" She stopped as she noticed Sparkpelt staring at them from the edge of the clearing.

The orange warrior's gaze flicked anxiously from Bramblestar to Squirrelflight. "Is everything okay?"

"Of course." Squirrelflight forced her fur to smooth and hurried toward Sparkpelt. "We were just discussing patrols."

Sparkpelt looked doubtful. "I wanted to talk to you both," she mewed hesitantly. "But I can come back later."

"No," Squirrelflight mewed quickly.

"You're not interrupting." Bramblestar padded to join them, his gaze softening as he greeted Sparkpelt with the touch of his nose.

Claws seemed to grip Squirrelflight's heart. She missed feeling close to Bramblestar.

Sparkpelt looked at them. "There's something I have to tell you."

Squirrelflight's pelt pricked with unease as she noticed how nervous Sparkpelt looked, and yet the young warrior's pelt was glossy and her eyes bright. She'd never looked healthier. What could be wrong?

"I'm expecting kits." Sparkpelt blinked at her.

"Sparkpelt, that's wonderful." Happiness surged beneath Squirrelflight's pelt. She glanced across the clearing to where Larksong was sharing a vole with Dewnose. The young tom was chatting to his denmate, his ears pricked, his eyes sparkling. Sparkpelt was going to be a mother, and her mate was a kind tom and a good warrior. Sparkpelt and Alderheart were both happy and settled. What more could she want?

And yet grief tugged at her belly. She longed for kits too—and a mate who still loved her. The possibility seemed suddenly far away. Her thoughts spiraled. Was she foolish for even wanting it? Should she resign herself to spending the rest of her days watching her Clan grow and change around her while she simply grew old and died?

"Squirrelflight?" Sparkpelt blinked at her anxiously. "You are pleased, aren't you?"

"Of course I'm pleased. And Bramblestar is too." She glanced at him.

Bramblestar was staring back at her, sympathy glistening in his eyes. Had he guessed what she'd been thinking? As she caught his eye, he looked away and touched his nose to Sparkpelt's head. "That's great news, Sparkpelt. We're very happy for you. When are the kits due?"

"I'm not sure." Sparkpelt was purring, her pelt fluffed with happiness.

Squirrelflight glanced at the young queen's belly. It was already beginning to swell. "It looks like it won't be too long," she mewed warmly.

Sparkpelt pressed her cheek against Squirrelflight's. "I can't wait to be a mother." She headed away. Larksong jumped to his paws and brushed against her as she reached him.

Squirrelflight turned back to Bramblestar, her feelings hardening once more. Were there any more rules he wanted to tell her about?

He was gazing at her kindly. "I know that must have been difficult," he murmured.

Squirrelflight stiffened guiltily, ashamed of the grief Sparkpelt's news had triggered. It was worse that Bramblestar had seen it. "I'm happy for her. I'm happy for them both."

"But I know how much you want more kits," he meowed.

She narrowed her eyes, anger flaring. "And I know how much you don't." She turned her tail on him and marched away. With every paw step, her anger melted and guilt took its place. Why had she said that? He was only trying to be kind. Overwhelmed, she headed to the medicine den. She needed to share her feelings with some cat. She remembered how relieved Leafpool had been when she'd returned to camp— surely she would understand.

She ducked through the brambles and saw Alderheart crouching beside the pool, sorting herbs. Leafpool was plucking old moss from one of the nests they kept for sick cats. She looked up as Squirrelflight entered, her eyes narrowing as she saw her sister's face. "Is everything okay?"

"Not really," Squirrelflight mewed huskily.

"Come and help me collect herbs," Leafpool mewed.

Alderheart looked up from his work. "We collected herbs this morning."

"I know." Leafpool whisked her tail. "But I think we need some more marigold. It won't flower forever." She crossed the den and bustled Squirrelflight outside. "What's happened?" she asked as they padded into the sunlight.

"It's nothing, really." Squirrelflight hesitated. "I'm probably being oversensitive."

Leafpool whisked her onward. "Is it Sparkpelt's news?" She reached the camp entrance and ducked through.

Squirrelflight hurried after her. "How did you know?"

"I've learned to tell when a cat is expecting kits." Leafpool stopped and met Squirrelflight's gaze. "And you've told me how much you want more of your own."

Squirrelflight stared at her. "I know I should be happy."

Leafpool swished her tail. "Come on. Some fresh air will do you good." She raced away, heading upslope toward the beech grove.

Squirrelflight followed, relishing the breeze as it streamed through her fur. The thrum of their paws on the forest floor was soothing. The familiar sight of the trees and brambles reassured her.

Leafpool slowed down as the trees opened into a small

clearing. Marigold clustered between the ferns, and she led Squirrelflight to a splash of orange where the flowers were growing thickly. Crouching beside it, the medicine cat tugged out a stalk with her teeth and dropped it on the ground. She looked at Squirrelflight. "It's okay to be sad."

"Is it?" Squirrelflight blinked at her.

"It must be hard to hear that Sparkpelt's expecting when you're not." Leafpool tipped her head sympathetically.

Squirrelflight looked at her paws. "I feel selfish."

"It's not selfish to want kits."

"I'm happy for Sparkpelt." Squirrelflight looked at Leafpool earnestly. "You know that, don't you?"

"Of course you are."

Squirrelflight sat down. "It's just going to be difficult." Guilt jabbed her again. "Watching my own kit have kits. I'm not ready to be that old. I want another chance. I know Sparkpelt deserves to be happy, but it's hard watching another cat get what I want so much."

"You deserve to be happy too." Leafpool's eyes rounded with sympathy.

"Bramblestar's angry with me, and I'm probably going to die without having more kits." Squirrelflight could feel herself sinking into self-pity, but couldn't stop. "I don't know if I'll ever be happy again."

Leafstar plucked another marigold stalk out with her teeth. "I'm not sure that's true."

"But it's how I feel." Squirrelflight glanced back toward the stone hollow. "Bramblestar says he's wondering whether he should replace me as deputy. And he's making up rules to test me. He doesn't trust my judgment anymore."

"He just needs time to calm down." Leafpool straightened and padded toward Squirrelflight. "He was really worried when you went missing. He thought you might be dead."

"Everything I do seems wrong at the moment. He tried to be kind to me just now, when Sparkpelt told us her news, and I snarled at him." Squirrelflight felt suddenly as heavy as stone. "And he's right. I shouldn't have gone off without telling him. But I just wanted to make him see that there's a way to stop the Clans fighting over land. And Sparkpelt . . ." Her shoulders sagged. "I hope she didn't see that I was upset. I'm happy for her, I really am, but it was hard to hide how I—"

Leafpool pressed her muzzle against Squirrelflight's cheek. "It's okay, Squirrelflight. You don't have to be perfect all the time." She purred softly, and Squirrelflight felt her pain ease as the warmth from Leafpool's cheek seeped into hers.

Squirrelflight drew away, suddenly appreciating her sister more than ever. She was still sympathetic, even after so much loss. "I can only imagine how hard it must have been for you all these moons. You've had to watch so many Clanmates having kits after you had to give your own away. While I was raising Jayfeather, Lionblaze, and Hollyleaf, and loving them as if they were my own, I never fully understood how much it must have hurt."

Leafpool met her gaze steadily. "I'm grateful you risked so much to make sure I didn't lose my place as medicine cat. And in a way, we raised them together. I was always there for them, and I could see them and take care of them."

Squirrelflight thought of Moonlight. *We are each mother to all the young.* "That's how the Sisters raise their kits. Each cat is mother to every kit, and sister to her campmates," she told Leafpool. "In the Sisters, no cat would have made you choose between your kits and being a medicine cat. There are no rules saying who can and can't have kits."

"But we're not with the Sisters; we're Clan cats." Leafpool's gaze hardened. "And no cat *made* me choose. I did what I thought was best." Her mew was suddenly brittle, and Squirrelflight knew that she'd touched a nerve. "There's no point imagining that it could have happened any other way. I did what I did, and it's no use regretting it. My bond with StarClan was too strong to think about giving it up." She narrowed her eyes. "Do the Sisters share with their ancestors?"

"I don't know. Moonlight mentioned ancestors, but I don't think they share with them like we share with StarClan. They were descended from kittypets, after all."

Leafpool huffed. "How can they even begin to understand the bond we have with StarClan and the sacrifices we make to honor it? There's more to being a medicine cat than knowing a few herbs or how to cure bellyache. I doubt these Sisters know what a prophecy is, and, from what you say, they are too busy living in the moment to think about what lies in their past or their future." She sniffed. "I wouldn't ever want to live like that."

Squirrelflight dipped her head. "I'm sorry. I shouldn't have said anything. It was just strange to see other cats living so differently." Squirrelflight couldn't help feeling that it might be nice to live in the moment, instead of being weighted down with rules and ancestors and traditions. She shook out her fur. "But the Sisters will move on soon, and SkyClan can have their land."

"If StarClan approves," Leafpool meowed sharply.

"Of course." Didn't Leafpool ever feel restricted by Clan rules and traditions? "Have you shared with them yet?"

Leafpool's gaze darkened. "They're still quiet."

"Perhaps they're okay with SkyClan moving."

"Perhaps." Leafpool looked unconvinced. "But until we have word, it's best that SkyClan doesn't make any decisions."

"Even if it means peace within the Clans?"

"StarClan knows best." Leafpool returned to the marigold patch and plucked out another stalk. Squirrelflight saw her ears twitching. She was clearly unnerved by StarClan's silence, and talk of the Sisters hadn't helped.

If only StarClan would share with her. They could let her know that it would be good for SkyClan to move to new territory. They might even know if Squirrelflight was destined to have more kits. Leafpool's words flashed in her mind. *Don't rush so much, Squirrelflight. Stop trying to sort out every problem at once.* Perhaps her sister was right. If she just waited, Bramblestar would get over his anger and they'd have more kits together, the Sisters would move on and SkyClan would find a new home, and the Clans would live in peace.

It was pointless trying to guess what the future held,

because no cat knew. Squirrelflight looked up through the branches at the afternoon sky. *Does StarClan know what will happen?* A shiver ran down her spine. If they did, they weren't giving anything away.

CHAPTER 8

Larksong slid past Squirrelflight and lifted his gaze, his mouth open. "There's a squirrel nest up there."

Branches twitched overhead, and leaves flickered in the sunshine that streamed through the canopy. Squirrelflight pricked her ears as she saw gray fur flash high in an oak. A fluffy tail bobbed along a branch, followed by another.

Blossomfall stopped beside her, following her gaze. She swished her tail. "It's too high up."

"I see it!" Mousewhisker looked into the branches, his pelt fluffing with excitement.

Larksong padded closer and peered up the trunk. "It'd be simple to climb." Sturdy branches jutted from the trunk of the oak tree. The bark was gnarled, easy to sink claws into.

"Let's leave the climbing to SkyClan." Squirrelflight beckoned Larksong back with a flick of her tail. She didn't want Larksong to risk such a long climb. Sparkpelt was with them, and she'd be uneasy seeing her mate hunting prey high overhead.

In the days since Sparkpelt had told her parents she was expecting kits, she and Larksong had been inseparable.

Larksong had come to Squirrelflight, asking to be assigned to the same patrols as Sparkpelt. Squirrelflight was touched by their protective love for each other, but it made her feel the loss of Bramblestar's affection even more.

She still shared Bramblestar's den and followed him up to the Highledge each night, settling self-consciously into the nest beside his. Without speaking, they both knew the importance of hiding the depth of the rift between them. The Clan must not know how divided their leader and deputy were, although Squirrelflight couldn't help thinking it must be obvious; she and Bramblestar hardly spoke to each other, and were formal when they did, and they never patrolled or hunted together anymore.

"Squirrelflight." Larksong's mew jerked her back to the present. "I can smell something strange." The black warrior's pelt was bristling along his spine. "It smells familiar, but I'm not sure what it is."

"It's a rogue!" Mousewhisker uncurled his claws. Blossomfall glanced around the forest. Larksong moved closer to Sparkpelt.

Squirrelflight tasted the air, stiffening as a scent she knew well bathed her tongue. *The Sisters.* What were they doing on ThunderClan territory? "Wait." She nodded to Mousewhisker, hoping she'd find the Sisters first. Surely they hadn't come to fight? Padding quickly ahead, she scanned the trees, her tail twitching as she glimpsed white fur moving through ferns. She hurried toward it, recognizing the pelt. "Snow?"

Snow turned her blue eyes on Squirrelflight. Squirrelflight

could see panic sparking in the she-cat's gaze.

"Who is it?" Blossomfall stopped beside Squirrelflight.

"It's Snow," she told her. "She's one of the Sisters."

Mousewhisker caught up to them. "What are you doing on ThunderClan land?" he snarled at Snow.

Blossomfall cut in. "She shouldn't be here." The tortoise-shell flattened her ears as Larksong and Sparkpelt reached them.

Sparkpelt blinked at Snow in surprise, then looked at Squirrelflight. "Why's she here?"

"She's trespassing on our land," Blossomfall growled.

Squirrelflight looked at Snow. "Why have you come here?" she asked gently.

"I was looking for you," Snow mewed. "You said you have medicine cats. They might know what to do. Sunrise needs help. She's been wounded."

Squirrelflight tensed. "Is it bad?"

"It's not our problem." Blossomfall curled her lip.

Snow kept her gaze fixed on Squirrelflight. "Can one of your medicine cats come and see her? She's not far from here."

Why had Sunrise been wounded so close to their territory? Squirrelflight shifted her paws uneasily. Blossomfall's fur was already bristling. She wouldn't be pleased if Squirrelflight treated this trespasser too kindly. "I'm not sure there's anything I can do."

"But your medicine cat might know, right?" Snow looked at her imploringly.

Squirrelflight hesitated. What would Bramblestar say if she helped the Sisters? Surely he wouldn't deny help to a wounded cat. And yet he'd been so angry that she'd found the Sisters in the first place. *If he knows Snow was looking for me, he might accuse me of bringing them here.*

"Let's just take a look at the wounded cat." Larksong padded to Squirrelflight's side. "It might not be as serious as Snow says. We can patch her up and send them on their way without bothering the rest of the Clan."

She looked at him, wondering. If they *could* fix this themselves, it would save questions about why the Sisters had been on their land. She frowned. But Bramblestar was bound to find out. The patrol would have no reason to keep this a secret. And yet she couldn't turn her back on an injured cat. She flicked her tail. "Show us where she is," she told Snow. "If I think she needs help, I'll send for our medicine cat."

"It might be a trap!" Blossomfall's hackles lifted.

Squirrelflight turned on her. "I know these cats well enough to know they won't hurt us."

Mousewhisker narrowed his eyes. "Are you sure? They held you captive, don't forget."

"They didn't harm me." Squirrelflight nodded to Snow. "Let's go."

Snow led the way past the ferns and followed a rabbit trail through brambles. She crossed a dried streambed and ducked beneath a juniper. On the other side, she halted.

Squirrelflight scanned the forest ahead. Where was Sunrise? "I don't see her."

Sparkpelt and Larksong stopped beside her, glancing nervously between the trees.

Mousewhisker padded toward the bushes, which lined the

slope ahead, and sniffed them warily. They quivered, and he recoiled in surprise, arching his back as Sunrise, Tempest, and Hawk slid out.

Blossomfall darted to his side, teeth bared. "I told you it was a trap!" Even with her pelt bushed, the Sisters were far bigger than her.

Tempest blinked at her in surprise. "Why would we trap you?"

"How should I know?" Blossomfall bristled.

Tempest ignored her and looked hopefully at Squirrelflight. "Have you come to help?"

"If we can." Squirrelflight could smell blood and saw that Sunrise was leaning heavily on Hawk. The yellow fur on her flank was stained red.

Larksong padded around the Sisters, his ears twitching. "What happened?"

"We got into a fight with some toms." As Hawk spoke, Sunrise collapsed to the ground.

Alarm sparked through Squirrelflight's pelt. There was no way they could fix this themselves. Sunrise needed a medicine cat.

"Should we fetch Alderheart?" Mousewhisker blinked at her.

"It would take too long," Squirrelflight told him. This was more serious than she'd imagined. "Let's carry Sunrise back to camp." She nodded to Snow, Hawk and Tempest. "You can go home. We'll take care of her."

Snow stiffened. "We're not leaving her."

Sparkpelt looked anxiously at her mother. "We can't let them all come to the camp." She leaned closer, lowering her voice so the others couldn't hear. "Bramblestar wouldn't be happy. He already thinks you're too quick to defend the Sisters."

"And he's right to be cautious." Blossomfall fluffed out her fur. "Don't forget what happened when ShadowClan took Darktail and his friends in."

"Darktail had always planned to destroy the Clans. He wasn't wounded when ShadowClan found him," Mousewhisker pointed out. "This cat really needs our help."

"Her *friends* aren't wounded," Blossomfall argued. "Why do they need to come?"

"To make sure our campmate is okay," Snow mewed. "We've met your Clanmates, remember? They weren't exactly friendly."

"We'll take care of her," Larksong promised.

Tempest lifted her chin. "We're coming with her."

Sparkpelt whispered in her mother's ear. "Bramblestar won't like it."

Squirrelflight pulled away, her heart quickening as blood spread wider over Sunrise's flank. "We have to help them." Flesh showed where the wound opened. She couldn't let a cat die. She'd deal with Bramblestar later. After all, things couldn't get any more strained between them, surely. It was a risk she'd have to take. "You'll have to carry her," she told Hawk and Tempest. She nodded to Larksong and Mousewhisker. "You can help."

She stood back as the toms ducked down and tucked their shoulders beneath Sunrise. Hawk and Tempest jerked their campmate up with their muzzles. Sliding beneath her, the four cats heaved Sunrise onto their backs and then, pressing together, began to head for camp. Sparkpelt walked close to Larksong's side, while Blossomfall circled the group uneasily as it made its way toward the streambed.

Squirrelflight padded ahead, scanning the forest to find the easiest route. Snow fell in beside her as she led the way up a gentle rise where the trees grew so thickly that the brambles had died away. She looked back as she reached the top. Tempest and Hawk walkedslowly, their gazes dark with concentration as they carried their campmate. Mousewhisker and Larksong pressed close, matching the Sisters' steps paw for paw. Sunrise lay limply across their backs. "We have to hurry."

As Squirrelflight picked up the pace, Sparkpelt caught up to them. "Sunrise is still breathing, but only just."

Squirrelflight kept her gaze on the trail. "We'll get her home in time." She hoped it was true.

"Alderheart will know what to do," Sparkpelt mewed.

"I didn't know if you would help." Snow blinked gratefully at Squirrelflight. "But I had to do something. We were so far from home."

"What were you doing here?" Squirrelflight returned her gaze. "You've never trespassed on Clan land before."

Snow's eyes darkened. "You're not the only Clan cats who are suddenly interested in the land we're using."

Squirrelflight's belly tightened. "What do you mean?"

"Yesterday, we smelled Clan scent on our side of your border," Snow explained. "Hawk thought you'd sent a patrol back, but you'd promised to leave us alone. Then Moonlight noticed that it was a different Clan scent and sent me, Tempest, Hawk, and Sunrise to investigate."

Sparkpelt pricked her ears. "Do you know which Clan it was?"

Snow shrugged. "Warriors all smell the same to me. We followed the scent into the pine forest that borders yours."

"ShadowClan!" Sparkpelt glanced at her mother. Why were they suddenly interested in the Sisters' land? Squirrelflight's pelt prickled uneasily. Had her suggestion at the meeting woken ShadowClan's curiosity about the land outside their border? Perhaps they wanted to check the land out for SkyClan too. Foreboding dropped like a stone in Squirrelflight's belly. Were they planning to take the land for themselves?

Sparkpelt blinked at Snow. "Is that how Sunrise got injured? Fighting with ShadowClan?"

Snow nodded. "We tracked two toms across the border and followed them into their territory. We stopped them and asked them what they were doing there. They attacked us."

Squirrelflight flicked her tail nervously. How would she explain to ThunderClan that Sunrise had been hurt fighting Clan cats? She pushed the worry away. The Sisters' fight had been with ShadowClan, not ThunderClan. Until a few moons ago, ShadowClan had been their enemy. Why should ThunderClan defend them?

"We hurt them pretty good," Snow meowed with obvious

satisfaction. "But one of them—Stonewing, I think that's what the other cat called him—managed to slice open Sunrise's flank before they ran away."

Sparkpelt's eyes glittered with alarm. "Should we help cats who hurt ShadowClan?"

Squirrelflight lifted her chin defiantly. "We're not ShadowClan's protectors. Besides, the Sisters were defending themselves."

"But Tigerstar won't be pleased if he finds out."

"Why should we behave without honor just to suit Tigerstar?" Squirrelflight returned Sparkpelt's gaze.

"Is that what Bramblestar would say?"

"Sunrise could die from this injury. If Bramblestar is more interested in pleasing ShadowClan than saving another cat's life, then he's not the cat I thought he was." Squirrelflight could see the camp in the distance. She glanced back at the others. "We're nearly there."

As she spoke, the bracken rustled ahead. Rosepetal and Bristlepaw burst out. They pulled up a tail-length from Squirrelflight, their eyes widening.

"What's going on?" Rosepetal looked past her to the Sisters.

"We found a wounded cat in the forest," Squirrelflight told her. "She needs our help."

Bristlepaw's pelt bushed. "Rogues!"

Snow dipped her head to the young she-cat. "We're the Sisters."

"The Sisters!" Bristlepaw stared at her. "What are you doing on our land?"

Squirrelflight pushed on. "I'll explain later." She padded down the slope toward the hollow and ducked through the tunnel into camp. "Jayfeather! Leafpool! Alderheart!" She called to the medicine cats as Larksong, Tempest, Hawk, and Mousewhisker carried Sunrise into the clearing and laid her down on the sunbaked earth.

Alderheart hurried from the medicine den, Leafpool at his tail. Jayfeather followed, his nose twitching. "Who's bleeding?" The blind medicine cat paused, his hackles lifting. "What are rogues doing here?"

"They're not rogues." Squirrelflight swept her gaze around the camp. Thornclaw was staring in amazement from beside the fresh-kill pile. Below the Highledge, Berrynose and Birchfall were sharing a rabbit. They blinked at the Sisters, hostility glittering in their gaze. Outside the warriors' den, Twigbranch and Finleap climbed warily to their paws. Hollytuft waved Flippaw back with her tail as the apprentice arched his back and hissed at Snow. Graystripe pushed away the mouse he was eating and narrowed his eyes. Squirrelflight ignored the tension sparking in the camp. "One of the Sisters needs our help."

Stones clattered on the rock tumble. "What's going on?" Bramblestar leaped down from Highledge. He stopped beside Squirrelflight and glared at her accusingly.

"Sunrise is injured," Squirrelflight told him. "She needs a medicine cat."

Sparkpelt moved closer to her mother. "Squirrelflight was scared Sunrise might die."

Bramblestar narrowed his gaze.

"I'll fetch cobwebs." Leafpool turned back toward the medicine den.

"Stop!" Bramblestar yowled with a flick of his tail.

Leafpool froze.

Squirrelflight stared at him. "Aren't you going to help her?"

He thrust his muzzle closer. "Why are you putting me in this position?" he hissed, so low only she and Sparkpelt could hear. "I thought I told you to run decisions past me first."

"Squirrelflight just wanted to help," Sparkpelt told her father earnestly.

"It's okay, Sparkpelt." Squirrelflight was grateful to her daughter, but this wasn't Sparkpelt's fight. She jerked her nose toward Sunrise, who lay unmoving in the clearing, her blood staining the ground. "I didn't think there was time for a meeting," she growled icily.

Bumblestripe padded forward. "You're going to help her, right?"

Thornclaw lashed his tail. "Why should we? We've only just rescued our Clanmates from these cats. We owe them nothing."

"But she's hurt." Finleap stared at the dark warrior in surprise.

Leafpool blinked at Bramblestar. "I can't stand by and watch her suffer."

Alderheart padded to her side. "That's not the medicine-cat way."

"We can't let her die." Mousewhisker gazed around his Clanmates. His pelt was stained with Sunrise's blood.

Blossomfall glared at him. "Didn't you hear Hawk say they attacked a ShadowClan patrol?"

Mousewhisker narrowed his eyes. "ShadowClan invaded their territory."

"Two warriors doesn't make an invasion!" Blossomfall hissed back. "The ShadowClan cats were outnumbered. These *Sisters* shouldn't have attacked them."

Thornclaw lashed his tail. "We can't treat rogues who attack warriors."

Hollytuft puffed out her chest. "The Sisters took our deputy captive and invaded ShadowClan land. They're no better than Darktail's Kin were. If we treat this cat, we'll make our enemies stronger."

Tempest blinked at her in surprise. "We're not your enemy."

"You held Squirrelflight hostage," Hollytuft shot back.

"You attacked ShadowClan," Birchfall snarled.

"Send them back to where they came from," Thornclaw yowled.

"Get them out of our camp!" Blossomfall chimed.

Squirrelflight's throat tightened. How could her Clanmates turn away such a gravely injured cat? She felt Sparkpelt move nervously beside her. Did her daughter want to send Sunrise away too?

Twigbranch padded forward. "It doesn't matter what they've done. Sunrise might die if we send her away."

"ThunderClan mustn't have another cat's blood on their paws," Finleap meowed in agreement. His Clanmates glanced uneasily at each other, as though they were unconvinced.

"What will Tigerstar say if he finds out we've taken her in?" Birchfall nodded toward the Sisters.

"Since when do we let Tigerstar dictate how we act?" Mousewhisker flicked his tail angrily. He looked at Bramblestar. "We can't let this cat die."

Bramblestar looked around his Clan. Anger flared in Thornclaw's eyes. Birchfall's ears twitched menacingly. Twigbranch and Finleap stared at him. "StarClan must decide," Bramblestar announced with a jerk of his muzzle toward Jayfeather. "Take Alderheart to the Moonpool and share with our ancestors. They will tell us what to do."

Squirrelflight blinked at him in surprise. "What does StarClan have to do with this? Do we need them to tell us how to be honorable?"

Bramblestar gazed back at her coldly. "These cats have threatened you and attacked ShadowClan. They clearly don't care who they harm or how. If we treat this cat, we show them we can be pushed around. And we might make an enemy of Tigerstar forever. StarClan has already told us that the Clans must stand together. For all we know, helping the Sisters might be no better than helping Darktail. We need StarClan's guidance. Jayfeather and Alderheart will travel to the Moonpool."

Hawk blinked at him. "Is the Moonpool far?"

Tempest padded closer. "There's no time to consult with ancestors." Panic edged her mew.

"We have no choice." Bramblestar turned to Jayfeather. "Be as quick as you can."

Squirrelflight could hardly believe her ears. Was Bramblestar going to risk this cat's life? He should act, not question.

"We have to help," she breathed.

Bramblestar didn't look at her. Instead he blinked at Leafpool. "Can you keep Sunrise alive until Alderheart and Jayfeather return?"

Leafpool stared anxiously at the bleeding cat. "I'll do my best."

As Jayfeather and Alderheart hurried toward the camp entrance, she ducked into the medicine den and returned with a thick wad of cobweb between her jaws.

Squirrelflight followed her to where Sunrise lay unconscious and hardly breathing. "Don't let her die," she whispered.

Leafpool began to draw the edges of the wound together. "If I can stop the bleeding—"

Squirrelflight hardly heard her. "How could Bramblestar let this happen?"

"He has to listen to his warriors." Leafpool wadded cobweb along the gash.

"Even when they're wrong?" Squirrelflight remembered how tenderly the Sisters had treated Leafstar's wound. Her heart seemed to twist inside her chest. Suddenly there seemed more honor among the Sisters than among her Clanmates. If Sunrise died because of ThunderClan's fox-heartedness, she wasn't sure if she'd be able to forgive them.

CHAPTER 9

Leafpool sat back on her haunches. "I've stopped the bleeding for now."

Anxiously, Squirrelflight sniffed the cobwebs wadded around the gash on Sunrise's flank. The blood there was growing stale. But Sunrise was still not moving; her eyes were closed and her breathing was shallow. The clearing beneath her was still damp with her blood.

Leafpool went on. "I need to make an ointment to keep infection at bay." She glanced toward the medicine den and then at Bramblestar.

The ThunderClan leader had padded to the entrance, where Alderheart and Jayfeather had disappeared a few moments earlier. He met Leafpool's gaze.

"May I fetch herbs?" she asked.

Please say yes. As Squirrelflight blinked at him hopefully, a growl rumbled in Thornclaw's throat. The warrior was glaring at the Sisters, who pressed close together at the edge of the clearing. His gaze flicked accusingly at Leafpool. "We're waiting for word from StarClan."

Blossomfall fluffed out her pelt beside him. "We can't do

anything until they tell us it's okay."

Squirrelflight stared at them, shocked by their coldness. "But she might die while we're waiting. What if StarClan says we can treat her then? We won't be able to treat a corpse."

Bramblestar crossed the clearing and stopped beside Leafpool. "Just keep her alive until Jayfeather and Alderheart return."

Leafpool straightened. "The Moonpool is a long way. They won't be back before moonhigh. The only way I can keep her alive is to stop infection forming in the wound." As she spoke, Sunrise stirred. She slowly opened her eyes and, with a flick of her tail, tried to lift her head.

Bramblestar whisked his tail. "She looks strong," he growled. "She'll be okay."

"She won't be unless I put ointment on the wound." Leafpool's fur twitched anxiously along her spine.

Snow crept closer to Sunrise. Fear showed in the she-cat's eyes. "Keep still," she breathed to her wounded campmate. "You'll reopen the wound."

Bramblestar glared at her. "Get back with the others."

As Snow flattened her ears and backed away, anger flared in Squirrelflight's belly. Was Bramblestar going to deny Sunrise even the comfort of her campmates? The Sisters had been far kinder to her when she'd been in their camp.

Outside the warriors' den, Mousewhisker shifted his paws. "Should we move her to the medicine den?"

Larksong lifted his tail hopefully. "We could carry her there."

"She'll be more comfortable out of the sun," Sparkpelt mewed.

Bramblestar glanced at them. "She'll stay where we can see her until Jayfeather and Alderheart bring word from StarClan."

Finleap padded forward. "Can we at least make her more comfortable?"

"I can fetch ferns," Twigbranch offered.

Bramblestar nodded, his gaze hard. "Very well." He turned away as they hurried out of camp.

Squirrelflight wanted to go with them, to make sure they picked the softest leaves, but she couldn't leave Sunrise. Someone had to fight for her.

The thorn tunnel shivered, and Hollytuft and Dewnose ducked into camp. Flippaw and Thriftpaw padded at their heels. They stopped as they saw the Sisters.

Hollytuft's eyes widened. "What's going on?" She looked at Sunrise.

"This cat has been hurt," Bramblestar told her. "Leafpool is taking care of her until we get word from StarClan."

"Word?" Hollytuft looked confused. "About what?"

Thornclaw crossed the clearing and stopped beside Bramblestar. "About whether we should treat her wounds."

Dewnose tipped his head. "Why do you need StarClan to decide?"

"These cats attacked a ShadowClan patrol," Blossomfall grunted.

Flippaw frowned. "I thought the Sisters never strayed onto Clan land."

Thriftpaw's hackles lifted. "Perhaps they think they can go where they like now."

"Rest," Leafpool breathed, touching her nose to Sunrise's cheek. She looked at Bramblestar again. "Can I get her poppy seeds?" she meowed. "She's in pain. Let me help—"

Thornclaw cut her off. "Why should we share our herbs?"

"I can't watch her suffer." Leafpool blinked at him.

As Thornclaw held her sister's gaze, Squirrelflight felt sick. Why had she brought the Sisters here? She'd trusted her Clanmates to take care of them. How could she have been so wrong?

"Poppy seeds can wait." Bramblestar flicked his tail briskly. "Flippaw and Thriftpaw," he meowed. "Go and help Finleap and Twigbranch find ferns." He nodded to Blossomfall. "Take Hollytuft and Mousewhisker hunting. We have extra mouths to feed. Rosepetal and Bristlepaw can help Birchfall strengthen the walls of the nursery." His gaze swept the Clan. "We can't ignore our duties just because we have visitors."

Thornclaw narrowed his eyes. "Are we sharing our fresh-kill with them?" He eyed Hawk and Tempest resentfully.

Tempest lifted her chin. "We can catch our own prey," she meowed.

Birchfall bristled. "Do you think we'd let you hunt on our land?"

Bramblestar looked suddenly weary. "They must eat, and since they can't hunt here, they must share our prey."

Squirrelflight couldn't help feeling a jab of pity for him. Every Clanmate seemed to want something different. How could he please them all? Guilt pricked momentarily beneath her pelt. Was she judging him too harshly?

Rosepetal and Bristlepaw headed toward the nursery, Birchfall at their heels, while Blossomfall led Hollytuft and Mousewhisker out of camp.

"Go with the hunting patrol," Bramblestar ordered, nodding to Larksong.

Larksong hesitated. "I'd rather stay with Sparkpelt."

Bramblestar stiffened. "Your patrol needs you."

"Can Sparkpelt come with me?" Larksong asked. "Squirrelflight let us join the same patrols. Now that she's expecting kits, I don't like to be away from—"

Squirrelflight flinched as Bramblestar swung his muzzle toward the black tom.

"I don't care what Squirrelflight did," he hissed. "Sparkpelt will be safe here with her Clan. Go join your patrol, as I ordered."

Sparkpelt blinked reassuringly at Larksong. "I'll be okay," she promised.

As Larksong dipped his head and hurried away, Squirrelflight glared at Bramblestar. How long was he going to keep trying to prove that *he* made the rules in ThunderClan, not her?

He stared back. "I want to speak with you in my den. You need to explain why your patrol brought the Sisters here."

Squirrelflight's paws pricked. Did he want another argument, even while a cat lay dying in the clearing? As he leaped up the rock tumble, she looked at Leafpool. "Will you be okay here?"

"Yes." Leafpool was watching Sunrise. "I'll do what I can."

Squirrelflight straightened and headed for the rock tumble.

"I'm coming too." Sparkpelt's mew surprised her. "I was part of the patrol."

"No." Squirrelflight felt a surge of affection for her daughter. "The decision was my responsibility."

Sparkpelt stuck out her chin. "I said I'm coming with you."

Squirrelflight dipped her head. She didn't want to argue with Sparkpelt too. She scrambled up the rock tumble, stones crunching beneath her paws. Sparkpelt followed and ducked after her into Bramblestar's den.

Bramblestar sat in the shadowy cave, his gaze icy. His ears twitched as he saw Sparkpelt. "I didn't ask to speak with you."

Sparkpelt met his gaze. "You said you wanted an explanation," she mewed evenly. "I was on the patrol. I can help."

Bramblestar grunted and flicked his gaze to Squirrelflight. "Why in StarClan did you bring them here?" Anger hardened his mew.

Squirrelflight bristled, pulling up short. "What did you want me to do? Leave Sunrise to die in the woods?"

"What would they have done if you hadn't found them?" Bramblestar didn't wait for her answer. "They would have taken their wounded home where they belong instead of making their problem our problem."

"But I did find them." Squirrelflight defended herself. She was not going to let him make her feel bad for trying to save a cat's life. "I couldn't turn my back on them."

Sparkpelt blinked at Bramblestar. "You couldn't have expected us to walk away."

"You could have taken them to the border and let their

campmates take care of them." Bramblestar's fur spiked along his spine. "Did you know they'd attacked a ShadowClan patrol when you brought them here?"

"Snow told me on the way to camp," Squirrelflight told him. "ShadowClan had been on their land. They were only trying to find out why. They didn't go looking for a fight."

"Do you think that's how Tigerstar will see it?" Bramblestar's gaze darkened. "How will he react when he finds out we're protecting them?"

Squirrelflight could hardly believe her ears. "Since when do you care what Tigerstar thinks?"

"Since StarClan told us there must be unity among the Clans!"

"So you'd let a cat die because Tigerstar might be upset?"

"I thought you wanted to keep the peace. Do you think this will help?"

Squirrelflight lifted her chin. "The Clans will understand when they find out what happened. We all follow the same code, and that code says nothing about letting cats die."

"It does say something about protecting your Clan," Bramblestar spat back. "How can you think that bringing a bunch of rogues into our camp is protecting ThunderClan?"

"They're not rogues!"

"They're not loners or warriors." Bramblestar curled his claws into the sandy floor of the cave. "What were you think-ing when you decided to bring them into our camp?"

Frustration surged in Squirrelflight's chest. "I was trying to save a cat's life. And they're *not* rogues! They're the Sisters!

There are more ways to live than being a warrior or a rogue!"

Bramblestar lashed his tail. "You spend two days in another camp and suddenly you're questioning our beliefs?"

"I'm not questioning our beliefs. I'm just pointing out that there are other ways to live."

"And how does that solve the problem that we are sheltering ShadowClan's attackers? How does that bring unity to the Clans?"

"Not everything is about the Clans!" Anger burned beneath Squirrelflight's pelt. There seemed so much more at stake here than whether the Clans were united. "What about the warrior code? What about honor and integrity? What about doing the right thing?"

"So you're the only cat who knows what's right?"

Squirrelflight felt Sparkpelt press against her.

"Please don't—" Her daughter's mew turned into a gasp. With a jerk, Sparkpelt dropped into a crouch.

Heart lurching, Squirrelflight twisted toward her. "Sparkpelt? What's wrong?"

"Cramp." Sparkpelt's eyes were glittering with pain. "My belly! The kits." Fear edged her mew.

Squirrelflight forced her fur to smooth. "Take a breath," she mewed. She lapped at Sparkpelt's shoulder, trying to calm her as she'd done when Sparkpelt was a kit. Her thoughts whirled. Were the kits coming? It was too early. She caught Bramblestar's eye.

He was leaning toward Sparkpelt, anxiety sparking in his gaze. "Fetch Leafpool."

"Wait." Sparkpelt blinked at her father. "It will pass. It's happened before. When I get upset."

Guilt seared Squirrelflight's pelt. Had she and Bramblestar caused this? "It's okay, Sparkpelt." She pressed closer. "We won't argue anymore. The kits will be fine."

"Will they?" Sparkpelt looked at her with round, anxious eyes.

"Of course." She remembered her own pregnancy. "I used to get cramps too. Usually when I'd eaten too much fresh-kill. It doesn't mean there's anything wrong."

Bramblestar was staring at her. "Should I fetch Leafpool?"

"Is the cramp easing?" Squirrelflight blinked at Sparkpelt.

"Yes." Pain still showed in her daughter's gaze, but her body was relaxing.

"Leave Leafpool with Sunrise for now," Squirrelflight mewed softly. She touched her nose to Sparkpelt's ear. "Cramps are normal. You just need to make sure you rest and don't get upset. In the days before Alderheart and you were born, I used to run to Jayfeather every night, certain the kits were coming too soon. He'd check me over, tell me there was nothing wrong, and send me back to the nursery. When the kits finally came, Daisy had to drag him out of his nest. He kept waving her away, telling her that I was just imagining the pain." She purred, the memory washing away her fear. "Can you imagine his surprise when he arrived to find you already born and Alderheart on the way? He stomped around the camp for a quarter moon, grumbling about queens who couldn't tell the difference between birth pains and indigestion."

A pang of longing tugged at her belly. If only she could have kits again. As the memory of her first litter filled her heart, she glanced at Bramblestar. He was listening, his gaze soft for the first time in days. He caught her eye and she saw love there. For a moment, it was as if they'd never quarreled. They'd been so happy together for so long that it seemed dumb to be arguing.

She blinked at him hopefully. If he was softening, was he ready to change his mind about the Sisters? "Please will you let Leafpool treat Sunrise?"

His gaze hardened in an instant. "Why don't you understand?" he snapped. "I can't help an enemy of the Clans without StarClan's blessing."

As he looked away, pain tightened its grip on Squirrelflight's heart once more. He wasn't ready to see sense.

He nodded curtly. "I'd better check to see that the Clan's okay." Stalking past them, he padded from the den.

"Don't worry." Squirrelflight brushed her cheek against Sparkpelt's. "It's all going to be fine." She wondered who she was reassuring, herself or Sparkpelt. "Stay here and rest. I'll go and see if he's all right. And I'll send Leafpool to check on you when she can."

Sparkpelt blinked at her gratefully and touched her nose to her mother's. "Be kind to him."

Squirrelflight flinched. *I wish he'd be kind to me.*

Bramblestar was talking with Thornclaw, their heads bent, as Squirrelflight scrambled down the rock tumble. She hesitated beside them, but they turned away and carried on talking. Disappointed, she walked on and stopped beside Leafpool. Thriftpaw and Twigbranch were gently tucking fern leaves around Sunrise. The wounded Sister hardly moved as they tried to make her comfortable. Pain glazed her eyes. "She needs poppy seeds," Squirrelflight whispered to Leafpool.

"And marigold." Leafpool touched a paw to Sunrise's flank. "I don't like how hot she's getting. It might be the beginning of infection."

Snow, who was watching from the edge of the clearing, leaned forward. "Why don't you do something?"

Leafpool glanced at Bramblestar. "I have to obey him," she whispered to the white she-cat.

Snow stared at her. "Can't you think and act for yourselves?" Frustration edged her mew. "First you have to consult with dead cats to see if you can treat her, and now you don't dare help a suffering cat because a tom tells you not to."

"He's our leader," Leafpool told her.

As she spoke, Thornclaw lifted his gaze and glared at Snow. "Stop talking," he hissed.

Squirrelflight's pelt prickled with anger. Had Thornclaw forgotten what it was like to need help? She shifted as Twigbranch nosed her softly aside and pressed a fern beneath Sunrise's shoulder. "Thank you." She blinked gratefully at the young warrior, relieved that not all her Clanmates were acting like fox-hearts, and leaned closer to Leafpool. "Can you check on Sparkpelt? She's in Bramblestar's den. She had some cramps. They've passed now, but I think she needs reassuring."

Leafpool nodded toward Sunrise. "Can you keep an eye on her?"

"Of course." Squirrelflight settled beside Sunrise, pressing her flank along the wounded cat's spine. Her heart ached as she watched her sister pad wordlessly past Bramblestar and climb the rock tumble. When had Bramblestar become so heartless? Did he really believe that Clan unity was worth paying for in another cat's blood?

Squirrelflight could see stars twinkling through the leafy canopy. The moon was high, and her Clanmates sat stiffly around the clearing, murmuring softly to one another, their gazes never straying for long from Hawk, Tempest, and Snow. She pressed closer to Leafpool. Beside them, Sunrise's breath had quickened and grown shallow.

Surely Jayfeather and Alderheart must return soon. Had StarClan given an answer? Squirrelflight sent another desperate prayer toward the glittering sky. *Please let us treat her.* Sunrise had slipped into unconsciousness as the sun had slipped below the trees. *At least it won't hurt now,* Squirrelflight had thought.

Leafpool had settled Sparkpelt into the nursery, where Daisy could keep an eye on her and reassure her if necessary. Larksong was there too. He'd hurried to check on Sparkpelt as soon as he'd returned with the hunting patrol.

Squirrelflight fluffed her pelt against the evening chill. "Shouldn't Jayfeather and Alderheart be back by now?" she whispered to Leafpool.

"They'll be here soon," Leafpool murmured.

As Bramblestar paced beneath the Highledge, Thornclaw sat motionless, eyes glinting like quartz in the moonlight. Birchfall, Blossomfall, Hollytuft, and Flippaw had gathered around the old warrior, and they sat close, staring with undisguised hostility at the Sisters.

Bramblestar had kept his word and shared the patrol's catch with their visitors, but the Sisters had eaten little. They had edged nearer to Sunrise, close enough now to breathe in her scent, which had grown hotter and sourer as the evening had drawn in.

"I pray StarClan will let us treat her," Leafpool murmured. "The wound is festering already. She needs those herbs."

Squirrelflight's heart quickened. Even she could see the swelling around the gash on Sunrise's flank. The cobweb was soggy now and couldn't hide the fiery red flesh beneath.

She pricked her ears as paw steps sounded outside the stone hollow. Bramblestar halted as the Clan shifted nervously around the edge of the clearing. Thornclaw got to his paws as Jayfeather led Alderheart into camp. Squirrelflight jumped up, straining to read Alderheart's expression. His round amber eyes gave nothing away.

"Well?" Bramblestar crossed the clearing to meet the two medicine cats. "What did StarClan say?"

Alderheart frowned. "We're not quite sure."

Bramblestar's pelt rippled along his spine. "But you're medicine cats! You must know. Did they say *anything*?"

"I had a vision," Jayfeather told him. "I spoke to Hollyleaf."

Squirrelflight held her breath. Surely StarClan must have

told him they could treat Sunrise! Perhaps Jayfeather hadn't understood their message. "What did she say?"

The medicine cat turned his blind blue gaze on her. "She said that clouds from the mountains will make it difficult to tell friend from enemy. But if the Clans stay united, the way forward will be clear."

Thornclaw grunted. "'Clouds from the mountains . . .'" He stared at the Sisters. "I think the message is clear. These cats bring trouble. We must send them away."

"No!" Squirrelflight hurried forward. "The message doesn't say they are the enemy, only that clouds will make it hard to tell *who* the enemy is."

Bramblestar frowned. "But they say the Clans must stay united. If we treat this cat, Tigerstar will see it as betrayal."

"You don't know that!" Squirrelflight flicked her tail angrily. "Sunrise needs herbs. Her wound is infected. StarClan would not ask us to let her die. And if they did, perhaps we shouldn't be listening to them." Silence gripped the Clan, and a chill ran beneath her pelt.

Bramblestar looked at her in disbelief. "If we turn our tails on StarClan, then we might as well turn our tails on the whole warrior code." His gaze hardened. "We might as well live like *them*." He flicked his muzzle toward Tempest, Hawk, and Snow. "Or would you prefer that?"

"Of course I wouldn't prefer that, but I can't stand by and let you decide to let a cat die. It's wrong!"

Thornclaw's ears twitched. "And what if the future of the Clans depends on it?"

Mousewhisker padded forward. "No future is decided by a single life!"

"We can't ignore StarClan!" Blossomfall called.

"We can't sit by while a cat suffers," Twigbranch countered.

Murmuring spread among the watching cats, as ears flattened and pelts prickled.

Squirrelflight looked imploringly at Bramblestar. "You have to decide! You have to save this cat!"

Bramblestar returned her gaze, his eyes glistening with doubt. "I can only try to do what's best."

Tempest started forward. "We'll take her home. She can at least die among friends."

"You should never have brought her here in the first place!" Thornclaw spat.

As Hawk and Snow clustered protectively around their campmate, Leafpool got to her paws. "You can argue until dawn for all I care." She turned toward the medicine den. "All I know is that StarClan hasn't told us to let this cat die. I'm fetching herbs to treat her. I will not sit vigil for a cat I could have saved." She began to head across the clearing.

"No!" Bramblestar leaped in front of her, squaring his shoulders as he stared at her. Leafpool froze, her eyes wide.

Squirrelflight's paws seemed rooted to the ground. Was Bramblestar going to fight her sister to stop her treating a wounded cat? As she blinked in disbelief, Sunrise let out a low groan. She was dying! Energy surged beneath Squirrelflight's pelt. She crossed the clearing and pushed in front of Leafpool, meeting Bramblestar's fierce gaze with her own. "Let her go," she growled.

Bramblestar stared at her miserably. "We can't keep doing this," he whispered only loud enough for her to hear. Desperation edged his mew. "If you keep undermining my authority, you could destroy the whole Clan."

Squirrelflight held her ground. "I have to do what I think is right."

"Even if it costs you your Clan?"

"ThunderClan is stronger than that," Squirrelflight spat. "At least I hope it is. If our future depends on letting a cat die, then it's not the Clan I thought it was."

Bramblestar stared at her. Uncertainty glittered in his gaze. "Why are you doing this to me?" His words pierced her heart. "You're my deputy. You're my mate. You're supposed to support me."

"Being a good deputy doesn't mean blindly following orders." Squirrelflight didn't move. "It means standing up for what I believe, and this time, I believe I'm right." The camp seemed to swim around her. She knew she was hurting him. But she had to convince him. As the Clan watched her silently, their eyes round in the moonlight, Bramblestar backed away.

His gaze flicked to Leafpool. "If you insist on treating Sunrise, go ahead. But take her to the medicine den. If she's out of sight, perhaps the Clan will feel less angry." He nodded toward the Sisters. "They can stay in the elders' den. Berrynose and Bumblestripe will stand guard tonight. Move Millie, Brightheart, Cloudtail, and Graystripe to the nursery." Around him, the Clan got to their paws. Mousewhisker and Twigbranch helped Tempest and Hawk lift Sunrise. Leafpool nosed her way into the medicine den. Bramblestar narrowed his eyes, his face like stone. Squirrelflight tried to drag her gaze from his, her heart cracking as he curled his lip. "StarClan wanted unity among the Clans," he snarled. "Thanks to you, there's not even unity in ThunderClan anymore."

CHAPTER 10

❧

Soft waves swished against the pebbles at the edge of the lake. A bright full moon dappled the water. Squirrelflight gazed toward the island as she padded along the shore toward the Gathering. Would Harestar and Tigerstar bring up the question of borders again? She glanced at Bramblestar beside her. "What are you going to tell them?" Would he mention that the Sisters were still in the ThunderClan camp nearly a quarter moon after they'd arrived?

"Nothing." He nodded toward the patrol of SkyClan cats in the distance, waiting to cross the tree-bridge. "Let the others do the talking. I have nothing to say."

They had hardly spoken in the past few days, not even trying to hide the rift between them from the Clan. Squirrelflight had grown used to keeping her thoughts to herself. From time to time, she missed the closeness she had once shared with Bramblestar, with a pang of grief that startled her. But tonight there seemed to be an unspoken agreement between them that, in front of the other Clans, they would pretend that nothing had changed. The ThunderClan patrol followed quietly, murmuring to one another. In the days since the Sisters had come to the camp, the Clan had been tense. At least Sunrise was healing thanks to Leafpool's treatment. Leafpool had remained in camp tonight to watch over her. Hawk, Tempest, and Snow were still in the elders' den.

"What do we tell the other Clans if they ask about the Sisters?" Thornclaw's terse mew sounded behind her.

Bramblestar glanced back at the tabby warrior. "There's no need for them to ask. As far as we know, the other Clans don't know that they are staying with us."

Hollytuft flicked her tail irritably. "But what if they ask if we've seen them? ShadowClan is bound to mention the attack on their patrol."

"We tell them we know nothing." Bramblestar jerked his muzzle forward, the fur prickling uneasily along his spine.

"You want us to lie?" Thornclaw frowned.

"Yes." Bramblestar kept his gaze ahead.

"We should have sent them home already," Bristlepaw growled.

Alderheart glanced at the young she-cat. "Sunrise needs more time to heal properly."

"The others aren't wounded," Bristlepaw shot back. The she-cat's gray pelt bristled. "They should have left days ago."

Irritation sparked in Squirrelflight's pelt. "They wanted to stay with their campmate."

Thornclaw huffed. "Who cares what they want? Did they care what we wanted when they held you captive? Who knows what they'd have done to you if we hadn't turned up and threatened to shred them!"

Alderheart lifted his chin. "Sunrise will be able to travel in a few days. Then they can all leave and things can go back to normal."

Squirrelflight's paws felt heavy. She wasn't sure things could ever go back to normal—for her and Bramblestar, at least. They'd argued too much over the past moon. So much had been said that couldn't be taken back. Her heart ached as she wondered if they'd ever be close again. She quickened her pace, eager to reach the island and let the clamor of voices and scents wash over her and crowd out her sense of loss.

SkyClan had disappeared into the long grass on the far shore by the time she reached the tree-bridge. She waited for Bramblestar to cross first, then followed, leading her Clanmates onto the island. She nosed her way through the grass and emerged into the clearing. WindClan and ShadowClan moved silently to make room for ThunderClan, their gazes solemn. RiverClan watched stiffly from the edge of the clearing while SkyClan clustered at the base of the Great Oak, their wary gazes flitting around at the other cats.

Tigerstar's gaze swung toward the ThunderClan cats and fixed darkly on Bramblestar. Squirrelflight tensed. Did the ShadowClan leader know that they were sheltering the Sisters?

Bramblestar crossed the clearing and leaped onto the low branch of the Great Oak. He gazed expectantly at the other leaders. There would be no time for gossip tonight.

Squirrelflight took her place on the arching roots of the oak. Hawkwing settled beside her as Crowfeather, Reedwhisker, and Cloverfoot joined them. Above them, Tigerstar sat beside Bramblestar. Mistystar followed, Harestar and Leafstar at her tail. The Clans drew closer, crowding beneath the oak's spreading branches, its shadow darkening their pelts.

Bramblestar lifted his muzzle. "Prey is running well in ThunderClan's forest—"

Tigerstar interrupted. "There are more important matters to discuss than prey." His dark gaze swept over the Clans. "We have a new enemy at our border. We need to react."

Murmurs of agreement rippled through the ShadowClan cats. WindClan's warriors were nodding solemnly. RiverClan cats exchanged knowing glances.

Squirrelflight's belly tightened. "What enemy?" she called, though she was afraid she knew exactly who he meant.

Tigerstar glared back at her. "You of all cats should know. They held you hostage, along with Leafstar. And now they have attacked and permanently wounded one of Shadow-Clan's finest warriors."

The fur lifted along Squirrelflight's spine. *Permanently wounded?*

Bramblestar blinked innocently at Tigerstar. "What happened?"

"The Sisters came onto ShadowClan land and attacked a patrol," Tigerstar told him.

Squirrelflight's paws prickled with indignation. Shadow-Clan had gone onto the Sisters' land first, surely. The Sisters had only tracked them to find out why they'd come. That was what Snow had told her. With a sickening feeling, she wondered which version of the story was true.

Tigerstar went on. "They shredded Strikestone's ear. The wound was so deep that the infection was hard to treat. He will never hear in that ear again."

Squirrelflight stiffened. She didn't realize Strikestone had been so badly injured. Growls of anger rose from the Clans.

"Fox-hearts!"

"They're no better than badgers!"

Harestar leaned forward. "The Sisters are clearly a threat to the Clans."

Tigerstar nodded. "We need to drive them away."

Squirrelflight stared at him. "There aren't enough of them to threaten us."

Leafstar nodded. "We outnumber them countless times."

"They are big cats, and dangerous." Tigerstar stared at the SkyClan leader. "You saw that for yourself." His gaze switched to Squirrelflight. "They could easily cross the border and pick off our patrols one by one."

"They'd never do that!" Squirrelflight's ears twitched with indignation. "They are peaceful."

"They don't look for fights," Leafstar chimed.

"Tell that to Strikestone." Tigerstar lashed his tail.

Yowls erupted from the ShadowClan, WindClan, and RiverClan cats.

"The Sisters must go!"

"Drive them out!"

Thornclaw watched them, satisfaction glittering in his gaze. Twigbranch and Molewhisker exchanged uneasy glances.

Squirrelflight blinked helplessly at Hawkwing. "Why is he picking on the Sisters?" she whispered. "They couldn't hurt us. They don't *want* to hurt us!"

Hawkwing met her gaze. "They permanently wounded one of his warriors," he murmured through the yowling of the Clans. "He has to react. And don't forget, ShadowClan nearly fell apart only a few moons ago. Tigerstar needs an enemy to unite his Clan behind him."

Squirrelflight blinked at him as she began to understand. "And if StarClan wants the Clans to be united, he has to pick a fight with outsiders."

"Exactly." Hawkwing's eyes glittered with unease.

"You don't think we should fight them, do you?" Squirrelflight was unnerved by the support of the other Clans for Tigerstar's plan.

"Why fight?" Hawkwing shrugged. "They'll be gone in a moon."

Above them, Bramblestar shifted on the branch. His tail swished ominously behind him as he stared out at the crowd. Gradually WindClan, RiverClan, and ShadowClan fell silent. Macgyver and Sandynose blinked up at him warily from among their Clanmates. ThunderClan's warriors moved closer to one another, avoiding the gazes of the other Clans.

"There is no need for war," Bramblestar yowled. "The Sisters have promised to leave soon. Why fight a retreating enemy? It's better to let them go."

Tigerstar flattened his ears. "It's just like ThunderClan to defend the enemies of ShadowClan."

"Are you sure they're your enemy?" Bramblestar challenged.

"They attacked us. They captured Leafstar."

Leafstar's ears twitched. "We were trespassing on their land—"

Tigerstar pressed on. "They took your deputy hostage. They should be your enemy too." Tigerstar stared at Bramblestar, then flicked his gaze toward the ThunderClan cats gathered below. "And yet ThunderClan is silent tonight. The Sisters were last seen heading for your territory. Their scent was detected on your border." He narrowed his eyes as he looked back at Bramblestar. "Do you know something about the Sisters that we don't?"

"Of course not." Bramblestar lashed his tail.

Squirrelflight saw Thornclaw look away. Beside him, Molewhisker dropped his gaze as Bramblestar went on.

"We haven't heard from the Sisters since they returned Leafstar and Squirrelflight to us unharmed."

Squirrelflight flinched. She hated hearing Bramblestar lie.

Leafstar fluffed out her fur. "I'm not sure you need to declare war on them. They treated us kindly while we were with them."

Squirrelflight nodded eagerly, relieved that Leafstar was defending the Sisters. "They fed us and treated Leafstar's wound."

Tigerstar huffed. "They *caused* Leafstar's wound!"

A breeze ruffled Harestar's pelt. "WindClan agrees with ShadowClan," he yowled. "StarClan has decreed that the Clans be united. So we stand with ShadowClan to honor our ancestors and strengthen our alliance."

Mistystar nodded slowly. "We stand with ShadowClan too. Leafstar has agreed to move to new territory—"

Leafstar bristled. "That decision isn't final!"

"And yet it would solve all the Clans' problems," Mistystar countered. "We need the fishing land we gave to Shadow-Clan. WindClan needs their moorland back." She blinked at the SkyClan leader. "The sooner we move the Sisters from your new territory, the sooner the Clans can reestablish their rightful borders."

Squirrelflight's heart filled with dread. Three leaders were determined to fight the Sisters. And she could see by the excited murmuring of the watching cats that they had the full support of their Clanmates. How could she expect any cat to resist the promise of a return to their traditional borders? She looked helplessly at Bramblestar. Surely he could find a way to stop them! She searched his gaze expectantly. Was he going to defend the Sisters, despite everything?

"We have a Clan mediator." Bramblestar lifted his chin. "Why not use him?"

Leafstar pricked her ears. "Tree." She scanned the crowd, her gaze settling on the yellow SkyClan warrior. Tree blinked back at him, pelt bristling in surprise. "Could you go to the Sisters and persuade them that it is in everyone's best interests for them to leave?"

Tree's gaze glittered with unease. "I mediate between the Clans, not with outsiders."

Mistystar narrowed her eyes. "But they're not outsiders to

you," she told Tree. "They're kin. Moonlight's your mother, right?"

Tree's hackles lifted. "I barely know her. She forced me out when I was a kit."

"In that case you won't mind asking her to leave," Mistystar shot back.

Tree looked away for a moment, then turned back to face Mistystar, clearly uncomfortable. "She won't *listen* to me," he said finally. "I'm happy to be a Clan cat; I'm happy to do my duty by mediating between the Clans. But please, if it's all the same to you, I would like to be left out of this. I much prefer my life without Moonlight or the Sisters in it."

Squirrelflight stared at the yellow tom in surprise. She heard murmurs of sympathy, and some shocked exclamations.

"So you want to be a Clan cat until we ask you do to something you'd rather not?" she heard Crowfeather mutter.

Squirrelflight raised her voice. "I think we should listen to Tree," she said, shooting Leafstar a glance. "Leafstar and I have seen the tension between him and Moonlight. Perhaps we should wait until we have no other voice."

Leafstar nodded at Squirrelflight, then raised her voice above the din. "Very well, Tree," she said. "We'll consider other options . . . for now. But if your connection to Moonlight might help—"

"It won't," Tree interrupted.

Bramblestar heaved a sigh. "Let's move on," he said. "In terms of moving the Sisters, I believe we must do nothing without the counsel of StarClan."

Hope flashed beneath Squirrelflight's fur. Perhaps that would stall them.

"StarClan has been silent lately," Harestar pointed out. "They must feel we can make our own decisions."

Squirrelflight saw Bramblestar hesitate. He pricked his ears, as though ready to speak, but said nothing. She wanted to call out for him, *But StarClan isn't silent!* They had shared with Jayfeather. But how could she tell them without giving away the secret of the Sisters' presence in the ThunderClan camp? Worse, if the Clans knew StarClan's message, with its talk of *enemies*, it might convince them that StarClan wanted war against the Sisters.

It was better to say nothing.

Bramblestar dipped his gaze for a moment, then lifted it to meet Harestar's once more. "They won't be silent on a matter of war," he growled. "And there is no unity among the Clans in this plan. SkyClan isn't with you." He glanced at Tigerstar. "And ThunderClan will not agree to any action against the Sisters without the approval of StarClan."

Squirrelflight felt a rush of pride. How could any leader argue with him? She watched as Tigerstar eyed Bramblestar ominously.

Then the ShadowClan leader dipped his head. "Very well." He exchanged glances with Harestar and Mistystar. "We will wait to hear from StarClan. Until then, we must all be vigilant. Who knows when the Sisters will strike again? And next time it might cost a cat more than their hearing." As he leaped from the branch, his Clanmates gathered around him, eyeing

ThunderClan and SkyClan defiantly.

Mistystar and Harestar scrambled down the trunk, and Leafstar jumped after them. The SkyClan leader nodded politely to Squirrelflight as she passed. Squirrelflight nodded back, longing to know when she would make the final decision to move her Clan onto the Sisters' territory. Suddenly she found herself hoping Leafstar would delay it. As long as she wasn't sure she wanted the Sisters' land, it would weaken the other Clans' support for Tigerstar's plan.

Squirrelflight's Clanmates were heading for the long grass. She watched them trail after the other Clans.

"Trust Tigerstar to find an excuse to turn this into a war," Jayfeather grumbled as he passed.

Alderheart padded beside the blind medicine cat, nervously twitching his whiskers. "Do you think any of the Clans suspected?"

"Hush!" Bumblestripe fell in beside him. "Let's wait until we get clear of the island before we say anything."

Fur brushed Squirrelflight's flank. Bramblestar was beside her, staring after their Clanmates. His ears twitched uneasily. "I've made liars out of my whole Clan," he murmured. He looked accusingly at Squirrelflight. "Are the Sisters worth sacrificing our honor and our pride for?"

Guilt wormed beneath Squirrelflight's pelt. She knew that asking his Clanmates to lie must have wounded Bramblestar deeply. "We couldn't have told the truth." She blinked at him. "Who knows what Tigerstar would have done?"

"I warned you he'd react badly."

"We can't live in fear of what Tigerstar might do."

"But what Tigerstar does matters, whether you like it or not."

Squirrelflight shifted her paws uneasily. "He seems determined to drive the Sisters off their land."

"Would it be such a bad thing if he did?" Bramblestar stared at her darkly.

Squirrelflight blinked back at him, shocked. "Moonlight's expecting kits," she gasped. "We have to protect them."

Exasperation seemed to flash in his gaze. Was he irritated that she was still worrying about kits? "And who will protect Sparkpelt's kits if Tigerstar finds out we're sheltering his sworn enemy?"

Squirrelflight's heart lurched. "He won't find out!"

"We won't give him the chance." Bramblestar watched their Clanmates disappear into the long grass. "Sunrise and her campmates must leave our territory tonight."

CHAPTER 11

Squirrelflight leaped down from the tree-bridge and headed along the shore. She could see the shapes of ShadowClan and Wind-Clan, moving like shadows over the stony beach as they trekked back to their territories. RiverClan had already crossed the shore and disappeared into the marshes. Her paws pricked. How was she going to break the news to the Sisters that they had to leave now, in the middle of the night?

Pebbles crunched behind her as Alderheart hurried at her heels.

She glanced at him as he fell in beside her. "Do you think Sunrise is well enough to travel?" she asked.

"She'll be okay if her campmates help her." Alderheart gazed across the lake as though his thoughts were elsewhere. "And she can rest once she's home."

"Do you think it's fair?" Squirrelflight's tail twitched.

"Do I think what's fair?" Alderheart looked at her.

"To make them leave. Now. Before they're ready?"

Alderheart returned her gaze steadily. "I think it's for the best."

"For *whose* best?" Squirrelflight asked crossly.

"Every cat's." Alderheart's hopped over a rotting branch that had washed onto the shore. "The Sisters will be safer on their own territory. And our Clanmates will be happier knowing they're gone. If Tigerstar wants war, it's dangerous having them in camp."

Squirrelflight looked away. She knew Alderheart was right, but she wished the Sisters could have seen ThunderClan at its best. Her Clanmates hadn't always been so unwelcoming and defensive. The Sisters had come at a bad time.

The patrol trailed behind them, murmuring to one another. Bumblestripe and Honeyfur walked side by side. Hollytuft shadowed Jayfeather while Bristlepaw and Thriftpaw padded behind. Bramblestar hung back with Thornclaw. As they neared camp, Squirrelflight's heart quickened. She wanted to break the news to the Sisters before Bramblestar ordered them out of camp. She turned and called to Bramblestar. "I'm going ahead to tell Leafpool that Sunrise has to leave."

Bramblestar narrowed his eyes. "Okay." He nodded to Bumblestripe. "Go with her."

Squirrelflight stiffened. Was he sending Bumblestripe to keep her safe, or because he didn't trust her? What did he think she would do? Hole up in the medicine den and fight for the Sisters to stay?

She nodded politely and pulled away from the patrol, breaking into a run. Bumblestripe fell in beside her and matched her, paw step for paw step, as she zigzagged between ferns and veered onto the rabbit trail that would bring her out close to the camp entrance. It was too narrow to run side by side here, and she slipped into the lead, speeding up as she neared home. She ducked first through the thorn tunnel and hurried into camp.

The clearing was hidden in shadow. The Clan must be asleep. Only Whitewing's pelt showed on the far side of the clearing, bright in the moonlight. She hurried forward as she saw Squirrelflight. "Did ShadowClan know the Sisters are here?" she whispered anxiously.

"No." Squirrelflight flicked her tail as Bumblestripe followed her into camp. "Bumblestripe will tell you what happened." As Whitewing turned away Squirrelflight padded quickly to the elders' den. She stuck her head through the entrance. The scent of the Sisters bathed her muzzle and she blinked, adjusting to the darkness. "Snow? Are you awake?"

The white she-cat lifted her head and blinked sleepily in the shadows. "What's happened?"

"You have to leave tonight," Squirrelflight told her.

Tempest jerked her head up. "Right now?" Alarm glittered in the tabby's bright gaze.

"As soon as Bramblestar gets back," Squirrelflight told her. "He wants you to leave tonight. He's following with the rest of the patrol. They'll be here soon."

Hawk scrambled to her paws. "Is Sunrise well enough to travel?"

"I hope so. I'm going to see Leafpool now," Squirrelflight blinked at her. "She'll know what to do." She ducked out of the elders' den, sensing Bumblestripe's gaze as she crossed the clearing. She ignored it and nosed her way through the brambles that draped the entrance to the medicine den.

Leafpool was sitting beside Sunrise's nest, her face hidden in shadow. She pricked her ears as Squirrelflight slid inside. "Was the Gathering okay?"

Sunrise shifted in her nest. "Did ShadowClan make trouble?" Anxiety glittered in her gaze.

Squirrelflight crossed the den. "ShadowClan wants to declare war against the Sisters. Leafstar and Bramblestar convinced them to hold off until we hear from StarClan." She gazed evenly at Sunrise. "But Bramblestar says you have to leave here tonight."

Leafpool's pelt prickled. "Tonight?" She glanced anxiously at Sunrise's wound. Squirrelflight guessed what she was thinking. The gash had closed, but a mistimed jump or a fall could reopen it. And the infection had sapped the she-cat's strength.

"I've warned Snow." As Squirrelflight spoke, the white she-cat pushed her way into the den, Tempest and Hawk at her heels. They crowded inside, appearing bigger than ever in the tight hollow.

Snow blinked at Leafpool. "Is she well enough to travel?"

Leafpool shifted her paws. "She'll have to be. If Shadow-Clan is talking war, it's too dangerous for you to stay."

"War?" Hawk asked, her eyes wide. "You didn't mention that before. Do you really think the other cats would attack because you've helped us?"

"You attacked their warriors," Leafpool replied evenly. "They would see it as defending their own."

"But we were only defending *our* own," Tempest meowed.

Leafpool's ear twitched irritably. "We could argue about who was in the right all day. What matters is that you must leave if we want to avoid violence." She caught Squirrelflight's eye nervously.

Does she think I'm going to argue? Squirrelflight felt uneasy about sending Sunrise home while she was still weak, but she realized Alderheart had been right, and Leafpool clearly felt the same way—if ShadowClan, WindClan, and RiverClan were ready to start a war with the Sisters, they wouldn't be safe here, and their presence would put ThunderClan in danger.

Leafpool flicked her tail. "I'll make up a bundle of herbs for you to take." She padded toward the cleft in the rock at the back of the den where the herbs were stored. "I hope you can find more when you get home." She crouched and began tugging leaves from the shadowy crack. "Use marigold, and goldenrod if you can find it. That wound will need to be kept clean until it's fully healed."

Snow dipped her head. "We are grateful for your care, Leafpool. Sunrise would have died without you."

"Alderheart and Jayfeather would have taken care of her if I hadn't," Leafpool meowed briskly as she pulled out a wad of thyme.

Squirrelflight shifted her paws. Would they have? Jayfeather and Alderheart had helped treat Sunrise's wound, but she'd felt their unease at having a cat some of the Clan considered an enemy in their medicine den. She suspected they'd be relieved when the Sisters left.

Sunrise shifted in her nest, her face taut with pain.

Hawk stiffened. "Are you sure she can travel?"

Leafpool wrapped the herbs in a leaf and carried them to Sunrise's nest. She opened the bundle and, with her pad, dabbed at a patch of poppy seeds pooled between the leaves. "Swallow these." She lifted her paw to Sunrise's mouth, and the yellow she-cat ducked to lick them off. "They'll help with the pain. There's more in the bundle for when you get home, but you'll have to find your own once they're gone."

Tempest was frowning. "Do the Clans always turn a fight into a war?"

Squirrelflight looked at her. "What do you mean?"

"Sunrise was hurt in a border fight," Tempest meowed. "Is that any reason to start a war?"

"Tensions are running high at the moment," Squirrelflight explained. "We changed borders recently, and it's not working out as well as we'd hoped. And the fight permanently damaged Strikestone's hearing. I didn't realize when we brought Sunrise back here that a Clan cat had been so badly hurt."

"Nor did we." Tempest's gaze darkened. "We didn't mean to harm him."

Snow lifted her muzzle. "We were defending ourselves."

Leafpool rerolled the bundle. "What's done is done." She pushed it toward Hawk.

"They're back." Squirrelflight blinked anxiously toward the den entrance as paw steps sounded in the clearing.

The brambles shivered and Bramblestar pushed his way in. "Are they ready?" He gazed darkly at the Sisters.

Snow nodded.

"I've given them herbs to take with them," Leafpool told him.

Bramblestar narrowed his eyes. "*Our* herbs?"

Leafpool met his gaze. "I'll pick fresh herbs to replace them."

Bramblestar flicked his tail toward the entrance. "It's time they were going." He nodded toward Snow. "Try not to be seen. And stay away from ShadowClan's borders. I don't want them picking up your scent."

"I'm going to escort them," Squirrelflight told him. "I can make sure they stay away from Clan borders."

Bramblestar looked at her suspiciously. "I'm sure they can manage by themselves."

"They'll manage better with a guide." Squirrelflight returned his gaze evenly. She wanted to check on Moonlight. Was the Sisters' leader close to kitting? "ShadowClan mustn't know they've passed through our territory."

Bramblestar frowned. "If you must go, I'm sending Bumble-stripe with you."

"Let him sleep," Squirrelflight mewed quickly. "It's late." She tipped her head to one side. "Or don't you trust me to do this alone?"

Bramblestar stared back at her, then shook out his pelt. "Go with them if you must," he growled. He nodded quickly to the Sisters and nosed his way out of the den.

"He doesn't sound pleased with the idea," Snow observed.

"These days, he's not pleased with anything I do."

Squirrelflight watched the brambles swish back into place, her heart heavy.

"There's no time to worry about that now." Leafpool helped Sunrise to her paws. As the wounded cat climbed unsteadily out of her nest, Hawk and Tempest hurried to support her. They pressed against her on either side, guiding her to the entrance. Snow picked up the bundle of herbs and followed them out.

Leafpool watched them go. "Don't travel too fast," she warned Squirrelflight. "Sunrise is very weak."

"I'll make sure she gets home safely," Squirrelflight promised.

Outside, Bramblestar hung back in the shadow of the Highledge, his eyes glittering in the moonlight. Thornclaw and Hollytuft watched from the fresh-kill pile as the Sisters moved slowly past them.

Larksong padded to the edge of the clearing and dipped his head to Tempest. His black pelt was no more than a shadow in the darkness. "Take care," he mewed.

"I'll look after them." Squirrelflight told him.

Larksong looked surprised. "Are you going with them?"

Squirrelflight lifted her chin. "I brought them here. I'll see them home."

Sparkpelt padded to her mate's side, her gaze shimmering with worry as she blinked at her mother. "Will you be okay?"

"I'll be among friends," Squirrelflight reassured her.

A low growl rumbled in Thornclaw's throat. Squirrelflight ignored it and followed Tempest and Hawk as they steered

Sunrise through the thorn tunnel.

In the forest, Snow fell in quietly beside Squirrelflight. She held the bundle of herbs between her jaws, staying close as Squirrelflight led the Sisters toward the abandoned Twolegplace.

The journey was slow, and they stopped from time to time to let Sunrise rest. The wounded cat made no fuss, but Squirrelflight could see from the bright pain in her eyes that she was struggling. An owl hooted in the trees, staying with them as they made their way through the forest, as though curious about their presence. Foxes screeched in the distance, and everywhere Squirrelflight could hear the rustle of prey in the undergrowth.

At the edge of Clan territory, Squirrelflight relaxed a little. From here, she wouldn't have to keep glancing over her shoulder for prying Clan eyes. She halted as Tempest and Hawk helped Sunrise across the border; then she let Snow take the lead. The white cat knew this territory better than she did. Tiredness was beginning to tug at her bones, and she was relieved when at last she recognized the trail that led into the Sisters' secluded valley.

She opened her mouth and, through the dank night air, tasted the scent of their camp. *Moonlight.* She smelled the she-cat's scent, feeling at home at once. Pricking her ears, she listened for movement. This late into the night, the Sisters must be sleeping.

At the fern entrance, Tempest lifted her muzzle and yowled. Instantly, dens rustled and paw steps pattered over grass.

"Snow? Is that you?" Moonlight's call sounded from the camp.

Squirrelflight fought the urge to race ahead, letting Tempest and Hawk ease Sunrise through the ferns before she followed them into the camp.

"You're home." Moonlight stood outside her den, her eyes shining. "Sparrow brought your message." Her gaze flitted toward Sunrise. "It looks like Squirrelflight's medicine cat managed to help."

Flurry hurried to her mother's side. "Hawk!" She rubbed her cheek against her mother's. "I'm glad you're back."

Sparrow wove around them, purring. "You were gone for ages. Moonlight was about to send a search party."

Squirrelflight was relieved that the gray she-cat hadn't. What would Bramblestar have said if even more Sisters had turned up on their land?

Sunrise sank down into the grass with a weary groan.

"Are you still sick?" Furze darted toward her.

"I'm recovering," Sunrise told her. "Slowly."

Snow dropped the herb bundle beside Sunrise. "Squirrelflight's campmates gave us these herbs to treat her."

Moonlight hurried across the clearing and stopped beside Snow. Squirrelflight eyed her swollen belly. "I'm glad you're safe." Her gaze flashed toward Squirrelflight, surprise lighting her face as though she'd only just realized Squirrelflight was with the returning patrol. "I must thank you for taking care of my campmates."

Squirrelflight's pelt prickled uneasily. What would

Moonlight say when she heard that ThunderClan had considered turning Sunrise away, even if it meant she died? "It was risky," she mumbled. She needed to explain. "Sunrise was injured in a fight with ShadowClan. Sheltering her was dangerous."

Moonlight dipped her head. "I'm sorry my campmates put your Clan in such a difficult position. Has it caused you trouble?"

"Not really." Squirrelflight told her. "ShadowClan doesn't know we helped her. But they are ready to declare war on you because of the fight with their patrol. One of their warriors lost his ear, and his hearing."

Moonlight tipped her head to one side. "Do they know we'll be moving on once my kits have been born?"

"Yes," Squirrelflight met her gaze apologetically. "But Tigerstar doesn't want to wait that long, and RiverClan and WindClan are willing to fight with him."

Moonlight blinked at her. "And your Clan?"

"Bramblestar is stalling them. He says we must have the permission of StarClan."

"They're your ancestors, yes?"

Squirrelflight nodded.

"And they live up there?" Moonlight looked into the sky. Pale blue was showing on the horizon, but the stars were still glittering in blackness overhead. "It seems a long way to travel. Perhaps that's why some choose to stay here."

Squirrelflight frowned. "What do you mean?"

Snow pricked her ears. "Don't you see them?"

"See who?" Squirrelflight shifted uneasily. The Sisters were staring at her as though she'd grown rabbit ears.

"The dead," Moonlight told her.

Cold wormed beneath Squirrelflight's pelt. "Only medicine cats share with StarClan."

Moonlight looked puzzled. "Don't the rest of you see them?"

Squirrelflight hesitated, remembering suddenly the great battle against the Dark Forest. "Once, many moons ago, our ancestors fought beside us." Her belly tightened. "But those days are over. Since then, the warriors of StarClan only show themselves to our medicine cats."

Moonlight met her gaze. "Perhaps it is simpler that way. The dead are all around us. They seem younger and sleeker than they did in life, as though death brings them peace."

"Do you speak to them?" A memory stirred at the edges of Squirrelflight's thoughts.

"Sometimes," Moonlight told her.

Tree! Squirrelflight caught hold of the memory. The loner that SkyClan had taken in was able to see the dead. He'd brought dead warriors from the shadows to speak with their living Clanmates. "Of course! Your son Tree sees the dead too!"

"Cats born of the Sisters have this skill." Moonlight gazed at her. "It keeps us connected to our ancestors."

"We all see the dead," Furze told her. "Sometimes they talk to us; sometimes they don't. Sometimes I'm not sure they even see me."

"I often see the same cat," Tempest told her. "If she wants to, she speaks to me; if not, she ignores me."

Squirrelflight wondered if the Sisters' dead had the same powers of prophecy as StarClan. "Do they ever tell you what will happen in the future?"

Tempest narrowed her eyes. "How would they know?"

"Our dead move among us," Moonlight explained. "They have no power to see what we cannot."

Squirrelflight glanced at the sky, frustration pricking in her paws. What use were the dead if they couldn't help the living? Dawn was creeping closer. She needed to get home. "Tell your dead friends to watch out for the Clans," she warned Moonlight. "Bramblestar has stopped ShadowClan for now, but once Tigerstar gets an idea, it's hard for him to let go."

Moonlight swished her tail. "We are bigger and stronger than Clan cats."

Squirrelflight gazed at her solemnly. "Maybe, but you're heavily outnumbered. Even rats are dangerous when they come in swarms."

Tempest and Furze exchanged nervous looks. Hawk shifted closer to her kits.

Moonlight held Squirrelflight's gaze. "You may be right," she conceded. "But we won't be here for long. Try to persuade the Clans to wait. We mean no harm to them, but my kits must be born here."

Squirrelflight dipped her head. "I will do what I can." Even as she promised, doubt gnawed at her belly. Maybe once, with Bramblestar on her side, she could have persuaded the Clans to keep their claws sheathed, for a while at least. But their experience with Darktail had made the Clans more wary. His Kin had posed as a harmless group of rogues, too—but then they'd infiltrated ShadowClan and eventually taken it over. Before he was done, they'd taken RiverClan's land as well, and horribly mistreated the cats in their care. Many cats died in the battle to defeat him, and ShadowClan was nearly destroyed. All the Clans had become more hostile to outsiders and less open to reason as a result. She knew the Sisters were no threat, but she wasn't sure that she could convince the Clans to leave them in peace.

CHAPTER 12

❧

"Stay with me." Squirrelflight nudged Ivypool with her nose, waiting while Twigbranch and Finleap checked the clearing. She wanted to give the two young warriors a chance to guide the hunt.

In the days since the Sisters had left the camp, she'd volunteered for every patrol. She wanted to keep busy. She was leading a hunting patrol now. They hadn't had much luck so far, finding prey scarce around the beech grove, but as they headed closer to the edge of the forest, prey-scents were becoming thicker. Ivypool paused beside her and watched Twigbranch and Finleap sniff their way through the ferns that pooled in a patch of sunlight.

Twigbranch lifted her head and called over the browning fronds. "There are squirrel scents here, but they're stale." She looked into the canopy. "Prey must be busy today building nests for leaf-bare."

Ivypool padded forward, pushing between the ferns. "They have to come out to find fresh bedding, just like we do."

Twigbranch shrugged. "If they do, they're not looking for it here."

Squirrelflight nodded toward the edge of the forest, where bright sunshine lit the trunks. "We could check the land beyond the stream."

"The moorland?" Ivypool looked unconvinced.

Finleap pricked his ears hopefully. "Moorland prey might be less shy." As he swished through the ferns, heading for the light, Twigbranch hurried after him.

"I don't see the point of hunting on the moorland." Ivypool fell in beside Squirrelflight as they followed the younger cats. "We'll be giving it back soon."

"Only if SkyClan agrees to move," Squirrelflight told her. "And even then, we have to wait for the Sisters to leave their camp."

"Not if Tigerstar goes ahead with his plan to chase them off," Ivypool reminded her.

Squirrelflight's belly tightened. "He promised to wait for word from StarClan." Bramblestar hadn't sent Jayfeather and Alderheart to consult with StarClan yet, and she guessed he was delaying on purpose. He didn't want any news that would encourage Tigerstar to start a war with the Sisters. Besides, Bramblestar already knew what StarClan thought. *Clouds from the mountains will make it difficult to tell friend from enemy. But if the Clans stay united, the way forward will be clear.* She wasn't surprised he hadn't shared the message with the other Clans. It could too easily be interpreted as an order to move against the Sisters.

Had the other Clans sent medicine cats to the Moonpool? Would StarClan give them the same message? Squirrelflight couldn't help but consider what that might mean: *What if StarClan* does *want us to attack the Sisters?* But how could that be? Squirrelflight knew many of the cats in StarClan; they were her own kin and Clanmates, good cats at heart. Why would they want the Clans to attack these harmless cats? For now, she decided, she was choosing to believe that wasn't what StarClan meant.

Judging from the silence from beyond ThunderClan's borders, Squirrelflight guessed that no message had been shared. But waiting was making her nervous. How long would Bramblestar resist the call to war against the Sisters if StarClan sent word to the other Clans?

She was heartened that he hadn't done more than send the Sisters back to their camp. He clearly wasn't prepared to push them farther away. Not yet, at least. Squirrelflight fluffed out her fur. He'd behaved with similar restraint in their relationship. Bramblestar kept his distance, eating and hunting with others, only speaking to her about Clan business, but he hadn't asked her to leave his den. They both slept there each night, in separate nests, sharing the silence.

Watching Sparkpelt's belly swell and her pelt grow glossier had sharpened Squirrelflight's grief at not having her own kits. The hope that she might have another litter with Bramblestar seemed to grow more remote with each passing day.

Sunlight bathed her face, jerking her from her gloomy thoughts. She and Ivypool had reached the edge of the forest. Twigbranch and Finleap were already crossing the stream.

Ivypool opened her mouth to let air bathe her tongue. The silver tabby's eyes brightened. "I smell rabbit." She hurried after Twigbranch and Finleap.

Squirrelflight followed, jumping from stone to stone across the stream and landing lightly on the far bank. WindClan scents rolled from the high moor as a warm wind ruffled her pelt. Ahead, Finleap dropped into a hunting crouch. Twigbranch and Ivypool froze. Heart quickening, Squirrelflight followed her Clanmates' gaze. Brown fur flashed between the heather bushes. *The rabbit!*

She held her breath as Finleap's stumpy tail swished eagerly over the earth. The heather quivered. Finleap shot forward. As he plunged through the bushes, Twigbranch and Ivypool dived after him. Squirrelflight darted through a gap in the heather. Branches scraped her pelt. Bushes crowded on either side, blocking her view, but she could hear paws thrumming and smell the rabbit's acrid fear-scent. Zigzagging between the stems, she tracked the patrol, breathing fast as she glimpsed Ivypool's silver tail-tip flashing. She chased after it, excitement sparking through her pelt.

A moment later, she slammed into Ivypool's hindquarters. The silver tabby had stopped without warning. Surprised, Squirrelflight fought to keep her balance as she stumbled to a halt. "What's wrong?"

Ivypool was staring through the heather, her pelt bristling. "Look."

Twigbranch and Finleap were backing toward her. Her pelt bristled with alarm as she smelled WindClan scent. *Breezepelt.* The black warrior was advancing on the ThunderClan patrol. His eyes were narrowed to hostile slits as he pushed through the heather.

Squirrelflight straightened and met his gaze as Ivypool, Twigbranch, and Finleap pressed around her. "What are you doing here?"

Breezepelt glared at her without answering.

Doubt tugged at Squirrelflight's belly. This was still ThunderClan land, wasn't it? For a moment, Squirrelflight wondered if they'd crossed the border by accident. She glanced around, her view blocked by the heather, then pushed her way out and padded onto the grass. The line of gorse that marked the border was a tree-length away. They were still inside ThunderClan territory.

Ivypool, Twigbranch, and Finleap followed her out, looking confused.

Ivypool eyed Breezepelt angrily as he slid from the heather. "What in StarClan do you think you're doing?" she snarled at him.

Finleap's hackles lifted. "You scared off our prey!"

"*Your* prey?" Breezepelt growled scornfully.

"Yes!" Finleap took a step closer to the WindClan warrior, unsheathing his claws.

Squirrelflight glimpsed pelts moving through the stretch of heather. Hootwhisker, Nightcloud, and Sedgewhisker were heading toward them. "Wait, Finleap," she warned.

Finleap lashed his tail. "But he scared off our prey."

"I don't want to start a fight." Squirrelflight shifted her paws uneasily as the other WindClan warriors neared. "I want to know what WindClan's warriors are doing here." As Finleap backed toward her, she caught Breezepelt's eye. "This isn't your territory," she told the black tom. "Why have you disturbed our hunt?"

Breezepelt met her gaze, his eyes flashing dangerously. "This land is wasted on ThunderClan," he growled. "You said so yourself at the Gathering."

Squirrelflight bristled. "That was an informal gathering between leaders and deputies. We never formally agreed to change the borders."

"And yet you said it," Breezepelt pressed.

"*Harestar* said the land was wasted on ThunderClan," she corrected him.

"But you agreed." Breezepelt stood motionless as his Clan-mates reached him and fanned out on either side, their hostile gazes fixed on the ThunderClan warriors.

Squirrelflight's ears twitched nervously. He was using her words against her. Harestar must have put him up to it. The black warrior hadn't been at that gathering. None of the warriors had. Only leaders and deputies. "I said we hadn't been using the moorland as much as we could," she growled. "But we're using it now."

Hootwhisker nodded toward the forest. "Why not hunt in the woods? It's what you're used to, and there's enough prey for you there."

Nightcloud's gaze flicked over the ThunderClan patrol. "You certainly don't look hungry."

"Hunger has nothing to do with it!" Finleap flattened his ears. "This is our territory, and we can hunt here whenever we want."

"You're trespassing," Ivypool snarled.

Squirrelflight kept her gaze on Breezepelt. "The leaders have agreed that the new borders will remain until SkyClan has made a decision. So I suggest you leave our land until our leaders agree to restore the old borders." Her pelt pricked nervously. Were the WindClan warriors looking for a fight?

Breezepelt's tail twitched. He leaned toward Nightcloud and whispered in her ear. The black she-cat looked at him, then jerked her muzzle toward Squirrelflight. "I suggest you discuss this with Bramblestar. He may have a clearer view on what is best for the Clans."

The insult jabbed Squirrelflight's belly like claws. "I *will* discuss this with Bramblestar," she growled. "But he won't allow borders to be ignored any more than I will. Without borders, there can be no unity among the Clans." She stared deep into Breezepelt's gaze, hoping he understood the implication. In crossing the ThunderClan border so blatantly, WindClan was disregarding StarClan's command for peace.

Breezepelt held her gaze for a moment, then looked away. He signaled to his patrol with a flick of his tail. "Let's head back to the high moor."

Without a word, his Clanmates turned and headed into the heather, climbing the slope toward the border. A low growl rumbled in Ivypool's throat. Twigbranch flexed her claws angrily. As the WindClan patrol crossed the line of gorse, Squirrelflight turned back toward camp. "We should go tell Bramblestar."

* * *

Squirrelflight made the journey back in silence, unease rippling through her pelt. Behind her, Ivypool, Finleap, and Twigbranch muttered angrily to one another. As they reached camp, Squirrelflight ducked first through the thorn tunnel. Bramblestar was sitting on the Highledge. She beckoned him with a flick of her tail.

His eyes widened and he leaped down the rock tumble and stopped as Ivypool, Finleap, and Twigbranch gathered around her. He searched Squirrelflight's gaze, his ears pricking anxiously. "What's happened?"

"WindClan," Finleap answered first, his tail flicking angrily behind him. "They say our moorland belongs to them."

Twigbranch growled.

Squirrelflight watched Bramblestar, looking for outrage to flare in his amber eyes. But he only blinked. "I will speak with Harestar. Today." He nodded to Squirrelflight. "Will you come with me?"

Squirrelflight's eyes widened as surprise sparked inside her. Was this how he was going to defend the borders he'd agreed to? "What are you going to say to him?"

Bramblestar lifted his chin. "I'm going to try to come to an agreement. If Harestar believes land is being wasted strongly enough to fight for it, then we need to listen to him."

Ivypool bristled. "Are you thinking about giving the moorland back?" She sounded shocked. "If we give land to WindClan *and* SkyClan, we won't have enough prey to make it through leaf-bare."

Bramblestar looked at her. "I won't let my Clan go hungry," he promised. "Trust me."

Ivypool held his gaze for a moment, then looked away. Flicking her tail, she beckoned Finleap and Twigbranch away. "I don't know what ThunderClan's coming to," she muttered as she led them around the clearing. "Protecting rogues and giving land away to any Clan that wants it."

"Thornclaw won't be happy, either, if you let WindClan take our land." Squirrelflight blinked at Bramblestar. The ThunderClan warrior had been sullen ever since Bramblestar had agreed to let Leafpool treat Sunrise.

"Thornclaw is just one warrior," Bramblestar grunted.

"But he speaks for others. Birchfall, Blossomfall—"

Bramblestar cut her off. "I'm only going to *speak* with Harestar. There must be a way to divide Clan land so that none is wasted."

"Not if we have to make space for SkyClan," Squirrelflight pointed out.

"Then it might be time to find a new space for SkyClan." Bramblestar shook his head. "I'm sorry, Squirrelflight, I know I've fought you on this. But perhaps you're right. There's no other way to solve the dispute fairly."

Squirrelflight stared at her mate, surprised. Relief washed over her like a warm breeze in newleaf. "I . . . Thank you."

Bramblestar nodded, his expression softening, and headed toward the entrance. "Let's speak to Harestar now. Waiting will only make tempers worse."

Squirrelflight followed him, pricking her ears. The warmth

she'd felt at Bramblestar's admission suddenly faded as a new concern occurred to her. Was Bramblestar really ready to admit that her plan to wait for the Sisters to move on could solve the border conflict? Or was he coming around to Tigerstar's plan to drive the Sisters off their land? "So you think SkyClan should move to the mountain territory?" She ducked through the thorn tunnel after him.

"Yes." He padded into the forest, taking the trail that led toward the moor.

Anxiety tightened Squirrelflight's belly. "When?"

Bramblestar glanced at her as she fell in beside him. "As soon as Leafstar is ready to make the decision to go." He turned his gaze ahead. "Not before. It must be SkyClan's decision. No Clan must pressure them into moving."

Squirrelflight's ears twitched. What if Leafstar made the decision tomorrow, or in a quarter moon, before Moonlight's kits were born? She tried to push the thought away. Surely Leafstar wouldn't knowingly endanger Moonlight or her kits. But what if she did? She glanced at Bramblestar. "Would you drive the Sisters away before they're ready to leave?"

"I'll try to keep the peace as long as I can, but the Clans' interests must come first."

Squirrelflight's pelt sparked with anger. Did Bramblestar really believe that the impatience of warriors was more important than the Sisters' needs? "Why?"

"Do you think we should put the comfort of rogues before ourselves?"

Squirrelflight bristled. "The Sisters aren't rogues!"

He looked at her, puzzled. "How are they different?" He didn't wait for an answer. "I can't let my Clan go hungry so that the Sisters can eat."

"No cat is going without food!" Squirrelflight stared at him. Bramblestar was twisting the argument. "We don't have the right to take land just because we want it."

"We *need* it," Bramblestar insisted. "And the Sisters have proved that they pose a threat to the Clans."

"What threat?" Squirrelflight's hackles lifted.

"They're willing to attack Clan cats and hold them hostage. I call that a threat."

"They were just defending themselves," Squirrelflight argued.

"And we're just defending *ourselves.*"

"So why are you holding Tigerstar back?" Squirrelflight's paws pricked with frustration. "Why not just let him start his war against the Sisters now?" She didn't want an answer. "You told him that we had to wait for word from StarClan. But we've *had* word from StarClan. Tigerstar could easily twist what Hollyleaf told Jayfeather into an excuse for war. Why not tell him what StarClan said and let him attack the Sisters?" She fixed his gaze, her heart aching. She wanted him to say that it was because he knew it was wrong to steal land, that he had pity for Moonlight and her unborn kits.

Bramblestar looked at her coldly. "There's no need for war with the Sisters until we know for sure that SkyClan wants their land."

Squirrelflight's heart sank. She knew that Bramblestar

was being honorable in his own way. He was putting the needs of the Clans first, as a leader should. And if he hadn't cared about the Sisters at all, he would have already shared StarClan's message and let ShadowClan start the war. Still, the coldness of his reasoning irked her. Couldn't he see that the Sisters deserved respect too? A warrior's way of life wasn't the only way to live.

Her tail drooped as she matched Bramblestar's paw steps. Around them, birds chattered and sunshine dappled the forest floor. There was no point in wishing Bramblestar were different. She was ThunderClan's deputy. She needed to focus her thoughts on what was best for her Clan. The confrontation with Breezepelt had been close to an open declaration of war. She must support Bramblestar now. If he could come to a compromise with Harestar at this meeting, they could maintain the uneasy peace among the Clans while still delaying the invasion of the Sisters' territory. Whatever was decided in the WindClan camp this afternoon might give Moonlight the chance to have her kits in the birthing den the Sisters had built for her.

At the WindClan border, they waited for a patrol. The wind in the heather covered the silence between them. Squirrelflight stared across the moor, relieved when she saw Larkwing, Slightfoot, and Oatclaw on the hillside.

"Slightfoot!" Bramblestar whisked his tail.

Slightfoot's pelt bristled. Larkwing narrowed her eyes. The patrol headed toward them, eyeing them warily.

"I want to talk to Harestar," Bramblestar told them as they neared.

Slightfoot looked unsurprised. WindClan must have heard about the encounter between Breezepelt and Squirrelflight by now. His stony gaze flitted over Bramblestar and Squirrelflight. "We'll take you to him."

He stepped aside, inviting them over the border with a nod of his head. Squirrelflight followed Bramblestar nervously between the gorse bushes. She'd known these WindClan warriors their whole lives, remembered their first Gathering as apprentices, and yet the hostility in their eyes made her keenly aware that she was treading on enemy territory. StarClan might demand that the Clans unite, but could the wishes of StarClan really undo countless moons of rivalry and suspicion?

Bramblestar stayed close to her as they followed Larkwing along the hillside, cutting through swaths of heather and winding between stiff bracken stems. She felt comforted by the brush of his fur against hers as Slightfoot and Oatclaw padded close at their tails.

At last they reached the tall gorse wall of the WindClan camp. Larkwing led them around it, then ducked through a tunnel hardly visible among the prickly branches. Bramblestar followed, and Squirrelflight hurried after, her pelt prickling anxiously as they emerged onto a wide stretch of uneven grass. Hummocks poked up here and there, and, around the clearing, gorse dens had been woven into the camp walls. Featherpelt, her sides heavily rounded, and Gorsetail were sharing a piece of prey near the edge of camp. The she-cats lifted their gaze as Squirrelflight and Bramblestar entered and stared at the ThunderClan cats through narrowed eyes.

Kestrelflight padded from his den. He caught Bramblestar's eye and greeted him with a respectful nod. Nightcloud got to her paws at the edge of the clearing as Slightfoot turned to Bramblestar.

"Wait here," he meowed. The WindClan warrior hurried toward a tightly woven den at the end of the clearing. Harestar was already sliding out, his nose twitching as the wind lifted his fur. He saw Bramblestar and Squirrelflight at once. "Bring them here," he called.

As Slightfoot hurried to Harestar's side, Oatclaw nudged Squirrelflight forward.

She shrugged him away. "I can find my own way across a clearing," she snapped.

Bramblestar gave her a warning look. "This is WindClan's camp," he told her. "We follow their orders."

She shook out her pelt and fell in beside him as he crossed the clearing, ignoring Larkwing and Oatclaw padding on either side.

As they reached the WindClan leader, Crowfeather nosed his way from the leader's den, his eyes glittering with interest.

Harestar met Bramblestar's gaze. "You wished to speak with me?"

"Breezepelt brought a patrol onto our territory today," Bramblestar meowed evenly.

Squirrelflight glared at the WindClan leader. "You sent him, didn't you?"

Harestar didn't answer.

Bramblestar narrowed his eyes. "Are you trying to reclaim our stretch of moorland?"

"ThunderClan has no use for it," Harestar answered. "Your scent floods the hillside like dog stench without the forest to disguise it. On open moor, prey can *smell* you coming. It flees to our side of the border and becomes our prey anyway. Why waste your time? Return our land to us."

"It's *our* land. We all agreed to the new borders." Bramblestar's pelt ruffled along his spine. "Don't forget we gave a lot of our territory to SkyClan."

"You could have your SkyClan land back if you wanted." Harestar shifted his paws. "You're the one who's delaying their move. You can be the one to suffer the consequences."

Squirrelflight glanced at Bramblestar. Was this demand for land WindClan's way of persuading ThunderClan to agree with ShadowClan's war on the Sisters?

Bramblestar's tail swished ominously. "While greenleaf lasts, there are no consequences to suffer," he told Harestar. "There is enough prey in the forest to feed ThunderClan. The Sisters will be gone by the time leaf-bare comes, and we can rethink our borders then."

"If you have enough prey, why should WindClan wait to reclaim our territory?" Harestar's gaze didn't waver. Crowfeather shifted closer to his leader, his hackles rising.

Bramblestar gazed silently at the WindClan leader for a moment. Squirrelflight wondered what he was thinking. It would be hard to argue with Harestar's logic. Bramblestar dipped his head. "Very well," he growled. "You may hunt on our stretch of moorland until SkyClan makes a decision. Our border will remain where it is, and we will mark it regularly. But we will share the land for the next couple of moons."

Crowfeather frowned. "Why should we let ThunderClan mark a border on our land?"

"It won't be for long." Harestar's mew was ominous. He met Crowfeather's gaze. The two cats seemed to exchange a single thought; then Harestar turned back to Bramblestar. "Very well."

Oatclaw's tail quivered. "What will Tigerstar say?"

Squirrelflight looked at the young warrior in surprise. "Who cares? This has nothing to do with Tigerstar."

Bramblestar's gaze darkened. "Oatclaw has a point," he murmured. "When RiverClan hears that we've given Wind-Clan hunting rights on their old land, they might insist on the same for the land they gave to ShadowClan."

Squirrelflight shifted her paws nervously. She nudged Bramblestar aside, lowering her voice. "If RiverClan takes its land back from ShadowClan, it might start a Clan war."

He frowned. "But Tigerstar knows StarClan wants peace."

"Then he'll try to take the Sisters' land and give it to Sky-Clan so he can have his old territory back." Squirrelflight blinked at him. Bramblestar might not be ready to defend the Sisters, but she knew he was ready to defend SkyClan. "I thought you didn't want Tigerstar telling SkyClan where they should live."

Bramblestar's gaze clouded with thought. He turned back to Harestar. "We have to keep this agreement secret from the other Clans."

"If that's what you wish." Harestar dipped his head.

Squirrelflight saw Crowfeather's eyes narrow. She stiffened. Was the WindClan deputy planning to make trouble by spreading word of this agreement?

Bramblestar must have been wondering the same. "Peace in the Clans depends on this remaining between us." His gaze burned into Crowfeather. Squirrelflight felt a rush of hope. This agreement with WindClan might give the Sisters the time they needed, as long as Tigerstar didn't find out.

CHAPTER 13

Squirrelflight shivered as gray drizzle washed the clearing. It had been two days since she had visited the WindClan camp with Bramblestar. The weather had grown chilly, and she could taste leaf-fall in the air. Around her, the Clan had settled down to share a midday meal. Larksong was eating hungrily beside the fresh-kill pile. Bramblestar shared a squirrel with Birchfall and Hollytuft. Bristlepaw dragged a vole into the apprentices' den, where Thriftpaw and Flippaw were sheltering from the rain.

Squirrelflight pushed the remains of the shrew she'd been sharing with Millie toward the deaf old she-cat. "You finish it," she mewed loudly.

"Are you sure?" Millie blinked at her.

"Sure."

Graystripe nosed his way out of the elders' den and glanced up at the overcast sky. He fluffed out his fur. "I'm hungry." He looked toward the fresh-kill pile, where a few mice lay in the mud, and wrinkled his muzzle. "I think I'll wait to see what this afternoon's patrol brings in."

Millie hooked the half-eaten shrew toward him. "Do you want this?"

As Graystripe examined it, paw steps thrummed beyond the thorn tunnel. He lifted his muzzle and glanced toward the entrance.

"Bramblestar!" Finleap charged, breathless, into camp.

Squirrelflight's pelt bristled in alarm. The young tom looked scared. He stood panting in the clearing, rain dripping around his face. She hurried to meet him as Bramblestar scrambled to his paws. "What's happened?" she asked.

"Tigerstar!" Finleap struggled to catch his breath. "He's on the border with Scorchfur and Berryheart. Mistystar's with them—"

Squirrelflight blinked at him. "Tigerstar *and* Mistystar?" Her belly tightened. Had they found out about the agreement with WindClan?

Finleap went on. "Mistystar brought Owlnose and Havenpelt with her."

Bramblestar stopped beside her. Anxiety darkened his gaze. "Two warriors each. It must be serious," he growled.

"Twigbranch and Thornclaw are escorting them here," Finleap puffed. "I ran ahead to warn you."

"Thanks, Finleap." Bramblestar waved him away with a nod of his muzzle and glanced around the camp. Bristlepaw blinked from the apprentices' den. Larksong left the mouse he'd been eating and padded closer, his hackles lifting. Birchfall and Hollytuft narrowed their eyes as Bramblestar addressed the Clan. "We're about to have visitors," he told them. "Be polite, but be on guard."

As his Clanmates exchanged anxious glances. Bramblestar looked gravely at Squirrelflight. "I hope they haven't found out about the border."

Squirrelflight wished she could reassure him, but she felt sure that their short moment of peace was at an end. "Why else would they come?"

"They brought two warriors each," Bramblestar mused, hardly listening. "Enough for a show of strength."

"Not enough to start trouble," Squirrelflight pointed out.

Bramblestar looked at her. "Not yet."

As he spoke, the thorn tunnel shivered, and Twigbranch and Thornclaw led Tigerstar, Mistystar, and their warriors into the camp.

Squirrelflight hung back as Bramblestar met them in the middle of the clearing; then she padded to his side. Tigerstar fluffed his damp pelt out against the rain. Mistystar stood beside him, her gaze stony.

"What brings you here?" Bramblestar asked evenly.

Tigerstar twitched his tail. "You know what brings us here." Behind him, Scorchfur and Berryheart exchanged glances. Owlnose and Havenpelt moved closer to Mistystar.

"Don't pretend you can't guess," the RiverClan leader growled.

Tigerstar flexed his claws. "You've reestablished your old border with WindClan."

"The new border still remains," Bramblestar told him calmly. "We mark it every day."

"But you let WindClan hunt on your stretch of moorland," Tigerstar accused.

Mistystar lifted her chin. "Which is the same as having no

border at all."

Squirrelflight moved closer to Bramblestar. "Our agreement with WindClan is ThunderClan business."

"We've discussed this." Tigerstar glared at her. "It becomes my business when Mistystar demands that we return River-Clan's marshland."

"We don't control what RiverClan does," Bramblestar replied stiffly. "WindClan and ThunderClan came to a peaceful agreement. There's no reason why you and River-Clan can't sort this out yourselves."

"Is that all you have to say?" Tigerstar's ears twitched angrily. "ThunderClan cats usually can't stop themselves telling other Clans what to do."

Bramblestar held his gaze. "Do you want me to tell River-Clan you won't give their land back?"

"No!" Tigerstar lashed his tail. "ShadowClan can fight its own battles."

"Then why are you here, disturbing our peace?" Bramble-star's ears twitched.

Squirrelflight looked at him. If he was going to refuse to get involved, she'd follow his lead. "What can *we* do?"

"Defend your border with WindClan so we can defend ours." Tigerstar growled. "We need the marshland."

Mistystar snorted. "ShadowClan was never going to do more with that land than catch a few frogs and butterflies. *We* can fish there," she snapped. "The borders are better this way."

"They might be better for you!" Tigerstar met her gaze, his

hackles lifting. "RiverClan didn't give half its land to Sky-Clan."

"ThunderClan gave land to SkyClan too," she shot back. "They don't seem to mind."

Tigerstar swung his muzzle toward Bramblestar. "Thunder-Clan enjoys stirring up trouble in other Clans. I'm asking you to put an end to it now."

"The situation is difficult," Bramblestar conceded. "But StarClan wants unity. I'm not going to fight over borders. Not with you, or with WindClan. They can keep the hunting rights to our stretch of moorland."

Tigerstar narrowed his eyes. "Then perhaps we should take our land back from SkyClan."

Squirrelflight's chest tightened. "You can't! They need territory, too."

Tigerstar swished his tail slowly. "Or you could help us drive the Sisters off their land so that SkyClan can move and we'll all have enough land. ShadowClan has to eat."

Alarm sparked through Squirrelflight's pelt. She glanced helplessly at Bramblestar. He mustn't let Tigerstar push him into war against the Sisters.

Bramblestar hesitated, his pelt ruffling along his spine. His gaze flitted from Tigerstar to Mistystar. "The border between RiverClan and ShadowClan has nothing to do with us. I suggest you settle your dispute yourselves." His gaze fixed on Tigerstar. "I'd think twice about threatening SkyClan. Leaf-star is still deciding whether she wants to move. Intimidation may make her dig her claws in. And ThunderClan will stand with her. SkyClan has been chased away too many times before. This time we won't sit by and watch. ShadowClan may find itself in a war it cannot win."

Tigerstar narrowed his eyes. "Is that a threat?"

Mistystar peered curiously at Bramblestar. "Have you been making secret alliances with SkyClan as well as WindClan?"

"ThunderClan hasn't made alliances with any Clan," Bramblestar growled.

Tigerstar's ears twitched. "And yet WindClan hunts on *your* land." He nodded to Scorchfur and Berryheart. "Come on," he told them. "We're wasting our time here." He turned away, flicking his tail across Mistystar's muzzle.

She ducked, snarling. "Let's go," she told Owlnose and Havenpelt. "Bramblestar clearly doesn't care about any cat's borders except his own."

Squirrelflight stifled a shiver as the RiverClan cats barged past Tigerstar and marched out of camp. Growling, Tigerstar, Scorchfur, and Berryheart followed them. She turned to Bramblestar. "Do you think they'll fight?"

Bramblestar stared after them darkly. "If they do, it's not our problem."

"But we have to do something."

"Like what?"

Squirrelflight blinked at him nervously. "If they don't turn on each other, they might turn on SkyClan."

"I know," he answered bluntly. "But until Leafstar makes a decision, we can only tread carefully."

Squirrelflight's thoughts whirled. "What if there's a Clan war?"

"I wish I had an answer for you." Bramblestar looked at her

hopelessly, then turned away. He padded back to where he'd left his squirrel and settled heavily beside it. Bending his head, he began to chew on the bedraggled carcass as rain streamed from his whiskers.

Squirrelflight's heart sank. Was there no solution that didn't involve war?

"Squirrelflight." Daisy called from the nursery entrance.

She stiffened. Sparkpelt had moved to the nursery, sharing a nest there with Larksong until the kits were born. She hurried across the clearing. "Is Sparkpelt okay?"

"Sparkpelt's fine," Daisy mewed brightly. "She felt the kits move and she wanted to tell you."

Squirrelflight purred, relieved to hear good news.

"I'm going to get some food," Daisy told her, and headed toward the fresh-kill pile. Squirrelflight padded to the nursery and squeezed through the brambles into the warm den. She shook out her pelt before heading for Sparkpelt's nest.

Sparkpelt lay among the ferns, her belly round with kits. She purred as she saw Squirrelflight. "Feel this." She glanced at her flank.

Squirrelflight touched her nose to Sparkpelt's belly. Happiness flashed beneath her fur as she felt the kits stir beneath her daughter's pelt. But longing surged in her chest. She wanted to feel her own kits moving inside her.

Sparkpelt blinked at her, alarm flashing in her eyes. "Is something wrong? You can feel them moving, can't you?"

"Yes." Squirrelflight reassured her quickly. Should she explain to Sparkpelt about her grief? "You're going to be a wonderful mother," she murmured. "I still remember how happy I was when you and Alderheart were born. I was so proud, even prouder of you than I was of my Clan. I miss feeling that way. I wish—"

The entrance shivered as Larksong pushed his way into the nursery. He looked tired, his eyes dull, his fur slicked by the rain. He brightened as he saw Sparkpelt. "How are you?" He slid past Squirrelflight and pressed his nose to his mate's cheek.

"I'm fine." She purred happily and licked his ear.

Larksong sat back on his haunches and burped.

Sparkpelt's whiskers twitched teasingly. "I hope you're not going to teach our kits those manners."

"Sorry." Larksong looked chastened. "I shouldn't have had that extra mouse. But nobody else seemed to want it, and the hunting patrol will bring fresh prey later." His mew was husky. Did he have a chill? He dipped his head to Squirrelflight, as though suddenly realizing she was there. "I promise I'll be the perfect father to your daughter's kits."

Squirrelflight purred. "I'm sure you will be." Sparkpelt was lucky to have such a good mate. "I think you're going to be very happy." Her heart ached with fondness, and she wondered how she had even considered telling Sparkpelt how much she wanted kits of her own. *Let her enjoy this,* she told herself. *She doesn't have to deal with your problems. She'll have enough to occupy her once the kits are born.*

Larksong shivered. "I was coming to lie down. I've been feeling tired all morning. I don't know why. I've only been on dawn patrol." He looked puzzled. "I don't seem to be able to catch my breath."

"It's probably the wet weather," Squirrelflight suggested. She blinked at him playfully. "You're going to have to get fit before the kits arrive. They'll keep you on your paws day and night."

Larksong purred. "Don't worry about that. I plan to make sure they have everything they need." He got to his paws. "I can't wait to give them their first badger ride." Padding up and down the den, he glanced over his shoulder. "Can you imagine them up there on my back?" He stopped suddenly.

Alarm sparked in Squirrelflight's fur as Larksong's gaze froze. Pain glittered in his eyes, as though he'd been swiped across the muzzle with powerful claws.

Sparkpelt must have seen it too. "Larksong?" Fear edged her mew.

Larksong's eyes grew suddenly dull. They rolled back as his paws buckled and he dropped to the ground.

"Larksong!" Sparkpelt darted to his side, bristling with horror. Squirrelflight pressed beside her, terror hollowing her belly. Larksong wasn't moving. His flanks were still. *He's not breathing!*

"Stay with him," she told Sparkpelt. "I'll fetch a medicine cat."

She pelted from the den, rain spraying her face as she raced for the medicine den and burst inside. "Help!"

Alderheart looked up sharply from the herbs he was mixing. "What is it?"

"Larksong! He's collapsed in the nursery." Squirrelflight fought back panic as Alderheart pelted past her, out of the den. She hurried after him.

Bramblestar looked up from his squirrel. "What's happened?"

"It's Larksong! He's sick!" Squirrelflight pushed her way into the nursery after Alderheart. Fear-scent flooded the den.

Alderheart pressed his ear to Larksong's chest.

Sparkpelt stared at him, her pelt spiked. "Is he okay?" Her mew came as a sob.

"His heart is beating." Alderheart sat up. "But we have to get him started breathing again."

Sparkpelt seemed to freeze. "Will he die?"

Squirrelflight slid in beside her. "Alderheart will do what he can."

"What's wrong with him?" Sparkpelt was trembling.

Squirrelflight pressed against her. "Breathe," she told Sparkpelt. "You don't want this to affect the kits."

Bramblestar had pushed his way into the den. He stared, his eyes wide.

Alderheart glanced at him. "Fetch Leafpool. She's in the elders' den with Millie. Tell her to come quickly. I need help. Now!"

Bramblestar raced out as the dark ginger medicine cat pressed his paws onto Larksong's flank and began pumping his chest.

Squirrelflight's paws seemed to freeze as she watched.

Sparkpelt was stiff beside her, gulping juddering breaths

as Alderheart worked on Larksong. "Don't let him die," she sobbed. "Please don't let him die."

Squirrelflight felt time slow as she watched Alderheart press harder and harder, pumping at Larksong's chest as though trying to shock him into life. He mustn't die now. He had to see his kits. He'd been so excited. They mustn't grow up without a father. Suddenly, Larksong gasped. A spasm seemed to grasp him and shake him into a long, trembling breath. Then he lay still. Squirrelflight heard blood roaring in her ears. "Is he alive?"

Alderheart bent his head to Larksong's chest.

Even before he sat up, Squirrelflight saw Larksong's chest moving. "He's breathing," she whispered. Relief swamped her. She looked at Sparkpelt. "He's alive!"

Sparkpelt slumped against her. As Squirrelflight moved, her daughter slid to the ground, staring at Larksong with wide, desperate eyes.

Chapter 14

Squirrelflight glanced anxiously at Sparkpelt. Her daughter was calmer now that they'd moved Larksong to the medicine den, but her eyes were still shadowed with fear as she watched over her mate, who lay unconscious in one of the nests at the edge of the small hollow.

Leafpool paced as Alderheart leaned over Larksong, wiping away the dark liquid pooling at the side of the warrior's mouth. Jayfeather rummaged quickly through the herb store once more.

"Should we give him more yarrow?" Alderheart asked the blind medicine cat.

Jayfeather shook his head. "He's too weak, and besides, we're not sure this is caused by something he ate."

Sparkpelt's pelt ruffled along her spine. "There must be something you can try."

Jayfeather tore open a bundle of chervil. "We could see if he can swallow a few of these leaves."

Leafpool stopped beside Squirrelflight. "Let's talk outside," she murmured.

Squirrelflight's belly tightened as Leafpool guided her

toward the entrance. "Is Sparkpelt all right?" As concerned as she was about Larksong, she was more afraid for Sparkpelt's kits.

"She's fine and so are the kits." Leafpool nosed her way through the brambles.

"But she's so upset." Squirrelflight followed her through. The drizzle had eased, but raindrops still dripped from the canopy into the clearing.

"I can feel the kits moving," Leafpool told her. "And Sparkpelt hasn't had any cramps. I've given her thyme to help with the shock. She's strong and sensible. She'll be okay." Her gaze darkened. "I just wish we knew what was wrong with Larksong. His breathing has steadied, but it's still shallow. And his heartbeat is weak."

Squirrelflight fought back fear. "Have you seen anything like it before?"

"No." Leafpool gazed toward the trailing brambles. "Even Jayfeather is baffled. He says he's never smelled a sickness like this. And we've never seen a sickness that stopped a cat breathing so suddenly."

"Could it be contagious?" Squirrelflight's heart lurched. Larksong had nuzzled Sparkpelt before he collapsed.

"We don't know." Leafpool looked at her helplessly. "He's bringing up bile, which makes us think that the sickness is in his belly. But that's all we know." She looked toward the clearing. Bramblestar sat at the edge with Thornclaw and Finleap. Twigbranch and Birchfall stood nearby. Outside the elders' den, Millie and Graystripe eyed the medicine den anxiously, while Hollytuft paced beside them. Leafpool called to Hollytuft. "You were on patrol with Larksong this morning. Did you see anything unusual while you were out?" Leafpool called.

Hollytuft twitched her tail. "Nothing out of the ordinary. We caught a squirrel, but we put it on the fresh-kill pile when we got back."

Leafpool glanced toward the pile. There was nothing left but the few bedraggled mice Graystripe had turned his nose up at earlier. "What did Larksong eat before he got sick?"

Squirrelflight frowned. "He said he'd had two mice before he came to the nursery."

Bramblestar got to his paws. "Check the prey," he told Hollytuft. "But be careful."

As Hollytuft hurried toward the fresh-kill pile, Twigbranch glanced at it nervously. "Do you think it was something he ate?" the young warrior asked.

"The prey might have been rotten," Finleap suggested.

"But we only caught it this morning," Thornclaw pointed out. "It was fresh."

"Perhaps he ate sick prey," Twigbranch mewed.

Squirrelflight narrowed her eyes. "Surely he would have smelled the sickness before he ate it?"

Outside the elders' den, Graystripe pricked his ears. "He might have been too hungry to notice."

Millie sniffed beside him. "No cat is too hungry to smell sickness in prey. Even a kit would know that kind of sourness."

Bramblestar fluffed out his fur. "If it's a new sickness, we wouldn't recognize it."

Hollytuft sat back on her haunches beside the fresh-kill pile. "It all smells fresh and healthy to me," she told Bramblestar.

"We should get rid of it anyway," Bramblestar answered.

"I'll see to it." Squirrelflight wanted something to keep her busy. She headed toward the pile.

"Help her, Hollytuft." Bramblestar nodded toward the black she-cat, then glanced toward the apprentices' den. Flippaw and Bristlepaw were watching anxiously from the entrance. "You two can help, too," he told them.

They hurried out eagerly, as though relieved to be given something to do.

Squirrelflight beckoned them with a flick of her tail and sniffed the mice. "Let's take them out of camp and bury them in the forest." She caught Hollytuft's eye. "We can dig a hole between the brambles at the top of the slope."

Hollytuft nodded. "We'll need to dig it deep to stop foxes finding them."

Flippaw blinked at her. "Why do we care if foxes get sick from this prey?"

"Sickness harms everyone," she told him. "Do you want a fox carcass rotting near the camp?"

Bristlepaw looked warily at the prey. "What if we get sick from carrying it?"

"We'll carry it carefully." Squirrelflight rolled one of the mice closer with her paw. "Let me show you." She nodded to Hollytuft. "Take Flippaw and start digging," she ordered. "We'll bring the prey."

As Hollytuft and Flippaw headed away, Squirrelflight touched the back of the mouse's neck with her paw. "This part is like a kit's scruff," she told him. "The skin's tougher here so its mother can carry it."

Bristlepaw blinked at her. "I never thought about prey having mothers."

"Everything has a mother." She pressed her paw into the mouse's scruff. "You can pick it up using your teeth, but hold it gently. Because the skin is tougher here, it's less likely to bleed. Draw your lips back and keep your tongue out of the way. You don't want to swallow any fur or blood."

Bristlepaw leaned down and took the mouse's neck gingerly between her jaws. She lifted it up, glancing uncertainly at Squirrelflight.

"That's good," she told her. "Now take it to Hollytuft. Be careful not to let it swing too much. The skin might tear."

As Bristlepaw padded slowly away, Squirrelflight picked up another mouse and headed after her. It had been a while since she'd trained an apprentice, and she'd forgotten the satisfaction of teaching warrior skills to young cats. Was she being selfish in wanting kits of her own? Being part of a Clan was what made warriors strong, not only having kin. Perhaps it was enough to pass her skills to the next generation, no matter whose kit it was. She thought of the Sisters and how they raised their young together. The Clans weren't so different. Surely her Clanmates were enough like family for her not to need more kin of her own?

* * *

Squirrelflight left Hollytuft and Flippaw scraping earth over the hole they'd buried the mice in and headed back toward camp. Her paws were muddy from digging and her muscles ached. Bristlepaw sat back on her haunches, looking pleased with her work.

Hollytuft called after her. "Should I take Flippaw and Bristlepaw hunting to find fresh prey?"

Flippaw and Bristlepaw pricked their ears eagerly.

"Good idea," Squirrelflight called back. "But don't hunt where you hunted earlier." She'd need to find out where today's prey had been caught before she organized tomorrow's patrols. If it was prey that had made Larksong sick, ThunderClan would have to be careful about the fresh-kill they brought into the camp.

She hurried through the thorn tunnel and crossed the clearing. Twigbranch and Finleap were laying rain-washed ferns over the bloody patch of earth where the fresh-kill pile had sat. Thornclaw and Birchfall murmured together, their muzzles close. Honeyfur, Berrynose, and Whitewing glanced anxiously at the medicine den.

The brambles at the medicine den's entrance shivered, and Sparkpelt pushed her way out. Her eyes were clouded with tiredness, her pelt ruffled and unwashed. Leafpool followed her out and began to guide her toward the nursery. Squirrelflight hurried to meet them. "How's Larksong?" she asked Sparkpelt, searching her daughter's gaze for a flash of hope. Sparkpelt looked back at her blankly.

"Larksong's still unconscious," Leafpool told her. "But he's stable for now. I'm taking Sparkpelt back to the nursery to rest."

"I want to stay with Larksong," Sparkpelt whispered.

"He's in good paws," Leafpool promised. "You need to rest. Away from all the fuss. You have to think about your kits."

"I guess." Sparkpelt's tail dragged as she padded toward the nursery.

Leafpool lowered her voice. "I wish I could give her hope, but we still don't know what's wrong with Larksong."

"Go back to the medicine den." Squirrelflight ignored the fear sparking in her chest. "I'll look after Sparkpelt." She hurried to follow her daughter into the nursery.

Inside, Daisy blinked from the shadows. The pale queen's eyes were round with worry. "Any news?"

Sparkpelt shook her head and slumped into her nest.

"Leafpool, Alderheart, and Jayfeather are doing everything they can," Squirrelflight told Daisy.

"Do they know what caused it?"

"They're not sure."

As Squirrelflight spoke, Sparkpelt lifted her head sharply. Anger flashed in her eyes. "It was something he ate!" She heaved herself to her paws and glared at Squirrelflight. "He said he felt tired after eating so much; then he collapsed and stopped breathing. It has to be the food! We should be doing something about it!"

Squirrelflight blinked at her. "We've cleaned out the fresh-kill pile. We can't do more than that."

"This should have never happened!" Sparkpelt was bristling.

"Of course not," Squirrelflight agreed.

"It'll be okay," Daisy soothed.

"I don't know why nobody is saying what's *obvious*!" Sparkpelt's whiskers trembled. "ShadowClan poisoned the fresh-kill pile! They were in the camp this morning, weren't they?"

"How could they have?" Squirrelflight stared at her in surprise. "We were watching them the whole time."

"SkyClan watched them too," Sparkpelt shot back. "But they still managed to poison Sparrowpelt."

Squirrelflight remembered how Juniperclaw, ShadowClan's former deputy, had nearly killed a SkyClan warrior by leaving prey laced with deathberries on SkyClan's fresh-kill pile. The act had driven Leafstar to lead SkyClan away from the lake and had nearly destroyed the Clans. Surely they wouldn't do it again?

She realized that Sparkpelt was still staring at her. "This isn't deathberry poisoning. Leafpool would know if it were. Besides, when Juniperclaw poisoned Sparrowpelt, he acted alone," she argued. "And he's dead now. Tigerstar would never let such a thing happen again."

"Really?" Sparkpelt looked unconvinced.

"Of course not." Squirrelflight's heart quickened.

"Even when ThunderClan keeps bullying him?" Sparkpelt glared at her. "We won't let Tigerstar get even with the Sisters after they hurt one of his Clanmates. Why did you have to bring them here in the first place?"

"I didn't mean to," Squirrelflight mewed defensively. "I was trying to help SkyClan."

Sparkpelt wasn't listening. "Now we've made a secret alliance with WindClan. For all we know, Tigerstar's found out that we sheltered the Sisters too. That would be enough to make him want to hurt us. Bramblestar keeps making decisions that make life hard for ShadowClan. Is he *trying* to make Tigerstar angry?"

"This isn't Bramblestar's fault." Squirrelflight lifted her chin. "Your father is just doing what he thinks is right."

"And he doesn't care who gets hurt!"

Daisy padded tentatively forward. "Bramblestar would never hurt any cat."

"He just wants peace," Squirrelflight chimed. "That's why he's trying to appease WindClan, and why he won't join a war against the Sisters."

Sparkpelt flattened her ears. "So it's okay if Larksong dies, as long as WindClan and the Sisters are happy!"

"No!" Frustration scorched Squirrelflight's pelt. Sparkpelt didn't know what she was saying. "Larksong's not ill because of what Bramblestar has done."

"I don't believe you!" Sparkpelt hissed. "If Bramblestar hadn't gone against Tigerstar so many times, Larksong would be fine now!"

The brambles rustled at the entrance. "What's going on?" Bramblestar nosed his way in, anxiety glittering in his gaze. "I heard yowling."

Daisy looked at him anxiously. "Sparkpelt's upset, that's all. She's had a difficult day."

Sparkpelt snarled at him. "Do you admit it?"

"Admit what?" He looked taken aback.

"If you hadn't done everything you could to make Tigerstar angry, Larksong would be fine now!" Sparkpelt's eyes narrowed into slits.

Bramblestar stared at her, his pelt ruffling along his spine. "I don't understand." He glanced questioningly at Squirrelflight.

"She's worried that ShadowClan might have poisoned the fresh-kill pile when they visited the camp earlier." Squirrelflight shifted uneasily. She was angry with Bramblestar, but he didn't deserve this. He had enough worries already. And yet Sparkpelt was clearly suffering. *Please don't argue.*

Bramblestar tipped his head to one side and blinked at Sparkpelt. "How could they have poisoned the prey? We were all here watching them."

"They've done it before!" Sparkpelt hissed.

Daisy looked anxiously from father to daughter. "Juniperclaw did that, and he's dead now," she repeated.

"All ShadowClan cats are the same." Sparkpelt flexed her claws. "They'd poison their own mothers for more territory."

"That's not true." Squirrelflight edged closer to Sparkpelt. She had to calm her down. This couldn't be doing the kits any good. "ShadowClan cats are warriors just like us. They wouldn't break the warrior code."

Sparkpelt held her ground. "They would if they were pushed far enough, and Bramblestar has done nothing but get in Tigerstar's way." She glared accusingly at her father.

"Bramblestar's been doing what's best for the Clans," Squirrelflight argued.

"Why are you sticking up for him?" Sparkpelt stared at her. "He's hardly spoken to you in days. He's been treating you like an apprentice. And you're defending him! Why are you being such a mouse-heart?"

Bramblestar's hackles lifted. "Don't talk to your mother like that!" he hissed. "I don't care how upset you are. Hurting cats who love you isn't going to help Larksong. It's just going to make everyone as miserable as you are. I'm sorry Larksong is ill, and we'll do everything we can to make sure he gets well again, but don't accuse your mother of being a mouse-heart. She's one of the bravest warriors I know. And I am doing everything I can to keep peace among the Clans. I have to stand up to Tigerstar, or he'll push SkyClan around forever." Hurt glittered suddenly in the ThunderClan leader's gaze. "It's hard standing up for what you believe in, and it's even harder when the cats who are supposed to support you undermine you instead."

As his gaze flashed from Sparkpelt to Squirrelflight, claws seemed to pierce Squirrelflight's heart. Bramblestar's tail swept the ground. "I'm trying to lead a Clan! How can I expect my warriors to follow me if my own kin challenge me at every turn?" Growling, he pushed his way out of the den.

Daisy shifted her paws. "It's been a difficult day for everyone." She gazed sympathetically at Squirrelflight. "Why don't you get some air, and I'll make sure Sparkpelt rests."

Sparkpelt was staring after her father, her eyes hollow with grief. "I'm sorry." She dragged her gaze to Squirrelflight.

"It's okay," Squirrelflight murmured. "I know you're upset." She felt suddenly weary. "You'll feel better in the morning.

And I'm sure Leafpool will have found a way to help Lark-song by then." She touched her nose to Sparkpelt's head, then headed out of the den, relieved to leave her daughter in Daisy's care for a while. She crossed to the medicine den. Had Leaf-pool, Jayfeather, and Alderheart come up with a cure? She ducked inside, disappointment dropping like a stone in her belly as she saw Leafpool and Jayfeather murmuring, heads close together at the back of the cave. They looked as worried as ever, and Alderheart was wiping another drop of bile from Larksong's lips.

Lilyheart, Larksong's mother, sat beside the nest, her eyes round with worry. She blinked at Squirrelflight when she saw her. "What could have caused this?"

Squirrelflight shook her head. "We don't know."

"Could it be deathberry poisoning?" Lilyheart fretted.

"There are *no* deathberries in the camp," Squirrelflight meowed, irritated.

"ShadowClan might have brought some. We know Puddle-shine uses them."

Leafpool looked up. "This isn't deathberry poisoning. We don't recognize these symptoms."

Lilyheart's pelt bristled. "They might have found another poison!"

Squirrelflight fixed Lilyheart's gaze with her own. "ShadowClan had nothing to do with this." She mustn't let rumors about ShadowClan's involvement in Larksong's ill-ness take hold. There was enough tension among the Clans already. "Larksong's illness is a shock and a tragedy. He's always been a strong, healthy warrior, and it's frightening to see him get so sick so quickly. But we're going to find out what caused it." She eyed Leafpool desperately. "And we're going to find out how to cure it." Fear wormed in her belly as Leafpool's gaze darkened. She was making Lilyheart promises they might not be able to keep, but she had to give the small, dark tabby hope. This sickness had come from nowhere. It could have been caused by anything. Larksong might be only the first cat to be struck down by a sickness the Clans had never experienced before. And if it spread, hope might be all that ThunderClan had.

CHAPTER 15

"I'm coming with you." Squirrelflight squared her shoulders as she faced Jayfeather.

Jayfeather narrowed his eyes. "This is between medicine cats."

Alderheart shifted beside the blind tom. "We're going to talk to Puddleshine, to see if he has seen anything like Larksong's sickness in ShadowClan."

"I have to put the Clan's minds at rest," Squirrelflight insisted. Through the night, rumors that ShadowClan had been the cause of Larksong's sickness had spread like fleas through the Clan. By morning, as the rain clouds cleared from above the camp, her Clanmates had barely listened to her orders for the day's patrols.

Lionblaze had paced the clearing with ruffled fur. "We should send a patrol to ShadowClan."

"They can't get away with poisoning a second Clan," Cinderheart had agreed.

Around them, Poppyfrost, Cherryfall, and Molewhisker had nodded, murmuring their agreement.

Bramblestar had scrambled down from the Highledge and

stood beside Squirrelflight. "We don't have any proof that ShadowClan caused this. And there's so much tension among the Clans that an accusation like this might lead to war."

The warriors had backed down and, grumbling, gone on patrol. But Squirrelflight was convinced that the rumors would rumble on unless some cat investigated the claims of poisoning.

Now she blinked hopefully at Alderheart and Jayfeather as they prepared to leave for the ShadowClan camp. "I'll tell ShadowClan I'm escorting you. I'll tell them that we're worried about the threat from the Sisters." Guilt pricked at her belly. The Sisters weren't a threat to any cat. But she had to get into the ShadowClan camp and find proof that ShadowClan was innocent.

Jayfeather's tail twitched impatiently. "You ought to ask Bramblestar's permission," he grunted. "We can't accuse ShadowClan without proof."

"I'm not going to accuse anyone," Squirrelflight told him. "I just want to see how ShadowClan acts when I tell them about Larksong. I'll be able to tell if they're guilty."

Jayfeather snorted. "ShadowClan is always guilty of something."

Squirrelflight held her ground. "I have to come with you."

Alderheart met her gaze nervously. "ShadowClan might take offense if we bring a warrior to their camp. You should get Bramblestar's permission."

Squirrelflight swallowed her frustration. "Bramblestar is out hunting," she reminded them. "I can't ask him now."

"We can't wait." Alderheart glanced anxiously toward the medicine den.

"If Puddleshine knows of a way to help Larksong, we need to hear it as soon as possible," Jayfeather chimed.

Squirrelflight gazed at them desperately. She was Clan deputy. If she wanted to travel with them, she could. And yet she knew they were right. Tensions with ShadowClan were already high. If her visit to their camp made things worse, ThunderClan could find itself facing battle. She needed Bramblestar's support for her mission. And, she realized, she needed his support as her mate. She was always better with him behind her. She should have realized that from the start. "Let's find him," she suggested.

"He could be anywhere," Jayfeather objected.

"He said he was going to hunt near the beech grove," she told him. "It's not far out of the way. We could stop and get Bramblestar's permission."

Jayfeather's ear twitched. "I guess we could," he conceded. "But I'm not going to wait around while you search the area. If we find him, great. If we don't, you ought to return home."

"Okay," Squirrelflight agreed reluctantly. She would respect her medicine cat's wishes.

She let Jayfeather and Alderheart lead the way through the thorn tunnel, relieved to be out of camp as they headed into the forest. She couldn't help Larksong, but hopefully she could put her Clanmates' minds at rest by proving that ShadowClan wasn't involved.

Jayfeather followed a rabbit trail into the swaths of

blueberry bushes that covered the forest floor around the hollow. Alderheart followed, his gaze darting here and there as though looking for prey.

"Are you hoping to hunt?" Squirrelflight called to him as she padded behind them.

"I'm looking for herbs," he called back. "New patches appear at the end of greenleaf. They'll be too young to harvest, but it's useful to notice where they'll appear again in newleaf."

Pride warmed Squirrelflight's pelt. She remembered Alderheart as a kit, hardly able to tell a good piece of prey from a bad one. He'd been a terrible warrior apprentice, but he'd found his feet as a medicine cat. Now he could recognize every herb in the forest. *He's grown up now,* she thought with a pang of grief. *He doesn't need me anymore.* She pushed away the longing as she imagined a nest of newborn kits.

The forest sloped. She pricked her ears. The beech grove was beyond the next rise. Opening her mouth, she let the air bathe her tongue, searching for Bramblestar's scent. What if he wasn't there? If she had to turn back, would Jayfeather and Alderheart be able to tell whether ShadowClan had been involved in Larksong's sickness? They hadn't known them as long as she had. She scanned the woods. Thick brambles crowded between the beeches. The forest was lighter here. Sunshine glimmered through delicate leaves. She felt its warmth on her pelt and slowed, narrowing her eyes as she searched for a sign of Bramblestar's hunting party.

Jayfeather, who was hurrying ahead, turned his face toward her, his blind blue gaze flashing through the green undergrowth. "We can't slow down," he told Squirrelflight. "Larksong is depending on us."

Alderheart pushed through a stand of ferns. "Bramblestar's not here." His eyes glittered with worry. "Are you going to head back?"

"We're not out of the beech grove yet." Squirrelflight padded onward, her breath shallow as she scanned the forest desperately for some sign of Bramblestar's patrol.

Jayfeather shrugged and pushed on, his tail flicking behind him.

Squirrelflight could see the shadows ahead where the beeches gave way to oak and pine beyond. She pricked her ears, listening for paw steps. Ahead, the brambles thinned, and Jayfeather padded softly into a clearing. As he crossed it, Squirrelflight's heart sank. *He isn't here.* Her paws tingled with the urge to keep moving, to go anyway, but in her heart she knew that wouldn't work. Between Jayfeather's objections and Bramblestar's possible reaction, it could have terrible results . . . and she just couldn't do that to Bramblestar again. So she wouldn't be able to visit ShadowClan after all. "Alderheart." She ducked from beneath a bramble.

He blinked at her. "What?"

"Will you ask Puddleshine whether the poison might have come from ShadowClan?"

His pelt ruffled. "I can't accuse his Clanmates."

"But you'll try to find out as much as you can," Squirrelflight pressed.

Jayfeather stopped in the clearing. "If Larksong's sickness has anything to do with ShadowClan, we'll find out," he promised. "But we're not going to start a fight. We're healers, not warriors."

"I know." Squirrelflight's paws pricked with frustration. She stopped as they headed toward the border, watching them disappear among the brambles on the far side of the clearing. Her heart sank. She hated feeling so powerless. As she turned back to camp, paws thrummed the ground. A squirrel shot from the brambles beside her and cut across her path. It disappeared into the bracken on the other side. Excitement flashed beneath her pelt. As she turned to chase it, a cat exploded from the brambles. Ginger fur blazed past her. *Cherryfall!* A second warrior burst from the brambles, then a third. Berrynose and Dewnose were on Cherryfall's heels, their pelts fluffed as they plunged into the bracken.

"Squirrelflight!" Bramblestar's mew made her jump. She turned as he scrambled to a halt beside her. His tail was bushed and his eyes shone. "What are you doing here?"

"Looking for you."

"Why?" Bramblestar was out of breath.

Squirrelflight nodded toward the brambles where the medicine cats had disappeared. "Jayfeather and Alderheart are going to consult with Puddleshine about Larksong," she explained quickly. "I want to go with them."

"To question ShadowClan about the sickness?" Bramblestar narrowed his eyes.

"I wasn't going to question them, but I want to see how they react when I tell them about Larksong. There are too many rumors in ThunderClan. I need to tell our Clanmates that I saw for myself that ShadowClan has nothing to do with this."

"Are you afraid some of our warriors will take revenge?"

"I just think there's enough tension on the border at the moment." She searched Bramblestar's gaze. Was he going to send her back to camp?

He whisked his tail. "I think it's a good idea."

"You do?" Surprise fizzed beneath her pelt. She could hardly remember the last time they'd agreed.

"There's no harm in warning ShadowClan that there might be sickness or infected prey around." Bramblestar looked toward the ShadowClan border. "And if you find any suggestion that ShadowClan might have been involved, at least we'll know the worst and be able to prepare."

She blinked at him. "So I can go?"

"I think you should hurry." Bramblestar peered through the trees. "Jayfeather's probably at the border by now."

Squirrelflight lifted her tail. "Thanks, Bramblestar." She broke into a run, racing along the route Jayfeather and Alderheart had taken. The scent of pines bathed her nose as she neared the border. She could see Jayfeather's gray pelt, pale in the shadows. Alderheart paced beside him.

They looked around, blinking as she crashed through a patch of ferns and pulled up beside them.

"I found Bramblestar," she puffed. "He thinks it's a good idea if I come with you."

Jayfeather flicked his tail and turned his muzzle back toward the border, tasting the air. "You made it just in time. Here comes a ShadowClan patrol."

Squirrelflight pricked her ears, listening for the sound of paw steps.

Alderheart stretched his muzzle forward, scanning the pines. "Where?"

As he spoke, pelts showed in the shadows. Squirrelflight recognized Snowbird's white pelt moving between the trees. Snaketooth and Cinnamontail were with her.

Snowbird's eyes narrowed as she headed toward the border, her hostile gaze fixed on Jayfeather. "What do you want?" she asked sharply as she reached them.

"We need to speak with Puddleshine," Jayfeather told her.

"There's sickness in our camp," Alderheart added. "We need his advice."

"And to warn Tigerstar," Squirrelflight mewed quickly.

"Warn him?" Snowbird narrowed her eyes. "About what?"

"I'll tell that to *him*," Squirrelflight meowed pointedly.

"Tigerstar's out hunting," Snaketooth grunted.

"I can speak to Cloverfoot," Squirrelflight told him. Would ShadowClan's deputy know as much as their leader?

Snowbird's nose twitched warily. "How do we know you're not bringing the sickness with you?"

"We're fine," Jayfeather promised. "A medicine cat would never knowingly spread illness."

Snowbird eyed him, then nodded. "Okay." She sniffed his pelt as he crossed the border. Alderheart followed. Squirrelflight glanced at Snaketooth and Cinnamontail, then padded after her Clanmates.

The ShadowClan warriors kept their distance as they escorted the ThunderClan patrol to the ShadowClan camp. Snaketooth and Snowbird exchanged glances but didn't speak until the camp wall loomed between the trees.

"Go straight to Puddleshine's den," Snowbird told Jay-feather as she ducked through the entrance tunnel.

"Why would I want to go anyplace else?" Jayfeather pad-ded after her.

Squirrelflight followed, Alderheart at her heels.

Acrid ShadowClan scent filled her nose as she emerged into the clearing. Sparrowtail and Whorlpelt were dragging old bedding from a den. Yarrowleaf and Berryheart sorted through the fresh-kill pile. Outside the elders' den, Light-paw and Pouncepaw were practicing battle moves in front of Oakfur and Ratscar. The apprentices paused as they saw the ThunderClan patrol, turning their heads to stare as Jay-feather and Alderheart crossed to Puddleshine's den.

Puddleshine ducked out, his eyes lighting as he saw Jay-feather and Alderheart. "It's good to see you." He stretched his nose forward, greeting them warmly, and led them inside.

"Can I speak with Cloverfoot now?" Squirrelflight asked Snowbird.

Snowbird swished her tail. "Wait here." As she headed across the clearing, Ratscar sat up and stared at Squirrelflight. Hostility sharpened his gaze. Sparrowtail and Whorlpelt uncurled their claws. Yarrowleaf pushed a vole to one side and padded closer, her hackles lifting.

Squirrelflight forced her pelt to stay smooth. ShadowClan clearly wasn't pleased to see her. They must resent the agree-ment ThunderClan had made with WindClan as much as their leader did. She felt their stares burning though her pelt as she waited for Snowbird to return with Cloverfoot.

Snowbird disappeared into a den at the far end of the camp. She emerged a few moments later, Cloverfoot at her heels. The ShadowClan deputy stared curiously at Squirrelflight, pausing for a moment before crossing the clearing.

Squirrelflight padded to meet her, stopping short as Cloverfoot fluffed out her gray tabby pelt, her gaze hardening into anger.

"What are you doing here?" Cloverfoot asked icily as she reached Squirrelflight.

"I came to warn you that one of our warriors is very sick." Squirrelflight dipped her head politely.

Cloverfoot frowned. "Why should we care?"

"We don't know what caused his sickness." Squirrelflight watched Cloverfoot carefully. Would the ShadowClan deputy give anything away? "He might have eaten tainted prey or picked up an illness in the forest. I thought ShadowClan should know, because we share borders and your warriors might be exposed to whatever made Larksong sick."

Cloverfoot narrowed her eyes. "Thank you for letting us know."

"Have any of your cats become ill?" Squirrelflight glanced around the camp, quickly reading the expressions of the other ShadowClan cats. She couldn't see guilt there, only curiosity.

"No." Cloverfoot whisked her tail. "Did you say Larksong might have eaten tainted prey?"

"He might have," Squirrelflight told her. "We're not sure yet." Cloverfoot wasn't showing any sign that ShadowClan might be responsible. "He's the only cat who's sick. So we're hoping it's an isolated incident."

"I hope so too." Concern flashed for a moment in Clover-foot's eyes. She blinked it away. "I think you should leave now and take your medicine cats with you."

"But they want to consult with Puddleshine about Lark-song's symptoms." Had they had enough time to probe for clues about ShadowClan's involvement in their Clanmate's sickness?

"They've had long enough." Cloverfoot grew brisk. "There are injured cats trying to rest in the medicine den."

"Injured cats?" Squirrelflight pricked her ears. Was ShadowClan in trouble? Another fight with the Sisters? Her chest tightened.

"A dispute with RiverClan border patrol," Cloverfoot told her. "Since they found out about your agreement with Wind-Clan, they've been pushing their border farther and farther, trying to reclaim their marshland." Anger ruffled her pelt.

Squirrelflight shifted her paws self-consciously. "I'm sorry to hear that."

"You caused it," Cloverfoot snapped.

The camp wall shivered. Squirrelflight stiffened as Tiger-star padded into camp. Dovewing, Strikestone, and Scorchfur followed at his heels. He glared at her. "What are you doing here?"

Cloverfoot answered for her. "Squirrelflight's come to report a sick cat in ThunderClan."

"There are *wounded* cats here thanks to ThunderClan." Tigerstar padded toward her, his hackles lifting.

"I'm sorry RiverClan is causing trouble," Squirrelflight

said, forcing her fur to remain flat. "But we can't be held responsible for borders that don't belong to us."

Tigerstar glared at her. "Even when you caused the dispute?"

"We don't control RiverClan." Relief washed Squirrelflight's pelt as Jayfeather and Alderheart padded from Puddleshine's den. They should leave. Tigerstar seemed ready for a fight. *Quick.* She beckoned them with a flick of her tail.

Tigerstar kept his gaze fixed on her. "How can you be so arrogant?" Anger hardened his mew. "You stop us finding new land for SkyClan—"

Squirrelflight interrupted him. "SkyClan hasn't agreed to move yet."

Tigerstar snorted. "Everyone knows that Leafstar thinks the mountain territory would make a perfect home for Sky-Clan."

"But moving there is SkyClan's choice, not yours," Squirrelflight insisted. "Besides, the Sisters still live there. In a moon, the Sisters will be gone and Leafstar will have made a decision."

"A moon!" Tigerstar lashed his tail. "How many warriors will have been injured in a moon?"

"None, if you and RiverClan agree to wait."

"Like you and WindClan agreed to wait?" Tigerstar spat. "How can we expect anything but hostility from RiverClan now that you've given WindClan their moorland back?"

"Perhaps you should think about giving RiverClan their marshland back—"

Tigerstar cut her off. "How dare you?" he hissed. "You tell

me that SkyClan must make their own decision, then tell me I should give RiverClan our land!"

"I'm just trying to help." Heat burned Squirrelflight's pelt. She could understand Tigerstar's frustration. But for the sake of the Sisters, he had to wait.

Jayfeather flicked his tail impatiently. "The last argument didn't solve this, and neither will this one." He turned his blind blue gaze on Squirrelflight. "We should get back to camp. Leafpool might need our help."

A growl rumbled in Tigerstar's throat. "Your medicine cat is right. *Leave.*" He nodded to Dovewing and Scorchfur. "Escort them to the border."

"We know the way," Squirrelflight told him, bristling.

"I want to make sure you go." Tigerstar eyed her darkly.

As Squirrelflight stalked past him, he called after her. "Tell Bramblestar that if our border dispute goes on much longer, we won't wait for StarClan to decide whether we can take the Sisters' land, or for Leafstar to make her decision. We'll take the land ourselves. RiverClan might even help us, for the sake of peace."

She ignored him, but her belly churned with fear. The Sisters were impressive and powerful cats, but could they defend themselves against the aggression of two Clans?

Alderheart fell in beside her, his gaze flitting anxiously around the camp. From all sides, ShadowClan cats were glowering at them menacingly.

Jayfeather padded behind, his tail twitching as Dovewing and Scorchfur followed. "Warriors," he grumbled. "All they think about is borders."

As they ducked out of the camp, Dovewing and Scorchfur fanned out. Scorchfur stared ahead, his pelt bristling along his spine.

Dovewing glanced nervously at Squirrelflight. "Tigerstar has a point," she murmured.

Squirrelflight looked at her, surprised. Dovewing had been raised in ThunderClan. She had kin there and had been a loyal ThunderClan warrior until she'd joined ShadowClan to be with Tigerstar so they could raise their kits together.

Dovewing dropped her gaze. "I just mean I can see ShadowClan's point of view now."

"I know they've lost territory," Squirrelflight conceded. "But if they just wait a moon—"

"It's not that." Dovewing moved closer, lowering her voice. "It's the way ThunderClan does things," she murmured. "I can see why the other Clans get irritated. ThunderClan cats only seem to be able to see their point of view. It's like they think they're better than everyone else. And Bramblestar always acts like he knows best, when he doesn't know any more than any other leader."

"But he's smart," Squirrelflight argued.

"So is Tigerstar," Dovewing shot back. "And Mistystar and the others. They can see that moving SkyClan to new land would solve everyone's problems, but Bramblestar is hung up on making sure SkyClan's feelings don't get hurt. Tigerstar is right—the mountain territory would be great for SkyClan. It would be great for any Clan."

Alarm sparked in Squirrelflight's pelt. "But what about the Sisters?"

"Who cares about the Sisters?" Dovewing blinked at her. "They're just a bunch of rogues who don't even *want* the land. They were planning to move on anyway; we just want them to do it a little sooner. It's not like chasing a Clan from their home."

Jayfeather sniffed beside them. "She has a point."

"No, she doesn't." Squirrelflight swished her tail crossly. "Being a warrior is more than being practical. It's about doing what's right. Bramblestar is only trying to make sure that Sky-Clan doesn't feel they're being pressured. It's important that they feel like the other Clans respect them. And the Sisters aren't rogues. They're more like a Clan than you think. And their leader is expecting kits. What kind of fox-heart would chase an expectant mother from her den?"

Dovewing shrugged. "I guess ThunderClan will never see that protecting your own Clan is sometimes more important than being right." She moved away, shadowing the patrol but keeping distance between herself and her old Clanmates.

Squirrelflight glanced at Jayfeather. "Does ThunderClan really think it's better than everyone else?"

Jayfeather grunted. "Every Clan thinks it's better than everyone else." He quickened his pace, his empty gaze on the forest ahead. "Isn't that part of the warrior code?"

Squirrelflight stared at him. Didn't cats believe in honor anymore? Couldn't they see that she and Bramblestar wanted the best for everyone? She shook out her fur. At least and she and Bramblestar agreed on *something* at last. The borders must stay the same until SkyClan and the Sisters were ready to move. A chill wormed beneath her pelt. But what if protecting the borders led the Clans into battle? War was the one thing StarClan had warned them against. She shivered. By protecting the Sisters, would she anger her ancestors?

CHAPTER 16

❧

Leaves, green and brittle, drifted at the roots of the oak trees. They rustled in the wind as Squirrelflight, Jayfeather, and Alderheart crossed the border and headed home through ThunderClan territory. Squirrelflight glanced over her shoulder. Strikestone had turned away, but Dovewing was still watching them through narrowed eyes. Squirrelflight used to wonder if the former ThunderClan warrior felt a pang of regret when she met her old Clanmates, but it seemed that every hair on Dovewing's pelt was ShadowClan now.

"I don't think they know anything about Larksong's sickness." Alderheart's mew jerked her from her thoughts. "Puddleshine had no idea what could have caused it. He was scared his Clanmates would catch it."

Relief washed Squirrelflight's pelt. The sickness had nothing to do with ShadowClan. At least now it wouldn't mean war. "Cloverfoot was surprised, and I didn't notice any of her Clanmates looking guilty." She glanced at Jayfeather. "What do you think?"

"I can't read thoughts anymore," Jayfeather grunted. "But Tigerstar wasn't hiding anything. I could hear it in his mew.

ShadowClan had nothing to do with Larksong's illness. He must have picked up the infection in the forest."

As he spoke, a pile of leaves shivered in front of them. Squirrelflight pricked her ears. Prey was rustling beneath it. She stopped, signaling with a flick of her tail for Jayfeather and Alderheart to wait. They paused beside her as she opened her mouth. Mouse-scent touched her tongue. "This was where Larksong was hunting before he got sick." Her pelt prickled. She glanced at the medicine cats. "Would you be able to tell if a mouse was tainted by examining it?"

Alderheart blinked at her. "I don't know."

"We could try," Jayfeather mewed. "But you'd have to catch one first."

"Okay." Squirrelflight dropped into a hunting crouch and crept forward, her belly brushing the earth. The leaves rustled again. She pictured the mouse underneath the pile, fixing with her gaze the place where it moved. Tensing, she bunched the muscles in her hind legs and leaped. She slammed her paws into the pile. Leaves exploded around her, fluttering to the ground as she jabbed her paws deep, feeling for soft flesh with outstretched claws. She hooked something warm. It wriggled in her grasp and squealed. *The mouse.* She tugged it out and, pinning it to the ground, gave a killing bite. Then she spat out the blood and flung the dead mouse toward Jayfeather and Alderheart. "Take a look." She scraped her tongue through her fur to clean any infection off it. "Can you see anything strange?"

Jayfeather ran his paw slowly over the mouse. "It feels okay.

How does it look?" He turned his blind gaze on Alderheart.

"Its eyes are clear." Alderheart told him. "Its pelt is clean and smooth. I can't see any blisters or scabs. It looks healthy."

"It might *be* healthy." Squirrelflight padded to join them. "It's unlikely we found a tainted one first try. But we might be lucky."

"I don't know if finding a poisonous mouse is lucky." Alderheart wrinkled his nose.

"Let's check inside." Jayfeather curled his claws into the carcass and tore it open. He sniffed at its innards. "It smells good."

Alderheart peered closer. "Everything looks pink and healthy."

Jayfeather sat back on his haunches. "Either we've killed a healthy mouse, or this sickness is impossible to detect."

Squirrelflight frowned, worry worming beneath her pelt. "Or Larksong's sickness wasn't caused by a mouse." She felt suddenly exhausted and sat down. Her head swam.

Alderheart looked at her sharply. "Are you okay?"

"I don't know." She gazed at him blearily. Tightness gripped her chest. She stiffened, alarmed. Did she have the same sickness as Larksong?

"Let's rest here for a while." Jayfeather padded toward her. He sniffed her muzzle. "Have you eaten today?"

"Not yet," she told him, dropping onto her belly. Weariness dragged at her bones. "I felt queasy this morning."

Jayfeather padded around her, sniffing her pelt. "You smell healthy. Are you expecting kits?"

She stiffened. Could it be true? Hope flashed beneath her pelt. Had she been arguing with Bramblestar all this time unaware that she was carrying his kits? She frowned, doubtful. Her last litter hadn't made her feel like this. She'd felt stronger than ever when she'd been carrying Alderheart and Sparkpelt. And yet perhaps this time was different. If she was expecting kits, she wasn't ready for Jayfeather and Alderheart to know.

"Are you?" Jayfeather repeated, his blind blue gaze fixed on her.

"No," she mewed quickly. "I'm probably just hungry." The dizziness was wearing off and she could breathe deeply again. "I'm starting to feel better."

"You should eat when we get back," Jayfeather advised.

Alderheart padded closer, anxiety glittering in his gaze. "Perhaps you're just tired," he meowed hopefully.

"Yes." She blinked at him. "That's probably what it is." She got to her paws and shook out her pelt. There was no point in worrying. "Let's get back to camp and tell them about ShadowClan."

Jayfeather padded beside her, turning his muzzle toward her from time to time as though worried.

"I'm feeling fine," she told him as they neared the camp. "Don't mention this to any cat. Sparkpelt has enough to worry about."

Jayfeather wasn't listening. His ears had swiveled toward the camp entrance. Alarm prickled through the fur along his spine. "Something's wrong."

Squirrelflight's heart quickened as he darted forward and ducked through the thorn tunnel.

She hurried after him. "What is it?"

As she burst into camp, she heard anxious murmuring. Jayfeather was already haring toward the medicine den, Alderheart at his heels. Squirrelflight quickly scanned the camp. Blossomfall and Ivypool were clustered around Lilyheart, their eyes dark with worry. Thornclaw and Berrynose leaned close to each other, talking in hushed voices at the edge of the clearing. Bristlepaw, Thriftpaw, and Flippaw sat like owls, watching their Clanmates in wide-eyed silence as Twigbranch paced distractedly below the Highledge.

Finleap hurried to meet her. "You're back." His eyes glittered with alarm.

"What's happened?" Panic shrilled through Squirrelflight's fur. "Is it Larksong? Is he . . ." *Dead?* She couldn't bring herself to say the word.

Finleap stared at her wordlessly.

It must be worse! Squirrelflight felt sick. "Sparkpelt?" Had the kits come? Had there been complications with the birth? Horror swamped her as Finleap nodded slowly.

"She's sick," he mewed.

Bramblestar pushed his way out of the medicine den. His eyes flashed as he saw Squirrelflight and he hurried across the clearing. "Don't be alarmed," he meowed as he neared. "She's a strong cat."

"What happened?" The breath caught in Squirrelflight's throat.

Bramblestar stopped in front of her, his eyes as round as moons. "She went to rest in the nursery," he told her. "She'd been complaining of a tight chest. I went to check on her and found she wasn't breathing."

The ground seemed to sway beneath Squirrelflight's paws. "Like Larksong."

"I fetched Leafpool," Bramblestar went on. "She got her breathing again, and we took her to the medicine den. Leafpool's with her now. She's unconscious, but her breathing is fine. If she has the same sickness as Larksong, it doesn't seem to have affected her as badly."

"But she stopped breathing!" Squirrelflight stared at him.

"Her heartbeat is strong," Bramblestar told her. "And the kits are still moving."

Squirrelflight's thoughts whirled. "What if you hadn't gone to check on her? What if she'd died without anyone realizing she was sick?"

Bramblestar thrust his muzzle against her cheek and held it there. "She didn't die," he meowed steadily. "I checked on her and she's alive."

Squirrelflight leaned against him, grateful for his warmth. She felt cold to the bone and fought to stop herself shivering. "Can I see her?" She drew away and looked deep into Bramblestar's eyes.

"Of course." His gaze shimmered for a moment; then he looked away.

Squirrelflight hurried across the clearing. She pushed through the trailing brambles, her heart racing. Sparkpelt was curled up in a nest beside Larksong's. Leafpool sat beside her. Alderheart watched anxiously as Jayfeather touched his nose to Sparkpelt's fur.

The blind medicine cat drew away, frowning. "I've never known a sickness that doesn't *smell* like sickness." He shook out his pelt, then nodded to Alderheart, as though coming to a decision. "We're going to check on every cat in the Clan," he told him. "If any of them is tired, or has difficulty breathing, we'll send them to the medicine den. That way we can stop it spreading." He glanced at Leafpool. "Okay?"

Leafpool nodded. "It's a good plan."

As Jayfeather led Alderheart out of the den, Squirrelflight met Leafpool's gaze. "You saved her life." Her heart ached with gratitude.

Leafpool dipped her head. "Bramblestar is the one who found her."

Squirrelflight felt a rush of affection for her mate. It was comforting to know that, whatever had happened between them, he was always there for their kits. She padded to Sparkpelt's nest. Her daughter looked suddenly small among the bracken fronds. Squirrelflight bent to touch her nose to Sparkpelt's fur, but Leafpool put out a paw. "Don't get too close," she warned. "Until we know what's causing this, it's best to stay clear."

Squirrelflight's heart seemed to crack. "But she's my daughter."

"That doesn't mean you won't catch it from her." Leafpool gazed gently at Squirrelflight.

"Will her kits be okay?" Squirrelflight asked.

"I felt them moving before you came in. They seem strong."

Squirrelflight hesitated. Should she tell Leafpool about feeling unwell on the way home? *No.* How could she help her Clan if she were confined to the medicine den? *But Leafpool should know about my kits in case I get sick.* "I think I may be expecting," she told Leafpool.

"Really?" Leafpool's eyes widened with surprise. "Are you sure?"

Doubt tugged in Squirrelflight's belly. Leafpool had said that she *always* knew when a cat was expecting kits. *Am I wrong?* She changed the subject. "How's Larksong?" She looked at the black tom's nest. Larksong was barely more than a shadow against the bracken.

"He still hasn't woken and he's had difficulty breathing," Leafpool told her. "But we're giving him tansy and chervil root. And we've managed to get a little water into his mouth."

Squirrelflight felt numb. What if he died? What if *Sparkpelt* died too, and their unborn kits? She headed for the entrance, shaking out her pelt before the thought could take hold. She pushed through the brambles, holding her face up to the sunshine. Perhaps the light could wash away the darkness she felt welling inside her.

Around the edge of the clearing, Jayfeather and Alderheart moved from warrior to warrior, leaning close as they checked them for symptoms. Finleap and Twigbranch moved aside as Graystripe padded from the elders' den, his eyes dark. Flippaw paced nervously around Hollytuft, while Bristlepaw and

Thriftpaw seemed rooted to the ground.

Thornclaw was blinking anxiously at Bramblestar. "Could Sparkpelt have eaten a tainted mouse too?"

"We haven't hunted anywhere near the place Larksong's mouse was caught," Bramblestar reasoned.

Graystripe padded closer. "Perhaps there are tainted mice all over the forest. Sickness spreads between prey just as it spreads between cats."

Bramblestar's pelt bristled along his spine. "It might not even be prey that's causing the sickness. What if Larksong picked up sickness in the forest and passed it to Sparkpelt?"

"Where could he have picked it up?" Thornclaw frowned. "We've never seen anything like it before."

Mousewhisker padded nearer. "It might be a sickness from outside the Clans."

Bramblestar blinked at him. "Larksong hasn't left Clan territory."

Squirrelflight tensed. A thought surfaced that she didn't dare acknowledge.

Thornclaw's gaze flashed suddenly. "But strange cats have come *onto* Clan territory." Squirrelflight stared at him, knowing what he was going to say next. The dark warrior growled. "The Sisters might have carried this sickness with them."

Bramblestar pricked his ears. Graystripe and Mousewhisker swapped glances. It made sense.

Squirrelflight padded quickly forward. "I'll visit them." If they'd brought this illness into the Clans, she had to warn them. "I'll see if they're sick." As she spoke, Alderheart nudged

Berrynose toward the medicine den. The pale warrior padded toward the trailing brambles, his eyes sparking with fear.

"Are you sick?" Mousewhisker asked Berrynose as he passed.

Berrynose glanced at him. "My chest is a little tight, that's all."

"I just want to keep an eye on him," Alderheart explained.

Jayfeather looked up beside Thriftpaw. The apprentice's ears were twitching nervously. "Thriftpaw is wheezing," he mewed.

Alderheart hurried toward the young she-cat and pressed an ear to her chest. He straightened. "You'd better go to the medicine den too."

Thriftpaw's eyes widened. "Am I sick?"

"You're probably fine," Jayfeather told her. Across the clearing, Ivypool got to her paws, her pelt spiking with alarm. "But it's best if we watch you for a while."

Ivypool hurried toward her kit, panic glittering in her gaze. "I'll go with her."

Jayfeather shook his head. "If this sickness is contagious, we need to keep the affected cats isolated until we've found a way to treat it."

Ivypool stared as Alderheart guided Thriftpaw toward the medicine den. Thriftpaw glanced at her mother as he passed. She blinked reassuringly, but Squirrelflight could see fear in the young cat's eyes.

"I'll go to the Sisters' camp now," she told Bramblestar. "If they do have this sickness, they might know a cure."

Bramblestar nodded. "Take a patrol with you."

She blinked at him, expecting him to choose warriors to go with her, but he turned and followed Alderheart toward the medicine den. Did he trust her to pick her own patrols again? She felt a flash of relief. "Ivypool." She nodded to the silver-and-white tabby. "I want you to come with me." Ivypool glanced toward the medicine den. "You can stay here if you want," Squirrelflight told her. "But you'll be more help to me than you will be to Thriftpaw right now."

Ivypool dipped her head. "I'll come."

"Twigbranch." Squirrelflight nodded to the gray she-cat. "I want you to come too. And Finleap."

Twigbranch glanced toward the medicine den. "Should we take a medicine cat, to examine the Sisters?" she ventured.

"Good idea." Squirrelflight flicked her tail. "Go and tell Leafpool that I need her."

As Twigbranch hurried away, Squirrelflight felt her chest tighten again. She tensed. Was she sick, and not expecting kits at all? She shook out her pelt. *It's just anxiety,* she told herself. *I'll be okay.* She forced herself to relax, letting her breath deepen. She couldn't be sick now. She had to find out where this mysterious illness had come from and how to cure it. Sparkpelt's life could depend on it.

CHAPTER 17

By the time Squirrelflight led the way down the thickly bram-bled slope toward the ferns that screened the Sisters' camp entrance, the moon was shining high above the small valley where they had made their home.

She stopped outside and raised her muzzle. "Moonlight? It's me."

Branches rustled beyond the ferns, and Snow's mew answered. "Squirrelflight?"

"Yes." Squirrelflight flicked her tail toward Ivypool, Twig-branch, and Finleap, signaling them to stay back. She didn't want the Sisters to think this was anything but a friendly visit. "Can I come in? I've brought some Clanmates with me."

Paw steps sounded in the grassy clearing. Voices echoed in the night.

"What are they doing here this time of night?"

"Why has she brought campmates?"

"Let's find out." Moonlight answered them briskly. "Come in, Squirrelflight. Bring your Clanmates."

Squirrelflight nosed her way through the ferns. The Sis-ters ringed the clearing, staring with wide, moonlit eyes as

241

the ThunderClan cats filed into camp. Moonlight's belly was more swollen than ever. She hung back, flanked by Snow and Tempest, and eyed the patrol warily. "It's late for a visit. Are you here with another warning?"

"I wanted to speak to you as soon as I could." Squirrelflight scanned the sisters, looking for signs of illness. Sunrise wasn't with them. "Are you all well?" She pricked her ears, searching Moonlight's gaze as the large gray she-cat answered.

"We are."

"And Sunrise?" Squirrelflight glanced anxiously at Leafpool.

"She's resting," Moonlight's ears twitched. She was clearly unnerved by the patrol's arrival.

Leafpool padded forward. "May I see her?"

"Her wound is almost healed," Moonlight told her.

"I'd like to check," Leafpool pressed.

"Okay." Moonlight nodded to Furze. "Take her to Sunrise's den."

Furze beckoned Leafpool with a flick of her tail and led her through a gap in the dogwood at the edge of the clearing.

As Leafpool disappeared, Squirrelflight glanced around at the Sisters. Their long, thick pelts were disheveled. Was that sickness, or was their fur simply ruffled by sleep?

Tempest shook out her fur, as though conscious of Squirrelflight's gaze. "Why bring so many Clanmates just to check on Sunrise?"

"Bramblestar told me to bring a patrol with me," Squirrelflight told her.

Amusement flashed in Moonlight's gaze. "Are you still trying to please him?"

Squirrelflight swished her tail. "He's my leader, and my mate." How could Moonlight understand? She had neither.

"Of course." Moonlight dipped her head. Her gaze was still firm when she lifted it again. "But you are not just here to check on Sunrise." As she spoke, Leafpool padded from the dogwood.

"She's healed well." Leafpool met Moonlight's gaze. "You found the herbs you needed?"

"Yes." Moonlight turned her questioning gaze back to Squirrelflight. "Is Sunrise why you came?"

"There is sickness in our camp," Squirrelflight told her. "We came to find out if you had it too."

"Were you worried that you'd passed it on to us?" Moonlight narrowed her eyes. "Or that we'd brought it to you?"

Squirrelflight avoided the question. "We were worried you might be sick."

"We're not." Moonlight eyed her curiously.

Relief washed Squirrelflight's pelt. She'd tried not to think how the Clans would react if they thought the Sisters had bought sickness to the forest. "Then it must be caused by prey. Be careful what you catch. We think there might be tainted prey in the forest."

Snow's pelt prickled. "We hunt here, not in your forest."

Leafpool padded to Squirrelflight's side. "We don't know what has tainted the prey, and whatever it is might have spread here."

Ivypool stepped forward, her eyes glittering anxiously. "Have you seen any sick prey?"

Moonlight narrowed her eyes. "Not that we've noticed. And nothing has made us ill."

Finleap shifted behind Squirrelflight. "If there's nothing to learn here," he mewed, "we should head back."

Twigbranch moved closer. "Do you think any other cats will have fallen sick while we've been away?"

"I hope not." Squirrelflight's belly tightened. She dipped her head politely to Moonlight. "I'm sorry we disturbed you."

As she turned to go, Moonlight's eyes narrowed. "What are the symptoms of this sickness?"

"It comes on quickly," Leafpool told her. "The patient feels tired, then suddenly collapses and stops breathing. We've managed to keep the first two victims alive, but they're unconscious and bringing up bile. If we can't treat them soon, they might die."

Moonlight looked at Snow. Flickers of recognition seemed to spark in their gaze.

Squirrelflight stiffened. "Do you know what's causing it?"

"We thought it was strange that you let meadow saffron grow in your forest," Snow meowed.

Moonlight sat down, her heavy belly resting on her hind paws. "We thought that Clan cats must be immune to its poison."

"Meadow saffron?" Squirrelflight had never heard of it. "What is it?"

"Haven't you seen the purple flowers?" Hawk asked. "We

saw a few while we were on your land."

Squirrelflight glanced at Leafpool. She hadn't noticed any unusual plants, but the medicine cats might have spotted it. "Have you seen any?"

"No." Leafpool looked perplexed. "But we weren't looking for it."

Moonlight's gaze had darkened with concern. "When we settle new land, we dig up any meadow saffron we find. Mice and shrews like to eat the roots and seeds. It doesn't hurt them, but it makes them harmful to us."

Leafpool pricked her ears. "How do you know this?"

"Our ancestors passed on the knowledge," Tempest explained. "The Twolegs they escaped from grew meadow saffron near their nest."

Squirrelflight's heart quickened. Had they found the cause of Sparkpelt's sickness? "But how did this plant get on *our* land?"

Hawk frowned. "It might have spread from Twoleg gardens."

Moonlight nodded. "If a Twoleg near your territory has planted some near their nest, birds will eat the seeds and drop them on your land."

Leafpool's eyes were wide. "Is there a cure?"

Moonlight shrugged. "Dandelion root will clear the poison from inside. But treatment must be fast, before the poison takes hold."

Ivypool's tail twitched impatiently. "We must get back!"

"Thank you." Squirrelflight nodded to Moonlight. "You

may have saved the lives of our Clanmates." As she turned toward the entrance, Ivypool hesitated.

"Thank you." The silver warrior's gaze flitted gratefully around the Sisters.

Moonlight dipped her head. "I'm glad we could help."

Squirrelflight pushed her way through the ferns. Hope sparked in her fur. But it was a long journey home. Would they make it back in time to save Sparkpelt?

As the patrol crossed the border and raced through the moonlit forest, Leafpool pulled up. "Wait." The medicine cat nodded to Twigbranch and Finleap. "Come with me."

Squirrelflight scrambled to a halt, alarm sending a shiver up her spine. "Where are you going?" She needed Leafpool with her. What if Sparkpelt hadn't made it through the night?

Leafpool met her gaze. "We won't be long. We need to gather dandelion roots. We'll bring them back to camp as soon as we can. You and Ivypool go ahead so you can be with Sparkpelt and Thriftpaw."

"Don't take too long." Squirrelflight glanced toward the camp.

"We'll be quick," Leafpool promised, and headed away into the shadows.

As Twigbranch and Finleap hurried after her, Squirrelflight glanced at Ivypool. The silver tabby's eyes were dark with worry. "Come on."

Squirrelflight charged onward through the forest. Dawn must be close, but clouds obscured the moon, throwing darkness over the forest, so deep she could barely see her whiskers. She skimmed blindly over the swath of blueberries and raced down the slope toward the hollow, scrambling to a halt outside the thorn tunnel. She paused as Ivypool caught up to her, and took a breath. *Please, StarClan, let Sparkpelt be alive.*

She hurried through the entrance, her heart lurching as she padded into a silent camp. It was quiet. Had she expected to find a body laid out in the clearing while her Clanmates sat vigil? She crossed the camp, Ivypool at her heels. "Wait here," she told the silver tabby as she reached the medicine den. With four sick cats, it must already be crowded. "I'll send Alderheart outside to talk to you." Ivypool nodded, staring with hollow eyes as Squirrelflight nosed her way through the trailing brambles.

The hot, stuffy air surrounded her as she blinked in the darkness. She could make out the shape of Jayfeather, crouching beside Larksong. Alderheart rested his paws on the edge of Sparkpelt's nest. They turned as Squirrelflight crossed the den.

Jayfeather sat up. "Are the Sisters sick?"

"No." Squirrelflight halted. "But they know what's caused the sickness. A new plant on our land. They saw it while they were here. It's called meadow saffron. Prey that eats it becomes poisonous." She leaned over Sparkpelt's nest. The orange tabby was unconscious. She fought back panic. Why was Sparkpelt so still? "How's she doing?"

"I gave her poppy seeds to make her sleep," Alderheart told her. "She was fretting over Larksong."

Squirrelflight glanced into the nest beside Sparkpelt's. Through the darkness, she could see Larksong's matted pelt, his bones jutting out as though he'd grown suddenly old. "Is he any better?"

"No." Alderheart's eyes glittered with worry.

Jayfeather flicked his tail impatiently. "Do the Sisters know a cure?"

"Dandelion root will clean the poison out," Squirrelflight told him. "But it must be given quickly." She glanced at Larksong's nest. "Leafpool's gathering some now. She'll be here soon."

Her heart leaped with hope as the brambles rustled at the entrance, but it was only Bramblestar.

"I saw you were back," he meowed, hurrying across the den.

Jayfeather stared at him blindly in the darkness. "The Sisters aren't sick, but they know what's caused this and how to treat it."

Bramblestar's pelt prickled with surprise. "Will they be okay?" He glanced at Larksong and Sparkpelt's nests.

Squirrelflight's heart twisted with fear. "We don't know if we found out in time." She glanced at the other nests beside the den wall. Thriftpaw and Berrynose were sound asleep, their muzzles tucked beneath their paws. "Are they sick?"

"Not yet," Alderheart told her.

"Ivypool is waiting outside," Squirrelflight told him. "She needs to know that Thriftpaw's still okay."

As she spoke, Leafpool crashed through the trailing brambles and dropped a bundle of dandelion root from her jaws.

"We didn't stop to gather much, but it should do for now." Her pelt was ruffled from running, and her tail was fluffed out.

Ivypool slid in after her, scanning the medicine den.

Alderheart hurried to meet her. "She's fine," he told the silver tabby, guiding her outside. Dawn light showed between the brambles as they pushed through. "There's no sign of sickness. We just want to keep an eye on her for a day or two."

Jayfeather scooped up a dandelion in his jaws and snapped off the thickest part. He began to chew it into a pulp.

Leafpool looked into Larksong's nest. "We should treat Larksong first." She frowned. "If we can get him to swallow it."

"What about Sparkpelt?" Bramblestar's eyes rounded.

"We'll treat her afterward," Leafpool told him.

Squirrelflight caught her sister's eye. "How are the kits doing?"

Leafpool leaned over the edge of the nest and pressed her ear against Sparkpelt's flank. "They're quiet now," she told Squirrelflight, straightening. "But I can still feel movement."

Squirrelflight glanced at Bramblestar, her heart pressing in her throat. Would the Sisters' treatment save Sparkpelt and the kits?

Jayfeather spat dandelion pulp onto his paw. "Hold his head," he ordered Leafpool.

As Leafpool lifted Larksong's head with a paw, Alderheart nosed his way back into the den and hurried to join them. Squirrelflight moved closer to Bramblestar, craving the warmth of his pelt against hers. Jayfeather held his paw in front of the black tom's muzzle. "If you open his mouth," he told Leafpool, "I can smear it on his tongue. That should—"

He stopped as Larksong jerked in his nest. The black tom's legs stiffened and his body twitched. A convulsion took hold of him; his back arched. He began to thrash wildly, as though a fox had seized his spine and was shaking him. Leafpool pressed her paws around his head. Alderheart leaped into the nest and pinned Larksong's shoulders into the bracken, holding him down as spasms contorted his body.

Squirrelflight's heart lurched. She pressed harder against Bramblestar.

"Larksong?" Sparkpelt's alarmed mew sounded behind her. Sparkpelt was struggling blearily to her paws, her terrified gaze fixed on Larksong. "What's happening to him?"

"It's a fit," Jayfeather told her. "It'll stop in a moment."

"It'll kill him!" Sparkpelt wailed.

Squirrelflight's paws seemed frozen to the earth. Was this going to happen to Sparkpelt next? On the far side of the den, Thriftpaw and Berrynose lifted their heads. Their eyes rounded in horror as they took in Larksong. Nervously, Thriftpaw climbed into Berrynose's nest and huddled beside the pale warrior. Squirrelflight glanced at them, then turned her helpless gaze back on Larksong. The spasms were easing. The convulsions seemed to loosen with each jerk until he lay as limp as fresh prey, his head hanging over the edge of his nest.

Alderheart hopped out. He was trembling.

"Will he live?" Bramblestar's mew was husky with fear.

Leafpool and Jayfeather exchanged glances.

Bracken crunched as Sparkpelt tried to haul herself from her nest. "Larksong." The name came as a sob.

Squirrelflight nudged her back. "Rest," she pleaded. "There's nothing you can do to help him."

"I can comfort him!" Sparkpelt grunted with effort as she pushed her mother away and padded shakily to Larksong's nest. She rested her head beside his cheek. "Larksong," she breathed, her gaze clouded with grief.

Squirrelflight's heart seemed to crack. She blinked at Jayfeather. "Are you going to give him the dandelion root?" The pulp was still smeared on his paw.

He reached for a leaf and wiped it off. "It's too late. He won't be able to swallow this." His blind blue gaze reached for Squirrelflight. "There's nothing more we can do for him."

"You have to save him," Sparkpelt breathed weakly.

Jayfeather pushed the leaf toward her muzzle. "Swallow this." He pointed his muzzle toward the pulp.

She didn't seem to hear him.

Squirrelflight bent closer to her. "Eat the dandelion root," she whispered. "It will help you and the kits."

Sparkpelt's gaze was fixed on Larksong.

"Please." Squirrelflight lifted the leaf and placed it beside Sparkpelt's muzzle. She glanced desperately at Bramblestar. "Tell her she has to," she pleaded.

Bramblestar leaned forward. "Sparkpelt," he mewed softly.

She lifted her gaze to him, then froze. Pain sparked in her gaze.

As Squirrelflight saw her flanks spasm, her heart seemed

to stop. Was she having a fit like Larksong?

Sparkpelt gasped. "My belly." She jerked from Larksong's nest and sat back on her haunches as another spasm made her gasp.

Leafpool pricked her ears. "The kits are coming!"

Squirrelflight's pelt spiked. Not now! They couldn't come now, not here. They were too early, and Sparkpelt was sick. "Is she strong enough?" She blinked at Leafpool.

"She'll have to be." Leafpool jerked her muzzle toward Alderheart. "Take Thriftpaw and Berrynose to the nursery," she ordered. "Now that we know the sickness doesn't spread, they don't have to be confined here. Stay with them."

Alderheart's eyes widened. "Don't you need me here?"

"I have Jayfeather. And some cat needs to keep an eye on them," Leafpool told him. "These symptoms come on fast."

Alderheart hurried away, bustling Thriftpaw and Berrynose, wide-eyed, from the den.

Sparkpelt crouched on the den floor, her breath coming fast as another spasm pulsed through her. Jayfeather eased her onto her side and began to lap her pelt with long, soothing licks. Leafpool crouched at her tail. "The first kit's coming."

Squirrelflight watched as a small, wet sack plopped onto the ground. The sack tore as it landed, and a tiny tortoiseshell kit, tinier than Squirrelflight had ever seen, struggled from the membrane. Leafpool grabbed its scruff and scooped it toward Squirrelflight. "Clean it and keep it warm."

Pelt prickling with surprise, Squirrelflight picked up the kit by its scruff. She sat down and placed it on the ground against her belly. Leaning down, she licked the remains of the membrane from its pelt and then washed it softly with her tongue. "It's a she-cat," she breathed, relieved to feel it squirming against her. Her heart swelled as kit scent filled her nose.

Bramblestar leaned closer, a purr throbbing in his throat. "She's beautiful," he murmured, touching his nose to the kit's head.

"She has a brother." Leafpool jerked another kit toward them.

Squirrelflight took him and cleaned him and pressed the little black tom next to his littermate. Sparkpelt groaned as another convulsion shook her.

"You're doing well," Leafpool told her.

Sparkpelt stretched her head back and gazed desperately at Larksong. In the pale dawn light Squirrelflight saw that the black tom's eyes were open, half focused on Sparkpelt. Did he realize what was happening?

Squirrelflight got to her paws. She lifted the tom-kit and swung him toward Bramblestar. "Keep this one warm." She placed him between his paws, then picked up the she-kit by the scruff. Carrying her gently, she took her to Larksong's nest. She placed her at the edge of the nest, beside his muzzle.

Sparkpelt grunted, her body convulsing again.

"This is the last one." Leafpool moved back as a tiny black-and-orange tom-kit slithered onto the floor. She pressed a paw onto Sparkpelt's flank. "Rest now," she meowed. "We'll take care of the kits."

Sparkpelt didn't respond. She was staring at Larksong

as the she-kit mewled beside his muzzle. His clouded gaze seemed to sharpen. He moved his head, touching his nose to the kit's flank.

Squirrelflight held her breath as Larksong blinked slowly, his eyes widening with joy. The kit wriggled and rubbed her head against his muzzle. Larksong gave a short, rasping purr. His gaze flicked toward Sparkpelt, glistening with affection. Then it grew dull, like twilight fading into night.

Shock pulsed through Squirrelflight. *He's dead.* Larksong's eyes stared blankly at Sparkpelt, but she knew he couldn't see her anymore.

"Larksong?" Sparkpelt stared back at him, panic edging her mew.

Jayfeather hurried to Larksong's nest and pressed his ear to the tom's chest. Squirrelflight quickly snatched the kit away and carried her back to Bramblestar, where she tucked her beside her littermate.

"Larksong!" Sparkpelt was struggling to her paws. She staggered toward Larksong, collapsed as she reached him, and laid her head beside his on the edge of the nest.

Squirrelflight blinked in panic at Leafpool. Would this be too much for Sparkpelt? But Leafpool was staring at the last kit. He lay lifeless on the ground. Blood roared in Squirrelflight's ears as grief threatened to overwhelm her. Beside her, Bramblestar sheltered the first two kits between his paws. Dread glittered in his gaze. He stared at Sparkpelt, hardly moving.

Squirrelflight struggled to breathe. She felt as though she

were drowning. Closing her eyes, she fought the grief. Spark-pelt mustn't know that one of her kits had died. She'd been through too much already, and she was still sick. Steadying her breath, Squirrelflight nudged Bramblestar with her nose. It seemed to shake him from his horror. He blinked at her questioningly.

"We must take the kits to Sorrelstripe," she told him.

"She's got her own kits." Bramblestar blinked at her.

"Then she'll have milk," Squirrelflight told him. "She can feed these with her own until Sparkpelt can nurse them. Daisy will be there to help look after them." She glanced at her daughter, her heart twisting as she saw raw grief in Spark-pelt's eyes. She wanted to comfort her, but she knew Sparkpelt was lost in misery. *I can't help Sparkpelt yet, but I can take care of her kits.* Squirrelflight shook out her pelt and scooped up the she-kit. "Bring the black kit," she told Bramblestar.

He glanced toward the third kit, his black-and-orange pelt dull in the half-light. "What about that one?" His mew was soft and Squirrelflight guessed that he, too, didn't want Sparkpelt to hear.

Squirrelflight gently laid the wriggling she-kit on the floor, then lifted the orange-and-black tom-kit, carrying him out-side the den. She laid him in a bed of leaves, then returned to Bramblestar and picked up the she-kit again.

"Where did you take him?" Bramblestar asked as he scooped up the black tom-kit.

Squirrelflight put down the she-kit and gestured to the leaves as they left the den. "We can plan a vigil for Larksong and his kit when these kits are safe," she said. "In the meantime, I don't want Sparkpelt to see."

She picked up the she-kit again and blinked at him. He seemed to understand, grief sparking in his gaze. As she headed for the trailing brambles, he followed her. Squirrelflight bent her head low to protect the kit from the prickles. They were going to get through this. No matter how much grief Sparkpelt was going to suffer, Squirrelflight was determined not to let her daughter down.

CHAPTER 18

❧

As the sun slid behind the trees, Squirrelflight ducked into camp. Patrolling the borders with Leafshade, Honeyfur, and Fernsong hadn't eased her grief. The forest usually soothed her, but the sadness, which gripped her heart like fox teeth, hadn't eased. It tightened as she saw Larksong's body laid in the clearing, ready for the vigil. His tiny orange-and-black kit lay at his side.

As she paused, gazing at them in the twilight, Fernsong stopped beside her.

"Will Sparkpelt be well enough to sit vigil?" the yellow tabby meowed.

"I don't know." Squirrelflight eyed the medicine den nervously. Leafpool had given Sparkpelt the dandelion root after she'd finished kitting. Had it washed out the poison yet?

Honeyfur gazed at her dead littermate. "I'll sit vigil."

"So will I." Leafshade paused at her sister's side. The tortoiseshell glanced at the stars, which were beginning to show in the darkening sky. "Larksong is with Snowbush now."

Honeyfur met her gaze. "They'll be watching over us."

Squirrelflight left them beside Larksong and headed

toward the medicine den.

As she nosed her way through the brambles, Leafpool got to her paws.

"The dandelion's working," Leafpool mewed. For the first time in days the tabby's gaze was lit with hope. "I gave some to Berrynose and Thriftpaw just to be on the safe side, but I don't think they were ever sick. I've sent them back to their dens."

Squirrelflight was hardly listening. Her heart quickened as she hurried to Sparkpelt's nest. Sparkpelt was curled like a dormouse at the bottom.

Leafpool followed. "Her heart is beating strongly now and her breath is steady."

"Then why is she still sleeping?" Worry nagged at Squirrelflight's belly.

"She's been sick, and she kitted this morning. She's exhausted. Sleep is the best remedy now." Leafpool pressed close to Squirrelflight. "She's going to be okay."

Squirrelflight blinked at her sister. "Did you tell her about the kit that died?"

"Yes." Leafpool's gaze glistened.

"How did she react?"

"I don't think she took it in." Distress glittered for a moment in Leafpool's eyes.

"Has she seen the other two yet?"

"Not yet."

"Has she asked after them?" Squirrelflight's pelt prickled nervously. What if Sparkpelt could only associate the kits with Larksong's death? She might never learn to love them properly.

"She's only woken once," Leafpool told her.

"And she didn't mention them?"

Leafpool's eyes rounded sympathetically. "She's been sick."

"Kits should be with their mother." Squirrelflight's thoughts whirled. Daisy would comfort them and Sorrelstripe would feed them, but the kits should have Sparkpelt's love.

"They are safe," Leafpool told her. "That's most important now. It's best they don't have Sparkpelt's milk until the poison is out of her system."

Squirrelflight shifted her paws. "What if she doesn't bond with them?"

"She will." Leafpool held her gaze steadily. "It takes more than loss and separation to stop a mother from loving her kits. I know that more than any cat."

Squirrelflight's throat tightened. Leafpool had been through so much and hadn't let it change her. Perhaps Sparkpelt would be okay. "I'm going to see the kits," she meowed.

Leafpool dipped her head. "Come back when you're done," she told Squirrelflight. "Sparkpelt will probably wake up soon."

Squirrelflight glanced at her daughter, still tucked up tight, and headed for the den entrance. Outside, night had settled over the camp. Her Clanmates moved quietly around the clearing as starlight dappled Larksong's pelt. His kit sheltered in his shadow. Someone had gathered soft moss and tucked it around them, as though hoping to keep them warm. Eyes pricking, Squirrelflight padded softly to the nursery.

Sorrelstripe was asleep in her nest, her own kits curled at her belly. Where were Sparkpelt's kits? As Squirrelflight blinked through the darkness, Daisy lifted her head. The queen was curled on a bed of bracken, her paws resting protectively around two tiny squirming bundles. "How's Sparkpelt?"

"She's recovering," Squirrelflight told her.

"Good." Daisy purred. "I expect these two will want to see their real mother soon." She nuzzled the kits fondly. "Sorrelstripe's been suckling them along with her own. It's exhausting for her, so I've been keeping them with me when they're not feeding." She unfolded her paws. The kits mewled indignantly as she revealed them to the chilly night air. Squirrelflight hurried across the den and nuzzled them. They reached instinctively for her. The smell of them filled her heart, and as they fidgeted blindly, pawing at her nose, she knew with a jolt that she wasn't expecting a litter of her own after all. It had never been more than desperate hope, and tiredness caused by worry. She'd been foolish to believe she was carrying Bramblestar's kits. Squirrelflight nuzzled the kits harder, purring, as longing hollowed her belly. If Sparkpelt didn't want these kits, she would take care of them as if they were her own.

Tiny claws scraped her cheek as the tortoiseshell she-kit rolled away and began pummeling Daisy's belly. The black tom-kit wriggled after his sister, pressing his face into Daisy's soft belly fur.

Daisy curled her paws around them once more. "They need

names." She hugged them gently.

Meadowkit. Gladekit. Bluekit. Names flashed in her mind, names she'd planned when she'd been dreaming of new kits of her own. She pushed them away and blinked at Daisy. "Sparkpelt should name them."

Daisy reached toward the moss piled in a soggy heap at the side of the bracken. She hooked a piece and offered it to the kits. Mewling, they lapped at it and began to suckle, each tugging at a corner. "This keeps them quiet while Sorrelstripe rests."

Squirrelflight was impressed by how quickly they'd adapted to such strange nursing. "They're going to be great warriors, just like Sparkpelt and Larksong."

"Of course." Daisy's eyes shone in the half-light.

"I'll see if Sparkpelt is ready to come and see them." Squirrelflight headed for the den entrance. She slid out and saw her Clanmates gathering around Larksong and the kit. Graystripe and Millie stood in the shadow of the elders' den. Thriftpaw, Bristlepaw, and Flippaw sat between Ivypool and Fernsong while their Clanmates ringed the clearing.

Bramblestar was heading toward the nursery. "I was just coming to fetch you."

"What about Sparkpelt?" Squirrelflight scanned her Clanmates.

"She's here." Bramblestar nodded toward a shadowy figure padding across the clearing.

Sparkpelt's green eyes glittered in the darkness as she reached Larksong's body. She lowered her head and pressed her muzzle against his lifeless cheek. Then she sat beside him and lifted her chin, as though bracing herself for a long night. An owl hooted above the camp.

Squirrelflight moved closer to Bramblestar. "Is she fit enough to sit vigil?"

"If she weren't, Leafpool wouldn't have let her come," Bramblestar whispered.

"What about the kits?" Squirrelflight glanced at the nursery. "She's hardly seen them."

"Let her mourn Larksong first." Bramblestar's eyes glistened as he gazed at his daughter. "She has moons to spend with her kits."

Lilyheart padded from between Honeyfur and Leafshade. She touched her nose to Larksong's shoulder. "Snowbush won't be lonely anymore." The small tabby lifted her head, her eyes clouded with grief. Honeyfur and Leafshade huddled beside her. Sparkpelt glanced at them, as though acknowledging their grief, then looked away.

Twigbranch padded from the shadows at the edge of the clearing. She stopped beside Lilyheart. "Larksong was lucky to have a mother like you," she mewed. "As a kit, I lost my own mother. I moved from one camp to another, lost and gained a sister and a father. Throughout it all, you were there for me, and Larksong was like a littermate." She dropped her gaze shyly. "I will miss him like a brother."

Lilyheart blinked gratefully at the young warrior as Twigbranch took her place beside Honeyfur and Leafshade.

Finleap hurried forward. "Larksong was a great mentor." He glanced around at his Clanmates. "It's not fair he died of sickness and not in battle. But I promise to become the best warrior I can be in honor of his memory." He backed away, pelt prickling self-consciously, and took his place again beside Plumstone and Eaglewing.

Bramblestar padded forward, stopping in a pool of moonlight. "ThunderClan has lost two brave warriors, for I know Larksong's kit would have followed in his father's paw steps. Larksong was always kind to his Clanmates and loyal to his Clan. May StarClan welcome him with open hearts. He can never be a father to his kits here, but his memory will live on in them and in the hearts of the cats he's left behind." Squirrelflight's heart flooded with grief as Bramblestar blinked affectionately at Sparkpelt. "We will miss him and the kit we never had the chance to know."

Squirrelflight fluffed her fur out against the wind. There was a chill in the air, and the heavy dew brought by the dawn hadn't yet lifted. She sat near the fresh-kill pile, eyeing the medicine den anxiously. Sparkpelt had returned there to sleep after her long night's vigil beside Larksong's body. She still hadn't been to the nursery to see her kits. As Squirrelflight wondered whether to wake her, the thorn tunnel shivered and Berrynose padded into camp. Plumstone, Mousewhisker, and Lionblaze trailed after him.

The patrol was clearly in the middle of a heated conversation. Mousewhisker stopped at the edge of the clearing, his gaze dark. "I'm just saying that all this trouble started when the Sisters showed up."

"It's a coincidence." Lionblaze sat down and began to

wash the mud from his paws.

"It's no coincidence that they're taking up land meant for SkyClan," Plumstone pointed out.

"And it's strange that a poisonous plant we've never heard of shows up in the forest at the same time as the Sisters." Berrynose lay down outside the warriors' den.

Squirrelflight glared at him. "The Sisters didn't cause the sickness. They're the ones who told us what it was, and how to cure it."

"They didn't tell us what this meadow saffron looks like. There are plenty of different plants with purple flowers," Berrynose answered. "How are we meant to find it and dig it up if we don't know what it looks like?"

"I didn't give them the chance to tell us." Squirrelflight felt like she was always defending the Sisters. "I wanted to get back so Leafpool could treat Larksong and Sparkpelt." She looked up at the Highledge, where Bramblestar was pulling apart a thrush. *Tell them to stop. This isn't the Sisters' fault.* Didn't they realize that the Sisters had probably saved Sparkpelt's life?

Bramblestar stopped eating when she caught his eye. He got to his paws and slithered down the rock tumble. Squirrelflight felt a prick of guilt. She shouldn't draw him into this. He looked tired. He'd sat vigil with Sparkpelt all night and been the first to help dig the hole where Larksong and his kit would be buried. He swiped his tongue around his mouth, wiping it clean. "It would be helpful to know what plants we need to dig up."

"I could visit them again and find out," Squirrelflight offered.

Berrynose grunted. "What you need to find out is when they're leaving."

"Why?" Squirrelflight flicked her tail irritably. "SkyClan hasn't even decided whether to move yet."

Mousewhisker sat down. "Perhaps Leafstar doesn't want to make a decision that might mean the Sisters have to move. She might be as fond of them as you are." He gazed accusingly at Squirrelflight.

"I'm not fond of them," she shot back. "I just happen to respect their way of life."

Bramblestar shifted his paws. "You used to respect *our* way of life," he grunted.

She looked at him, surprised. She'd thought they'd settled their differences. Was he still angry with her? "I still do!"

"Then why do you keep talking about the Sisters?" Bramblestar held her gaze.

"Mousewhisker and Berrynose started it!" Squirrelflight defended herself.

Berrynose sat up. "I just think it will be better when they're gone. As long as they're living on our border, Tigerstar will be bristling for a fight, Leafstar will be dithering over whether SkyClan should move, and you two will be bickering." His gaze flashed toward Bramblestar.

The ThunderClan leader's ears twitched. "Maybe it's a good idea to pay them a visit. They can tell us when they're planning to leave and what meadow saffron looks like. I want to organize a patrol to destroy any of those plants on our land."

"I'll go," Squirrelflight offered again. She didn't trust her Clanmates to treat the Sisters with the respect they deserved.

"Blossomfall and Cherryfall can go with you," Bramblestar meowed.

"I don't need a patrol," Squirrelflight objected.

"You'll be a long way from home," Bramblestar pointed out.

Squirrelflight shifted her paws. She wasn't going to let Berrynose accuse them of bickering again. "Okay," she agreed. "But I want to go now."

"Take Leafpool with you, too," Bramblestar ordered. "A medicine cat should learn all they can about this new plant."

Squirrelflight's heart lifted. It would be good to have Leafpool at her side. She headed toward the medicine den. "I'll see if she's ready."

"I'll let Blossomfall and Cherryfall know," Bramblestar told her.

Squirrelflight nosed her way into the medicine den. Sparkpelt was alone with Leafpool. The orange tabby sat in her nest, staring blankly at the den wall. "How are you?" Squirrelflight crossed the den and touched her nose gently to her daughter's head.

Sparkpelt ducked away distractedly, as if Squirrelflight had interrupted a thought.

"This grief will pass," Squirrelflight told her.

Sparkpelt lifted her empty gaze to meet her mother's. "I don't want it to pass." Her mew was hollow.

"But what about your kits?" Squirrelflight blinked at her, worry pricking through her fur. "You haven't even named them yet."

"I can't think about names." Sparkpelt turned her gaze

back to the wall. "It hurts too much."

Squirrelflight glanced anxiously at Leafpool. Her sister blinked back encouragingly, and Squirrelflight tried again to connect with her daughter. "Sorrelstripe is exhausted," she told Sparkpelt. "For her sake, you need to feed your kits. Besides, you're their mother. They need you."

"Do they?" Sparkpelt looked puzzled.

"Of course they do!"

"I guess I'd better feed them." Sparkpelt heaved herself to her paws. "Where are they?"

"In the nursery, of course." Squirrelflight swallowed back frustration. Sparkpelt was so caught up in misery, she barely seemed to know where she was. "Do you want me to come with you?"

"Why?" Sparkpelt stared at her. "You can't feed them."

Leafpool padded forward and nudged Sparkpelt toward the den entrance. "Go and feed them," she mewed matter-of-factly. "You can come back here afterward. Daisy can keep them warm."

Squirrelflight's heart ached as she watched Sparkpelt pad limply from the den. "Doesn't she care?" She turned her gaze on Leafpool.

"She's numb with grief," Leafpool told her. "It will pass. Feeding the kits might help."

"Might?" Squirrelflight stiffened.

"Larksong only just died," Leafpool reminded her gently. "Give Sparkpelt time."

Squirrelflight closed her eyes. *I must be patient.* She blinked them open and flicked her tail. "Can you come with me to visit the Sisters?"

"Of course." Leafpool tipped her head to one side. "Why?"

"Bramblestar wants to know what meadow saffron looks like, and I want to see if Moonlight's had her kits yet. She looked close to kitting last time we saw her."

"Are you wondering when they're going to move on?"

"It would be better if they could leave soon," Squirrelflight confessed. "Mousewhisker and Berrynose think the Sisters are responsible for the sickness and unrest. I'm worried that if all the Clans turn against them, they might be in danger."

Leafpool nodded. "Come on." She headed for the den entrance. "Let's go."

"Squirrelflight!" Tempest met the patrol at the top of the valley, lifting her tail as she caught sight of them. She hurried along the ridge to meet them. "How are your sick Clanmates?"

Squirrelflight dipped her head. "Larksong died."

Tempest's eyes widened. "Didn't the dandelion root work?"

"There wasn't time to give him any. He was too sick." Squirrelflight glanced over her shoulder at Blossomfall, Cherryfall, and Leafpool. Their fur was ruffled from the journey. A brisk, chilly wind was whisking over the valley.

"I'm sorry to hear that." Tempest blinked sympathetically at Squirrelflight. She began to head down toward the camp. "Come on. It's cold here."

"We managed to save another cat, though." Squirrelflight followed her along the winding trail, Leafpool, Cherryfall, and Blossomfall at her heels. "Actually, it was my daughter."

"I'm glad to hear it." Tempest pushed through the ferns at the camp entrance, the fronds brushing her long fur flat.

Squirrelflight followed her through. "How's Moonlight?"

"She's well." Tempest stopped on the grassy clearing.

Furze poked her head from a den. "Why did you come?"

"I need to know what meadow saffron looks like," Squirrelflight told the ginger cat. "Too many plants have purple flowers."

Moonlight's den rustled. "It's a tall purple flower." The gray she-cat squeezed out. She padded heavily across the grass, her belly so wide that she looked like a badger. Squirrelflight saw Leafpool frown. Was something wrong? She stiffened as Moonlight went on. "It's easy to spot. The leaves die back before the flower opens. It's quite strange, poking up from the forest floor without leaves. Like an owl without feathers."

Flurry padded from behind the dogwood, followed by Snow, sliding from between the bushes. They blinked at the ThunderClan patrol.

Snow narrowed her eyes. "You're back soon."

Blossomfall's pelt prickled. "We need to know when you plan to leave."

"Once the kits are ready." Moonlight looked at her belly. "They will come soon. We'll leave once they've opened their eyes."

Leafpool narrowed her eyes. "You've been expecting kits for a long time."

Moonlight looked back at her wearily. "It feels like moons since I first felt them move."

Squirrelflight shifted her paws. "Sparkpelt found out she

was expecting kits soon after we met you. She's had them now." *Surely you should have had yours.* But Sparkpelt's kits had come early.

Moonlight purred. "Congratulations. Are they well?"

Squirrelflight dropped her gaze. "The youngest died. A tom."

Moonlight's gaze darkened. "I'm sorry to hear that. Such a loss is never easy." She glanced at Snow. "We could perform a small ceremony for him."

Blossomfall bristled. "We've sat vigil," she mewed sharply. "That's ceremony enough."

Leafpool's ears pricked. "I'd be interested to see the Sisters' ceremony."

Blossomfall huffed. "Don't expect me to join in."

"We expect nothing of you but to witness it," Moonlight told her. "A spirit so young needs guiding. He won't understand what he's lost and who waits for him beyond death. We must help him find a place in the hearts of the living and the dead so that he can know both."

She beckoned Snow, Furze, and Creek nearer with a flick of her tail. Then she nodded to Tempest. "Do we have colts-foot?"

"I'll fetch some." Tempest slipped quickly into one of the dens and returned holding a small bunch of yellow flowers between her jaws. She carried them across the clearing and dropped them at Moonlight's paws.

As Squirrelflight leaned closer, curiosity prickling in her pelt, Cherryfall pricked her ears uneasily. "Will StarClan approve?"

Leafpool looked at her. "Why shouldn't they? The Sisters are honoring the dead." She turned her gaze back to Moonlight as the gray she-cat began to claw away a small patch of grass. Then she dug a small hole and dropped the flowers into it. Covering them up, she glanced at her campmates. They formed a circle around the hole, closed their eyes, and lifted their muzzles.

Squirrelflight held her breath as, silently, the Sisters held their faces to the sky. Then Moonlight murmured, "Safe journey, kit." Furze, Tempest, Snow, and Flurry echoed her mew. "Safe journey, kit." Together they repeated the words, chanting them softly, then raising their voices until their mews became wails and their wails broke into a fierce yowling. Their cry rang around the small valley, splitting the air.

Squirrelflight stared, her heart pounding. *What in StarClan are they doing?*

Blossomfall moved closer to Cherryfall. "What a lot of nonsense," she growled.

"Hush!" Leafpool flicked her tail impatiently at the tortoiseshell warrior. Her gaze was fixed on the Sisters as they fell suddenly silent. They stood unmoving for a few moments, then broke sharply from their circle, as though waking from a dream.

Squirrelflight searched Moonlight's gaze. The Sisters had claimed to see the dead. Had they seen Sparkpelt's kit?

Moonlight blinked softly. "We have encouraged your daughter's kit to walk with ThunderClan, both the living and the dead. His spirit can be nurtured and loved there."

"You saw him?"

Tempest nodded. "He had orange-and-black fur."

Squirrelflight felt a chill ripple through her pelt. She hadn't described the dead kit. Moonlight really must have seen him.

Snow frowned, looking puzzled. "A black tom was with him." She blinked at Squirrelflight. "Do you know who that was?"

"Larksong." Blossomfall shifted uneasily beside Squirrelflight.

"The kit's father," Squirrelflight told Moonlight. "He died at the same time."

Moonlight nodded. "I thought they were kin. He seemed very protective of the young spirit in his care."

Leafpool's pelt prickled. "Why did you yowl? Is it part of the ceremony?"

"It wards off dark spirits that might wish to harm the dead," Moonlight told her. "It's our warning that those we remember are protected for as long as we remember them."

"Thank you." Squirrelflight dipped her head gratefully to the Sisters. As she did, she made a silent promise to Larksong. *We will remember you both.* How strange the Sisters ceremony had seemed, but was it so different from a vigil? These cats honored the dead by remembering them, just as the Clans did. Was it possible that, in their own way, the Sisters had a link with StarClan?

CHAPTER 19

❧

Squirrelflight sat back on her haunches and watched as Leafpool dropped into a hunting crouch. A sparrow was rummaging through fallen leaves a few tail-lengths ahead, sunshine dappling its feathers. Leafpool's tail flicked excitedly.

Quick! Squirrelflight held her tongue. Would her sister know not to wait too long? She was a medicine cat, not a warrior. One breath of wind and the sparrow might take fright and flutter into the branches overhead.

Squirrelflight was still surprised that Leafpool had asked to join the hunting patrol. "I need to stretch my legs," Leafpool had told her, hurrying after them as Squirrelflight had headed out of camp with Twigbranch, Finleap, and Honeyfur. "I've been crouching in the medicine den sorting herbs for too long."

"I would think you'd rather go gathering herbs." Squirrelflight blinked at her.

Leafpool had flicked her tail. "I want *warm* fresh-kill," she insisted. "It's always cold by the time it reaches the pile."

Finleap whisked his tail happily. "We'll catch more prey with another pair of paws."

"I didn't know medicine cats hunted," Twigbranch mewed.

"Of course we hunt," Leafpool had snorted. "When we get time." She slid past the patrol and headed out of camp.

Twigbranch, Finleap, and Honeyfur had stopped nearby to investigate a mouse nest dug deep into the roots of an oak while Leafpool had led Squirrelflight to this dip in the forest floor. It was shady and alive with bugs. "Always hunt where prey looks for prey," Leafpool had mewed.

Squirrelflight had recognized the old hunting rule at once. "That's what Dustpelt used to tell me."

"I know." Leafpool purred fondly. "You used to come back to the apprentices' den after training and tell me everything you'd learned."

Squirrelflight tried to remember. It seemed such a long time ago. "Did you tell me all about herbs?"

"Of course." Leafpool's whiskers twitched. "But you usually fell asleep halfway through."

Squirrelflight felt a rush of guilt. "Did I?"

Leafpool purred again. "It's okay. I know how hard Dustpelt made you work." As she spoke, a sparrow flitted down from a tree. Leafpool lowered her voice. "I'm just glad you showed me some of the skills you learned."

Quick! Leafpool was still staring at the sparrow, her eyes slitted now. *Before it flies away.* Squirrelflight held her breath as Leafpool finally leaped. She was impressed by her sister's speed as Leafpool caught the sparrow before it could flutter up into the branches, then killed it with a bite.

"Well done!" Squirrelflight got to her paws, her mouth

watering at the juicy tang of blood. She padded to Leafpool's side and sniffed her sister's catch.

Leafpool sat back purring. "Should we eat it now?"

Squirrelflight scanned the clearing, listening for Twig-branch, Finleap, and Honeyfur. "We'd have to do it quickly before the others catch up with us." Wind rustled the branches overhead, and birds chattered in the sunshine. "Dustpelt would have put me on tick duty for a moon if he'd caught me eating prey before it reached the fresh-kill pile."

"I'm a medicine cat," Leafpool purred. "I don't have to follow *every* warrior rule. And it's my catch."

Squirrelflight shot her a look. Her sister was tempting her. "Okay," she purred, feeling suddenly as playful as a kit. "But I'm a warrior, so I'll have to catch something for the Clan before we go back."

"If that's what it takes." Leafpool tore the sparrow in two and pushed one half toward Squirrelflight.

Squirrelflight hooked it and took a mouthful. She closed her eyes, the warm blood delighting her. The flesh was soft and sweet. She swallowed it happily.

"Have you visited Sparkpelt today?" Leafpool asked.

Squirrelflight paused, forgetting suddenly the sweetness of the sparrow. "I saw her this morning."

"I'm glad." Leafpool was chewing. "She needs company. Daisy is with her, and a few other cats have visited. Storm-cloud stopped by this morning. But she needs to feel part of the Clan as much as possible."

Squirrelflight's belly tightened as she remembered

Sparkpelt lying in her nest, staring blankly as her kits played with Daisy. "She doesn't seem to be getting better."

"It'll take a while for her to get over Larksong's death." Leafpool swiped her tongue around her lips.

"But she's missing out on motherhood," Squirrelflight fretted.

"There's no rush." Leafpool took another mouthful. "Flamekit and Finchkit will be kits for a while yet. And she's tough." Leafpool crunched through a bone. "Like her mother."

Squirrelflight picked at the sparrow distractedly. *Am I tough?* She didn't feel it right now.

They ate in silence until there was nothing left but feathers; then Leafpool rolled onto her side. "Have you talked to Bramblestar yet?"

Squirrelflight sat up and began to wash. She knew what Leafpool was getting at. If she wanted to heal the rift between her and Bramblestar, she'd have to talk to him. "It's not easy."

"Why not?" Leafstar stretched. "He's your mate."

"What if I ask him about kits and he still doesn't want them as much as I do?" Squirrelflight gazed distractedly between the trees. "Or I ask him about the Sisters and he says they have to leave? I know he's still angry that I went off and found them in the first place. I'm sure he thinks it's my fault the Clans are fighting."

Leafpool huffed. "The Clans are always fighting."

"I guess." Squirrelflight felt suddenly weary. "But this time Bramblestar blames me."

"Are you sure?" Leafpool glanced at her.

Squirrelflight twitched her tail. "I'm not sure of anything right now."

"Why don't you ask him?"

"It might make things worse."

Leafpool sat up. "Will they get better if you keep quiet?"

"Maybe." Squirrelflight was beginning to think silence was the only way things might get better. "We only spend time together when we're playing with Flamekit and Finch-kit." Pleasure fluttered faintly in her chest as she pictured Bramblestar giving them badger rides around the nursery. "I think Bramblestar loves them even more than I do."

Leafpool eyed her steadily. "Do you still want more kits with him?"

"Of course I do." Squirrelflight felt the familiar twinge of longing in her heart. "But I can't see that happening now. We barely talk."

As she spoke, paw steps thrummed at the top of the rise. Twigbranch, Finleap, and Honeyfur charged down the slope carrying prey. They scrambled to a halt and dropped their catch beside Squirrelflight.

"Leafpool caught a sparrow," she told them proudly.

Finleap eyed the pile of feathers, his gaze sparking with amusement. "Was it tasty?"

"Very." Leafpool purred. She glanced at Squirrelflight. "We should catch another for the Clan."

Honeyfur nodded toward the sunny glade ahead. "There'll be plenty over there."

"Let's catch as many as we can," Twigbranch mewed. "The

Clan will want a big meal before tonight's Gathering."

As the young warriors hurried away, Squirrelflight got to her paws. "I'm not looking forward to this Gathering," she confided to Leafpool.

"It will be tense," Leafpool agreed. They headed after their Clanmates. "Do you think ShadowClan and RiverClan have come to an agreement about their border?"

"I hope so." Squirrelflight ducked beneath a branch. "Otherwise, Tigerstar might insist on pushing the Sisters off their land."

"Perhaps the Sisters have left by now," Leafpool mewed hopefully.

"I doubt it." Squirrelflight's pelt prickled nervously. Moonlight must have kitted by now, but the kits wouldn't be ready to travel for a while.

Ahead, Honeyfur stopped beside an oak and scraped her fur against the rough bark. Squirrelflight padded past her and gazed into the sunny glade. Twigbranch and Finleap were already charging through the ragged blueberrybushes. What if the Sisters *had* moved on? Everything would be solved. SkyClan could move onto their land, and the Clans would have no reason to fight. She and Bramblestar could forget their differences, and life could go back to how it was.

Her paws felt suddenly heavy. Nothing was ever that simple.

Night folded itself around the lake, swathing the valley in darkness. After the long walk from camp, Squirrelflight sensed tension as soon as she slid from the long grass. Shadow-Clan, WindClan, and RiverClan hung back at the edges of the island clearing, their gazes glittering with hostility as they eyed one another. Scorchfur tugged Flaxpaw back by his scruff as the ShadowClan apprentice began to head toward RiverClan. "Not tonight," he growled.

"I was only going to talk to the other apprentices." Flaxpaw looked at his mentor hopefully.

"You might as well talk to foxes," Scorchfur hissed.

Lightpaw, Pouncepaw, and Shadowpaw stood close to Dovewing while Tigerstar wove around them protectively. Only SkyClan seemed relaxed. They watched the other Clans, tipping their heads as though puzzled by the unfriendliness. Leafstar hurried to meet Bramblestar as soon as he crossed the clearing.

"What's wrong with every cat?" The SkyClan leader blinked at him. "I didn't realize things had gotten worse. Stonewing lashed out at Mallownose before you arrived." She glanced nervously at the star-specked sky, where wisps of clouds trailed above the forest. If the truce was broken, clouds would hide the moon and the Clans would have to go home, their grievances unresolved.

Bramblestar glanced around at the gathered cats, his pelt prickling along his spine. "There's more tension over the borders," he told the SkyClan leader. "But that doesn't mean you must make a decision before you're ready."

Leafstar caught Squirrelflight's eye. "Have you heard from Moonlight? Has she had her kits?"

"She must have," Squirrelflight told her. "But newborn kits won't be ready to travel for a while."

Bramblestar flicked his tail impatiently. "I wish she'd hurry up before we're all at war," he growled. He padded toward the Great Oak and leaped onto the lowest branch.

Leafstar dipped her head. "I'd better go too." Anxiety glittered in her gaze as she turned away and leaped up beside Bramblestar.

Tigerstar, Harestar, and Mistystar followed, eyeing one another accusingly as they took their places in the oak.

Squirrelflight hesitated as the Clans streamed around her. Crowfeather, Reedwhisker, and Cloverfoot jostled for position as they climbed onto the roots of the oak and sat, stiffly ignoring one another as Squirrelflight finally joined them. Only Hawkwing acknowledged her with a polite nod.

As the crowd settled in front of her, pelts shifting in the moonlight, Tigerstar stepped forward. "ThunderClan has given WindClan its land back. RiverClan wants to move our border, and ShadowClan cannot accept that. The only way to avoid war now is to drive the Sisters from their camp."

Scorchfur whisked his tail eagerly. "That's right. Why fight one another when *they've* got our land?"

Dread wormed beneath Squirrelflight's pelt as yowls of agreement rose among the Clans.

"We must wait!" Bramblestar's growl silenced them. He eyed Tigerstar sharply. "Has StarClan sent word yet? Did any medicine cat get an answer from them at their half-moon meeting?"

"Not yet," Tigerstar snorted. "But silence could mean anything. You're just playing for time. Why are you so loyal to these rogues?"

Bramblestar bristled. "I'm not loyal to them."

"Then why are you determined to defend them?"

Bramblestar narrowed his eyes. "I don't think we should take the Sisters' land until SkyClan has agreed to move there."

"SkyClan would be mouse-brained to turn down that land." Tigerstar lashed his tail. "It's good land, and we won't let them stay on our territory forever."

"You *gave* them that territory!" Bramblestar glared at the ShadowClan leader.

Tigerstar curled his lip. "And we can take it back, just like WindClan took *its* territory back."

"I gave it to them," Bramblestar retorted. "I was trying to keep the peace,"

Tigerstar rounded his eyes innocently. "That's all I want," he meowed. "To keep the peace."

"By starting a war against the Sisters?" Bramblestar stared at him indignantly.

Squirrelflight realized she was holding her breath. Bramblestar was defending the Sisters. Hope flashed beneath her pelt.

Tigerstar's tail flicked ominously. "I will fight the Sisters if it means peace among the Clans. Isn't that what StarClan wants?"

Bramblestar held his ground. "You're trying to force SkyClan to move again! Look what happened last time you drove them out. A storm nearly killed us all."

"This time SkyClan *wants* to move!" The ShadowClan leader swung his muzzle toward Leafstar. "You want SkyClan to have the new territory, right?"

Leafstar hesitated.

"Right?" Tigerstar glared at her.

"I don't want the land if it means hurting the Sisters," Leafstar told him, her gaze clouding with uncertainty.

A snarl rang from the back of the clearing as Emberfoot jeered at the SkyClan leader. "You'd rather see war in the Clans than chase a few rogues from land they don't even want?"

Yowls of agreement exploded around him and rippled through the crowd.

Squirrelflight froze. She pictured the Sisters going about their duties, unaware of the storm building here, ready to sweep them away. Her paws pricked with fear.

Leafstar stared desperately at Tigerstar. "Why can't we wait until the Sisters leave?"

Harestar flattened his ears. "Why should we?"

"The Sisters don't need that land!" Mistystar snapped.

Tigerstar held Leafstar's gaze. "Is SkyClan willing to move?"

"Not yet," Leafstar answered shakily.

"But would you move once the Sisters are gone?" Tigerstar pressed.

Leafstar stared at him, then nodded. "Yes."

Tigerstar rounded on Bramblestar. "SkyClan has made its decision. They want to move. Now ThunderClan must support us. The Sisters have to leave."

Squirrelflight's heart pressed in her throat as Bramblestar hesitated. *Why don't you object?* She lifted her muzzle. "None of us want—"

"Silence!" Bramblestar cut her off with a look. It glittered with rage. "My deputy does not speak for me." As he dragged his gaze back to Tigerstar, Squirrelflight felt numb. She stared at him. Was Bramblestar going to declare war on the Sisters? Five Clans against a small band of she-cats, and possibly a squealing litter of newborn kits. Shame washed Squirrelflight's pelt. Was there no honor left in the Clans?

Bramblestar squared his shoulders. "ThunderClan won't join a war," he growled.

Tigerstar's gaze flashed. "But you won't stop us?"

Bramblestar looked away. "No." Squirrelflight stared at him, unable to believe her ears as he went on. "I don't care what happens to the Sisters. They've made it clear that they're no better than rogues. But Leafstar must be heard. Her opinion must be respected."

"She's been heard." Harestar flattened his ears. "She wants their land."

"Only after they've left." Bramblestar lashed his tail. "And she doesn't want them hurt."

Leafstar stepped to the edge of the branch. "Perhaps the Sisters can be reasoned with," she mewed hesitatingly.

"Why?" Mistystar looked unconvinced. "Reason hasn't worked so far."

Leafstar aimed a meaningful glance at Tree. "Perhaps it's

time for them to hear from their own kin."

Tree groaned, looking suddenly put on the spot. "I've told you, it won't—"

"I know you think it won't help," Leafstar interrupted. "But if it could prevent a war—if it were the difference between life and death for Moonlight and her kits—surely you would consider it?"

"I—" Tree began to speak, then stopped himself. He looked around the Gathering, then began again. "I do want peace."

"Of course you do, Tree," Bramblestar said smoothly. "So do what you can. Talk to your mother on our behalf."

Tree looked down at his paws. He shuffled them uncomfortably, then closed his eyes. "All right. I still don't have high hopes, but I'll try, if you want me to." Tigerstar shrugged. "I guess it's worth an attempt."

Harestar nodded. "Why fight if we don't have to?"

Murmurs of approval rippled through the crowd as Tigerstar whisked his tail.

"It's decided," the ShadowClan leader growled. "Tree will talk to the Sisters."

Below him, Breezepelt rolled his eyes. "Why send a loner to do a warrior's job?"

Hawkwing bristled beside Squirrelflight. "Tree is no loner!" he snarled, eyeing Breezepelt. "He's a loyal Clan cat now."

Across the clearing, Violetshine's gaze glowed with affection at her father, and her Clanmates shifted around her, scowling at the WindClan tom.

"Hawkwing's right." Leafstar lifted her chin. "Tree is as much a warrior as any SkyClan cat. And if he goes to the Sisters, I'll go with him."

Tigerstar looked at her surprised. "Why?"

"I know them." Leafstar glanced at Squirrelflight. "So does Squirrelflight. We can both go with him. We might be able to help."

Tigerstar's ears twitched. "If that's what you want." He eyed Tree menacingly. "You'd better find a solution," he growled. "Or the next patrol we send to the Sisters won't be so friendly."

Squirrelflight caught Bramblestar's eye. He looked at her, his gaze unreadable. Was she supposed to say she wouldn't go? He'd silenced her just now. He clearly didn't want her to be involved. As Tigerstar and the other leaders jumped down from the branch, signaling the end to the meeting, Bramblestar didn't move.

"Are you coming?" Hawkwing hopped off the root and looked back at her as the crowd began to disperse.

"I'll wait for Bramblestar." Squirrelflight watched the Clans head for the long grass. She shifted her paws nervously as the clearing emptied, then looked up at Bramblestar again. He stared past her, then leaped from the tree. Thorns pierced her heart as he shook out his pelt and stalked across the clearing without her. She watched him go, feeling desolate. Had they grown so far apart that they'd never agree on anything again?

CHAPTER 20

"You go ahead." Tree swished his tail as they headed out of Clan
territory onto the Sisters' land. It was the morning after the
Gathering, and the sun was glittering through the trees. "I
want to practice my speech." He hung back and let Squirrelflight and Leafstar take the lead.

"He has a speech?" Squirrelflight was surprised that any
cat would have to practice to speak with his mother. She
understood that the relationship between Tree and Moonlight was strained, but it surprised her that it was *this* strained.
She blinked at Leafstar as they followed the steep path out of
the forest. She glanced over her shoulder. Tree was murmuring softly to himself.

"He and Hawkwing went over what he was going to say
to Moonlight before we left." Leafstar slid under a drooping
willow branch.

Squirrelflight ducked under another branch. "I don't know
why Tree needed to come, if he doesn't want to see his mother
again. We could have passed on the Clans' message without
him."

"He does have a talent for slicing open a problem so it can

be looked at easily. It's why I made him our mediator. Besides, I don't think the Clans would let us come without him." Leafstar gazed ahead. "Tigerstar's already frustrated that we've stopped him from taking this land before now. He wouldn't want me and you in charge of the negotiation."

"But it's not a negotiation, is it?" Frustration clawed at Squirrelflight's belly. "It's a threat. If the Sisters don't leave, the Clans will drive them away by force."

"I know." Leafstar flicked her tail as the land flattened beneath her paws. She headed between the thinning trees. "But we might be able to give the Sisters enough time to prepare for the journey and to leave with a little dignity. And besides, Tree *is* Moonlight's son."

Squirrelflight nodded. "If she won't listen to us, she might listen to him."

"That's what I'm hoping." Leafstar stopped as they broke from the forest and mountain territory opened ahead of them.

Paw steps brushed the ground behind them as Tree caught up.

"I think I've got it," he meowed. "I know exactly what I'm going to say."

"Do you think she'll agree?" Squirrelflight glanced at him anxiously.

"If she were reasonable, she'd agree." Tree gazed over the rolling landscape. "But we're talking about my mother."

Unease wormed beneath Squirrelflight's pelt. Moonlight had seemed reasonable to her. She could be peaceful and kind. But there was also a stubborn streak running through her fur.

Persuading her to leave the mountain territory might be like asking a badger to leave its set.

They reached the camp at sunhigh. Sunshine bathed the valley. The bushes crowding the Sisters' camp looked blowsy and tattered. As Squirrelflight led Tree and Leafstar down the winding path to the entrance, guilt pricked at her belly. How could she stand by as a queen and her tiny kits were forced from their home? She pushed the thought away. Perhaps the kits were strong and healthy, and the Sisters were already preparing to leave.

"Squirrelflight?" Snow's mew took her by surprise. As the white she-cat slid from the ferns at the camp entrance, suspicion glittered in her gaze. "What are you doing here?"

"Has Moonlight had her kits?" Squirrelflight asked eagerly.

Snow narrowed her eyes. "No."

Disappointment dropped like a stone in Squirrelflight's belly. It should be past time. "We have to speak with her."

Stiffening, Snow looked past them to Tree. "Why?"

Leafstar padded closer. "It's important."

"Moonlight's close to kitting," Snow told them, her gaze still on Tree. "She's moved to the birthing den."

"But we can still see her, right?" Leafstar shifted her paws impatiently.

Snow bristled. "Do you expect me to let a grown tom into our camp?" She glared at Tree.

Squirrelflight blinked at her. "But Tree is your kin, isn't he?"

"The Sisters don't believe in kin," Tree snapped. "Not *male* kin, anyway."

"Hold your tongue," Leafstar snapped. "You're meant to be our negotiator."

"Sorry." Tree met Snow's gaze stiffly. "I've come from the Clans. I must speak with Moonlight. She will want to hear my message."

Snow hesitated, her ears twitching. Then she headed through the ferns. "Follow me."

Squirrelflight pushed her way through, blinking as she saw the grassy clearing; Sparrow, Sunrise, and Hawk were sharing a thrush. Tempest and Furze lay in a patch of sunshine.

Creek, resting beside Flurry, bristled in surprise as he saw Tree and scrambled to his paws. "Why is a tom here?"

"You're a tom, aren't you?" Tree stared back at him.

"But you're too old to be here." Creek shifted nervously.

"You'll be old one day," Tree grunted.

As Snow slid into the birthing den, Squirrelflight glanced apologetically at the Sisters. "I'm sorry to disturb you again, but we have to talk to Moonlight."

Sunrise blinked at her, chewing, no sign of her injury.

Tempest lifted her head. "Do you want some prey?" She flicked her tail toward a pile of fresh-kill at the edge of the clearing. "We caught plenty."

"No thanks." Guilt prickled through Squirrelflight's fur. The Sisters were so kind. Couldn't they guess why she was here? "We just want to speak to Moonlight."

Hawk blinked at Leafstar. "How's your injured leg?" she asked.

"Healed." As Leafstar turned to show her where the fur had grown back, Snow ducked out of the birthing den.

"She'll see you," she told them. Her gaze glittered sharply as it flitted over Tree. "Even you." Her nose wrinkled.

"Thank you." Squirrelflight's heart quickened as she ducked into the den. Leafstar and Tree padded after her.

The nursery was warm and well padded with bracken and moss. Cocooned from the sunshine, it glowed with a rosy half-light. Moonlight lay on a nest of fresh ferns, her broad head dwarfed by the size of her belly.

Squirrelflight stared at it. "Your kits must be overdue."

"Perhaps." Moonlight's gaze flitted from Squirrelflight to Leafstar. "It's good to see you again, Leafstar." She ignored Tree. "Snow says you've brought a grown tom into our camp."

"He's been sent by the Clans, to speak for them," Squirrelflight told her.

Moonlight's gaze rounded. "Don't they think your voices are enough?"

Leafstar's tail twitched. "They wanted someone impartial."

"So they sent my son." Amusement glinted in her eyes.

Squirrelflight's chest tightened. Was Moonlight going to take this seriously? "Please listen to Tree. He's your best chance for peace."

Moonlight flicked her gaze to Tree for the first time. "It's good to see you again, Earth."

"I told you," he meowed firmly. "I'm not Earth anymore. I'm Tree."

"Of course." She dipped her head politely. "And you've come with a message from the Clans."

"Not a message," he told her. "I've come to persuade you to leave this territory."

She held his gaze coolly. "Really." She sounded unimpressed.

"You already know that SkyClan wants this land," he began. "The land around the lake is not big enough to support five Clans. It was decided that SkyClan should move here. But they can't while you're here."

"I've told Leafstar already that she can have the land when we move on," Moonlight told him.

"You need to move on *now*. The Clans are already fighting over land. Every moment you stay here puts another warrior at risk." Tree stared at her urgently. "For the sake of the Clans, you have to go."

Moonlight tipped her head. "I thought the Clans *enjoyed* fighting. They attacked us for no good reason. They nearly killed Sunrise."

"You were trespassing," Tree reminded her. "And you maimed one of their warriors."

"If they'd simply asked us to leave, no one would have been hurt."

Tree's fur ruffled along his spine. "That's what they're doing now," he meowed. "Asking you to leave so that no one gets hurt."

Moonlight narrowed her eyes. "Is that a threat?"

Squirrelflight's heart quickened. Moonlight was being difficult. She shot Tree a warning glance.

He dipped his head. "I came here to reason with you, not to threaten."

"Then reason with me." Moonlight's gaze suddenly hardened. "Don't quote words given to you by someone else. You're my son. I hope I taught you to have a mind of your own."

"I *was* your son," Tree answered. "I speak for the Clans now."

"The Clans!" Moonlight snorted. "Do you think like a Clan cat too? Dividing land out like prey to be given to others." She scowled at him. "Have you forgotten that as a tom, you are protector of the land? You should wander it, not own it!"

"You've never believed in borders!" Tree snapped back. "You've never believed in home. But some cats *want* to belong. They want a home that will *always* be a home."

Squirrelflight stepped forward. "I realize this is an emotional time," she meowed evenly. "Perhaps it wasn't the best idea to ask your son to reason with you. But he's not trying to threaten you. And if his words are someone else's, it's because he's trying so hard not to. But the truth is, if you don't move, you will face a battle with more cats than you have ever seen, every one of them trained in fighting."

Leafstar shifted beside her. "You say you want to have your kits here, but they would be in danger here."

Moonlight glared at her. "Is the land really worth that much to the Clans? Would they harm kits to get their paws on it?"

A chill ran along Squirrelflight's spine.

Tree lashed his tail. "Why argue?" he growled. "You're outnumbered. There's no way you can defend this valley. You certainly couldn't defend the hunting land around it. Why don't you just accept that you have to leave?"

Moonlight lifted her chin. "The Sisters will not be bullied.

We will not move. If the Clans wish to attack us, we will defend ourselves."

Squirrelflight could hardly believe her ears. Was Moonlight crazy? ThunderClan would not hurt a queen and her kits, but ShadowClan might, or even WindClan. A battle could easily rage out of control. She stared urgently at Moonlight. "Please leave," she whispered. "Don't risk your kits' lives." *And bring shame on the Clans.* If the Sisters didn't leave, the Clans might prove her worst fear—that they were capable of self-interest so ruthless, it wouldn't matter which cats stood in their way.

Moonlight returned her gaze unwaveringly. "I've told you. We will not move."

Tree flattened his ears. "You always put your beliefs before the needs of your kits." Curling his lip, he pushed his way out of the den.

Tail drooping, Leafstar followed. Squirrelflight glanced at them as they left. Perhaps it hadn't been such a good idea to ask Tree to mediate with his mother. She turned her gaze on Moonlight. The queen stared back at her coldly. "Please," Squirrelflight mewed. They'd shared a camp, if only for a short while. They'd helped build this den together. She'd stood up for Sunrise when her Clanmates had wanted to send her away. They had a connection. Surely there was something she could say now to make Moonlight change her mind?

Moonlight stared at her, unblinking. "Leave."

Dread settled in Squirrelflight's belly. Trembling, she nosed her way outside. They'd failed. The Sisters were staying and the Clans would attack. Her thoughts whirled. Preying on the vulnerable was not part of the warrior code. If ThunderClan attacked the Sisters, could she fight alongside her Clanmates? She wanted to prove her loyalty to ThunderClan, but could she risk hurting an expectant queen?

CHAPTER 21

Around the island, the lake had turned to flame, lit by the setting sun. Squirrelflight and Bramblestar had come as soon as Squirrelflight had returned from the Sisters, sending Berrynose to fetch Harestar, while Leafstar had sent word to Tigerstar and Mistystar. Now the leaders from every Clan moved restlessly on the shore of the island, anger sparking between them as Leafstar and Squirrelflight reported Moonlight's reply.

"They won't move?" Outrage sparked in Tigerstar's eyes.

Mistystar's pelt prickled indignantly. "This is an insult. Don't they know who they're dealing with?"

"We could destroy them in a single battle!" Harestar flexed his claws.

Squirrelflight swallowed back desperation. She could still save the Sisters. She didn't care whether Bramblestar wanted her to keep quiet. The Clans mustn't attack them. "But why *should* they move? Moonlight is expecting kits!"

"*Why should they move?*" Tigerstar repeated Squirrelflight's question as though he couldn't believe his ears.

Squirrelflight stared at him. "If we just leave them alone, they'll be gone in a moon."

Harestar flicked his tail. "I don't think they'll ever move," he snarled. "They know we want that land, and they're determined to keep it for themselves."

Mistystar nodded. "This is a matter of honor. How dare these rogues defy us!"

Bramblestar shifted his paws. "I'm not sure honor has much to do with it," he meowed evenly. "But it does seem that we are going to have to chase these cats away sooner or later."

"And it might as well be sooner," Harestar snapped.

"We should have done it already," Tigerstar grunted.

"They're clearly determined to hang on to this land for as long as they can." Bramblestar glanced at Squirrelflight.

She blinked at him. "Moonlight only wants to wait until she's had her kits. Is that so unreasonable?"

"It *is* when the peace of the Clans is at stake," Bramblestar answered.

Anger burned beneath Squirrelflight's pelt. "There's no need for the Clans to fight one another!"

Tigerstar growled. "Not every Clan is willing to give their land away as easily as ThunderClan." His gaze moved pointedly from Bramblestar to Harestar. "We want to keep our borders until SkyClan has moved."

"We want our marshland back!" Mistystar snapped.

Bramblestar met Squirrelflight's gaze. "Do you see? There can be no peace until the border disputes are settled once and for all. We have to make the Sisters leave."

"And they're clearly not going to leave until we drive them away," Harestar growled.

"Even if it harms unborn kits?" Squirrelflight dug her claws into the earth. How could she be the only cat here who didn't see how unfair the Clans were being?

"A cat can have kits anywhere," Mistystar pointed out. "Especially a rogue."

"The Sisters aren't rogues!" Squirrelflight looked helplessly at Leafstar. Why hadn't she spoken up?

Leafstar eyes glittered in the dying sunlight. Was that an apology in her gaze? "I think Moonlight *is* being unreasonable. She could move if she wanted to. She must know that she's putting her kits in danger, and yet she insists on staying."

Squirrelflight stared at her. Leafstar had been her only ally, and now she was siding with the others. Her heart lurched. "Do *you* think we should drive them out too?"

"Not drive them out, exactly," Leafstar murmured. "But if the Clans sent a patrol big enough to show Moonlight what the Sisters are up against, she might change her mind."

"That's right!" Tigerstar's eyes lit up. "If we show up in force, Moonlight will see that it's pointless trying to stand against us."

"We wouldn't have to unsheathe a claw," Harestar agreed.

Bramblestar looked at Squirrelflight. "You must agree that's reasonable," he meowed. "No one would be harmed, and SkyClan would get their land now."

Squirrelflight's paws pricked with anger. "You don't know Moonlight," she shot back. "If you show up in her camp, she won't just back down. She's more likely to fight."

"Even if she's outnumbered?" Mistystar blinked at her.

"Especially if she's outnumbered," Squirrelflight insisted.

Tigerstar narrowed his eyes. "If she wants to fight, then we'd fight. But it would be Moonlight's choice."

Squirrelflight looked helplessly at Bramblestar. "You can't let this happen," she breathed. "Sending a patrol to scare the Sisters away is the same thing as attacking them."

Bramblestar stared back at her, his gaze determined. "Trying to guess how Moonlight will react is not my problem. I have to do what's best for the Clans."

"Then it's settled?" Harestar looked at him hopefully.

"I'll bring a patrol," Bramblestar told him.

"We should leave at dawn," Tigerstar meowed. "Each Clan should bring its strongest warriors."

"Where do we meet?" Mistystar asked.

"You can meet on our territory," Leafstar offered. "Where our border meets ThunderClan's. You can cross into the mountain territory easily there." She glanced nervously at Tigerstar. "But SkyClan won't be sending a patrol."

"It was your suggestion!" Harestar blinked at the SkyClan leader.

Leafstar ignored him and pressed on. "We won't risk a war on unborn kits. But if you want to chase the Sisters out, we won't stand in your way."

Squirrelflight's heart felt as heavy as stone. Tomorrow, the Clans would force the Sisters from their home. It didn't matter whether the Clans planned to attack first or not. The Sisters might not mean any harm, but she knew how stubborn Moonlight could be. This confrontation would escalate into violence, and she was powerless to stop it.

Bramblestar dipped his head to the other leaders. "I'll see you all at dawn." He turned and padded away without looking at Squirrelflight. She stared after him. Was he ashamed? Or was he angry with her? Surprise jabbed at her belly. *Does he even still care what I think of him?*

"You'd better hurry." Mistystar eyed her pointedly. "It looks like he's not going to wait for you.

Heat burned beneath Squirrelflight's pelt. "I can find my own way home," she snapped. As she turned away, Harestar sniffed.

"It's good to see Bramblestar taking charge of his Clan at last," the WindClan leader murmured.

Squirrelflight jerked her muzzle toward him. "In Thunder-Clan, we're allowed to have our own opinions," she snarled, lashing her tail as she walked away.

She didn't try to catch up with Bramblestar, but crossed the tree-bridge and trailed him along the shore. He didn't wait for her, and she could see by the set of his shoulders, his head hanging low, that he wanted to be left alone. *In ThunderClan, we're allowed to have our own opinions.* Was that true anymore? He'd been angry ever since she'd suggested Sky-Clan move to new territory at the leaders' meeting. Why? ThunderClan used to be a Clan where everyone's ideas were given a hearing. Had her longing for more kits put him on edge? Clearly she'd been pressuring him, without knowing it, into doing something he didn't want to do. Her heart ached. They used to want the same things. Now they seemed to think and feel differently about everything.

When she padded into camp, Bramblestar was already organizing the patrol that would go with him in the morning to the Sisters' camp. In moonlight pooling at the center of the clearing, he looked around at the warriors crowding excitedly in front of him.

"Thornclaw, you'll come with me," Bramblestar told the dark warrior.

"Can I come?" Blossomfall pushed her way to the front.

"Me too." Mousewhisker whisked his tail.

Twigbranch hung back with Finleap and glanced hopefully at Squirrelflight as she passed, as if hoping she would keep the other cats from forcing the Sisters out.

Squirrelflight looked away. There was nothing she could do to stop this. She slunk into the shadow of the Highledge, huddling away from the rest of her Clan. She didn't want to hear their eager voices. How could so many of her Clanmates approve of this plan? Would they be acting like this if she were leader? She hunched tighter, crouching against the earth. What was the point in wondering? She'd never be leader, just like she'd never go along with this fox-hearted plan.

The shadows deepened as evening gave way to night. Squirrelflight fluffed her fur against the chill.

"What about you?"

Bramblestar's question took her by surprise.

She looked up. He stood over her, his gaze dark. Behind him the clearing was empty. "What do you mean?" She sat up.

"Can I count on your support tomorrow?" There was hostility in his mew. "You are my deputy, after all."

"And your mate." Her pelt pricked uneasily. What did he expect her to say? "But that doesn't mean I have to support you in everything. I can't support you when I don't agree with you."

"You're my deputy. I expect you to support me no matter what," he snapped. "How can the Clan trust my decisions when you constantly challenge me?"

"You're their leader. They'll support you," she mewed. "No matter how wrong you are."

Bramblestar bristled. "So you doubt your Clan too?"

"That's not what I said."

"It's what you meant."

"You haven't understood what I've meant for a moon!" Squirrelflight flattened her ears. "If you did, we wouldn't be arguing now, and you wouldn't be leading a battle patrol against an expectant queen!"

"Is that all that matters to you?" Bramblestar's eyes blazed with frustration. "Some rogue and her kits? There's more to life than kits!"

"And there's more to life than fighting!"

"Of course there is!" Bramblestar held her gaze. "Do you think I don't know that?"

"You're acting as if borders and battles are the only thing you care about," Squirrelflight spat.

"And you're acting like the Sisters are the only *cats* you care about!" Hurt edged his mew.

"You think I don't care about ThunderClan?" Thorns seemed to pierce Squirrelflight's heart. "Of course I care! I care about them, and I care about *you*! More than anything!

But you don't seem to respect me anymore—not as your mate, not as your deputy—and I don't know why."

"Of course I respect you." Bramblestar's mew softened. "But you don't seem to agree with anything I say or do. I have a Clan to lead. How can I lead them when the cat I care most about thinks I'm doing everything wrong?"

Squirrelflight gazed at him through the darkness. "Do you really believe you're doing the right thing by attacking the Sisters?"

"I'm not attacking them! I'm just making sure they leave."

"But you must know there'll be a battle if you show up."

Bramblestar's eyes flashed. "I don't know anything of the kind, and I'm not responsible for how Moonlight might react. I know that you're worried, but I'm not going there to fight. I don't want the Sisters to be hurt. I will do everything in my power to make sure we move her without bloodshed." He looked suddenly helpless. "I promise I'm only trying to do what's best, Squirrelflight. I can't let the Clans fight among themselves. StarClan has told us there must be peace. This is the only way we can ensure that peace."

Pity swelled in Squirrelflight's chest. She suddenly saw how torn he must feel. SkyClan's arrival beside the lake had sent shock waves through the Clans that they were still struggling to cope with. She understood why Bramblestar wanted to protect the Clans' fragile harmony. But if everyone could just take a breath and *wait*, she felt sure that a battle with Moonlight and the Sisters could be avoided. "Don't you see that I can't agree with you?" she murmured. "The Clans are threatening unborn kits because they can't wait one moon for extra land. It's greedy and heartless."

"But more land for each Clan will mean a lasting peace." Bramblestar stared at her desperately. "Don't you see that?"

"Is peace in the Clans so important?" There hadn't been peace among the Clans while she was growing up, and the sky hadn't fallen in.

"I have to obey the wishes of StarClan." His eyes glimmered with doubt. "I'm a Clan leader. StarClan trusted me enough to give me nine lives. I can't betray them."

Squirrelflight's heart ached. Bramblestar sounded wretched. He needed her. She lowered her mew to a whisper. "Even if I don't agree with what you're doing, I love you."

"You do?" Hope glimmered in his eyes.

"Of course I do."

Pelt smoothing, Bramblestar leaned forward and pressed his muzzle to her cheek. "I love you too."

Peace washed Squirrelflight's pelt for the first time in a moon. She felt the warmth of Bramblestar's check and breathed in his scent. He smelled of the forest and the night, dew catching in his fur. "I wish you weren't taking a patrol to the Sisters' camp. I wish this could be settled another way. But if this is what you feel you must do, my loyalty will lie with you and with ThunderClan."

He leaned against her, a soft purr trembling in his throat. "Thank you."

"Come on." She began to lead him toward the rock tumble. "Let's get some sleep. We've got a long journey to make in the morning."

* * *

That night, Squirrelflight dreamed a terrible dream. Battle raged around her. Cats shrieked on every side, writhing as they fought. As she strained to see through blinding sunshine, paws slammed into her shoulder. She hit the ground with a thump and glanced desperately around, scanning the confusion for a face she recognized. Fear-scents bathed her muzzle. Who were these cats? Her paws felt as heavy as stone, the earth dragging at her pelt like water.

As she tried to struggle to her paws, a shadow fell over her. Claws glinted in the sunlight as a tom slashed at her muzzle. Terror shrilling through her pelt, she rolled out of the way and hauled herself up, lashing out as she leaped to her paws. Her claws met something soft and ripped through. It crumpled under her blow. She squinted against the light, trying to see what she'd hit. On the ground in front of her, she saw a small body. Its orange-and-black pelt was matted with blood. *Sparkpelt's lost kit*. Horror seared her belly. She felt the blood on her claws seep into her fur, warm and wet, filling the air with a terrible sweetness. *I killed him!*

She woke with a jolt, her pelt clammy. Blinking into the darkness of the den, she struggled to catch her breath. *It was just a dream.* But the horror lingered in her belly. She slid away from Bramblestar and climbed out of their nest. It was more than a dream. She was sure. *It was a warning.* Heart lurching, she darted out of the den. She had to check on Sparkpelt. She had to see that the kits were safe.

She slithered as quietly as she could down the rock tumble and hurried through the moonlight to the nursery. Nosing her way in, she blinked, adjusting her eyes to the darkness.

Sparkpelt was asleep in her nest, Flamekit and Finch-kit pressed against her belly. Daisy snored softly in the nest beside them. Relief washed Squirrelflight's pelt. They were safe. It had been just a dream.

As she crept from the nursery, movement caught her eye. A shadow shifted outside the medicine den. She glimpsed white paws in the darkness and recognized Leafpool. What was she doing up? It wasn't even close to dawn. She padded toward her. "Leafpool?" she whispered. "Are you okay?"

Leafpool's eyes glinted in the shadows. "I couldn't sleep."

"Why not?" Squirrelflight's belly tightened.

Leafpool frowned. "I'm not sure, but I have a terrible feeling that something is wrong." She shuddered. "Why are you awake?"

"I had a nightmare," Squirrelflight told her. "About a kit." She glanced toward the nursery. "I thought Sparkpelt's kits might be in trouble."

Leafpool's gaze shimmered with alarm. "Are you sure the dream was about *Sparkpelt's* kits?"

Squirrelflight stiffened. "Who else could they be?"

"Moonlight's." Her mew was barely more than a whisper.

Alarm sparked through Squirrelflight's fur. Was the dream a warning? Were Moonlight's kits in danger? "We have to go." She raced for the camp entrance. "If her kits are in danger, we have to save them."

CHAPTER 22

Squirrelflight scrabbled between boulders, climbing the hill that would bring them close to the Sisters' camp. She could hear Leafpool panting behind. The sky was still as black as raven feathers, glittering with stars as they pushed onward, but light was pooling at the horizon. The Clan patrols would be gathering at the border soon.

"We're nearly there, right?" Leafpool puffed. "I recognize this track."

Squirrelflight glanced over her shoulder. Her sister's pelt was ruffled, her eyes glittering with exhaustion. "It's just over this hill." She paused as they reached the top and looked down into the valley. The Sisters' camp was hidden among the thick overgrowth at the bottom. "I hope we're in time. My dream was really bad. If it was about Moonlight's kits, she must need us."

Leafpool stopped beside her. "I had a dream too."

Squirrelflight looked at her. "About the kits?"

"Yes." Leafpool eyed her uncertainly. "There were wounded kits everywhere, more than I could treat. I had the sense they were Moonlight's kits." She shrugged. "I don't know why

306

StarClan would send me a dream about the Sisters. They're not Clan cats. But it felt important." As she spoke, she pricked her ears. "Do you hear that?"

Squirrelflight listened. A wail drifted from the valley. Her heart lurched. There was pain in the cry. "Moonlight!" She pelted down the hillside, zigzagging between bushes. As she plunged through a wall of bracken, another wail rose from the camp. Her paws skidded on the earth, sending stones spraying behind her. She could hear Leafpool's paw steps thrumming at her heels as she slewed past a bramble. Heart pounding, she crashed through the fern entrance.

Leafpool burst out behind her as she slowed to a stop on the grassy clearing. The wail sounded again. Squirrelflight jerked her muzzle around, scanning the moonlit camp.

Snow was hurrying toward the birthing den. Creek and Flurry crouched, wide-eyed, at the edge of the camp, while Furze paced anxiously beside them.

Snow stopped and stared. "What are you doing here?"

Squirrelflight ignored the question. "Where's Moonlight? Is she okay?"

"She's kitting."

Squirrelflight saw fear in Snow's gaze.

Leafpool hurried forward. "Take me to her," she ordered briskly.

"But she's *kitting*!" Snow blinked at her.

"I'm a medicine cat, remember?" Leafpool told her. "I treated Sunrise."

"Hawk and Tempest are taking care of her." Snow sounded

uncertain. "They know what to do." A screech echoed from the birthing den.

"It sounds like they need help." Leafpool pushed past Snow and disappeared inside.

Squirrelflight blinked at Snow, trying not to betray her fear. "She's helped deliver countless kits in ThunderClan, including my own. She knows what she's doing."

"I hope so." Snow's pelt prickled along her spine. "Moonlight's been kitting since sundown. She's had one kit but something's wrong. We've never seen anything like this. Perhaps it's because she was expecting for so long. The kits might be too big. The next one won't come. I think it's stuck."

Pressing back panic, Squirrelflight darted after Leafpool. She blinked, adjusting to the darkness, as Snow squeezed after her.

At the edge of the den, a newborn kit mewled at Tempest's paws while Hawk crouched beside Moonlight. The queen was stiff with pain as she fought against a spasm. Her thick pelt was matted. Her eyes rolled wildly and she let out another shriek. Squirrelflight was shocked to see strong, stubborn Moonlight so overwhelmed. Her suffering must be terrible.

Leafpool ran her paws over Moonlight's belly.

"Snow says a kit is stuck," Squirrelflight told her.

"I know." Leafpool didn't take her eyes from Moonlight. "It's facing the wrong way. I can feel it. We need to ease the pain and give Moonlight the strength to push." She looked at Hawk. "Do you know what raspberry leaves look like?"

Hawk nodded.

"What about ragweed?" Leafpool asked.

Snow blinked at her eagerly. "I know ragweed."

"Find some." Leafpool's gaze flitted to Squirrelflight. "Go with them. Bring as much as you can, but be quick. We need to get this kit out before Moonlight exhausts herself completely."

Squirrelflight nodded, relieved that she could help. As she ducked out of the den, Hawk and Snow pushed past her and raced out of camp. She followed, chasing Snow's white tail as it flashed away between the bushes. Branches poked at her pelt. Loose earth crumbled beneath her paws. She followed Snow to the top of the hill and out onto a stretch of grass. The white she-cat had stopped and was staring toward the distant horizon, her eyes narrowed against the wind that streamed through her fur. The land was lit now with pale dawn light. Hawk was already streaking down the hillside ahead of them, skimming the grass like an owl swooping for prey.

"She's fetching raspberry leaves," Snow told Squirrelflight. "Ragweed is this way." She bounded downhill toward a shallow stream.

Squirrelflight hurried after her, catching up as Snow reached it. The water chattered over pebbles, and Snow waded in and hopped out the other side. Squirrelflight splashed after her, gasping as the chilly water tugged her belly fur. As she scrambled onto the bank, she saw Snow stop beside a swath of tall yellow flowers. They swirled in the breeze as the white she-cat reached up and tore down a pawful of blossoms. Squirrelflight stopped beside her and helped, ripping the pungent petals from their stems.

Snow heaped more on the ground. "How much do we need?"

Squirrelflight glanced at the pile uncertainly. "That must be plenty," she guessed. "If we need more, I can fetch some." She grasped a bunch between her jaws and raced back to camp. Moonlight's wail split the air as Squirrelflight charged through the fern entrance and made for the birthing den. She pushed her way inside and dropped the ragweed beside Leafpool. "I can fetch more if you need it," she panted.

Leafpool took a mouthful, chewed it, and spat the pulp onto her paw. She ran her tail over Moonlight's trembling flank and, leaning close, held her paw to the queen's muzzle. "Swallow this," she told her.

Moonlight groaned, her gaze clouded with pain, and turned away as Snow burst into the den and dropped more ragweed beside Leafpool.

"She needs to swallow this." Leafpool looked imploringly at Snow.

The white she-cat nodded curtly and crouched beside Moonlight's head. "It will help," she promised the queen. "Just swallow it."

Moonlight looked at her, fear in her gaze, then quickly lapped the pulp from Leafpool's paw.

Leafpool glanced at Squirrelflight. "Did you find raspberry leaves too?"

"Hawk's fetching some."

As she spoke, the den shivered and Hawk slid through the entrance. Squirrelflight glimpsed faint daylight outside.

She stiffened. She could picture the patrols gathering at the edge of Clan territory. Her paws pricked nervously. What had Bramblestar thought when he'd woken to find her gone? Would he have guessed that she'd come here?

Hawk's flanks heaved as she caught her breath. She dropped a mouthful of raspberry leaves beside Leafpool, who quickly chewed them and held out more pulp for Moonlight to lick. As Snow lapped the queen's cheek encouragingly, Squirrelflight blinked at Hawk. "The Clans are coming," she warned.

"Now?" Hawk narrowed her eyes.

"They're probably on their way," Squirrelflight told her. "They're coming to tell you to leave."

Hawk's eyes widened. "How can we leave now?" She looked at Moonlight in alarm.

Squirrelflight shifted her paws nervously. "I don't know." Would the Clan patrols retreat once they saw Moonlight was kitting? What would happen if they didn't? She pushed the thought away and leaned closer to Leafpool. "How's she doing?"

"We can't do anything until the herbs start to work." Leafpool sat back on her haunches, her gaze dark as another spasm rippled through Moonlight. The queen groaned limply, helpless against the pain.

Squirrelflight looked toward the den entrance. Weak sunlight was beginning to show through it. Every hair on her pelt seemed to tremble. *Please let Moonlight kit in peace.* She hoped that StarClan could hear her prayer. No cat spoke as they waited for the herbs to take hold. The first and only kit to be born mewled again and settled at last against Tempest's belly. Moonlight groaned softly as dawn brightened into day.

At last, when Moonlight had stopped moaning, Leafpool placed her paw on the queen's belly. She lifted her head and looked at Leafpool. For the first time, her gaze was sharp. Leafpool met it. "Ready?"

"Ready." Moonlight rolled onto her paws and crouched, her tail stiff.

"Wait for the pain," Leafpool murmured.

Squirrelflight held her breath.

Moonlight pressed her paws harder against the earth as a spasm jerked along her flank. She lifted her head and let out a screech and pressed her hindquarters against the earth. With a shudder, the second kit slithered onto the ground behind her. Snow darted toward it and quickly lapped the membrane from its pelt.

Squirrelflight's breath caught in her throat as silence gripped the den.

"It's not breathing." Snow looked desperately at the lifeless scrap of fur.

Leafpool pushed past her. "Take care of Moonlight." As Snow crouched at Moonlight's cheek, Leafpool stretched the kit out and hooked its mouth open with a claw. Squirrelflight flinched. What was she doing? Leafpool placed a paw on its chest and pumped with small, fierce jabs.

Hawk stared at her with wide eyes. "Be careful!"

Leafpool ignored her and nipped the kit's scruff, then lifted the kit's body and shook it.

The kit jerked, lifted its head, and wailed.

It's alive! Relief surged in Squirrelflight's belly.

Quickly, Leafpool carried it to Tempest and put it beside its littermate. "It's another she-kit."

"She's a fighter, like her mother." Tempest scooped the kit close to her belly and bent to wash her.

As Leafpool turned back to Moonlight, the queen jerked and shuddered, and a third kit slipped onto the ground. Squirrelflight held her breath as Leafpool licked the membrane clear of its muzzle.

The kit mewled, squirming at Leafpool's paws.

"A tom." Leafpool's eyes shone. "He's the last." She lifted him between her jaws and passed him to Squirrelflight. "Put him with his littermates," she mewed. Squirrelflight's heart swelled as she breathed in the kit's scent. She padded toward Tempest and placed the kit gently between his sisters. She blinked at Leafpool, who was smoothing Moonlight's ruffled pelt with a paw while Snow touched her nose to the queen's cheek.

Squirrelflight tensed. "Is she okay?"

"She's tired, but she's fine." Leafpool sat back on her haunches.

Squirrelflight's pelt rippled with pleasure. They had saved Moonlight and her kits. She blinked happily at Snow, a purr throbbing in her throat. Then she froze. Snow had stiffened. Ears pricked, the white she-cat stared toward the den entrance. Heart lurching, Squirrelflight followed her gaze. Outside the camp, bushes rustled. Something was pushing between them.

Muted paw steps scuffed the earth.

Hawk's eyes glittered with panic. "Are they here?"

Squirrelflight padded to the entrance and peered out. Creek, Furze, and Flurry had backed toward the center of the clearing, their hackles high. The air around them was thick with Clan scents. As the bushes around the edge of the camp shivered, alarm shrilled through Squirrelflight's pelt. "Leaf-pool," she mewed huskily. "The battle patrol is here."

CHAPTER 23

Leafpool pushed past her and looked out. "We've got to stop them."

"Don't let them see you." Squirrelflight nosed her away. "They mustn't know you're here."

Outside, Sunrise had joined Furze, Creek, and Flurry, and they were backing toward the birthing den, backs arched, growling softly. Their gaze was fixed on the shivering dogwood at the far side of the clearing. It twitched as warriors slid out. Slowly, cats crept like shadows from the bushes, their eyes flashing in the early morning light.

Squirrelflight swallowed back panic. There was no way out. She was trapped here with the Sisters.

Tigerstar stalked into the clearing. His gaze flitted around the camp then settled on Furze. "Where's Moonlight?"

Furze stared back wordlessly as Mistystar, Harestar, and Bramblestar fanned out around the ShadowClan leader. At the edge of the camp, their warriors bushed out their pelts menacingly. Furze flexed her claws. "You're trespassing," she growled.

Beside her, Flurry's hackles lifted. "Get out of our camp."

Harestar flicked his tail. "We've come to speak with your

leader." His eyes glittered with hostility.

Squirrelflight's belly tightened. *Please don't fight!* Would the Sisters try to defend Moonlight? They'd have to if the Clans didn't back down. Moonlight couldn't defend herself right now. She ducked away from the entrance and nodded toward the stricken queen. "We have to get her out of here." If Moonlight was safe, the Sisters would have less reason to fight.

Moonlight lifted her head weakly. Her gaze flitted around the den. "Where are my kits?" Tempest nudged the kits toward her. With slow stumbling steps they found their mother and snuggled eagerly against her belly. Moonlight curled around them protectively. Her nose wrinkled. "What's that stench? Have foxes broken into the camp?"

"The Clans are here." Leafpool's eyes were dark with fear.

Squirrelflight padded closer. "They want you to leave."

Moonlight tried to struggle to her paws but, weak from the birth, slumped helplessly beside her kits. "They shouldn't have come," she growled.

"But they have," Squirrelflight told her. "We have to get you and your kits to safety."

"I'm not going anywhere." Moonlight swished her tail.

"If you stay here, you'll be putting your kits in danger. And your sisters will die trying to protect them, and you." Outside, the Sisters' growling had hardened into warning yowls. Squirrelflight thrust her muzzle close to Moonlight's. "You're outnumbered! All the pride in the world won't save you." Before Moonlight could answer, she jerked her muzzle toward Snow. "We have to get Moonlight and her kits out of here."

Snow stared at her. "She's just kitted. They won't harm her, surely?"

"Tigerstar wants this land, and he wants it now." Squirrelflight lashed her tail. "He's made it clear that he won't back down. You need to get Moonlight away while I try to stop them fighting."

"We can't make Moonlight travel so soon." Hawk's eyes were wide. "It might kill her, or her kits!"

"You have to get her clear," Squirrelflight snapped. There wasn't time to discuss this. "If fighting breaks out, she won't be safe here." Daylight glinted through the branches at the back of the den. The wall was thin there. Squirrelflight hurried toward it and began to tear at the vines. "Make a hole here and take Moonlight and her kits out the back. Get them to somewhere safe." Her thoughts whirled. Was anywhere safe now that the patrol was here? It didn't matter. Right now, she must persuade the Sisters to leave the den. "Find somewhere you can hide."

Tempest glanced at Snow. "The cave," she mewed quickly.

Snow's gaze hardened. "We can't let them drive us away without a fight."

Squirrelflight turned on her. "Get Moonlight somewhere safe; *then* think about fighting!" she snarled.

Snow held her gaze for a moment, then looked at the narrow gap Squirrelflight had torn. "Okay." She grabbed a vine and ripped the gap wider.

"Leafpool." Squirrelflight blinked at her sister. "I'm going to go out there and try to keep the Clans talking. You help

Tempest and Snow carry the kits. Hawk can help Moonlight."

Leafpool stared at her. "You can't let our Clanmates see you here!"

"I have no choice." Squirrelflight ignored the fear clutching at her belly. *Will Bramblestar be surprised to see me here? Or will he have guessed?* "It's the only way to get Moonlight clear."

"What if they attack?" Leafpool's gaze was bright with fear.

Squirrelflight pushed the thought away. "Let's hope it doesn't come to that."

Leafpool narrowed her eyes. "Remember, Squirrelflight," she murmured darkly, "you're a warrior, not a Sister. You must live among your Clanmates long after the Sisters are gone."

Squirrelflight padded past the kits, still damp from their birth and as small as prey. "I must do what's right." Avoiding Leafpool's eye, she pushed her way out of the den.

The warriors stared. Eyes widened. Pelts spiked as Squirrelflight slid between Flurry and Sunrise and squared her shoulders against the bristling warriors. They lined the clearing like a pack of hungry foxes. She could see Bramblestar at the edge of her gaze, but she avoided looking at him.

"What are you doing here?" Tigerstar stared at Squirrelflight.

Crowfeather didn't give her the chance to answer. "She came to warn the Sisters!" He padded forward, his tail flicking ominously behind him.

Mistystar narrowed her eyes. "We know you wanted to undermine your leader," she growled, "but we didn't think you'd go so far as to betray him."

"I've betrayed no cat!" Squirrelflight snapped. "I came to make sure Moonlight was okay."

Flurry moved closer. "Don't tell them about the kits," she hissed under her breath. "They mustn't know Moonlight is weak."

Furze nodded. Creek flicked his tail. Squirrelflight glanced at them. "You have to," she whispered urgently. "It's your only chance to make them leave."

Crowfeather's eyes flashed with rage. "She's plotting with the enemy!"

Squirrelflight swung her muzzle toward the WindClan deputy. "The Sisters aren't your enemy!"

Tigerstar's ears twitched angrily. "They maimed Strikestone!"

Flurry lashed her tail. "He nearly killed Sunrise!"

Outraged yowls exploded from the warriors.

"They invaded our territory!"

"We were just defending our border!"

Alarm spiraled in Squirrelflight's chest. Tempers were flaring. She eyed Tigerstar. "You wanted to show the Sisters how strong the Clans are," she yowled above the noise. "You've done that. You can leave now and let them decide what to do. If they have any sense, they will leave. But it's not fair to bully them like this."

Sunrise bristled beside her. "We can handle bullies."

"We don't need you to speak for us," Flurry snarled at Squirrelflight.

Squirrelflight lowered her voice so that only the Sisters

could hear. "Moonlight's had her kits. She's okay. Leafpool and the others are taking them away from the camp." She could only hope that once they knew that Moonlight and the kits were safe, they wouldn't want to fight.

Flurry narrowed her eyes. "Did the Clans tell you to send Moonlight away?"

"No!" Surprise sparked in Squirrelflight's pelt. "I did it to protect her and the kits."

"Bramblestar." Tigerstar's gaze slid toward the Thunder-Clan leader. "How does it feel to be wrong for a change?" He sounded pleased.

A chill ran along Squirrelflight's spine. What was the ShadowClan leader talking about? She turned her head slowly toward Bramblestar.

He was staring, puzzled, at Tigerstar. "What do you mean?"

"You chose the wrong cat to be your deputy." Tigerstar's voice was as smooth as honey. "It seems that Squirrelflight prefers rogues to her own Clanmates."

"That's not true!" Squirrelflight's heart lurched. She stared desperately at Bramblestar, but his gaze was fixed on Tiger-star.

"What Squirrelflight does is up to her," he meowed coldly.

Surprised murmurs rippled from the ring of warriors.

Breezepelt's hackles lifted. "She's disloyal!"

"That's not true!" Squirrelflight glared at him.

"And it's not the first time," Breezepelt went on. "You raised your sister's half-Clan kits and told your Clanmates and Bramblestar they were your own! You're a liar."

"Liar!" Ripples of agreement spread among the warriors.

Squirrelflight flattened her ears. Did the Clans still care about that? It had been so long ago! And Leafpool's kits had gone on to help save all the Clans.

Bramblestar eyed Breezepelt angrily. "We came here to talk to the Sisters, not rake up old bones."

Breezepelt flashed him an accusing look. "We didn't expect to find your deputy here, mixing with the enemy! Squirrelflight's disloyal. She's been disloyal before. She can't be trusted!"

Squirrelflight hissed at Breezepelt. "You don't get to lecture me on loyalty! Who did you fight for in the battle with the Dark Forest?" Anger pulsed in her belly.

Crowfeather padded forward, swishing his tail as he brushed past his son. "We can listen to Squirrelflight's explanation later," he growled. Squirrelflight forced her pelt to stay flat as foreboding wormed in her belly. He nodded to her. "Move out of the way. We've come to move the Sisters."

"You came here to *warn* the Sisters," Squirrelflight reminded him.

"We've heard your *warning*, and we're not moving." Sunrise stepped forward, her head high.

"Please don't fight." Squirrelflight's mew trembled. She caught Bramblestar's eye. He had to stop this.

He stared back at her, his gaze unreadable.

Creek bushed out his tail. "This camp is ours," he growled. "If you want to take it, you'll have to take it by force." The young cat stared at Tigerstar.

He's not even old enough to be an apprentice, Squirrelflight thought desperately. *He can't fight warriors.*

Furze lifted her broad head. She was almost twice as big as some of the warriors, and, for a moment, Squirrelflight wondered if the Sisters could win this battle. How many cats would be hurt?

"Please!" She stared desperately around her fellow warriors. "Just go, and let the Sisters leave in their own time."

"A warrior never backs down." Harestar flattened his ears and dropped into a battle stance.

Sunrise narrowed her eyes to slits. "Neither does a Sister." With a snarl, she leaped for the WindClan leader.

The clearing exploded into battle. Shock pulsing through her pelt, Squirrelflight backed away. Sunrise, Furze, Flurry, and Creek disappeared beneath a throng of writhing pelts. The stone tang of blood filled the air.

I promised Bramblestar that I would support him, she remembered. But how could she? Working so hard to save Moonlight's kits had connected her to the Sisters even more. She was a ThunderClan cat—she knew that—but she couldn't shed the blood of cats she knew meant the Clans no harm.

At the edge of the clearing, Twigbranch stared at the fighting cats as though frozen to the ground. Squirrelflight was surprised to see her. She hadn't approved of this patrol. Had Bramblestar made her come, or had she volunteered so that she could help keep the peace? The gray she-cat's eyes rounded with disbelief. "We weren't supposed to fight."

Bramblestar didn't seem to hear her. He shouldered his way to the middle.

"No!" Squirrelflight tried to catch his eye. He mustn't fight. He'd never forgive himself if he knew he was threatening newborn kits, hiding only a few tail-lengths away.

Harestar reared out of the swarm. Sunrise rose with him, slashing viciously at the WindClan leader's muzzle. Trading blows, they sank beneath the sea of pelts like cats drowning. Creek rolled out from the pack, turning as soon as he was clear and hurling himself at Cloverfoot. He hooked his claws into the ShadowClan deputy's shoulders and dragged her onto her back. Leaping on top of her, he struggled to pin her to the ground and aimed a swipe at her cheek. Cloverfoot tried to twist free, but, straining with every hair on his pelt, the young tom held her fast. As his paw swung toward her, Crowfeather leaped from beside his Clanmates and slammed into Creek's side. He sent Creek crashing into a bramble and leaped after him, paws flailing. Breezepelt, Scorchfur, and Gorsetail raced to help him.

You'll kill him! Squirrelflight stared in horror as Creek disappeared beneath a swarm of warriors. *Please stop!*

Twigbranch's pelt flashed past her. "Wait!" Squirrelflight hooked her claws into her Clanmate's pelt and dragged her away from the fighting.

Paws churning, Twigbranch wrestled free from her grip. She turned on Squirrelflight. "What in StarClan—" Her mew trailed away as she saw Squirrelflight.

"We can't let this happen." Squirrelflight stared pleadingly at the young warrior. "Moonlight has just kitted. She's very weak, and the kits have hardly taken their first breath. Their first memory can't be a battle! Help me stop them!"

Twigbranch glanced around the camp. "Where are the kits?"

"Leafpool and the others have taken them somewhere safe. Flurry, Furze, Sunrise, and Creek are on their own."

Twigbranch nodded. "I'll tell Blossomfall and Mouse-whisker," she promised. "I'll make them stop." She turned and pushed her way between Emberfoot and Yarrowleaf, who were scrabbling to get deeper into the fray. Squirrelflight began to nose her way between Oatclaw and Duskfur. She had to find Bramblestar and explain about the kits. He'd see why the Sisters *had* to fight. They were defending their young. As she ducked past Oatclaw, Sunrise flashed past her. Squirrelflight spun as the she-cat broke free of the patrol and fled across the clearing.

"Retreat!" Sunrise called to her campmates. "We can't win here!"

Furze ripped herself free from Shimmerpelt and Petalfur and raced after her, yowling over her shoulder. "Creek! Flurry! This way!"

The battle seemed to stumble to a halt as the Clan patrol realized that their enemies were on the run. Creek leaped to his paws and hared after his campmates, speeding over the grass like a bird. Together, they crashed through a bramble and disappeared.

Tigerstar watched them go, his eyes narrowing with determination. "Let's make sure they're gone!" Like a pack of wolves, the warrior patrol gave chase.

As the clearing emptied, Squirrelflight stared shakily at

the bloodstained grass. Her breath caught in her throat as she saw Flurry, lying on the ground. Her ginger-and-white pelt was matted. Scratches crisscrossed her muzzle. Squirrelflight hurried toward her, heart pounding. She crouched beside the wounded cat. Was she dead?

"You care more about the Sisters than your Clanmates."

Bramblestar's mew took her by surprise. Squirrelflight turned. He was staring at her.

She met his gaze. "I care about any injured cat," she mewed.

"Even an enemy?"

"A life is a life." She got to her paws and faced him.

"Why are you here?" Confusion clouded his gaze.

"Last night I dreamed a kit was in trouble," she told him. "Leafpool dreamed it too. We had to come." She padded closer. "Moonlight needed help. She was having trouble kitting and she needed a medicine cat. Leafpool saved her and her kits. She finished kitting just before the patrol arrived."

Bramblestar blinked at her. "Where is she?"

"Leafpool and the others have taken her and the kits somewhere safe."

Bramblestar stiffened as yowls echoed from the head of the valley. "Where?"

Squirrelflight shrugged. "A cave. I've never seen it before, but it can't be far."

Bramblestar blinked at her. "Do you think that's where the others have fled?"

Alarm pricked in Squirrelflight's paws. *Get Moonlight somewhere safe; then think about fighting!* "They might think they can defend it from the Clans."

Just then, a breathless Crowfeather appeared at her side. "Did you say Leafpool is in a cave?" His blue eyes were wide with alarm, and concern. Of course he was concerned, Squirrelflight realized—they had once been forbidden mates. And while both cats had moved on with their lives, Squirrelflight knew that those feelings never completely went away.

"They'll be trapped," Bramblestar growled, digging his claws into the earth. "Tigerstar and the others will have them cornered."

"Then we have to stop them fighting!" She glanced at Bramblestar, but his gaze had flitted behind her. Something was moving across the grass toward them. As she turned, ginger-and-white fur flashed at the edge of her vision. With a snarl, Flurry knocked her aside. As she staggered to keep her balance, Squirrelflight saw the she-cat crash into Bramblestar. Hissing, Flurry sank her teeth into Bramblestar's neck. He stumbled beneath the huge she-cat's massive weight, screeching as she pressed hard into his neck. He dropped onto his belly and rolled onto his back. Tucking his hind legs under her, he began to kick out, grunting with pain. Flurry let go and, pressing a forepaw into his chest, swiped his cheek with her other paw. Bramblestar's muzzle was knocked sideways. He struggled to escape, but Flurry pinned him down and struck him again and again.

Squirrelflight's pelt spiked with horror. Flurry was trying to kill him! She unsheathed her claws and leaped.

"They've trapped the kits!" Twigbranch burst from the

bushes and hared across the clearing toward her.

Squirrelflight's leap jerked into a stumble. Struggling to keep her balance, she spun to meet Twigbranch's horrified gaze.

"The kits?" Flurry jerked her muzzle toward the young warrior. In an instant she was off Bramblestar and pelting across the clearing. Tail bushed, she plunged through the gap where the others had fled.

Squirrelflight darted to Bramblestar's side. "Are you okay?" Her heart seemed to miss a beat as he lay limp. She lapped his bloody cheek urgently. "Bramblestar!"

With a groan, he nudged her away. Staggering to his paws, he looked at her, his eyes clouded with pain. "Were you going to let her kill me?"

"No! I was—"

Before she could finish, Bramblestar limped after Flurry. "Come on. It sounds like the kits are in trouble."

Squirrelflight followed him as he tracked the patrol through ragged undergrowth. "I was going to pull her off."

He ignored her. Angry mews sounded ahead. She pricked her ears. *The kits.* She broke into a run. As she burst from the bushes, she saw the warrior patrol lined at the edge of a rough clearing. Ahead, a sheer cliff rose like an open wound in front of them. A landslide had stripped away the stone, and now raw earth glowed red in the early morning light. At the bottom, large boulders formed a cave, roofed by the branches and rubble that had recently fallen from the cliff. Flurry and Sunrise stood inside, staring out from the shadows.

"That's no place to hide kits," Bramblestar stopped beside her.

Twigbranch was with him. She followed his gaze. "It's no more than a pile of rubble."

Bramblestar peered past Flurry and Sunrise. "Are the kits in there?"

Twigbranch nodded. "With Moonlight and the rest of the Sisters."

"Where's Leafpool?" Squirrelflight narrowed her eyes as she tried to see past Flurry.

"She's in there too."

Squirrelflight glanced along the line of warriors. They were staring at Flurry and Sunrise, their hackles up.

Tigerstar padded forward. "Are you ready to leave yet?" he snarled at the Sisters.

A shape moved in the cave behind them. Moonlight limped slowly from the shadows and stood between her campmates. Her eyes were hollow with exhaustion. Squirrelflight's heart quickened. The gray she-cat was in no state to fight. Moonlight looked along the line of warriors and curled her lip. "We stay," she croaked.

Harestar narrowed his eyes. "But you're outnumbered."

"We can defend this cave for as long as we have to," Moonlight hissed.

"Then we'll flush you out." Tigerstar nodded to Cloverfoot and Scorchfur. "Climb on top of the cave and start digging."

"Be careful!" Squirrelflight hurried forward as Cloverfoot and Scorchfur leaped up and began to pick their way across the debris piled on top. Soil began to rain down across the opening.

Flurry glanced up, narrowing her eyes against the dirt. Sunrise growled at the warriors, her pelt bristling with rage. Moonlight showed her teeth.

Bramblestar padded to Tigerstar's side. "We could starve them out." He glanced nervously at the warriors on top of the cave as they began to dig. "There's no need to endanger the kits like this."

Tigerstar jerked his muzzle toward the ThunderClan leader. "Kits? No one mentioned that the kits had been born."

As he spoke, Moonlight lunged forward. "Attack!" The Sisters streamed from the cave, pelts bushed, ears flat. They hurled themselves at the line of warriors. Squirrelflight ducked away as Moonlight smashed into Tigerstar and sent him crashing into a bramble. Shrieks exploded around her. Hawk leaped onto Duskfur's back. Flurry swung a heavy blow at Snaketooth. Tempest hooked Reedwhisker's pelt with her claws and dragged him to the earth. At the entrance to the cave, Thornclaw and Creek tumbled across the ground, paws churning as they tore at each other's pelts.

Squirrelflight stared at them desperately. This battle could end only in blood. She froze as a rumble sounded from the cave. A branch moved, creaking ominously as the wood began to split. She saw the roof shift. It was crumbling. Dirt showered the entrance. Stones rolled from the edges. The cave was collapsing, with Leafpool and the kits inside!

Squirrelflight hared toward the opening. "Landslide!"

She barged past Creek and Thornclaw and plunged into the shadows. A branch split above her head, showering splinters of wood over her. "Leafpool!" Her shriek echoed in the darkness. Blindly, she stumbled over stones. "The roof's caving in!"

"Over here!" Leafpool's mew echoed from the back of the cave as pebbles showered onto Squirrelflight's back. Squirrelflight blinked, desperately trying to adjust her eyes to the dark. She could just make out Leafpool. "Where are the kits?"

Leafpool lifted a small bundle and hurried toward her. She thrust it at Squirrelflight. "The others are at the back." Earth was falling like rain. Stones tumbled, thumping and cracking onto the ground. Squirrelflight grasped the kit and turned. She smelled Hawk's fear-scent in the darkness and felt the she-cat in front of her. Hawk must have seen the roof crumbling too. She swung the kit toward her. Hawk grabbed it and Squirrelflight turned back for the next.

She could hear Leafpool scrabbling in the dirt. "I can't find them!" Leafpool wailed.

Squirrelflight darted to her sister's side, ears pricked as the roof rumbled ominously above them. She felt something soft against her paw. "I've found one." The kit mewled pitifully, and she bent to scoop it up. Narrowing her eyes against the falling dirt, she carried it toward the entrance.

Hawk was back, silhouetted against daylight as stones fell around her. She hurried forward and took the kit from Squirrelflight.

"Leafpool's looking for the last one," Squirrelflight told her quickly and turned back. Her pelt bristled in panic as she peered through the darkness. She could just make out her sister's pelt. "Have you found it?"

Leafpool didn't reply. She was digging frantically through the earth piling against the back of the cave. Squirrelflight glanced around, trying to see through the haze of falling dirt and stones. The acrid scent of wet earth filled her nose. Had the kit managed to find its way to the entrance? Perhaps one of the Sisters had already carried it out. Blood roared in Squirrelflight's ears. A creak sounded above her and she looked up. A thick branch that was holding back rocks shifted. Shards of wood exploded from it as it began to split. "Leafpool!" Panic jolted through her pelt. "The roof's collapsing!"

"I've found it!" Leafpool hauled a small body from the earth and swung it toward Squirrelflight.

"Let's get out of here." Squirrelflight took it from her and darted toward the entrance. Hawk was there. Squirrelflight jerked the kit toward her, relief swamping her as Hawk took it and hared out of the cave. She turned back. "Leafpool!" Squirrelflight saw her sister's eyes flash in the shadows as a deafening crack split the air. The branch snapped and, with a roar, dirt and rocks thundered down. Earth cascaded around her. Terror seared Squirrelflight's belly as the falling dirt pressed her to the ground.

"Leafpool!" She strained to see through the deluge. "Where are you?"

A hard blow slammed against the back of her head and flung her into blackness.

CHAPTER 24

Squirrelflight felt soft grass beneath her. She half opened her eyes, remembering the landslide and expecting to feel pain. Hadn't something hit her head? Sunlight dazzled her. Was she still in the Sisters' valley? She lifted her head, surprised that she felt so well. She scrambled to her paws and blinked at the flower-dappled meadow rolling away into soft green hills. In the dip below her, a shining pond glittered in sunshine. Around it, willows draped branches toward the water. She shook out her pelt. Her head felt clear, her body strong. She glanced around. Where was everyone? Was the battle over?

Leafpool lay a tail-length away, curled into a small dip in the grass.

Squirrelflight's chest tightened. Was she hurt? Her sister had been at the back of the cave when it had collapsed. She nudged Leafpool with her muzzle. "Are you okay?"

Leafpool lifted her head blearily and blinked open her eyes. "I think so?" She glanced around, surprise flashing in her eyes. "What are we doing *here*?"

"Do you know where this is?" Squirrelflight looked at her.

Leafpool looked away without answering.

She must still be groggy. Squirrelflight scanned the landscape. "The others must have carried us here," she guessed. "It's probably near the Sisters' camp. It doesn't look like Clan territory."

Leafpool got to her paws. "It's not," she mewed softly.

Squirrelflight glanced at her sister. There was a faraway look in her eyes. Unease fluttered in her belly. How could Leafpool know this place?

Leafpool's pelt rippled along her spine. "Squirrelflight. We're in StarCl—"

"No!" Squirrelflight froze. "We can't be dead. There's too much left to do. We must be near the Sisters' camp." She looked around frantically. "We need to find some cat. Bramblestar will be nearby. He wouldn't leave me alone."

Leafpool's gaze flitted past her. Squirrelflight followed it, dreading what she would see. *Larksong!* The black tom was padding across the grass toward them. Starlight rippled in his fur.

Squirrelflight backed away. The ground seemed to shift beneath her paws. "Did the landslide kill us?"

"You're not dead yet." Larksong dipped his head as he reached them.

Relief washed Squirrelflight's pelt. She glanced down at her own pelt and realized that she and Leafpool didn't sparkle as Larksong did. *We aren't StarClan—yet.*

Leafpool frowned, puzzled. "Is this a vision?"

"No." He met her gaze somberly. "You were both hurt in the landslide," Larksong told them. "Your bodies are in the ThunderClan camp. Alderheart and Jayfeather are trying to save you. While they try, you have paws in each world: two in the forest and two in StarClan."

Squirrelflight stared at him. "*Trying* to save us?"

Larksong met her gaze. "We don't know if you'll live. But you'll stay here until we find out."

"I can't die!" Squirrelflight's pelt bushed. "Bramblestar thinks I betrayed him! Sparkpelt needs me." She stared urgently at Larksong, wondering why he was sent to guide them. *Because he died so recently? Surely he'll understand. . . .* "You must send me back."

"It's not in my paws," he told her.

Leafpool tipped her head. "Can I see my body?"

"You can, if you wish." Larksong glanced toward the shining pond. "You can watch from there."

Squirrelflight pricked her ears. "Do you mean we can see ourselves in ThunderClan?"

"Yes." Larksong headed downslope toward the pond.

Squirrelflight hurried after him. "Will I be able to see Bramblestar?" She needed to know if he still believed she'd been willing to let Flurry kill him.

"You might," Larksong told her. "It depends."

"On what?" Leafpool followed, pricking her ears.

"I'm not sure. Sometimes the view is clouded."

As they neared the pool, Larksong crouched at the edge and dipped a paw in.

Squirrelflight gazed down. As he swirled the water, she saw, beyond the dazzling surface, a shadowy forest. She began to make out a hollow among the trees. *ThunderClan's camp.*

She leaned closer. The scene seemed to open, cats and dens coming into focus, and she could see her Clanmates moving around the clearing. Bramblestar was pacing outside the medicine den, his pelt matted and unkempt, still stained with the blood of battle. She tried to see his face. Was he angry? Betrayed? But a moment later, the vision darkened and suddenly moved inside the medicine den. "Is that me?" Her paws pricked as she recognized flame-colored fur in a nest at the edge of the den.

"Yes." Larksong nodded.

Her body lay limply on the bracken while Alderheart leaned over her, his forehead furrowed with worry. Leafpool lay in the next nest, unmoving, while Jayfeather sat beside her. Squirrelflight backed away from the water. Numbness seeped beneath her pelt. Was this real? She glanced at Leafpool.

Her sister was staring curiously into the pond. She lifted her face to Larksong. "Do you watch us from here?"

His eyes darkened. "I've been coming here to watch Sparkpelt and the kits." He looked at Squirrelflight. "I miss her so much. If you go back, please tell her that I'll never truly leave her."

If. The word filled Squirrelflight with fresh dread. She pushed it away. "Of course I'll go back. Alderheart won't let me die."

Larksong held her gaze. "Alderheart might not be able to keep you alive."

"But Sparkpelt needs me!"

Larksong didn't move. "She needed me too," he growled.

Despite the sunshine, a chill ran through Squirrelflight's fur.

Leafpool reached a paw toward the water. "Can I see anything I want to?" She touched the surface and the water shivered. The vision shattered and the pool once more reflected sunlight. Disappointment clouded Leafpool's gaze.

"You still have paws in the waking world," Larksong told her. "The view will be better when you are truly in StarClan."

Leafpool gazed toward the rolling hills. "Where is everyone?"

Squirrelflight suddenly realized that the meadows and hills were deserted. "Do we have to wait until we're dead to see the rest of our Clanmates?"

"No." Larksong's eyes brightened. "I came to welcome you. We didn't want to overwhelm you."

As he spoke, Squirrelflight saw figures on the crest of the hill, silhouetted against the sky. She narrowed her eyes, trying to make them out. Familiar scents touched her nose. *Cinderpelt. Sorreltail. Ferncloud.* Her heart leaped. Then her father's warm scent touched her nose. It smelled just as it had when she'd been young. "Firestar!" She saw his flame-colored pelt, sparkling now with stars, and raced up the slope to meet him.

Firestar wove around her when she reached him, purring loudly. "I've missed you," he meowed.

She blinked at him proudly. "Bramblestar made me deputy! Did you see?"

"Of course I saw." His eyes sparkled. "And you're a great deputy."

As he spoke, Cinderpelt, Sorreltail, and Ferncloud paced

eagerly around them. Squirrelflight turned to greet them, overwhelmed as she glimpsed Hollyleaf. Joy flooded her pelt. "Hollyleaf!"

The black she-cat slid between her Clanmates and touched her nose to Squirrelflight's cheek. "Hey, Squirrelflight!" Hollyleaf's fur sparkled in the sunlight.

"You look great." Squirrelflight flicked her tail. For a moment, she hardly remembered the landslide and the battle.

"Hollyleaf!" Leafpool reached them, purring. Eyes bright, she pressed her muzzle deep into Hollyleaf's neck fur. "It's so good to see you."

"And you."

As Hollyleaf nuzzled her mother, Cinderpelt blinked at Squirrelflight. "We didn't expect to see you so soon."

Sorreltail's eyes rounded with worry. "Firestar said you may not be with us for long."

"Of course not." Cinderpelt nudged her Clanmate sharply. "She needs to get back to ThunderClan. Bramblestar will be lost without her."

Ferncloud wove between them. "While she's here, I know two kits who'd love to see her." She pushed her Clanmates aside, and Squirrelflight's breath caught in her throat. Dandelionkit and Juniperkit were staring shyly at her, their small paws buried in the thick grass. Squirrelflight's heart seemed to crack as she saw them. These were Alderheart and Sparkpelt's littermates—the kits who'd died before she'd had the chance to raise them. She hurried to greet them, nuzzling them and running her tail along their spines.

"Are you coming to live with us?" Dandelionkit blinked at her eagerly.

"I don't know." Her eyes clouded. Why did she want to go back and help Sparkpelt's kits when she had kits of her own here in StarClan?

"We can show you all the best places to hunt," Juniperkit told her. "Longtail and Mousefur have been training us."

Mousefur? Longtail? Squirrelflight's heart skipped a beat. Longtail and Mousefur had been elders in ThunderClan for a very long time when Squirrelflight was younger. Her pelt prickled with happiness as she saw them padding toward her. She stared at them as Dandelionkit and Juniperkit, purring, wove around her legs. How many times had she cleaned out their bedding and helped pick fleas from their pelts? They looked like young warriors now, muscles rippling beneath their glossy fur. A tom-kit was hurrying after them. Squirrelflight froze as she recognized his orange-and-black pelt. It was Sparkpelt's dead kit. As she stared at the tiny tom, Larksong bounded up the slope. He scooped the kit up and dropped him onto his own back, where the kit hung on, his eyes shining with excitement.

"I've named him Flickerkit," Larksong meowed proudly.

Squirrelflight's heart soared. "I can't wait to tell Sparkpelt!" This might be just what Sparkpelt needed to lift her from her grief. She stiffened as gray fur moved at the edge of her vision. She recognized it at once. *Ashfur.* The gray tom had caused so much trouble for her and for Leafpool's kits. And yet he was here. He dipped his head as she saw him, then glanced at Hollyleaf. Was Leafpool's daughter okay with Ashfur being here?

Hollyleaf blinked calmly at the gray tom. There was no sign of anger in her gaze. Had the two cats learned to live in peace here in StarClan?

Squirrelflight nodded curtly to Ashfur. She wasn't sure she could be as forgiving as Hollyleaf. After all, Ashfur had threatened to destroy the happiness she'd found with Bramblestar, and almost succeeded. She lifted Dandelionkit and Juniperkit onto her back and padded past him to greet Longtail and Mousefur. "You look so well," she told the elders.

"We are." Mousefur looked far happier here than she had in her last moons in ThunderClan. "We were in the elders' den far too long. It's good to be able to hunt and explore again."

"Mousefur is the best hunter in StarClan," Dandelionkit squeaked.

"No she's not." Juniperkit plucked the fur between Squirrelflight's shoulders with thorn-sharp claws. "Longtail's the best!"

Squirrelflight could still see Ashfur out of the corner of her eye. She leaned closer to Hollyleaf. "It seems strange that he didn't end up in the Dark Forest," she whispered.

Hollyleaf shrugged. "I guess, but he's apologized. I think he's changed."

Longtail narrowed his eyes. "I wouldn't wish the Dark Forest on any cat."

"What's left of it," Mousefur grunted.

Squirrelflight looked at her. "What do you mean?"

"Since the Great Battle, the Dark Forest has been nearly empty," Mousefur told her. "Most of the cats who lived there were defeated and passed on. I think the forest is overgrown now and the trees are crumbling."

Squirrelflight's eyes widened. "Then what happens to bad cats when they die?" She thought of Darktail—surely he *belonged* in the Dark Forest, if any cat did.

Longtail shrugged. "Who knows? They don't show up here."

Dandelionkit scrambled down from her back. "What's the Dark Forest?"

"That's where the scary cats go." Juniperkit leaped down after her.

"Let's be scary cats!" Dandelionkit darted between Mousefur's legs. Growling excitedly, Juniperkit chased after her. Flickerkit leaped down from Larksong's back and joined in.

Leafpool tore her gaze from Hollyleaf and blinked at the kits happily. "I feel so at home here," she purred.

Squirrelflight shivered. It was good to see so many old friends, but she wasn't ready to stay. ThunderClan's forest was home, not here. Her gaze flitted around her old Clanmates. They were glancing anxiously at Leafpool. Had her sister said something wrong?

Firestar's tail twitched. "I'm glad you're happy here," he meowed. "But I'm not sure you can stay."

Squirrelflight pricked her ears. "Does that mean we're not going to die yet?" She looked at him eagerly.

Firestar's gaze darkened. "We don't know," he mewed. "But even if you do, you may not be allowed to stay in StarClan." His gaze flitted from Squirrelflight to Leafpool. "Either of you."

Shock sparked in Squirrelflight's belly. "What do you mean?"

Leafpool's eyes widened. "Does StarClan think we're bad?"

Squirrelflight stiffened. Had Bramblestar been right? Had she betrayed her Clan by supporting the Sisters? She was Clan deputy after all. Had StarClan seen her hesitate before defending Bramblestar against Flurry's attack? *I was about to save him.*

Leafpool shifted beside her. "It's because I lied about my kits, isn't it?" She moved closer to Hollyleaf. "I had to. I had no choice. Giving up my medicine-cat duties would have been as much of a betrayal."

"It's not me but the whole of StarClan you have to convince." Firestar stared at her gravely. "They believe that you broke the warrior code." His gaze moved to Squirrelflight. "You both did. You lied to your Clan."

Squirrelflight stared at him. "Every cat makes mistakes," she blurted.

"Yes." He shifted his paws uneasily. "But you must be held to account for yours before you're allowed into StarClan."

"How?" Leafpool's question was barely more than a whisper.

"StarClan must review your lives." He turned to Mousefur. "Take the kits away. They don't need to watch this."

"But we want to stay with Squirrelflight!" Dandelionkit's eyes rounded with alarm.

Juniperkit stuck his fluffy tail in the air indignantly. "Please let us stay."

"You'll see them afterward," Mousefur told him. She caught Firestar's eye. "I hope." Ignoring their complaints, the dusky brown she-cat nosed them away and swept Flickerkit after them with her tail.

Squirrelflight's paws pricked with alarm. Where were they going?

"Follow me." Firestar led her across the hillside while their Clanmates trailed behind and Leafpool padded at her side.

"What's going to happen?" Squirrelflight whispered.

Leafpool glanced at her nervously. "I don't know."

Firestar followed the meadow to a forest that reached down into a valley. He led them between trees and brambles to a wide, grassy clearing. As he stopped in the middle, Squirrelflight glanced around. "Where are we?" The place reminded her of Fourtrees, where the Clans had gathered every moon before the Great Journey to the lake.

"This is where StarClan meets to decide the fate of every cat," Firestar told her. As he spoke, starlight glittered between the trees. On every side, StarClan warriors padded from between the trees. Their pelts, sparkling with countless stars, lit the shadows as they gathered at the edge of the clearing.

Leafpool moved closer. "Where will we go if StarClan won't take us?" Fear shimmered in her gaze.

Firestar's gaze clouded. "I don't know," he mewed huskily.

Squirrelflight could hardly believe her ears. What if there wasn't anywhere else? Did that mean she and Leafpool would just disappear? Would they become nothing but a fading memory for the living? Or would they end up wandering the forest forever? Perhaps Tree would be able to see them. Or the

Sisters. "How will you decide?" she breathed.

Firestar shifted his paws. "*I* won't decide," he croaked. "I could never turn you away from StarClan. It is up to others."

A black-and-white tom with a long, thin tail padded from between the trees. His pelt sparkled with starlight. Squirrelflight recognized him at once. *Tallstar.* As he stopped at the head of the clearing, a large, blue-gray she-cat took her place beside him. Firestar dipped his head to her. "Bluestar." Squirrelflight felt Leafpool's fur bristle against her flank as a large brown tom with a twisted mouth crossed the clearing. "That's Crookedstar," Leafpool whispered. More stars glittered in the tom's glossy pelt.

A skinny, battle-scarred she-cat followed, with bright wide-set orange eyes. "Yellowfang." Firestar greeted her as she stopped beside Tallstar, Crookedstar, and Bluestar, and then dipped his head to a snow-white she-cat who was padding across the clearing. "Moth Flight." He blinked politely as a small brown tabby tom followed. "Littlecloud." As they lined up beside the others, Firestar's gaze flicked back to Squirrelflight. "These cats will decide if you deserve a place in StarClan."

Squirrelflight tried to read their gazes. Would they be sympathetic?

Leafpool was staring at Firestar. "How will they decide?"

"They'll hear what you have to say," he told her. His tail twitched uneasily. "You're lucky in a way. Most cats don't have the chance to speak for themselves. Their fate is decided before they reach us."

Squirrelflight stared at him, fear jabbing her belly. "Are we supposed to be grateful?" She and Leafpool had served their Clan since they'd been given their apprentice names. They shouldn't have to plead for a place in StarClan.

Firestar eyed her nervously. "Please think before you speak, Squirrelflight," he whispered.

She dipped her head apologetically and forced her pelt to smooth. "Okay."

Moth Flight lifted her muzzle. "Leafpool. We'll start with you."

Leafpool's eyes flashed with alarm.

Squirrelflight blinked at her reassuringly. "Just tell them the truth," she murmured. "No cat could blame you for the choices you made." She watched, her throat tightening as Leafpool padded in front of the snow-white she-cat.

Tallstar, Yellowfang, and Bluestar shifted their paws, their expressions giving nothing away. Crookedstar narrowed his eyes. Littlecloud flicked his tail as though he was impatient to begin.

"Leafpool." Moth Flight frowned. "You had kits even though you were a medicine cat. I know how that feels. I was the Clans' first medicine cat. I gave up my kits and it broke my heart. That's why I made the rule that no future medicine cat should have kits. I wanted to save you all from such pain."

"I fell in love," Leafpool mewed simply.

Littlecloud's pelt ruffled. "Do you think that is an excuse?"

"Every cat falls in love at least once," Tallstar mewed. "You didn't have to act on it."

"You broke my rule." Moth Flight's gaze was still fixed on Leafpool.

"I had to." Leafpool lifted her chin. "But being a medicine cat was too important to give up."

"Was it worth lying for?" Moth Flight pressed.

"What else could I do?"

Moth Flight eyed her coldly. "You put your feelings before your Clan."

That's not true! Squirrelflight want to yowl out, but she could see Firestar's pelt pricking. *Think before you speak.*

She blinked at Leafpool. *Tell them how giving up your kits broke your heart too! Tell them it was the hardest decision you've ever made!* Her sister was staring back at the StarClan cats, her eyes round. Wasn't she going to defend herself?

Bluestar nodded to her. "Have you nothing to say?"

Leafpool met the old she-cat's gaze, unblinking. "I'm waiting for you to say that the father of my kits was from another Clan." Around the clearing, the gathered StarClan cats murmured softly to one another, their pelts shimmering beneath the shadow of the trees as Leafpool went on. "Why defend myself from one accusation only to face another?"

Squirrelflight stiffened. Leafpool sounded angry.

"All right." Moth Flight's tail twitched ominously. "You had kits with a cat from another Clan."

"Have you no respect at all for the warrior code?" Littlecloud's eyes flashed.

"I'm not a warrior," Leafpool straightened. "I'm a medicine cat. And being a medicine cat means more to me than anything. I gave up Crowfeather. I gave up my kits. Yes, I broke the code, but I chose my Clan over myself." She faced them, her pelt prickling defiantly. "If you want to keep me out of StarClan, it's up to you."

Bluestar's pelt sparkled as she stepped forward. "Would you make the same choices again?"

Leafpool hesitated. "Of course I would! I can't imagine my life without Lionblaze, Jayfeather, or Hollyleaf. I'd never choose a life without them." She narrowed her eyes. "If they'd never been born, we might *all* have been lost to the Dark Forest."

Bluestar frowned. "That has nothing to do with you breaking the code," she snapped.

Yellowfang glanced at the ThunderClan leader. "Didn't you have kits with a cat from another Clan, Bluestar?" she mewed softly.

"Bluestar wasn't a medicine cat," Moth Flight growled.

Yellowfang tipped her head to one side. "You had kits, Moth Flight, before you decided you were the first and last medicine cat who could. Is that fair?"

"It was for the good of the Clans." Moth Flight glared at her.

"It seems to me"—Yellowfang's ears twitched—"that Leafpool sacrificed everything she loved to be a loyal medicine cat to her Clan. Can we ask more than that?"

"Of course we can!" Littlecloud glared at his Clanmates. "What's the point in having rules if cats can break them whenever they like?"

"Leafpool didn't just have kits," Crookedstar reminded them. "She had kits with a cat from another Clan and lied about it to every cat."

Yellowfang flicked her tail crossly. "She gave them up to be a medicine cat, just as Bluestar gave up her own kits to be a leader. I did the same in my time, and I am still a member of StarClan."

Bluestar held her gaze for a moment, then dipped her head. "Yellowfang has a point. We can't condemn Leafpool for breaking rules we've broken ourselves."

Crookedstar spoke for the first time. "Leafpool is right about her kits. They helped save the Clans from the Dark Forest."

"Only because we chose them," Moth Flight snapped. "We could have chosen any cat."

Around the clearing, the StarClan warriors shifted uneasily. Squirrelflight's pelt pricked. Moth Flight seemed determined to keep Leafpool out of StarClan. Was her word enough to overrule the others? She looked anxiously at Leafpool. Her sister's pelt was smooth as she gazed calmly at the StarClan leaders.

"Don't argue over me," Leafpool mewed suddenly. "I don't regret having my kits. Only that I lied about being their mother. I wish I'd had more courage, but I thought I was doing the best for everyone by choosing to remain a medicine cat. If you decide that I can't join StarClan, then I must accept your decision. But please don't turn Squirrelflight away."

Squirrelflight's heart leaped into her throat. *Don't sacrifice your place in StarClan for me!*

Leafpool went on. "Everything she did was out of loyalty to me. I couldn't wish to have a better sister. She wanted to protect my kits and me, and she was willing to sacrifice everything to keep us safe. If some cat must be punished for what we did, punish me, not her."

Squirrelflight's gaze clouded. Star-flecked pelts swam before her eyes. She could only focus on Leafpool, awaiting the judgment of StarClan. Squirrelflight pressed against Firestar. "She deserves to be here," she whispered.

"So do you." Firestar nudged her forward.

Squirrelflight's pelt spiked. Bluestar was looking at her expectantly. Heart quickening, she padded toward the ThunderClan leader. Leafpool blinked encouragingly, but Squirrelflight could see fear in her sister's gaze.

Crookedstar padded forward and glared at Squirrelflight. "You lied to your Clan," he told her bluntly. "You lied to your mate. You told them that Hollyleaf, Lionblaze, and Jayfeather were yours. Why should such a deceitful cat have a place in StarClan?"

Squirrelflight looked at her paws. Her pelt burned. "That was my only lie," she mumbled. "I have been loyal to my Clan in every other way."

"Really?" Bluestar's mew was sharp. "We have seen you choose the Sisters over your Clan time and time again in the last moon. They are strangers to the forest, and yet you put your own Clan at risk to protect them."

"Some cat had to!" Squirrelflight raised her head.

"Why?" Bluestar's eyes flashed.

"Moonlight was expecting kits."

Crookedstar frowned. "Cats can have kits anywhere. If

you'd let the Clans drive her off sooner, she could have had her kits far from Clan territory. No cat would have been hurt. Instead you put the kits in danger, as well as the Sisters and your Clanmates."

"My Clanmates were never in danger," Squirrelflight insisted.

Bluestar's eyes widened. "Have you forgotten the landslide already? Doesn't that count as danger?"

Guilt clawed at Squirrelflight's heart. "I was just trying to protect every cat." She stared helplessly at the StarClan cats. "That's all I've ever wanted to do. I wanted to protect Leafpool when I lied for her. I wanted to protect Bramblestar when I lied to him. Does it matter if rules get broken if it's to stop cats getting hurt?"

Crookedstar's gaze darkened. "Without the warrior code, we are nothing but rogues."

Bluestar glared at Squirrelflight. "Are you saying we should live without it?"

"No!" Panic flared in Squirrelflight's belly. "This isn't fair! I'm just trying to explain . . ." Her mew trailed away. *Think before you speak.* Firestar was watching her, his eyes glittering with worry. She blinked at Bluestar. "I'm sorry. I know that a warrior shouldn't lie. And that they must put their Clan before everything. I have failed you. I've failed my Clan."

Tallstar's ears twitched. "Bluestar." He blinked at the ThunderClan leader. "Why be so hard on her?"

"She broke the rules."

"She told you why she did it," Tallstar pressed.

Yellowfang narrowed her eyes thoughtfully. "Is it such a crime to protect those you care about?" She met Bluestar's gaze. "Surely it matters more *why* she broke the warrior code than the fact that she did? If Squirrelflight broke rules, it was out of compassion. Is that so bad?"

Squirrelflight's heart swelled with gratitude. "I know the warrior code is important," she blurted. "I never would have broken it if I hadn't felt I was doing the right thing. I hope that the mistakes I've made, I've made out of love."

Crookedstar swapped glances with Bluestar, then nodded to Leafpool and Squirrelflight. "Thank you." With a flick of his tail, he turned away and padded into the shadow of the forest. Bluestar, Tallstar, Moth Flight, and Littlecloud followed.

Squirrelflight stared after them, hardly able to breathe. *Was that it?* "Are we allowed into StarClan?"

Yellowfang glanced at her. "We'll let you know once we've discussed it." With a nod, she headed after the others.

Firestar hurried across the clearing. He stopped beside Squirrelflight and Leafpool, his pelt rippling nervously along his spine. "You spoke well, both of you."

"I hope so." Leafpool gazed anxiously at Squirrelflight. "If they stop you joining StarClan because of me, I'll never forgive myself."

Squirrelflight touched her nose to her sister's cheek. Leafpool's scent hadn't changed since they were kits, and she breathed it in fondly. "Whatever they decide, you're the best sister I could have asked for."

"So are you." Leafpool pressed against her, her breath warm on Squirrelflight's neck.

Pulling away, Squirrelflight saw affection shining in her eyes. She purred. "Whatever happens, we'll face it together."

"Squirrelflight." Firestar's mew jerked her attention away. He was staring across the clearing. Bluestar, Crookedstar, and the others had returned from the shadows.

"We've made our decision." Crookedstar beckoned Squirrelflight and Leafpool forward with a flick of his tail.

Squirrelflight's chest tightened. She felt her breath quicken. Staying close to Leafpool, she crossed the clearing and stopped in front of him.

"We've decided that both of you did more good than harm. If this is truly the end of your lives, you may remain in StarClan." The RiverClan leader's eyes shone. "But remember that we are still watching. If your lives are not over, we'll reconsider them when you return. You still have to earn your place in StarClan."

Squirrelflight nodded. "Of course. Understood."

"And thank you!" Leafpool pricked her ears. She turned to Squirrelflight. "If this *is* the end . . . we'll always be together now."

Squirrelflight blinked at her. This was what she wanted. Leafpool would always be safe now. StarClan would welcome her. She waited for happiness to spread beneath her pelt, but a chill gripped her. "I'm not ready to die," she whispered. She turned to Firestar. "I have to go back to ThunderClan. I can't leave things like this."

Firestar's eyes rounded sympathetically. "I know it's hard to leave the living behind." He touched his nose to her head. "But if your time has come to die, there's nothing you can do."

Leafpool pressed against her. "Alderheart and Jayfeather might save us."

Squirrelflight closed her eyes. *I hope so.*

"In the meantime . . ." Firestar's mew was suddenly brisk. He ran his tail along Squirrelflight's spine. "You can explore our territory. One day this *will* be your home. There's no harm in looking around."

CHAPTER 25

❧

Squirrelflight tore another piece of flesh from the rabbit carcass. It was so sweet that she closed her eyes for a moment to savor the taste, her fur prickling along her spine. A light breeze swirled around the sandy ravine where Firestar had brought them, an echo of the ravine where ThunderClan had made their camp in the forest before the Great Journey.

Dandelionkit and Juniperkit were playing moss-ball nearby with Larksong, Flickerkit, and Briarlight, while Leafpool and Hollyleaf lay happily beside Squirrelflight, paws outstretched, eyes closed, in a pool of sunshine. Firestar and Sandstorm were sharing a squirrel near the fern wall. The scents and sounds of the ravine were so familiar that Squirrelflight suddenly felt as though nothing had changed since she was a kit.

Dustpelt sat beside her, his tail flicking contentedly. He gazed around the ravine. "Do you remember the old camp?"

"Of course." Squirrelflight purred.

Leafpool lifted her head. "That's where we stood after we were given our apprentice names." Leafpool nodded to the edge of the clearing.

Squirrelflight remembered. "We were waiting for Dustpelt

and Cinderpelt to take us into the forest for the first time."

"You were always so impatient." Dustpelt's gaze flashed teasingly at Squirrelflight. "But you were a quick learner."

"I had to be!" Affection for her old mentor warmed Squirrelflight's heart. "You had so much to teach me."

Cinderpelt lay a tail-length away, sharing a squirrel with Longtail and Mousefur. She looked up from her meal. "Leafpool was always patient," she mewed fondly. "Especially with the elders. She could listen to them complain for moons."

Mousefur pricked her ears. "I hope you don't mean me," she mewed sharply.

Squirrelflight saw Cinderpelt and Leafpool swap a knowing glance. She blinked innocently at Mousefur. "Of course she didn't. You never complained." As she spoke, Squirrelflight noticed a gap in the ferns at the far end of the clearing. "Look, Leafpool." She nodded toward it. "That's where we used to sneak out of camp and go exploring."

Leafpool purred. "We'd pretend we were fetching mouse bile from the medicine den and slip out when no cat was watching."

Dustpelt's eyes widened. "*That's* why I could never find you."

On the other side of the clearing, Ashfur got to his paws. He signaled to Dustpelt with his tail. "Do you want to come hunting?" he called. "I'm meeting Whitestorm by the river."

"Sure." Dustpelt acknowledged the gray warrior with a nod. "I'd better go. Whitestorm will be waiting." Dustpelt dipped his head. "I'll see you when I get back."

Will you? Squirrelflight shifted uneasily. However nice it was to hang out with her old Clanmates, she wanted to be back with the living. She watched as Dustpelt met Ashfur at the entrance. "Isn't it weird having Ashfur around?" she asked Hollyleaf.

"Not really." Hollyleaf licked a paw absently. "After a while, what happened in the forest seems less important."

Firestar swiped his tongue around his jaws. "It's strange how distant the living Clans seem now. These days I recognize more pelts in StarClan than I do in ThunderClan."

Sandstorm pulled the squirrel carcass closer and picked delicately at the bones. "No cat fights in StarClan," she mewed between bites. "But then, we're never hungry, or cold. I suppose there's less to fight over."

"Squirrelflight!" Juniperkit's mew made her turn. He was hurtling toward her, his tail sticking straight into the air. He bundled into her, purring. "Do you want to play moss-ball with us?"

Dandelionkit hurried after him. "Briarlight says it's more fun if we all play."

"I said no such thing." Briarlight bounded to the edge of the clearing and blinked at Squirrelflight. She looked lean and fit, her pelt sparkling with starlight. It was hard to believe she'd been crippled for so long. She grabbed Juniperkit and scooped him onto her back. "Do you want a badger ride?"

"Yes!" Juniperkit squeaked.

"Me too!" As Dandelionkit scrambled onto Briarlight's back, Larksong and Flickerkit crossed the clearing.

"Let's have a race," Larksong called.

"Can we?" Flickerkit's eyes lit up.

"We can do anything we want." His father ducked low enough for him to climb onto his back.

Squirrelflight purred as Briarlight and Larksong charged away, the kits squealing with delight as they clung on. Her purr suddenly died in her throat. They'd always be like this. "Are they sad that they'll never become warriors?"

Firestar shrugged. "They learn warrior skills," he told her. "And even though they won't ever get warrior names, they can hunt and explore where they like. It's safe here. And there are always plenty of other kits to play with."

Sandstorm followed Squirrelflight's gaze. "They spend a lot of time with Mosskit," she told her.

Squirrelflight jerked her muzzle toward her mother. "Mosskit." The name rang a bell. She'd heard nursery stories about her. "Wasn't that Bluestar's kit? The one who went missing?"

"Yes." Cinderpelt shifted onto her belly. "She and Bluestar are inseparable now."

Leafpool glanced around the camp. "Why aren't they here?"

"Why should they be? There are no borders in StarClan," Cinderpelt reminded her. "Cats roam where they please. Bluestar lives with Oakheart now. They can be the family they never were in life."

Squirrelflight wondered what it was like to live without borders. She tipped her head to one side. "How can the Clans live in peace here but not beside the lake?"

"I told you." Sandstorm flicked her tail. "There's less to fight about."

Cinderpelt got to her paws. "I promised Yellowfang I'd hunt with her this afternoon." She blinked at Leafpool. "Do you want to come too?"

"Of course." Leafpool blinked at Squirrelflight. "Do you want to join us?"

"No thanks." Squirrelflight wanted to make the most of the time she had here in StarClan. She could wake up at any moment and find herself in the ThunderClan medicine den. "I'll stay with Sandstorm and the kits." She watched Leafpool and Cinderpelt hurry toward the gorse tunnel, their pelts fluffed with excitement. Cinderpelt seemed happier here, and Leafpool happy to be with her again.

Firestar closed his eyes, and Sandstorm began to wash his ears as though he were a kit. Mousefur rolled onto her side, clearly relishing the sunshine. How comforting it was to know that those who'd left them would never truly be gone.

Hollyleaf caught Squirrelflight's eye. "Can I show you around?"

"What about Sandstorm and the kits?" Dandelionkit, Juniperkit, and Flickerkit chased one another's tails on the other side of the clearing.

"They can come too," Hollyleaf told her. "Don't forget, kits aren't confined to camp here. They can go wherever they like in StarClan. There's nothing to hurt them here."

Squirrelflight glanced at her father. He was dozing now, gently snoring. "Should we wake him?"

"He likes to have a nap in the afternoon," Sandstorm told her. "He'll be fast asleep until sunset."

Squirrelflight got to her paws. "Dandelionkit! Juniperkit!" They stopped playing and looked at her eagerly. "Do you want to come look around with us?"

"Yes!" Dandelionkit raced toward her, Juniperkit on her tail.

"Can we come too?" Larksong and Flickerkit hurried after them.

"Sure!" Hollyleaf shook out her pelt. "Maybe we'll catch some squirrels while we're out." She headed for the thorn tunnel. "Tree hunting is the best."

"*Tree* hunting?" Squirrelflight pricked her ears nervously. "Isn't that dangerous?"

"Not here." Hollyleaf ducked through the entrance.

Juniperkit lifted his tail happily. "You can't hurt yourself, even if you fall."

"It's like flying without wings." Dandelionkit pushed past her and raced through the gorse tunnel, Juniperkit at her heels.

Squirrelflight hurried after them, her belly tightening. Even in StarClan, she didn't like the idea of her kits falling.

"Don't worry." Sandstorm must have seen her pelt prickling. She ran her tail along Squirrelflight's spine. "They're perfectly safe."

Squirrelflight raced along the oak branch. A ginger tail bobbed just ahead. As the ground blurred far below, she felt no fear. She reached the end and leaped. Air streamed through her fur. The tree beyond seemed to reach toward her, and she landed among its branches, breathless at the thrill. She hesitated, scanning the tree for the squirrel. There it was, swarming up the trunk! She hauled herself upward, her claws digging easily into the soft bark, and scrambled onto a crooked branch as the squirrel doubled back.

Hollyleaf was watching from the branch above. As the squirrel neared her, she slithered down, blocking the squirrel's path. It turned, eyes widening as it saw Squirrelflight. She leaped for it and hooked it up, then killed it with a single bite. Its blood sang on her tongue, and she sat back on her haunches, satisfaction pulsing beneath her pelt.

Hollyleaf stopped beside her. "Good, huh?"

Squirrelflight purred. "Very." She peered down through the leaves. She could see Juniperkit and Dandelionkit running along a branch below. It was strange to see kits so young climbing trees. They weren't fast enough to catch squirrels, but they moved with such nimbleness they looked like tiny warriors.

"Let's take this down and rest," Hollyleaf mewed. The sky was darkening as the sun dipped in the sky. "Firestar will be awake soon."

She picked the squirrel up between her jaws and scrambled down the trunk.

Squirrelflight followed, the forest floor soft as she landed.

Leaves rustled above her head, and Juniperkit and Dandelionkit dropped down beside her. They sniffed the squirrel excitedly.

"Can we taste it?" Dandelionkit asked.

"Aren't you too young to eat fresh-kill?" Squirrelflight pricked her ears with surprise.

Juniperkit rolled his eyes. "This is StarClan," he told her. "We can eat anything we like."

"Okay, then." As they padded around the squirrel, searching for the best place to take a bite, Squirrelflight looked around the woods. "Where's Sandstorm?"

"I'm here." Her mother padded from between the trees, Larksong at her tail. Flickerkit followed them, dragging a mouse by its tail. His catch was almost half his size.

"Did you catch that yourself?" Juniperkit sounded impressed as he hurried to sniff the mouse.

Flickerkit let the mouse flop onto the ground. "Larksong flushed it out and I killed it."

Larksong stopped beside his son and puffed out his chest. "He learns quickly."

Squirrelflight's belly felt suddenly hollow. How would Sparkpelt feel when she heard that Flickerkit was learning warrior skills without her? She blinked at Larksong. "Should I tell Sparkpelt that you're happy here?"

Larksong's gaze darkened. "I'm not happy, exactly.," he murmured. "I still miss her." Grief glittered in his eyes.

Flickerkit looked at him. "Will Sparkpelt be joining us soon?"

"Not yet." Larksong touched his nose to Flickerkit's head.

Guilt pricked Squirrelflight's pelt. She'd forgotten about Sparkpelt and Bramblestar while she was hunting. They'd be sick with worry. She should be with them, not here. "I need to see my Clanmates. Take me to the pond." She stared at Sandstorm. If there was a way to see her living Clanmates, perhaps she could send them a message. "I need to go back."

Sandstorm frowned. "I don't know if you can."

"I have to try." Squirrelflight padded past her mother and headed for the meadow where she'd woken. Sandstorm followed, Larksong, Hollyleaf, and the kits at her heels. Even the kits kept up as she broke from the forest and crossed the meadow to the pond. The surface shimmered in the fading light as she stopped beside it. She peered in, anxiety sparking in her belly as she saw nothing but her reflection. "How do I see them?"

"See who?" Leafpool's mew took her by surprise. Her sister was hurrying toward her, Cinderpelt at her side.

"I want to see Sparkpelt." Squirrelflight touched her paw to the water. As ripples spread around it, she glimpsed the ThunderClan camp. She dropped into a crouch and peered harder into the pond. The medicine den opened before her. Alderheart hadn't moved. He was still huddled beside her nest. Leafpool lay next to her, Jayfeather at her side. In the hazy shadows she could make out Bramblestar. His eyes were hollow with grief. Her heart twisted inside her chest. "I must get to them. I have to tell them I'm coming back."

"You can only watch." Sandstorm's flank brushed hers softly.

"There must be some way to send them a message." Squirrelflight looked again, her heart lurching as she realized that she couldn't see her daughter. "Where's Sparkpelt?"

"She's probably with her kits," Sandstorm murmured.

"Or she could be grieving," Larksong mewed. "I can never see her when she's really upset. It's like she's swallowed by shadows."

Foreboding trickled like ice water through Squirrelflight's pelt. "She needs me." Her words felt thick. She sat up. "They all need me."

Leafpool padded closer. "There's nothing we can do," she mewed gently.

"But you hear from StarClan all the time," Squirrelflight insisted. "There must be a way to reach them. How do you share with StarClan when you're at the Moonpool?"

Leafpool shrugged. "I just touch my nose to the water and I'm there with them."

Squirrelflight jabbed her nose into the pond. Water raced up her nose and made her sneeze.

Leafpool ran her tail along Squirrelflight's spine. "They'll be okay," she soothed.

"No, they won't!" Panic fluttered at the edge of Squirrelflight's thoughts. "I have to reach them." She stared urgently at Leafpool. "Perhaps if you try too. We have two paws here and two paws beside the lake. If we try hard enough, we have to be able to find our way back."

Leafpool shook her head. "I don't want to go back yet. It's been so long since I've seen Hollyleaf, Sandstorm, and Firestar. I want to stay with them while I can."

"But Sparkpelt needs us." Squirrelflight blinked at her.

"Sparkpelt needs *you*," Leafpool murmured softly. "Not me."

Squirrelflight saw calmness in Leafpool's gaze. *She's happy to be here.* She shook out her pelt. *Well, I'm not!* "I'm going to find my way back." She turned toward her kits.

Dandelionkit was chasing Flickerkit around her brother. She stopped as she saw Squirrelflight padding toward them. "Have you seen all your Clanmates in the pond?"

"Not yet." Squirrelflight ignored the guilt pricking beneath her pelt. "I have to go back."

"Now?" Juniperkit's eyes widened.

"But you only just got here," Dandelionkit mewed.

"I'll return," Squirrelflight promised. "You just have to be patient a little while longer." She glanced at Flickerkit and Sandstorm. "And you have friends here, and kin. I'll be back before you know it."

"Don't you *want* to stay?" Sadness glistened in Juniperkit's gaze.

"I can't stay yet," Squirrelflight told him. "There are cats I left behind. They still need me. More than you do."

"Okay, then." Dandelionkit lifted her chin bravely. "I can wait," she mewed.

Juniperkit glanced at his sister uncertainly. "So can I, I guess."

Squirrelflight touched her muzzle to his head, then nuzzled Dandelionkit's ears. "Be good," she murmured softly. "Keep practicing your hunting skills."

Juniperkit flicked his tail. "By the time you get back, we'll be able to catch whole squirrels."

"I'm sure you will." Squirrelflight's chest tightened as she turned back toward the pond.

Larksong padded closer. "If you reach Sparkpelt, tell her I love her. Tell her not to be unhappy. I'll take care of Flickerkit until she can join us. But she has to be happy. She has to make a life without me. I don't want her to grieve."

Squirrelflight nodded solemnly. "I'll tell her if I can." She turned to Sandstorm. "Say good-bye to Firestar for me." She ignored the grief tugging at her belly. She knew what she had to do. The pond was her link to ThunderClan. It must be the only way to reach them. Taking a gulp of air, she leaped. As she plunged into the water, her breath caught in her throat. Cold pierced her fur. Eyes stinging, she ducked beneath the surface and fought her way down into the shadowy depths.

CHAPTER 26

❧

Squirrelflight's thoughts raced as darkness enclosed her. What if the pond was bottomless? Would she drown? She glanced back toward the surface, but it was hidden in shadow. She forced herself on. If she could see ThunderClan in these waters, there had to be a way through. The weight of the water crushed her fur. Blood roared in her ears. Panic shrilled in her pelt as her lungs screamed for air. *I must go back!* She floundered, jerking her muzzle around, looking for escape. In the shadows, she glimpsed an opening. She pushed toward it, but tangled roots blocked the way, and only deeper shadow lay beyond. She spun around, the weight of the water tugging at her limbs. Was there any way out?

Hope flashed in her chest as she spotted a light in the distance. She kicked out, pushing herself toward it, and pressed her mouth tighter shut, fighting the urge to breathe. *Sparkpelt! Bramblestar!* She had to get back to them. Dizzy with fear, she fought on.

Slowly, as though she were waking from a nightmare, the chill eased and the water loosened its grip. She felt weightless. Her hunger for breath vanished as the water around her seemed to dissolve into air. She pushed faster toward the light glittering ahead, feeling its warmth as it embraced her. The shadows melted away, and she felt earth grow solid beneath her paws.

She looked around. The ThunderClan camp! She was standing in the clearing. Afternoon sunshine washed her pelt as she watched her Clanmates move around her. Berrynose picked a shrew from the fresh-kill pile. Bristlepaw and Thriftpaw dragged old bedding from the elders' den, while Leafshade pawed fallen leaves into a pile at the edge of the clearing. They worked quietly, and Squirrelflight could sense sadness like rain in the air, ruffling fur and shadowing gazes.

She stood still, expecting at any moment to be seen, but her Clanmates seemed unaware of her presence.

"Do you want the rest?" Stormcloud pushed a half-eaten mouse toward Hollytuft. "I'm not very hungry."

"Neither am I." Hollytuft gazed dully at the mouse.

Squirrelflight felt suddenly far away. Loneliness rang like an echo in her chest. She pushed it away and hurried to the nursery.

Inside, Sparkpelt lay in her nest while Daisy played with the kits. Sorrelstripe and her kits were outside.

"Come on, Flamekit." Daisy ducked down and encouraged the black tom-kit to climb onto her back, where Finchkit was already sitting.

Finchkit puffed out her chest. "I got here first."

"Only because you pushed me out of the way!" Flamekit flicked his tail indignantly and scrambled up beside her.

Finchkit tried to bat him away as he barged past her. "Hey! I want to go in front."

"No fighting!" Daisy scolded. "There's enough room for both of you."

Squirrelflight glanced at Sparkpelt. Wasn't she going to tell her kits to behave? Sparkpelt didn't move, her gaze blank as though she was hardly aware of Daisy or her kits. Squirrelflight hurried across the den and crouched beside her. "Sparkpelt! Your kits need you!" Flamekit and Finchkit had a Clan to take care of them, but they still needed their mother. Didn't Sparkpelt realize what she was missing? "Don't give in to grief." Squirrelflight remembered the closeness she had felt with her kits—it had always made her heart sing. "Sparkpelt!"

Sparkpelt's ear twitched, but her gaze didn't change. *She doesn't even know I'm here!* Frustrated, Squirrelflight backed away as Daisy rolled, purring, to the ground, and sent Finchkit and Flamekit tumbling into the soft depths of her nest.

They squealed with delight and scrambled out.

"Do it again!" Finchkit clawed her way back onto Daisy's shoulders. Flamekit clambered after her.

Sparkpelt didn't move.

Heart pounding, Squirrelflight ducked out of the den. *I have to live. Sparkpelt needs me.* She hurried to the medicine den and pushed through the brambles. The small hollow was gloomy despite the sunlight seeping down from the opening above the pool. Alderheart leaned into one of the nests, and as Squirrelflight padded closer, she could see him press his ear to the flank of the she-cat inside. Unease wormed through her pelt as she saw her body, unmoving. Leafpool lay beside her, and Jayfeather crouched with his chin resting on the edge of the nest. His blind blue gaze seemed empty of hope. If only he knew that Leafpool was probably chasing Cinderpelt across meadows in StarClan now, energy pulsing through her paws.

"Is there any herb we haven't tried?" Alderheart blinked at Jayfeather expectantly.

Jayfeather stared ahead. "We've tried everything. We can only hope now."

Squirrelflight wondered if prayers were any use. StarClan seemed as helpless to change destiny as any living cat. Her heart filled with love for Jayfeather and Alderheart. It seemed that they hadn't moved for days. She'd been a mother to both of them, and her heart broke to see their sadness. She padded to Jayfeather's side, the memory of StarClan's judgment still fresh in her thoughts. *Why should such a deceitful cat have a place in StarClan?* How must it have felt for Jayfeather to discover that she wasn't his mother? She'd lied to him since birth. Leafpool had too. Was that why he was so sharp with his Clanmates? Had bitterness hollowed out his heart? And yet she knew there was warmth there. His harshness was like snow in leaf-bare, hiding buds that would blossom when greenleaf returned. *I have to live!* She had so much still to share with him. "I'm sorry we deceived you," she whispered, wondering if there was any way he might hear. *He is a medicine cat, after all.* "It was wrong of us. But I hope that one day you will let go of the hurt we caused you." She swished her tail along his spine, hope sparking in her chest as she saw his pelt smooth a little.

Movement in the shadows at the edge of the den made her stiffen. Bramblestar had been there all along! She could taste his scent, but it was faint, as though he were far away. He padded to the nest where her body lay and sat beside Alderheart. "I wish I'd listened to her." Bramblestar's mew was husky with grief. Alderheart glanced at him, his pelt ruffling self-consciously as Bramblestar went on. "I ignored how strongly she felt. I didn't want to hear about the Sisters. It made things too complicated. It was easier just to think about the Clans. But Squirrelflight could see beyond that. She knew that honor doesn't mean anything if it can't reach beyond our borders. Any cat can respect those they know and love. But respecting cats we don't understand is truly being a warrior."

"Don't be so hard on yourself," Alderheart murmured. "You were fighting for your Clan."

"But Squirrelflight was my deputy," Bramblestar argued. "And my mate. I should have taken her opinion seriously instead of brushing it aside." His shoulders drooped. "If she dies, I don't know if I can carry on being leader. I will be responsible for her death. I am not fit to lead my Clanmates if I don't listen to them fairly."

"No!" Squirrelflight darted to his side. "ThunderClan is more important than I am. Who else can lead it like you do?" She stared at him, willing him to hear, her heart aching with love for him, but he stared hopelessly at his paws.

"How did we lose sight of what mattered?" His mew was barely a whisper, but Squirrelflight could hear it as loudly as the wail of a kit. "Now I can feel it as strongly as ever. How did I forget how much I loved her?"

Squirrelflight pressed her muzzle against his. It felt like no more than air. But his scent was stronger now. It filled her mouth, bathed her tongue, flooded her chest. "Our love will always be there," she breathed urgently. The ache in her heart seemed to draw his scent deeper. "Even when we lose sight of it, our love will still be there."

Bramblestar slumped as though defeated.

Alderheart shifted his paws anxiously. "I'm sure she knew that you still loved her." But he looked away, as though uncertain of his words. He got to his paws and headed for the entrance. "I'm going to get some fresh air."

Squirrelflight hurried after the young tom as he nosed his way through the brambles. "I'm coming back!" she called after him as he padded into the clearing. Jayfeather had seemed comforted by her presence. Maybe Alderheart, too, could sense her assurances in some way? He crossed the camp. "Don't worry." She ducked after him through the entrance tunnel. "I'll find my way back, I promise."

Outside camp, a warm breeze tugged leaves from the trees. Alderheart paused on the slope and looked up as they showered around him. He seemed to be searching the canopy. What was he hoping to see? Squirrelflight's heart leaped. Was he looking for a sign from StarClan? *A sign!* That was how StarClan communicated with the medicine cats while they were awake—with an omen. Could she send him one? Something to tell him she was okay and was trying to get home?

She looked around frantically. Could she affect anything

in the forest? She darted among the trees and pushed through ferns, hoping to stir them. They didn't move, but a blackbird shrilled an alarm above her head. Could it sense her? She spotted it calling from the branch of an oak and raced toward the trunk. It fluttered away as she neared. She could scare prey! She spun around, her heart pounding. Alderheart was still standing outside the camp, gazing upward. She had to be quick. She zigzagged between the ferns, hoping to flush out a mouse. Bark splinters sprinkled her back. She looked up. A squirrel was bobbing along the branch above her head. A *squirrel!* It was perfect. If she could send it running across Alderheart's path, he might see it and wonder what a squirrel was doing so close to the camp. Prey was usually wise enough to stay clear. He would *have* to realize it was a sign! She leaped for the trunk and hooked her claws into the bark. Not long ago she'd been chasing squirrels in StarClan. This was far more serious. She had to let ThunderClan know that she was trying to get home.

The squirrel looked over its shoulder as she hauled herself onto the branch. Confusion clouded its gaze, but its pelt fluffed in alarm. If it couldn't see her, it could sense her. It raced to the end and leaped into the branches of the next tree. Squirrelflight chased after it, flinging herself from the oak, paws outstretched. Her heart leaped into her throat as she glided through the air. With a gasp, she caught hold of the flimsy twigs jutting from a branch and jerked herself forward, scrabbling onto the thicker wood beyond. The squirrel was near the trunk. It looked up. She couldn't let it climb higher.

She had to chase it toward Alderheart. She pushed hard against the bark, driving herself forward, and leaped for the trunk. Startled, the squirrel turned, fear-scent pulsing from it, and flung itself from the branch. It landed nimbly on the forest floor. Squirrelflight jumped after it, landing as softly as a shadow. She darted in front of it, startling it into turning, then chased it toward the camp.

Excitement fizzed through her pelt as it darted past Alderheart. His gaze flashed toward it, his eyes widening in surprise. She pulled up and blinked at him. Had he understood the message? *It's me, Squirrelflight. I'm coming home.*

Alderheart seemed to freeze. He stared after the squirrel; then he shook out his pelt and padded back into camp.

Frustration knotted her belly. *Please understand!* Was this what it was like to be a StarClan cat—trying to communicate with the living, and never being sure if they understood? For the first time she wondered how many signs from StarClan they missed every day without knowing.

She sat back on her haunches. She'd done all she could. Her pelt prickled with unease. What if she could never get back? Would she be stranded in the forest forever, like the dead cats the Sisters saw? She shivered and pushed the thought away. What had happened to the Sisters? The battle seemed to have left the rest of ThunderClan unscarred. Had the Sisters escaped so lightly? What had happened to Moonlight's kits?

As her thoughts quickened, the forest blurred around her. She blinked, suddenly dizzy, and found herself in the Sisters' camp. Startled, she looked around. Hawkwing was yowling orders to a SkyClan patrol.

"We'll build the warriors' den over there." He nodded toward a space between the birthing den and the den where Squirrelflight and Leafstar had slept. "And that gorse bush will make a good den for the elders."

Macgyver and Plumwillow sniffed around the gorse. Macgyver slid beneath the branches and popped out a moment later.

"We can dig out a hollow around the stem," he told Hawkwing. "The earth is dry and sandy. It won't take long."

Sandynose pushed through the fern entrance. "There are plenty of brambles and vines we can gather." He padded toward Hawkwing. "We can get the camp weatherproof by leaf-bare."

"Good." Hawkwing looked pleased.

Squirrelflight tasted the air for faint signs of the Sisters. Where were they? SkyClan had clearly claimed this land as their own. Her heart quickened. Had they driven the Sisters away?

She hurried across the clearing and followed the trail of tattered bushes to the site of the last battle. Her tail twitched as she saw the cave where the Sisters had taken shelter. It was a pile of rubble and stone now, branches sticking out like bones from rotted prey. She could see where earth had been dug out. Was that where her Clanmates had pulled out her body and Leafpool's?

"Hey!" A mew made her jump. She spun, unsheathing her claws, instinctively dropping into a defensive warrior stance.

Then she realized—some cat could see her!

She blinked as she saw the ghostly shape of a tabby she-cat padding from beside the landslide. She could see through it. She shivered, her pelt spiking. This cat was dead.

The cat lifted her tail in a friendly greeting. "You're new here." She dipped her head as she neared. "Did you die recently?"

Squirrelflight bristled. "I'm not dead." She lifted her muzzle.

"Really?" The tabby reached out a paw and swept it through Squirrelflight's forelegs.

Squirrelflight leaped away. "Hey!" Energy buzzed through her paws like the sparks from dry grass.

"You look dead to me," the tabby mewed.

"It's just temporary," Squirrelflight told her. "While my body mends."

"Sure." The tabby sniffed, clearly unconvinced. "My name's Blade."

"I'm Squirrelflight."

"Hi, Squirrelflight." Blade nodded politely. "How did you die—I mean"—she corrected herself—"get injured?"

Squirrelflight nodded toward the landslide. "I was in there when it collapsed."

"I hope it didn't hurt too much." The tabby swished her tail. "I got hit by a monster. I was dead before I could feel anything."

"Did you live around here?" Had this cat seen the Sisters?

"Close enough." Blade shrugged. "I lived with Twolegs,

beyond the hills there." She nodded toward the cliff face.

"You're a kittypet?" Squirrelflight blinked at her.

"Aren't you?"

"I'm a warrior," Squirrelflight told her.

"Really?" The tabby's eyes widened. "Is that why you have such a weird name?" She didn't wait for a reply. "I've never met a warrior before. Especially not a dead one. I wondered where you went after you died. I've only seen the Sisters since I died."

Squirrelflight pricked her ears. "Do you know the Sisters?"

"Quite well." Blade sat down and began to wash her ears. "They can see dead cats," she mewed between licks. "I used to chat quite often with some of them."

"Who?"

"One was called Moonlight," Blade told her. "And I think another was Tempest?" She looked unsure.

Squirrelflight leaned forward. "Do you know what happened to them?"

"Those other cats." Blade jerked her muzzle toward the Sisters' camp. "They're warriors too, right?"

"Yes." Squirrelflight's pelt twitched.

"When they came to look at the mess after the battle, they took the Sisters away. They were pretty beaten up."

"Did they take Moonlight away?"

"I guess."

"And her kits?" Squirrelflight stared desperately at Blade.

"Yes." Blade tipped her head.

But no cat died, right? Squirrelflight was too anxious to ask.

She searched the kittypet's eyes. She'd have said if any cat had died, surely? "Where did they go?"

Blade shrugged. "I heard the big gray tom tell his friends to take them back to camp."

The SkyClan camp? Squirrelflight could hardly believe her ears. Of course—Leafstar hadn't let her warriors take part in the battle. If they were to shelter with any Clan, it would be with SkyClan. Hope flashed beneath her pelt. Were the Sisters safe at last?

"Thanks, Blade." She turned and began to head for the forest. She had to see for herself if the Sisters were okay. The valley became hazy around her, and the ground seemed to shift beneath her paws. A moment later she found herself in the SkyClan camp. She flicked her tail. This instant traveling was useful! She wished she could do it while she was alive.

Pain burst inside her head like burning ice. She winced, her paws trembling beneath her, as it hardened and grew sharper. Closing her eyes, she stood still, relief melting inside her as slowly it eased. *What was that?* Foreboding welled at the edge of her thoughts. She pushed it away. Perhaps Alderheart was trying a new treatment.

She forced herself to focus on the SkyClan camp, startled as Fidgetflake brushed past her, oblivious as he sent sparks fizzing through Squirrelflight's fur. Squirrelflight shook her pelt out as Fidgetflake ducked into the medicine den. Quickly, she followed, blinking as her eyes adjusted to the shadows inside.

Moonlight was lying in a wide, bracken nest while Frecklewish sorted herbs beside her. The gray she-cat's eyes were closed, and gashes crisscrossed her flank. Her muzzle was clogged with dried blood.

"Has she woken yet?" Fidgetflake asked softly.

Frecklewish shook her head. "I wish she were doing better." She tore a bunch of dried marigold apart. "I've put new ointment on her wounds, but the infection is hard to get rid of"

"Her kits are doing well," Fidgetflake told her. "They're nursing happily, and Violetshine says she's got plenty of milk now that her own kits are weaned. I've told Leafstar that she'll need extra fresh-kill to keep her strength up."

"Good." Frecklewish crumbled leaves into a pile. "How are the other Sisters?"

"Quiet." Fidgetflake glanced toward the entrance. "They wish they weren't here, but they know it's the best place for Moonlight."

"I just hope we can heal her." Frecklewish's eyes glittered with worry as she glanced at the gray she-cat.

Fidgetflake stiffened and blinked suddenly at Squirrelflight.

Squirrelflight froze. *Can she see me?* Her breath caught in her throat. Then she realized that the young medicine cat wasn't staring at her; she was staring straight through her.

"I can smell ThunderClan." Fidgetflake frowned.

"It's probably left over from the battle," Frecklewish told her.

As she spoke, the entrance rustled. Tree poked his head in. "I'm going hunting. Does Moonlight need fresh-kill yet?"

"Not yet."

As Frecklewish got to her paws, Tree's eyes widened. Surprise flashed in his gaze. Squirrelflight's pelt spiked with alarm. *He's looking straight at me!* Hope flashed in her heart. *Of course! He can see ghosts.*

"Tree?" Frecklewish narrowed her eyes. "Are you okay?"

He blinked and shook out his pelt, snatching his gaze away from Squirrelflight. "Y-yeah," he mewed. He ducked out of the den.

Squirrelflight followed him out. "You can see me, can't you?" She followed him as he padded quickly across the camp.

"I can't talk to you here," he hissed under his breath. He led her out of camp and a little way into the forest. Scanning the trees, he halted. He stared at her, his eyes rounding with sympathy. "I'm so sorry."

"Sorry?" Squirrelflight frowned. What was he sorry about?

"That you died," he mewed. "I knew you got hurt, but we all hoped you'd survive."

"I'm not dead yet." Squirrelflight swished her tail. "I'm kind of . . . in between StarClan and ThunderClan at the moment."

Tree's ears twitched. "I didn't know that was possible," he mewed.

"Neither did I." Squirrelflight sat down. "But apparently it is."

"Is Moonlight with you?" He peered past her. "She's been unconscious for days. Frecklewish isn't sure she's going to make it."

"I haven't seen her," Squirrelflight told him, wondering suddenly if Moonlight's spirit was roaming the forest nearby.

As she glanced between the trees, another pain seemed to pierce her eyes and stab into her head. It burned along her spine, and she staggered, gasping at the intensity.

"Squirrelflight?" Tree stepped closer, alarm spiking through his pelt. "Are you okay?"

"I don't know." She took a breath as the pain eased a little. She was trembling.

"You started to fade." Tree sounded scared.

Squirrelflight's blinked at him, her paws pricking. "I don't think I can stay here." Had Alderheart found a way to wake her at last, or was StarClan tugging her back? *Am I dying?* Her heart lurched. "If I don't wake up," she breathed urgently as the forest began to glitter around her, "you have to give Bramblestar a message."

Tree leaned toward her. "What?"

"You must tell him to go on without me. He has to lead ThunderClan. They need him. Tell him I love him and I'm waiting for him in StarClan. Tell Sparkpelt that I've seen Larksong. He's named their kit Flickerkit. They're with Firestar and Sandstorm." Starlight filled the forest, dazzling her. "Tell Alderheart . . ." Pain flared in her head once more, and before she could finish, darkness swallowed her.

CHAPTER 27

❧

Squirrelflight struggled to open her eyes. Weak light surrounded her, and she felt stiff stalks of bracken beneath her. Her head throbbed. Pain scorched her hind leg as though a fox were tearing at it. She tried to look at it, and paws slipped beneath her head, cradling it like a kit.

"Where am I?" Was she home?

"In the medicine den."

She recognized Jayfeather's mew. She strained to make sense of the shadows moving around her. Scents flooded her nose—Alderheart, Jayfeather, Bramblestar, the tang of herbs, and a sickly, sweet scent that filled her with dread. The shadows shifted and became clear. She could see the roof of the den, and the gap where light filtered down to the pool.

The paws behind her head moved, and she saw Jayfeather leaning over her. She flinched as he dripped sap into her mouth, then recoiled as the bitter taste bathed her tongue.

"It will help." Alderheart's mew sounded close to her ear. She realized, as he gently lowered his head, that his paws were the ones supporting her. She struggled to sit up, but pain split her head, and the fox seemed to tear more viciously at her leg.

"Don't try to move." Bramblestar was close. She felt his warm breath on her cheek and breathed in his scent, her heart aching with relief. She was home and she was with him. He loved her again.

An idea worried at the edge of her thoughts. Who was taking care of Leafpool? Alderheart and Jayfeather were both at her nest. Was her sister already awake? Squirrelflight craned to see. "Leafpool?"

Jayfeather moved and blocked her gaze.

"Leafpool!" Alarm sparked in Squirrelflight's belly as she recognized the sweet, sickly scent for what it was. Flailing her paws, she pushed him away. She ignored the pain piercing her leg and struggled to the side of her nest. Leafpool lay limp in her nest. Horror hollowed her belly as she realized her sister's blank, cloudy gaze could mean only one thing. Leafpool was dead.

"Leafpool!" She heard herself wail as though hearing an owl hoot way off in the forest. It couldn't be true. Grief seemed to rise up like a flood from the earth and drag her once more into darkness.

"Leafpool!" She opened her eyes. Her pain was gone.

"Squirrelflight?" Leafpool was leaning over her. Sunshine sparkled around her. "You came back."

Relief swamped Squirrelflight. She scrambled to her paws and pressed her cheek against Leafpool's. "I thought I'd lost you. But you're here." Soft grass rippled around her paws. Meadows stretched away on every side, dazzling in bright daylight. She stiffened and pulled away as she understood. This was StarClan's territory. She blinked at Leafpool. "Did I die too?"

"Not yet." Leafpool's eyes shone with love. Stars studded her pelt so that she glittered like the Moonpool.

Squirrelflight stared at her, grief tearing at her heart. "But you did." Her words were no more than a whisper.

"I'm glad to be here." Leafpool's eyes glistened. "I have so many friends here."

"But you have friends in ThunderClan." Squirrelflight stared at her. Could she really be glad to be dead?

"They'll join me eventually." Leafpool looked across the meadow. Firestar and Sandstorm were padding toward them, Hollyleaf beside them.

Squirrelflight's thoughts whirled. "Why am I here? Am I going to die?" Bramblestar's scent still lingered on her tongue. "I want to go back!"

"Be patient," Leafpool murmured. "You can't change what will happen by wishing."

Firestar reached them, Sandstorm and Hollyleaf at his side. "She might be able to change this." He blinked calmly at Squirrelflight.

Leafpool looked puzzled. "What do you mean?"

"Jayfeather and Alderheart's herbs are working." Firestar held Squirrelflight's gaze. "She can live if she fights. But her spirit must be willing to go back."

"Of course I want to go back!" Squirrelflight pricked her ears eagerly.

Sandstorm's gaze was dark. "You were badly hurt," she told Squirrelflight. "You can choose to live, but your life in ThunderClan might be very different from the one you know now. What if your injured leg doesn't heal properly? You'll have a limp. Will you be able to be deputy? Will Bramblestar *want* you as deputy? You defied his authority when you helped the Sisters. I know this is hard to hear, but what if he doesn't want you, even as a mate?"

"That's why I *have* to go back!" Squirrelflight stared at her mother. "I don't care what happens. I have to make things right with my Clan and with Bramblestar. And my kits are there."

"You have kits here, too," Sandstorm pressed. "You'll be able to care for Juniperkit and Dandelionkit. And Leafpool will be here. Don't you remember what I told you after your apprentice ceremony? As long as you have each other, you'll both stand tall."

Squirrelflight flicked her tail. "What's the good in standing tall in *StarClan*? ThunderClan needs me. Lionblaze and Jayfeather need me. If Leafpool is dead, I can't let them lose me too."

Sandstorm's eyes glistened. "I don't want you to suffer any more than you have. Look how happy Briarlight is here. You don't want to return to a life like hers, do you?" Sandstorm's eyes rounded imploringly. "Didn't you promise that you wouldn't let anything drive you and Leafpool apart?" She glanced at Leafpool. "Why not join her here? Then you'll always be together. You'll be safe."

Firestar touched his nose to Sandstorm's cheek. "Squirrelflight must make her own decision," he mewed softly. "Just as she's always done."

Leafpool's star-speckled fur rippled along her spine. "Death won't separate us." Squirrelflight's heart twisted as Leafpool met her gaze. "We promised always to stick together, and it won't be any different now. If you go back, I'll watch over you. And one day, we will be together again."

Squirrelflight's throat tightened. "I'll miss you," she whispered.

"We've been apart before," Leafpool told her. "It only made our relationship stronger."

Squirrelflight closed her eyes for a moment. Leaving Leafpool would be hard. "If I can go back, perhaps you can too, if you try." She blinked hopefully at her sister.

Leafpool shook her head. "ThunderClan doesn't need me. I know I'll be missed. But Jayfeather and Alderheart can take care of all the medicine-cat duties. Jayfeather and Lionblaze will still have you. I'll be happy here. I feel like I've come home." She blinked lovingly at Firestar and Sandstorm, then looked at Hollyleaf and purred. "I've been away from them too long."

Firestar tipped his head to one side and blinked at Squirrelflight. "Are you going back?"

"Yes."

"I'm proud of you," he mewed.

She lifted her chin. "My Clan needs me."

"They're lucky to have you." He narrowed his eyes. "But

you must tell them to turn toward StarClan, not away from us. We can help—"

Squirrelflight blinked at him. "We're not turning away from StarClan." What did he mean? "You've been quiet lately, that's all. We've been listening for messages that don't come."

"Perhaps you haven't been listening hard enough!" Firestar flicked his tail.

Squirrelflight frowned. Had the Clans been missing the signs StarClan had sent them? She knew now how hard it was to communicate with the living. "We'll try harder to hear you." She touched her nose to Firestar's muzzle. "I must go now. Bramblestar will be wondering what happened."

She brushed her mother's cheek with her own. "Tell Dandelionkit and Juniperkit that I'll be back. And when Bramblestar joins us, we'll be a family."

"Take care." Sandstorm pulled away and blinked anxiously at Squirrelflight. "Whatever happens, be brave."

"I will." Squirrelflight turned to Leafpool. "I'm sorry I have to leave you."

"I understand why you do," Leafpool mewed. "Tell Jay-feather and Lionblaze that I always loved them with a mother's love and I always will. Tell them I'm sorry for the lie. I was trying to protect them, not hurt them. I'll never forgive myself for the pain I caused, and I'll be watching over them, and you." She ran her tail along Squirrelflight's spine. "Even when you feel I'm a long way away."

Squirrelflight gazed at her sister, fixing a picture of her in her mind—her eyes bright, her pelt sparkling, a purr in her throat. She wanted to remember this, if she was going back to bury her body. "Okay." She nodded at Firestar. "I'm ready." She glanced across the meadow, looking for the pond.

Firestar seemed to guess what she was thinking. "You don't need to swim back this time. StarClan is ready to let you go. Close your eyes."

Squirrelflight closed her eyes and saw brightness. The blue of the sky seemed to swirl down and wrap her in a dazzling embrace. The ground disappeared from beneath her paws. As she fell, memories flashed in her thoughts.

"Squirrelkit! Come and play!" She was in the Thunder-Clan nursery, back in the old forest. Leafkit was calling to her from the entrance.

"Be careful!" Sandstorm called as Squirrelflight raced into the clearing, chasing Leafkit.

"You can't catch me!" Leafkit glanced over her shoulder, her pelt fluffed with excitement.

"Yes I can." Heart quickening, Squirrelflight hared after her, the wind in her fur.

The camp seemed to shift, and suddenly Leafpaw was standing beside her. They were apprentices again.

Leafpaw purred. "I can call you Squirrelface if you like."

Squirrelflight blinked at her. "You haven't called me Squir-relface in moons." Her heart ached with longing.

"Come on." Leafpaw padded across the clearing toward Cinderpelt and Dustpelt. "Let's tell them to hurry up."

This wasn't what had happened. "We waited for them to finish talking." Squirrelflight hurried after her. Were

Leafpaw's memories different from hers?

"Hurry up!" Leafpaw whisked her tail as she reached Cinderpelt. "I've got so much to learn. We have to hurry. I won't be around forever."

As Cinderpelt turned, the forest blurred and then flashed into focus once more. She was in the lake camp now, and Brambleclaw was glaring at her. "Couldn't you have told me the truth?"

She remembered his words. They were seared into her heart. He was talking about the lie she and Leafpool had told about Jayfeather, Lionblaze, and Hollyleaf. She'd told him they were his kits. He'd been so angry. "It was never my secret to tell," she breathed. "Leafpool had so much to lose."

"She lost everything anyway!" Brambleclaw snarled.

"No I didn't." Relief washed Squirrelflight's pelt as she heard Leafpool's mew. Her sister was facing Brambleclaw, pride rippling through her fur. "I watched my kits grow into fine warriors, and I still serve my Clan with all my heart."

And suddenly they were older, lying in the warmth of the setting sun.

"You said you were going to be Clan leader." Leafpool swished her tail over the ground. "We were going to rule the whole forest and be the most powerful cats who ever lived."

Squirrelflight purred as the memory warmed her. "We were very young." She gazed across the clearing to where Lionblaze and Jayfeather were sharing a rabbit with Sparkpelt and Alderheart. Bramblestar was scrambling down the rock tumble toward them.

Leafpool got to her paws. "Take care of them." She blinked lovingly at Squirrelflight and padded away.

As Leafpool faded into shadow, Squirrelflight closed her eyes. She felt solid earth beneath her and bracken sticking into her pelt. She was home. *Good-bye, Leafpool.* Her sister had had been her best friend. Without her, ThunderClan would never feel the same. Grief pulled at her heart as she drifted into darkness. *I'll miss you.*

CHAPTER 28

❧

"Can you hear me?"

Squirrelflight felt Alderheart's breath on her muzzle. Like a drowning kit dragging itself from the water, she struggled into consciousness. Her head throbbed. Pain burned in her leg. But it felt easier now, as though the fox had loosened its grip. She opened her eyes.

Alderheart was staring at her, hope glittering in his eyes. He pricked his ears as she met his gaze.

"Hi," she croaked weakly.

"Jayfeather!" Alderheart called out without taking his gaze from hers. "She's awake!"

"I'll fetch Bramblestar."

Squirrelflight heard the brambles rustle, and light flicked on the roof of the medicine den.

"He'll be here in a moment," Alderheart told her gently. "How do you feel?"

"Like I've fallen off a cliff." Squirrelflight tried to prop herself up on her front paws, but she didn't have the strength, and they crumpled beneath her. Her belly tightened as she recalled Sandstorm's words. *You may never fully recover.* She looked at Alderheart, searching his gaze. "How badly am I hurt?"

He ran his paws quickly over her flank and down each leg. "Can you feel that?"

"Yes." She grunted as he lifted her hind paw.

"Can you push against me?"

She stretched her leg against his paw, wincing. He lowered it gently and tried the other paws in turn, asking her to push each time.

"Any pain?"

"Only my hind leg," she told him. "And my head."

Alderheart nodded. "That's what we thought, but we couldn't be sure until you woke up." He peered into her eyes as though searching for something. "Do you know where you are?"

"In the ThunderClan medicine den."

"Do you know who I am?"

"Of course. How could I forget my own kit?"

He looked relieved. "You're going to be fine." He sat back on his haunches. "You've wrenched your hind leg, and there was some swelling to your head and body where the rocks hit you. But it's starting to go down."

Squirrelflight was hardly listening. Her injuries didn't matter. She peered over the side of her nest. "Is Leafpool still here?"

Alderheart straightened. "She . . ." He hesitated, alarm flashing in his eyes. "We—we moved her. I'm afraid—"

"It's okay." She wanted to save him the pain of breaking

the news. Her mew thickened as she swallowed back grief. "I know she's dead."

"How?" He blinked at her in surprise.

"I saw her when I woke up last time. Her eyes . . ." Her mew trailed away. She didn't want to remember. Should she tell him that she'd been in StarClan with her sister just a moment ago?

Paw steps sounded outside, and Bramblestar crashed through the brambles at the entrance. "She's awake?" Fear glittered in his gaze. "Is she okay?"

"She will be." Alderheart moved aside and Squirrelflight met Bramblestar's gaze. Her heart leaped as his face softened. He suddenly looked like the young warrior she'd fallen in love with. As he rushed toward her, she stretched out her muzzle, breathing in the warmth and the scent of him as he pressed his cheek against hers. He began to lick her head, as urgent and as gentle as a mother lapping her kit.

She purred. "I'm sorry I scared you."

"Don't be sorry." He pulled away and looked into her eyes. "Don't be sorry for anything. I was so worried. I love you so much. We should never have let things get so bad. I'll never let it happen again."

Squirrelflight tried again to push herself up, finding enough strength this time to hoist herself into an awkward sitting position. She saw Lionblaze hesitating beside Jayfeather at the entrance.

"Hi, Lionblaze."

He shifted his paws, as though he didn't know what to say. "I'm glad you're okay." He looked relieved, and then his gaze flitted to Leafpool's empty nest. It darkened.

"I know about Leafpool." She pushed herself higher. "I know you'll miss her as much as I will."

Lionblaze met her gaze. She saw conflict there, as though he wasn't sure what to feel. How hard it must be not to know which mother was his true mother. One had kitted him and one had raised him. Which one should he love? Surely there was a place in his heart for both of them.

He looked away. "It was a dumb accident," he growled. "We should have let the Sisters move in their own time. That land wasn't worth dying for."

Bramblestar's tail twitched. "What's done is done," he murmured.

Squirrelflight didn't want to think about it. Of course it was dumb. That was what she'd been telling them all along. But what was the point in saying so now? She glanced past Lionblaze expectantly. "Did Sparkpelt come too?"

Jayfeather crossed the den briskly. "She's feeding her kits." He avoided her gaze.

Worry sparked in Squirrelflight's pelt. "Is she okay?"

"She's healthy." Jayfeather leaned into the nest and sniffed her injured leg. "We can make you a splint," he told her. "To help you get around."

Squirrelflight didn't care about splints. "Are the kits well?" she pressed.

Bramblestar purred. "They're very well," he told her. "They want to explore outside the nursery already. Poor Daisy is exhausted."

"And Sparkpelt?" Was she playing with them yet?

"She's had a hard moon," Bramblestar mewed. "But she'll come around, I'm sure. She just needs a little more time. Seeing you get well will cheer her up."

"I'll be better in no time." Squirrelflight shifted until she sat up straight. She winced as pain shot through her hind leg.

"I'll get you some poppy seeds." Alderheart hurried to the herb store.

"Thanks." Squirrelflight glanced around the den. Lionblaze had padded closer, and Bramblestar was smoothing the bracken inside her nest.

Jayfeather followed Alderheart to the store. "You might as well fetch her some comfrey while you're there," he mewed. "We can wrap her leg in it before we attach the splint."

She purred. It was good to be back.

"I'm glad you woke up before her vigil." Bramblestar helped Squirrelflight from the medicine den. Dusk was turning into night, and the camp was bathed in shadow. "We couldn't have buried her without you."

Leaning on him heavily, Squirrelflight tried not to betray the pain jabbing her wrenched leg. The splint helped, but she still couldn't put weight on her hind paw, and the smell of the comfrey leaves bound around her leg was making her queasy.

She could see Leafpool now, lying in the middle of the clearing.

Millie looked up as Squirrelflight reached them. Their Clanmates were ringed around the body, murmuring softly to one another as they waited for the vigil to begin. "We will miss her," Millie told Squirrelflight softly.

"Thank you." Squirrelflight dipped her head. "She looks so peaceful." She waved Bramblestar back with her tail and limped to Leafpool's stiff, lifeless body, comforted by the thought that, in StarClan, Leafpool would be racing across meadows, warmed by endless sunshine.

She felt the gazes of her Clanmates flitting around her like moths, and wondered if they'd forgiven her for helping the Sisters. No one had called her a traitor, but that was what they must have thought when she'd emerged from Moonlight's den. She looked at Bramblestar uncertainly, seeking reassurance. He gazed lovingly back, as though he could see only her. Graystripe caught her eye and nodded to her from the edge of the clearing. Thornclaw blinked at her fondly. They *had* forgiven her. Grateful, she sat down, carefully easing her wrenched leg to one side.

The moon shone in a soft blue evening sky as Bramblestar padded forward and silenced the murmuring of his Clanmates with a flick of his tail. "Leafpool was a loyal and dedicated medicine cat. She helped her Clanmates when they were sick and watched over them when they were well. She couldn't mother her kits, and so she mothered all of you." His gaze swept around the Clan, and Squirrelflight saw her Clanmates dipping their heads in agreement. "She wouldn't sleep if she knew any cat was suffering, and would go without food or rest to care for her Clan. She fought for what she believed in and protected those who couldn't protect themselves.

ThunderClan will miss her. We were lucky to have her."

Millie padded forward and touched her nose to Leafpool's pelt. "Leafpool cared for Briarlight better than any cat. She made sure her life was long and comfortable despite her broken spine. She would sit up all night when Briarlight was in pain, talking to her and sharing stories to keep her spirits up. She thought up new exercises and games that would keep Briarlight healthy, and, at the end, Leafpool never left her side." Emotion glistened in the old she-cat's eyes. "I hope they will hunt together in StarClan."

As she stepped back, Alderheart padded to Leafpool's side. "I was lucky to have Leafpool as a mentor. She taught me so much about herbs and how to care for my Clanmates, not just their bodies but their spirits. I'll miss her skill and wisdom, and I'll miss her friendship more." He looked expectantly at Jayfeather.

Jayfeather pricked his ears as the Clan fell silent.

"Jayfeather," Alderheart prompted. "Do you want to speak?"

Jayfeather huffed. "Do you want me to say what a great medicine cat she was, or what a great mother she was?" There was bitterness in his mew.

It clawed at Squirrelflight's heart, but she forced her pelt to stay smooth. "Say whatever you want, Jayfeather."

Jayfeather flicked his tail. "She was a good medicine cat. She trained me well and I loved her for it." He frowned. "Then I discovered she was my mother and that she'd lied to me since I was born. Hollyleaf died defending her lie even though Leafpool had abandoned us."

On the other side of the clearing, Lionblaze bristled. He glared at Jayfeather. "What else could she do?"

"Tell the truth?"

"*Then* what?" The golden warrior's eyes flashed. "Did you want her to give up being a medicine cat for you? Would *you* give up being a medicine cat for anyone?" He flattened his ears when Jayfeather didn't answer. "No. I thought not."

Jayfeather eyed him angrily. "You didn't give me chance to finish. I was about to say that I forgave her eventually. Even though I could never love her as a mother after what she'd done, I respected her as a medicine cat and loved her as a Clanmate." He narrowed his eyes. "Don't pretend you loved her any more than I did."

Lionblaze's eyes glittered with grief. "I wish I'd loved her more." His mew was husky. "She deserved to be loved. She was loyal and good and kind."

Squirrelflight's eyes pricked. "She *was* loved." She got to her paws, wincing at the pain. "I loved her. Her final act was to save a litter of kits. They were the kits of an outsider—a stranger to our land, and to our code. But Leafpool saw every life as important, and she died saving something she cherished most of all—kits." She glanced at Jayfeather and Lionblaze. "She told me to tell you that she always loved you as your mother and she always will. She only lied to protect you." Lionblaze looked at his paws. Jayfeather gazed blindly into the gathering darkness as Squirrelflight went on. "She said that she'd never forgive herself for the pain she caused you, but I hope she finds peace in StarClan, because she deserves to be happy." Night hid her Clanmates in shadow, but she could see their eyes glistening in the moonlight. "Leafpool was the best littermate I could have had. I will miss her so much, but I know that she will always be with me, watching from StarClan."

As she finished, a breeze sent leaves showering into the clearing. They drifted down, as pale in the moonlight as Leafpool's amber eyes. *Is she sending me a message?* Squirrelflight looked at the stars, her heart pricking with hope. Even though Leafpool was in StarClan, Squirrelflight knew she wasn't very far away.

CHAPTER 29

Squirrelflight nosed her way into the nursery. It had been a long night, and she was stiff from sitting vigil beside Leafpool's body. Bramblestar had sat with her, pressing close to protect her from the chill. It had felt good to spend the time with Leafpool, to breathe in her scent for the last time and honor her memory with their Clanmates. Bramblestar was helping to bury her now. Squirrelflight had chosen the spot, in a quiet grove where Leafpool had loved to gather thyme.

Daisy sprawled near the nursery entrance, letting Flamekit clamber over her. Quivering with excitement, Finchkit pressed her belly to the ground and, like a warrior stalking prey, watched Daisy's tail flicking back and forth.

"Squirrelflight!" Flamekit's happy mew jerked her from her thoughts. The black tom-kit raced toward her and rubbed around her legs, purring.

Finchkit looked up, pricking her ears. "Are you better now?" she asked.

"I am," Squirrelflight told her.

Flamekit sniffed at the splint on her hind leg. "Why have you got this?"

"It's to support my leg while it heals."

"Does it hurt?" Finchkit sniffed the splint too.

"It's sore, but it'll improve in a few days." Squirrelflight glanced across the den. Sparkpelt lay in her nest, her chin hanging listlessly over the edge.

Stormcloud was with her, pushing a mouse a little closer to her muzzle. "Just try a bit," he murmured. "It might help you feel better."

Sparkpelt didn't look at him. "Why would I want that?"

"Your kits need you," Stormcloud edged the mouse a little nearer.

"I'm feeding them, aren't I?" Sparkpelt pushed the mouse away.

"Which means you need more food, not less." Stormcloud's eyes darkened with worry. "You must be hungry. You hardly ate yesterday."

Daisy sat up. "He's been coming every day," she whispered to Squirrelflight. "Trying to persuade her to eat and cheer her up." She sighed softly. "I'm beginning to think he's wasting his time."

"Does she ever play with the kits?" Squirrelflight asked quietly.

"She only gets out of her nest to make dirt." Daisy shook her head sadly. "If she doesn't take an interest in the kits soon, they're going to think I'm their mother."

Squirrelflight lifted her chin. What could she say to help Sparkpelt out of her grief? She crossed the den and stopped beside Sparkpelt's nest. "I thought you might come to the vigil," she mewed softly, trying to catch Sparkpelt's eye.

Sparkpelt stared at the ground. "I've had enough of vigils," she growled.

"Let's hope it's the last for a while," Stormcloud meowed darkly.

"Vigils are a part of a warrior's life,'" Squirrelflight told him briskly. "You can't wish them away. You have to deal with them as they come." She looked sternly at Sparkpelt. "You can't let grief spoil what you still have."

Sparkpelt didn't react.

"Your kits are a blessing," Squirrelflight went on. "You should enjoy them while you can. They'll be grown before you know it."

Sparkpelt stared ahead blankly as Flamekit and Finchkit chased each other between Daisy's legs.

"I saw Larksong," Squirrelflight mewed softly.

Sparkpelt jerked up her head. "Where?"

"When I was hurt," Squirrelflight told her. "I saw him in StarClan."

"You were never in StarClan," Sparkpelt grunted. She circled in her nest, tramping the bracken into a fresh hollow before slumping heavily into it. "You're making it up to make me feel better."

"He had Flickerkit with him," Squirrelflight pressed.

"Flickerkit?"

"That's what he named your kit." Squirrelflight searched her daughter's gaze, searching for a glimmer of happiness.

Sparkpelt lifted her chin. Interest sparked in her emerald

eyes. "That's the name we chose for him. No one knew it but me and Larksong."

"Larksong told me to tell you he loves you and he's okay. He's going to look after Flickerkit until you join them, and he wants you to be happy. He wants you to make a good life without him. He doesn't want you to grieve."

Sparkpelt stared at her mother, her gaze suddenly far away.

Squirrelflight's heart ached as her daughter's eyes glistened. She wished she could make her pain go away, but she knew Sparkpelt must face it alone. Time would help, and love. She called to the kits. "Come play with your mother."

Flamekit looked at her, puzzled. "But Daisy *likes* playing with us. Sparkpelt just wants to sleep."

Sparkpelt sat up. "No I don't," she mewed earnestly. "Not anymore."

Squirrelflight pricked her ears. It was the first flash of energy her daughter had shown since Larksong's death. She hurried to Flamekit and scooped him up by his scruff.

"Hey!" Flamekit churned his paws in the air as Squirrelflight carried him across the den. "I was playing with Finchkit."

Squirrelflight dropped him in front of Sparkpelt. "Finchkit can come too." She beckoned his sister over.

Sparkpelt blinked nervously at her kits, as though she didn't know what to do.

"Here." Stormcloud quickly tore a lump of moss from her nest and rolled it into a ball. He bowled it past the kits

Flamekit leaped after it instantly, his pelt fluffing with excitement. Finchkit's eyes rounded with determination. She lunged for the ball and knocked it away.

Squirrelflight nodded to Sparkpelt. "Go on," she encouraged.

Sparkpelt hesitated, then reached out a paw and scooped the moss ball away from the kits. They turned on her, pelts prickling with indignation.

"That was ours!" Finchkit told her.

"Then you'd better catch it!" Sparkpelt knocked the moss ball across the den floor.

Squeaking happily, Flamekit and Finchkit chased after it. Sparkpelt's eyes glowed. She hurried after her kits and hooked the ball away again, this time tossing it high above their heads. Flamekit leaped for it, spinning as he jumped.

"Great catch!" Sparkpelt mewed as he snatched the moss ball from the air.

"Throw it again!" Finchkit stared eagerly at her mother. "I want to catch it too!"

Sparkpelt purred and threw the moss ball high, watching proudly as Finchkit batted it away before it hit the ground. "You're going to be great hunters," she told them.

"Can we go and practice on real prey?" Finchkit blinked at her.

"Not yet." Sparkpelt's eyes were bright now. "But we can go outside if you like."

"It's a perfect day for chasing leaves," Stormcloud told her.

"Outside the den?" Flamekit's pelt bushed with excitement.

Finchkit stuck her tail in the air and marched to the den entrance. "I'm going first."

"No you're not!" Flamekit hared after and tried to barge past as she reached the opening in the brambles. Finchkit pushed him away and scrambled out of the den.

"Be nice!" Purring now, Sparkpelt hurried after them. "And fluff out your fur properly! It's chilly outside."

Stormcloud watched her go. "Do you think she's going to be okay?"

"It will take time." Hope glimmered in Squirrelflight's chest. "But with the help of her kits and her Clan, she'll find a way to get over Larksong's death." She ducked out of the den. Flamekit and Finchkit were already chasing across the clearing as the wind whisked a leaf ahead of them. Sparkpelt bounded after them, her tail fluffed with excitement as a fresh flurry of leaves showered down and the kits leaped for them, squealing with delight.

Squirrelflight sat down to rest her leg. Why had she wanted kits of her own so much? There would always be kits in the Clan. It didn't matter that they weren't hers. The Clan was like kin, and their kits would be her kits too. The Sisters weren't the only cats to believe that a kit belonged to every cat. Had she forgotten that warriors had been helping to raise one another's kits for moons? She purred to herself. That would never change.

A brisk wind swished through the branches above the camp. Fluffing out her fur, Squirrelflight headed toward the entrance. For the first time since she'd left the medicine den, her hind leg felt strong enough for her to make the journey to

SkyClan's camp. She wanted to see how Moonlight was doing. Had the Sisters moved on? She quickened her pace. She hoped not. She wanted to speak to them one last time before they left.

She waited at the border until she spotted Hawkwing, Sparrowpelt, and Blossomheart moving through the undergrowth a tree-length away. "Hawkwing." Her mew rang between the trees.

Hawkwing turned his broad face toward her. He pricked his ears. "Hi, Squirrelflight." He hurried over while Sparrowpelt and Blossomheart sniffed at the roots of an alder. "It's good to see you." His gaze flitted over her. "Are you well?"

"Yes, thank you."

"I'm sorry about your loss."

His reminder sent fresh tremors of grief through her heart. "She's in StarClan now." It was a reminder to herself as much as him. *She's happy.* "I've come to see the Sisters."

"They've moved to a temporary camp on the edge of our territory." He nodded between the trees.

Squirrelflight followed his gaze. "Do you think they'll mind if I visit? I want to see how Moonlight is doing."

"Moonlight is dead."

Squirrelflight's breath caught in her throat. "But Frecklewish and Fidgetflake were taking care of her."

"They did their best." Hawkwing's gaze was dark. "But she was too badly injured in the battle." His tail twitched angrily. "Four Clans against a small group of loners. I'm just glad Sky-Clan wasn't involved."

Shame washed Squirrelflight's pelt. She wanted to apologize

for her Clan's part in the attack, but she knew Bramblestar had only done what he thought was right at the time. "I hope next time, ThunderClan won't be involved either."

"Let's hope there isn't a next time." Hawkwing looked toward his camp. "The Sisters will be moving on once Moonlight's kits are weaned. Violetshine is feeding them since none of the Sisters can. We'll probably be in our new camp by the time they leave."

"Then the battle was for nothing." Squirrelflight blinked at him. "We could have waited until they left, and Moonlight would still be alive." Anger surged beneath her pelt.

"You want to see them? Tempest and Snow are in our camp right now."

"I'd like to talk to them before they go," Squirrelflight told him. "I want to tell them I'm sorry for their loss. Moonlight will be missed."

Hawkwing nodded her across the border. "You can speak to them there, and meet Moonlight's kits. They're growing fast."

Squirrelflight blinked at him gratefully. "Thanks."

He called to Blossomheart and Sparrowpelt. "Carry on hunting," he told them. "I'll catch up with you once I've seen Squirrelflight to the camp."

Blossomheart flicked her tail without looking up. She was stalking something between the brambles.

Hawkwing led Squirrelflight toward the camp.

"Do you think you'll like your new territory?" Squirrelflight asked.

"Yes." Hawkwing ducked under a low branch. "It's fine

land and there's good hunting there. I'm looking forward to getting out of the forest. I never could get used to living in the dark." He purred teasingly. "You and ShadowClan live like owls."

"We'll be warm in leaf-bare," she told him.

"So will we." Hawkwing shook out his pelt. "That valley seems pretty sheltered. I can see why the Sisters chose it."

They were nearing the camp now; SkyClan scents washed Squirrelflight's muzzle. She could smell the Sisters too. Snow's scent hung in the air at the entrance. Squirrelflight ducked through it after Hawkwing and padded into the SkyClan camp.

Leafstar was sharing a rabbit with Harrybrook and Sandynose at the far end of the clearing. She looked up as Squirrelflight crossed the camp. "Welcome." She got to her paws.

"Hi." Squirrelflight dipped her head politely as Leafstar reached her. "Hawkwing told me about Moonlight."

"I was sorry that she died." Leafstar glanced toward the nursery. Violetshine was tugging old bedding outside while Rootkit and Needlekit chased after the trailing bracken. Snow was outside, curled around two gray, fluffy kits while Tempest washed a third gray kit, who mewled in complaint.

"I'm not dirty!" the kit wailed indignantly.

"You've got moss stains behind your ears," Tempest told him between laps.

"Can I speak to Snow and Tempest?" Squirrelflight's heart quickened.

"Of course." Leafstar nodded and turned back toward her meal. "Take as long as you like."

Snow looked up as Squirrelflight neared, her eyes shining. The gray, fluffy kits clambered over her flank and charged away. They flung themselves onto the bedding Violetshine was dragging.

"Don't make a nuisance of yourselves!" Snow called after them.

"It's okay!" Rootkit began to help Violetshine haul the bracken to the edge of the clearing, while Needlekit bounced around it, making faces at the two younger kits.

"I want to play too!" The third kit ducked away from Tempest and raced toward the others.

Tempest watched him go, her eyes shining. "He's going to be trouble," she mewed affectionately.

"He's a tom," Snow joked as she got to her paws. She nodded to Squirrelflight. "I'm glad to see you looking so well."

"You too." Squirrelflight felt a surge of fondness for the white she-cat. "Moonlight's kits look happy here."

"They are," Snow told her. "It's good of Violetshine to feed them."

"But we want to leave as soon as we can, to make sure they don't become warriors," Tempest mewed.

Squirrelflight understood. Warriors had killed their leader. "I'm sorry to hear about Moonlight."

Snow's gaze glistened with sadness. "She died defending her kits," she mewed. "It was an honorable way to die. Besides, we still see her."

Of course. Squirrelflight's pelt prickled. The Sisters could see the dead. "Do you talk to her?"

"Yes." Snow brightened. "She wanted me to thank you for saving her kits from the landslide. And for trying to save us from your Clanmates. It was a courageous thing to do."

"I'm sorry it turned into a battle." Squirrelflight blinked at her earnestly. "I wish I could have persuaded the Clans to wait."

"You did what you could." Tempest shrugged. "They have our land now, which is what they wanted. I just hope it brings them the peace that they're looking for." She looked doubtful.

Snow shook her head. "Toms never want peace," she sniffed. "We're better off without them."

"Some toms like to fight," Squirrelflight mewed quickly. "But Bramblestar never wanted it to go so far. He was outnumbered by the other Clans."

"At least you stood up for us," Tempest mewed.

"Even though *you* were outnumbered too." There was an edge to Snow's mew. "We know what it cost you." Her gaze darkened. "Tree told us about Leafpool. We're sorry she died. Our kits owe her their lives. Sunrise does too." She glanced toward the kits, who were chasing Rootkit and Needlekit across the clearing. "Moonlight will always be grateful."

"Where will you go?" Squirrelflight asked.

"Moonlight says we should head across the lake," Snow told her. "Beyond the moors. We haven't been there before."

"Will she travel with you?" Squirrelflight wondered if dead cats could wander wherever they pleased.

"For a while," Snow murmured. "Until the kits are grown. She'll move on then."

"Where will she go?" Did the Sisters have their own version of StarClan?

Snow shrugged. "Who knows?" Her gaze flitted past Squirrelflight.

Tree was approaching. "Hi, Squirrelflight." He pricked his ears happily. "It's good to see you looking well."

"Will you escort me to the border?" Squirrelflight nodded to the camp entrance. It was time she got back to her Clan. Sparkpelt was going to give Finchkit and Flamekit their first taste of mouse, and she wanted to be there to see if they enjoyed it.

"Sure." Tree whisked his tail.

"Travel safely." Squirrelflight dipped her head to Snow and Tempest.

"Thanks for everything you did." Snow blinked.

Tempest shifted her paws. "You didn't ask what we'd named the kits."

Squirrelflight pricked her ears. "What?"

Snow purred. "Leaf, Squirrel, and Moon."

Squirrelflight's pelt pricked self-consciously. "I'm honored." She wondered if Leafpool was watching. Did she know that the Sisters had named a kit after her? "Thank you." She padded away, Tree at her side.

As they ducked out of camp, he looked at her eagerly. "I'm so glad I didn't have to deliver your message." His pelt prickled as though remembering made him nervous. "I didn't think you'd make it. I've never spoken to a ghost that wasn't dead before."

"Do you see Moonlight now?"

Tree fluffed out his fur. "I don't want to," he grunted. "She abandoned me in life. Why should I have to put up with her in death?"

Squirrelflight heard bitterness in his mew. "But you're sorry she's dead, right?"

"Of course." Tree followed the track around a swath of bracken. "Her kits deserve to have a mother, even if only for a short while."

"They'll have the Sisters."

"I guess." Tree stared along the trail. "But Rootkit and Needlekit will have a father and a mother for as long as they need them, and if they're in trouble, they'll always have a Clan to turn to."

Squirrelflight purred. She was glad that Tree seemed to have finally learned to appreciate Clan life. "You're starting to sound like a warrior."

CHAPTER 30

Squirrelflight gazed at the moon through the fluttering leaves of the Great Oak. In front of her, the Clans murmured softly to one another as their leaders took their places on the lowest branch. She remembered the last Gathering, where tempers had flared and the Clans had bayed like foxes for war against the Sisters. Now Moonlight was dead, and so was Leafpool; SkyClan had new territory, and the borders had been redrawn once again. Had those borders been worth two deaths? *Of course not.* She shook out her pelt.

"How are Moonlight's kits getting on?" she whispered to Hawkwing, who sat beside her with the other Clan deputies at the foot of the oak.

"They're thriving." Hawkwing's eyes sparkled fondly. "They'll be ready to travel in a half-moon."

"I expect Violetshine will miss them."

"She will." Hawkwing shifted his paws. "But she'll be glad to lose the Sisters. A new mother gets enough advice from her Clanmates. She doesn't need extra help from outsiders."

Squirrelflight pressed back a purr. She could imagine that the Sisters had strong opinions about raising kits, and they wouldn't be shy about offering them. "Have they helped you settle into their old territory?"

"They showed us where we can find the best hunting and the freshest streams," Hawkwing told her.

"That was kind of them after what happened."

"SkyClan didn't attack their camp." Hawkwing's gaze flashed reproachfully toward the ShadowClan and Wind-Clan warriors moving in the moonlight in front of him. "I think the Sisters respect us for it."

Squirrelflight followed his gaze, searching for a glimmer of shame in the eyes of the warriors. They had killed a queen who'd been protecting the kits she'd just given birth to. Her pelt prickled with fresh anger. They'd behaved more like rogues than warriors. "Do you think the Clans will ever admit they were wrong to do what they did?"

"I think it's best forgotten." Hawkwing swished his tail. "It can't be undone."

Dust showered from the branch above as Leafstar stepped forward and addressed the Clans. "SkyClan has moved to our new territory. We've almost finished building our camp. There is plenty of prey. We haven't seen any foxes or snakes inside the borders, but the Clan is on high alert while we adapt to the new landscape."

"What about the Sisters?" Scorchfur called from among the ShadowClan cats. "Have they left yet?"

Leafstar glared at the ShadowClan warrior. "How can they leave when you killed the mother of their newborn kits? Some cat must nurse them! We owe them that much after murdering their mother."

"It wasn't murder!" Strikestone bristled. "It was a battle."

"A battle for land we could have had in a moon if we'd simply waited." Leafstar's hackles lifted.

Tigerstar's ears twitched. "The Sisters may stay on Clan territory until the kits are weaned," he meowed, his gaze unreadable. "They no longer pose a threat to the Clans."

Squirrelflight flexed her claws. "They never did!"

Tigerstar's gaze flashed toward her. "They managed to turn you against your Clan."

"That's not true!" Shock sparked beneath her pelt.

"Then why did you warn them about our patrol?" he snapped. "We found you in their camp!"

"I was worried about Moonlight's kits," Squirrelflight shot back. "And with good reason!"

"Squirrelflight would never betray her Clan!" Bramblestar's yowl took Squirrelflight by surprise. The ThunderClan leader stared at the gathered cats, his eyes glittering with indignation. Then he dipped his head. "But let's not argue. Each Clan has enough territory to see them through leaf-bare. We've done what we set out to do. We may never agree on how we did it, but it's in the past now. We can't change what happened."

The Clans shifted uneasily as a soft murmur rippled through the crowd. Bramblestar went on, his fur smoothing. "Moonlight's death was regrettable, but SkyClan has done what it can, offering shelter to her kits until they are strong enough to travel. One of our Clanmates died saving them, too. We should honor her. She died trying to save others, which is how she lived."

Squirrelflight's throat tightened as the Clans fell silent. Puddleshine's eyes glistened with grief. Among the Wind-Clan cats, she saw warriors dip their heads.

"Leafpool will be remembered for as long as there are warriors to remember her." Willowshine's mew rang in the chilly night air. Murmurs of agreement rippled through the Clans.

Kestrelflight lifted his muzzle. "She will find peace in StarClan."

"Leafpool." Jayfeather called her name to the stars.

"Leafpool." Kestrelflight echoed his mew.

"Leafpool! Leafpool!" Her name spread through the Clans as others began to chant, their voices lifting like a breeze into the night sky.

Squirrelflight shivered. She'd never realized how respected Leafpool was among the other Clans. Beside her, Crowfeather was staring ahead, grimly silent, as though fighting back emotion. She saw his pelt ripple and felt a twinge of pity. Had he loved Leafpool all this time?

What did it matter if he had? She'd lived and died without him. As she pushed the thought away, Bramblestar shifted on the branch above. He nodded toward Squirrelflight. "My deputy has news to share from StarClan."

"Your deputy?" Tigerstar pricked his ears. "What news can she possibly have from StarClan? She's not a medicine cat. The medicine cats say StarClan is still silent."

"If you listen," Bramblestar grunted, "she'll tell you."

Squirrelflight got to her paws and gazed around the gathered cats. "When I was wounded after the landslide, I spent time in StarClan." Ears pricked and pelts prickled among the watching cats. She went on, trying to explain. "I was close to death. Close enough for StarClan to allow me into their hunting grounds." She tried not to think about how she'd had to argue for her place there after death. "I was reunited with kin and Clanmates, and I spoke with Leafpool. She is happy there, and though she will miss her life in the forest, she was ready to move on." Surprised murmuring sprung up among the older warriors, who exchanged glances. Squirrelflight went on. "Firestar gave me a message for the Clans. He said we must turn toward StarClan, not away."

"But they don't always answer when we turn to them," Emberfoot complained. Around him the other WindClan warriors nodded.

"That's true," Mallownose added.

Bramblestar flicked his tail. "StarClan knows what they're doing," he meowed solemnly. "If they want us to turn toward them, then we will."

"And what if they don't answer?" Shimmerpelt fluffed out her glossy pelt.

Squirrelflight gazed around the Clans. "Perhaps we haven't been hearing their answers." She remembered how hard it had been trying to share with the living when she'd only been *close* to death. "We should try harder to listen."

Puddleshine nodded. "We will listen harder," he promised.

"StarClan will guide us," Willowshine added.

As the Gathering broke up and the Clans swished away through the long grass, Squirrelflight hung back, not wanting to leave yet. This was the first Gathering she'd been to without her sister. Bramblestar had stopped at the edge of the deserted clearing as Jayfeather, Thornclaw, and Lionblaze followed their Clanmates to the tree-bridge. "Are you coming?" he called to her.

"I need a moment to remember Leafpool," she told him.

Bramblestar padded to join her. His pelt brushed hers as he stood beside her. The wind was chilly, and she leaned against him, relishing his warmth.

"I'm glad we're not arguing anymore," she breathed.

"So am I." He touched his muzzle to her ear. "I don't know what I would have done if you'd died. I don't think I could've gone on without you."

"Of course you could." She nuzzled his cheek. "Your Clan needs you. I know you would never let them down."

"I'm only strong because of you." A purr throbbed in his throat. "Promise me we'll never argue like that again. That we'll always talk things out before they get too bad."

She looked into his eyes. "You have to trust me," she murmured. "You must always know that you and ThunderClan are the most important things to me. I would never let you down."

"I know," he breathed. "And I'm sorry I ever doubted you. Ever since you were an apprentice, you've challenged me. And it's always made me stronger. You've helped me see things in a different way." His gaze shone and she shivered, sensing his love like a breeze enfolding her.

"Look." He looked up. "Is that a new star?"

She followed his gaze into the star-specked sky. A bright

star glinted among the others. Her heart quickened. "Do you think it's her?"

"Leafpool?"

"Yes."

"I don't know, but I know she's watching over you." Bramblestar pressed closer.

"She's watching over the whole Clan." A lump pressed in Squirrelflight's throat. "She always will."

READ ON FOR AN
EXCLUSIVE MANGA ADVENTURE . . .

CREATED BY
ERIN HUNTER

WRITTEN BY
DAN JOLLEY

ART BY
JAMES L. BARRY

BRAVELANDS

CHAPTER ONE

Swiftcub pounced after the vulture's shadow, but it flitted away too quickly to follow. Breathing hard, he pranced back to his pride. *I saw that bird off our territory,* he thought, delighted. *No rot-eater's going to come near Gallantpride while I'm around!*

The pride needed him to defend it, Swiftcub thought, picking up his paws and strutting around his family. Why, right now they were all half asleep, dozing and basking in the shade of the acacia trees. The most energetic thing the other lions were doing was lifting their heads to groom their nearest neighbors, or their own paws. They had no *idea* of the threat Swiftcub had just banished.

I might be only a few moons old, but my father is the strongest, bravest lion in Bravelands. And I'm going to be just like him!

"Swiftcub!"

The gentle but commanding voice snapped him out of his

dreams of glory. He came to a halt, turning and flicking his ears at the regal lioness who stood over him.

"Mother," he said, shifting on his paws.

"Why are you shouting at vultures?" Swift scolded him fondly, licking at his ears. "They're nothing but scavengers. Come on, you and your sister can play later. Right now you're supposed to be practicing hunting. And if you're going to catch anything, you'll need to keep your eyes on the prey, not on the sky!"

"Sorry, Mother." Guiltily he padded after her as she led him through the dry grass, her tail swishing. The ground rose gently, and Swiftcub had to trot to keep up. The grasses tickled his nose, and he was so focused on trying not to sneeze, he almost bumped into his mother's haunches as she crouched.

"Oops," he growled.

Valor shot him a glare. His older sister was hunched a little to the left of their mother, fully focused on their hunting practice. Valor's sleek body was low to the ground, her muscles tense; as she moved one paw forward with the utmost caution, Swiftcub tried to copy her, though it was hard to keep up on his much shorter legs. One creeping pace, then two. Then another.

I'm being very quiet, just like Valor. I'm going to be a great hunter. He slunk up alongside his mother, who remained quite still.

"There, Swiftcub," she murmured. "Do you see the burrows?"

He did, now. Ahead of the three lions, the ground rose up even higher, into a bare, sandy mound dotted with small shadowy holes. As Swiftcub watched, a small nose and whiskers poked out, testing the air. The meerkat emerged completely, stood up on its hind legs, and stared around. Satisfied, it stuck out a pink tongue and began to groom its chest, as more meerkats appeared beyond it. Growing in confidence, they scurried farther away from their burrows.

"Careful now," rumbled Swift. "They're very quick. Go!"

Swiftcub sprang forward, his little paws bounding over the ground. Still, he wasn't fast enough to outpace Valor, who was far ahead of him already. A stab of disappointment spoiled his excitement, and suddenly it was even harder to run fast, but he ran grimly after his sister.

The startled meerkats were already doubling back into their holes. Stubby tails flicked and vanished; the bigger leader, his round dark eyes glaring at the oncoming lions, was last to twist and dash underground. Valor's jaws snapped at his tail, just missing.

"Sky and stone!" the bigger cub swore, coming to a halt in a cloud of dust. She shook her head furiously and licked her jaws. "I nearly had it!"

A rumble of laughter made Swiftcub turn. His father, Gallant, stood watching them. Swiftcub couldn't help but feel the usual twinge of awe mixed in with his delight. Black-maned and huge, his sleek fur glowing golden in the sun, Gallant would have been intimidating if Swiftcub hadn't known and loved him so well. Swift rose to her paws and greeted the great lion affectionately, rubbing his maned neck with her head.

"It was a good attempt, Valor," Gallant reassured his

daughter. "What Swift said is true: meerkats are *very* hard to catch. You were so close—one day you'll be as fine a hunter as your mother." He nuzzled Swift and licked her neck.

"*I* wasn't anywhere near it," grumbled Swiftcub. "I'll never be as fast as Valor."

"Oh, you will," said Gallant. "Don't forget, Valor's a whole year older than you, my son. You're getting bigger and faster every day. Be patient!" He stepped closer, leaning in so his great tawny muzzle brushed Swiftcub's own. "That's the secret to stalking, too. Learn patience, and one day you too will be a *very* fine hunter."

"I hope so," said Swiftcub meekly.

Gallant nuzzled him. "Don't doubt yourself, my cub. You're going to be a great lion and the best kind of leader: one who keeps his own pride safe and content, but puts fear into the heart of his strongest enemy!"

That does sound good! Feeling much better, Swiftcub nodded. Gallant nipped affectionately at the tufty fur on top of his head and padded toward Valor.

Swiftcub watched him proudly. *He's right, of course. Father knows everything! And I will be a great hunter, I will. And a brave, strong leader—*

A tiny movement caught his eye, a scuttling shadow in his father's path.

A scorpion!

Barely pausing to think, Swiftcub sprang, bowling between his father's paws and almost tripping him. He skidded to a halt right in front of Gallant, snarling at the small sand-yellow scorpion. It paused, curling up its barbed tail and raising its pincers in threat.

"No, Swiftcub!" cried his father.

Swiftcub swiped his paw sideways at the creature, catching its plated shell and sending it flying into the long grass.

All four lions watched the grass, holding their breath, waiting for a furious scorpion to reemerge. But there was no stir of movement. It must have fled. Swiftcub sat back, his heart suddenly banging against his ribs.

"Skies above!" Gallant laughed. Valor gaped, and Swift dragged her cub into her paws and began to lick him roughly.

"Mother . . ." he protested.

"Honestly, Swiftcub!" she scolded him as her tongue swept across his face. "Your father might have gotten a nasty sting from that creature—but *you* could have been killed!"

"You're such an idiot, little brother," sighed Valor, but there was admiration in her eyes.

Gallant and Swift exchanged proud looks. "Swift," growled Gallant, "I do believe the time has come to give our cub his true name."

Swift nodded, her eyes shining. "Now that we know what kind of lion he is, I think you're right."

Gallant turned toward the acacia trees, his tail lashing, and gave a resounding roar.

It always amazed Swiftcub that the pride could be lying half asleep one moment and alert the very next. Almost before Gallant had finished roaring his summons, there was a rustle of grass, a crunch of paws on dry earth, and the rest of Gallantpride appeared, ears pricked and eyes bright with curiosity. Gallant huffed in greeting, and the twenty lionesses and young lions of his pride spread out in a circle around him, watching and listening intently.

Gallant looked down again at Swiftcub, who blinked and glanced away, suddenly rather shy. "Crouch down," murmured the great lion.

When he obeyed, Swiftcub felt his father's huge paw rest on his head.

"Henceforth," declared Gallant, "this cub of mine will no longer be known as Swiftcub. He faced a dangerous foe without hesitation and protected his pride. His name, now and forever, is Fearless Gallantpride."

It was done so quickly, Swiftcub felt dizzy with astonishment. *I have my name! I'm Fearless. Fearless Gallantpride!*

All around him, his whole family echoed his name, roaring their approval. Their deep cries resonated across the grasslands.

"Fearless Gallantpride!"

"Welcome, Fearless, son of Gallant!"

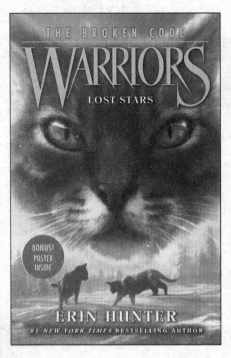
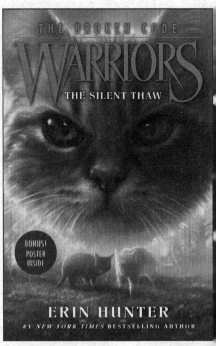

How many have you read?

Dawn of the Clans
- ○ #1: The Sun Trail
- ○ #2: Thunder Rising
- ○ #3: The First Battle
- ○ #4: The Blazing Star
- ○ #5: A Forest Divided
- ○ #6: Path of Stars

Power of Three
- ○ #1: The Sight
- ○ #2: Dark River
- ○ #3: Outcast
- ○ #4: Eclipse
- ○ #5: Long Shadows
- ○ #6: Sunrise

The Prophecies Begin
- ○ #1: Into the Wild
- ○ #2: Fire and Ice
- ○ #3: Forest of Secrets
- ○ #4: Rising Storm
- ○ #5: A Dangerous Path
- ○ #6: The Darkest Hour

Omen of the Stars
- ○ #1: The Fourth Apprentice
- ○ #2: Fading Echoes
- ○ #3: Night Whispers
- ○ #4: Sign of the Moon
- ○ #5: The Forgotten Warrior
- ○ #6: The Last Hope

The New Prophecy
- ○ #1: Midnight
- ○ #2: Moonrise
- ○ #3: Dawn
- ○ #4: Starlight
- ○ #5: Twilight
- ○ #6: Sunset

A Vision of Shadows
- ○ #1: The Apprentice's Quest
- ○ #2: Thunder and Shadow
- ○ #3: Shattered Sky
- ○ #4: Darkest Night
- ○ #5: River of Fire
- ○ #6: The Raging Storm

Select titles also available as audiobooks!

HARPER
An Imprint of HarperCollinsPublishers

www.warriorcats.com • www.shelfstuff.com

SUPER EDITIONS

- ○ Firestar's Quest
- ○ Bluestar's Prophecy
- ○ SkyClan's Destiny
- ○ Crookedstar's Promise
- ○ Yellowfang's Secret
- ○ Tallstar's Revenge

- ○ Bramblestar's Storm
- ○ Moth Flight's Vision
- ○ Hawkwing's Journey
- ○ Tigerheart's Shadow
- ○ Crowfeather's Trial
- ○ Squirrelflight's Hope

GUIDES   FULL-COLOR MANGA

- ○ Secrets of the Clans
- ○ Cats of the Clans
- ○ Code of the Clans
- ○ Battles of the Clans
- ○ Enter the Clans
- ○ The Ultimate Guide

- ○ Graystripe's Adventure
- ○ Ravenpaw's Path
- ○ SkyClan and the Strange

EBOOKS AND NOVELLAS

The Untold Stories
- ○ Hollyleaf's Story
- ○ Mistystar's Omen
- ○ Cloudstar's Journey

Tales from the Clans
- ○ Tigerclaw's Fury
- ○ Leafpool's Wish
- ○ Dovewing's Silence

Shadows of the Clans
- ○ Mapleshade's Vengeance
- ○ Goosefeather's Curse
- ○ Ravenpaw's Farewell

Legends of the Clans
- ○ Spottedleaf's Heart
- ○ Pinestar's Choice
- ○ Thunderstar's Echo

Path of a Warrior
- ○ Redtail's Debt
- ○ Tawnypelt's Clan
- ○ Shadowstar's Life

HARPER
An Imprint of HarperCollinsPublishers

www.warriorcats.com • www.shelfstuff.com